THE PENGUIN CLASSICS

FOUNDER EDITOR (1944-64): E. V. RIEU

FYODOR MIKHAILOVICH DOSTOYEVSKY was born in Moscow in 1821, the second of a physician's seven children. His mother died in 1837 and his father was murdered a little over two years later. When he left his private boarding school in Moscow he studied from 1838 to 1843 at the Military Engineering College in St Petersburg, graduating with officer's rank. His first story to be published, 'Poor Folk' (1846), had a great success. In 1849 he was arrested and sentenced to death for participating in the 'Petrashevsky circle'; he was reprieved at the last moment but sentenced to penal servitude, and until 1854 he lived in a convict prison at Omsk, Siberia. Out of this experience he wrote *Memoirs from the House of the Dead* (1860). In 1861 he began the review *Vremya* with his brother; in 1862 and 1863 he went abroad where he strengthened his anti-European outlook, met Mlle Suslova who was the model for many of his heroines, and gave way to his passion for gambling. In the following years he fell deeply into debt, but from 1867, when he married Anna Grigoryevna Snitkina, his second wife helped to rescue him from his financial morass. They lived abroad for four years, then in 1873 he was invited to edit *Grazhdanin*, to which he contributed his *Author's Diary*. From 1876 the latter was issued separately and had a great circulation. In 1880 he delivered his famous address at the unveiling of Pushkin's memorial in Moscow; he died six months later in 1881. Most of his important works were written after 1864: *Notes from Underground* (1864), *Crime and Punishment* (1865-66), *The Gambler* (1866), *The Idiot* (1869), *The Devils* (1871), and *The Brothers Karamazov* (1880).

DAVID MAGARSHACK was born in Riga, Russia, and educated at a Russian secondary school. He came to England in 1920 and was naturalized in 1931. After graduating in English literature and language at University College, London, he worked in Fleet Street and published a number of novels. Since 1948 he has mainly been working on translations of the Russian classics. For the Penguin Classics he has translated Dostoyevsky's *Crime and Punishment*, *The Idiot*, *The Devils* and *The Brothers Karamazov*; *Dead Souls* by Gogol; *Oblomov* by Goncharov; and *Lady with Lapdog and Other Tales* by Chekhov. He has also written biographies of Chekhov, Dostoyevsky, Gogol, Pushkin, Turgenev and Stanislavsky; and he is the author of *Chekhov the Dramatist*, a critical study of Chekhov's plays, and a study of Stanislavsky's system of acting.

THE BROTHERS KARAMAZOV

FYODOR
DOSTOYEVSKY

TRANSLATED
WITH AN INTRODUCTION BY
DAVID MAGARSHACK

VOLUME
I

PENGUIN BOOKS

Penguin Books Ltd, Harmondsworth, Middlesex, England
Penguin Books, 625 Madison Avenue, New York, New York 10022, U.S.A.
Penguin Books Australia Ltd, Ringwood, Victoria, Australia
Penguin Books Canada Ltd, 2801 John Street, Markham, Ontario, Canada L3R 1B4
Penguin Books (N.Z.) Ltd, 182–190 Wairau Road, Auckland 10, New Zealand

—

This translation first published 1958
Reprinted 1960, 1963, 1964, 1966, 1967, 1969, 1970, 1971, 1972, 1973, 1974, 1975,
1976, 1977, 1978

—

Copyright © David Magarshack, 1958
All rights reserved

—

Made and printed in Great Britain
by Hazell Watson & Viney Ltd,
Aylesbury, Bucks
Set in Monotype Bembo

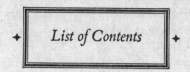

List of Contents

VOLUME ONE

PART TWO

Book Four: Heartaches

Book Five: Pro and Contra

Book Six: The Russian Monk

VOLUME TWO

PART THREE

Book Seven: Alyosha

Book Eight: Mitya

PART FOUR

Book Ten: The Boys

Book Eleven: Ivan Karamazov

DOSTOYEVSKY *began writing* The Brothers Karamazov, *his last and his greatest novel, in June 1878, and finished it in October 1880, about three months before his death.*

'You can't imagine,' *he wrote to the Slavophil poet and critic Ivan Aksakov on 21 September 1880,* 'how busy I am at present. I am working hard day and night. Yes, I am finishing the Karamazovs and reviewing in my mind the work which I, at any rate, think highly of, for there is a great deal of my own in it. I am, as a rule, highly strung when working – my work gives me a great deal of pain and worry. When working hard, I am even physically ill. Now I am striking a balance of what I have been revolving in my mind for three years, drafting it and writing it down. It has to be done well, that is to say, at least as best as I can. . . . The time has come when it has to be finished and finished without any further delay. . . . In spite of the fact that I have been writing it for three years, I keep re-writing some chapters again and again. I write and reject. . . . Only the inspired passages come off at once, the rest requires a great deal of hard work. . . .'

As a matter of fact, Dostoyevsky had been revolving the subject of his last novel in his mind for much longer than three years. All his four masterpieces are essentially murder stories, but each of them deals with a different aspect of murder. Crime and Punishment *revolves round the idea whether the murder of an evil old woman, an unscrupulous moneylender, can be justified if it helps to provide the means for a brilliant career of an impecunious student;* The Idiot *deals with murder as a result of carnal passion set against the Christian ideal of forgiveness; in* The Devils *the motive for murder is political, while in* The Brothers Karamazov *it is the most heinous form of murder that comes under close scrutiny – parricide, a subject that seems to have exercised a powerful fascination over Dostoyevsky since early childhood.* 'As a boy of ten,' *Dostoyevsky wrote to a correspondent on 18 August 1880, from Staraya Russa, where he usually spent the summer* months, 'I saw a performance of Schiller's *Robbers* and, I assure you, the powerful impression it made on me then had a very fructifying influence on my spiritual development.' Dostoyevsky's wife Anna records in her diary that while engaged in writing The Brothers Karamazov her husband again re-read The Robbers, and on one occasion read it aloud to his family. Schiller's play deals with the subject of parricide and the rivalry between two brothers.

This theme Dostoyevsky introduces at the very beginning of his novel by a direct reference to Schiller's play. 'This,' Fyodor Karamazov tells Father Zossima, pointing to his second son Ivan, 'is my most respectful Karl Moor, while this son of mine, Dmitry, who has just come in and against whom I am seeking justice from you, is my most disrespectful Franz Moor, both from Schiller's *Robbers*, which, I suppose, makes me the Regierender Graf von Moor.' The old man, though, made a mistake: it was Ivan and not Dmitry who, like Franz Moor, had been plotting his father's death and was in love with his elder brother's fiancée.

The genesis of The Brothers Karamazov, however, shows an even closer link with Dostoyevsky's past. For it was during his imprisonment in Siberia that he met a man serving a twenty years' sentence for parricide, who was to supply him with the central idea of the plot of his last novel. He relates this meeting in The House of the Dead, the first great work he wrote after his return from Siberia. The condemned parricide was, like Dmitry Karamazov, a retired lieutenant of a line regiment, by the name of Ilyinsky. (In the first drafts of The Brothers Karamazov the name of Ilyinsky occurs side by side with that of Karamazov.) In the first chapter of The House of the Dead, which appeared in 1861 in Time, the monthly periodical Dostoyevsky published with his elder brother Mikhail, he gives the following account of his meeting with Ilyinsky:

'There is one parricide in particular I cannot forget. He was of noble birth and was regarded by his sixty-year-old father as a kind of prodigal son. He led a riotous life and got himself heavily into debt. His father tried his best to restrain him and persuade him to change his mode of life. But his father owned an estate and was reputed to have money, and so his son murdered him in order to inherit his fortune. The crime was only discovered after a month. The murderer himself had informed the police that his father had disappeared and that his whereabouts were unknown. He spent the whole of that month in a most dissolute fashion. At last the police discovered the body in his absence. There was an open sewer, covered by planks, running across the whole length of the yard. The body lay in that sewer. It was dressed and carefully laid out, the grey head was cut off and placed beside the trunk, and the murderer had put a pillow under it. He did not confess; he was deprived of his rank and sentenced to twenty years' hard labour in Siberia. All the time I spoke with him he was in a most cheerful frame of mind. He was a muddle-headed, thoughtless, and extremely irrational fellow, but not by any means a fool. I never noticed any special streak of cruelty in him. The convicts despised him not because of his crime, to which they never referred, but because of his folly, because he did not know how to behave himself. In his conversations with me he sometimes spoke of his father. One day, talking to me of the healthy constitution which was characteristic of all the members of his family, he added: "My father, you know, never complained of his health to the very day of his death." Such brutal insensibility is, of course, uncommon; it is a phenomenon, a sort of flaw in a man's make-up, a physical and moral deformity still unknown to science, and not just a crime. I did not actually believe in this crime. But people of his town who ought to have known all the particulars about him told me everything about the case. The facts were so clear that it was impossible not to believe.

'The convicts,' Dostoyevsky concludes his account, 'overheard him shouting in his sleep one night: "Hold him! Hold him! Cut off his head, his head!"'

But in a subsequent issue of Time Dostoyevsky published the following correction in a note before Chapter VII of The House of the Dead:

'In the first chapter of The House of the Dead I said a few words about a parricide of noble birth. The other day the editor of Time received news from Siberia that the criminal had been right all along and had served ten years of imprisonment for nothing; his innocence had been officially established. The real criminals had been found and had confessed and the unhappy man had been released from prison. The editor has no reason to doubt the authenticity of his information. . . . There is nothing more to be said. There is no need to dilate on the tragic significance of this fact and on the dreadful fate of the young man whose life had been ruined by that terrible accusation. The fact needs no comment: it speaks for itself.'

Ilyinsky was the victim of a miscarriage of justice, which forms the main subject of Dostoyevsky's last novel.

The parricide theme, however, occurred to Dostoyevsky long after he had conceived the idea of writing 'a huge novel' dealing with another great theme of The Brothers Karamazov, the theme of atheism and the existence of

God. This idea of his proposed novel Dostoyevsky first discussed in a letter to the poet Apollon Maykov from Florence on 23 December 1868, ten years before he began writing The Brothers Karamazov.

'I have now in mind,' Dostoyevsky wrote, 'a huge novel under the title of Atheism (for God's sake this is strictly between ourselves), but before I can sit down to it I must read almost a whole library of books written by atheists, Catholics, and Greek Orthodox writers. Even if I get an offer for this work, it will be finished no sooner than in two years' time. I have the chief character. A Russian who belongs to our social set, an elderly man, not very well educated, but not entirely uneducated, either, a man of some rank, who suddenly in his old age loses his faith in God. All his life he was only interested in his job in the Civil Service, never left the rut, and had done nothing in particular up to the age of 45. (A psychological explanation, a serious man, a Russian.) His loss of faith in God makes a tremendous impression on him (the background and the action of the novel are conceived on a large scale). He gets mixed up with the younger generation, the atheists, Slavophils, and Europeans, Russian religious fanatics, monks, and priests; gets deeply involved, among others, with a Jesuit propagandist, a Pole; sinks as low as the sect of the flagellants and in the end – regains his faith in Christ as well as in Russia, the Russian God, and the Russian Christ, (for God's sake don't tell anyone about it: so far as I am concerned, I am going to write this last novel even if it kills me. I am going to speak my mind no matter what).'

Fifteen months later, however, he changed the title and to a certain extent the contents of his proposed novel.

'This will be my last novel,' he declared, as it turned out prophetically, in a letter to Maykov from Dresden on 6 April 1870. 'It will be as large as War and Peace and, I am sure, you would approve of the idea of it, at least that is what I have gathered from the talks I have had with you. This novel will consist of five long stories (about fifteen folio pages each; during the last two years the whole plan has matured in my head). The stories will be quite independent of each other, so that they could even be sold separately. The action of the first story takes place in the forties. (The general title of the novel is The Life of a Great Sinner, but each story will have a different title.) The main question that will be discussed in all the parts is one that has worried me, consciously or unconsciously, all my life – the existence of God. During his life my hero is at times an atheist, at times a believer, a fanatic, a dissenter and, again, an atheist. The second story will take place in a monastery. I put all my hopes on this second story. Perhaps people will at last say that not everything I have written is a lot of nonsense. (I am telling this to you alone: I want to make Tikhon Zadonsky the chief character of the second story, under another name, of course, but he too will be a bishop living in retirement in a monastery.) A thirteen-year-old boy, who took part in a criminal act, precocious and dissipated (I know the type), the future hero of my novel, is put into a monastery by his parents (our own set, cultured), where he is to be educated. A wolf-cub, a nihilist, the boy makes friends with Tikhon (you know Tikhon's character and personality, don't you?). . . . It is true,' he concludes, 'I shall not create anything but only show the real Tikhon whom I have taken to my heart long ago. . . . The first story will deal with my hero's childhood. . . .' (Dostoyevsky had made an attempt to introduce Tikhon in The Devils, and in June 1879 he paid a visit to the bishop at the Optina monastery, together with the young philosopher-poet Vladimir Solovyov. They spent a week at the monastery, and Dostoyevsky incorporated his impressions of his visit in the descriptions of the monastery in The Brothers Karamazov. Father Zossima, too, was modelled on Tikhon.)

Dostoyevsky wrote in almost identical terms to the critic Strakhov, concluding his letter by the assertion that he had decided to make 'this idea of mine into the culmination of my career, for I can't expect to live and write for more than another six or seven years'.

In the meantime however, the political events in Russia, where he had returned on 20 July 1871, and, particularly, the growing revolutionary terrorist movement there, made him postpone his plan of writing his 'huge novel' and write The Devils instead. He also resumed his journalistic work by editing the conservative periodical The Citizen, in which he began publishing his extreme reactionary views in his Diary of a Writer, which he subsequently published independently, the last two issues appearing shortly before his death. 'During these years,' a close friend of his records, 'he never regained the composure which is natural to people who carry on quietly with their work. His inner tension hardly ever left him. He was in a constant state of nervousness and irritability, especially during the last years of his life.' By the time he began writing The Brothers Karamazov he had become, according to the same authority, extraordinarily emaciated and the slightest effort exhausted him. He suffered from emphysema, and it was a burst blood vessel in his lungs, complicated by an attack of epilepsy, that finally killed him: he died on 9 February 1881.

Dostoyevsky jotted down the first draft of The Brothers Karamazov *in the autumn of 1874, about four years before he actually sat down to write the novel. This draft follows closely the Ilyinsky episode, and contains most of the elements of Mitya's story.*

'*13th Sept./74,' Dostoyevsky wrote. 'Drama. In Tobolsk, twenty years ago, something like the Ilyinsky episode. Two brothers, an old father, one of the brothers has a fiancée with whom the second brother is secretly and enviously in love. But she loves the elder one. The elder brother, a young lieutenant, leads a riotous and foolish life. He quarrels with his father. The father disappears. Nothing is heard of him for several days. The brothers discuss their inheritance and suddenly the police arrive: they dig up the father's body from the cellar. The evidence points to the elder brother (the younger brother does not live with them). The elder brother is tried and sentenced to hard labour in Siberia. (N.B. He quarrelled with his father, boasted about his mother's inheritance, and other foolish things.) When he entered the room even his fiancée recoiled from him. He was drunk and said: "Do you, too, believe I did it?" (The evidence has been cleverly fabricated by the younger brother.) The public is not sure who the murderer is.*

'*The scene in Siberia. The convicts want to kill him. The prison authorities. He does not betray them. The prison governor reproves him for having killed his father.*

'*Twelve years later. His brother comes to see him. A scene in which they understand each other without uttering a word. Seven years pass after that meeting. The younger brother is a person of high rank and occupies an important post in the Civil Service. But he is greatly worried, a hypochondriac. Tells his wife that it was he who killed his father. "Why did you tell me that?" He goes to see his brother. His wife, too, arrives. The wife implores the convict on her knees not to tell and to save her husband. The convict says: "I'm used to it." They make it up. "You're punished as it is," says the elder brother.*

'*The younger brother's birthday party. The guests assemble. He comes in. "I am the murderer." They think it's a stroke.*

'*The end: the elder brother is released, the younger brother sent to Siberia. The younger brother asks the elder one to be the father of his children. "He has entered upon the right path!"* '

At the time these notes were written Dostoyevsky was working at his novel The Adolescent, *and it was during that period that he jotted down a great number of notes which he afterwards made use of in his plot of* The

Brothers Karamazov. *In one of these notes he already outlines the life-histories of the three Karamazov brothers.*

'*Preparations for the marriage of the second brother Fyodor,*' *he wrote.* '*The younger one goes out and meets Lambert. Tells him about his family.* "*Is there a devil?*" *the third brother asks the elder one. Meanwhile the rebellion of the children. And so one brother is an atheist and in despair. The other one is a fanatic. The third – the coming generation, a living force, new men. (And the newest generation – children.)*'

The children theme is first elaborated in notes for a separate novel: 'A novel about children, only about children and the child-hero. N.B. (save a suffering child, stratagems, etc.). We found a child left on our doorstep. Fyodor Petrovich (a lover of children and wet nurses). Fyodor Petr., addressing the children after he had carried out their commissions, says: "*Children, I've done what you told me and I'm going to give you a full account of it now.*" *Or,* "*Children, I've read this or that book,*" *and then he tells them about politics, etc. N.B. (he is a grown-up child himself and is full of the deepest and liveliest feeling of love for children). The children plot to organize their own children's empire. Children's arguments about a republic or a monarchy. The children get in touch with the delinquent children in prison. The children – fire-raisers and wreckers of trains. The children convert the devil. Children – debauchees and atheists. Lambert. Andrieux. Children – parricides (Moscow News No. 89. 12 April). A civil servant, his marriage, a foundling [illegible], home for delinquent children, he accepts a bribe, resigns.*'

The maltreatment of children is touched upon in the draft of yet another novel: 'A fantastic poem-novel: the future society, the Paris revolution and Commune, victory. 200 million heads, terrible sores, dissipation, destruction of the arts, libraries, a tortured child. Quarrels, lawlessness. Death.

'*Children. Mother marries a second time. A group of orphans. Half brothers and half sisters. The champion of truth. Death of the worn-out mother. The children's protest. Run away? They go out into the street. The champion alone. Wanderings, etc.*'

In his notes for the year 1877 are also indications that Dostoyevsky was contemplating writing novels under the titles of 'The Russian Candide', 'A Book on Christ', and 'The Forties'. The last-named novel contains a number of notes that bear a direct relationship to some of the themes in The Brothers Karamazov: '*The Forties. Book of Wanderings. Ordeals (1, 2, 3, 4, 5, 6, etc.). Satan: We were all deceived. [Young man]: What maddens me most of all is that you have been appointed to look after me. . . . Why, you even accept God as something that has been cast off.'*

Another brief note contains the following chapter heading that must have been intended definitely for The Brothers Karamazov: 'The Devil. Ivan Fyodorovich's Nightmare.' A further note, later elaborated in the chapter of Ivan and the devil, reads: 'The man who shot himself and the devil, something like Faust. Can be joined to the poem-novel.'

The first mention of Lizaveta Smerdyashchaya occurs in Dostoyevsky's notes as early as in 1874-5: 'Lizaveta Smerdyashchaya. Send me, the stinking one, not to thee into paradise, but into hell, so that out of the torment and the fire I may cry to thee: thou art holy, holy, and I have no other love. . . .'

At first Dostoyevsky intended to deal with one of the main themes of The Brothers Karamazov, the disintegration of the Russian family and the Russian State, in a separate novel under the title of 'Disorder'. The note referring to it is dated 26 August 1875: 'The title of the novel is "Disorder". The whole idea of the novel is to show that universal disorder now reigns everywhere in society, in its affairs, in its leading ideas (which for that reason do not exist), in its convictions (which do not exist, either), in the disintegration of family life. If passionate convictions do exist, they are only destructive ones (socialism). There are no moral ideas left, not a single one remains, and the main thing is that he talks as if they never existed. "But you are religious, aren't you?" "You did not expect me not to be, did you?"'

All these themes, roughly sketched in the notes quoted above, Dostoyevsky finally incorporated in his last novel. But even when he began writing it, his idea of its ultimate form was still very vague. In his foreword to the reader, he reduced the five novels of his first plan to two, the second of which was to be the main novel and was to deal with the life of Alyosha Karamazov 'in our time', as he put it. But, as always with Dostoyevsky, his first intentions never worked out as he planned them. Alyosha, as he appears in the later books of the novel, plays quite an insignificant part in the development of the plot and becomes a very shadowy figure indeed when compared with the figures of his father, his two brothers Mitya and Ivan, and his half-brother Smerdyakov. It is obvious that Dostoyevsky himself lost interest in him, and that the few pages he devotes to him in Book Seven was all he had to say about him.

The idea that Dostoyevsky did not finish his novel, based on his rather *confused foreword to the reader, is entirely unsubstantiated. Dostoyevsky himself admitted it in his letter to Ivan Aksakov, quoted at the beginning of this introduction, and in another letter to one of his closest friends, written from Staraya Russa on 7 September 1880. 'In spite of the lovely weather,' he wrote, 'I sit day and night over my work – I am finishing the Karamazovs. I shall finish it by the end of September and then return [to Petersburg].' On the other hand, he realized more than anyone else perhaps that the novel in its final form was far from perfect. 'I know,' he wrote to a correspondent in April 1880, 'that, like many other writers, I have many faults, for I am the first to be dissatisfied with myself. . . . At the moment when I am trying to review my life's work, I often realize with pain that I have literally failed to express one-twentieth part of what I had wanted to, and perhaps could have expressed. The thing that comforts me is the constant hope that one day God will grant me so much inspiration . . . that I shall be able to express myself more fully, that, in short, I shall express all that is locked in my heart and in my imagination. . . . I cannot help feeling that there is much more hidden in me than I have hitherto been able to express as a writer. And yet,' he concludes, 'speaking without false modesty, there is a great deal that is true and that came from my heart in what I have expressed already.'*

The Brothers Karamazov, then, is, first of all, a picture of Russia as Dostoyevsky saw it in the turbulent years at the end of the seventies and at the beginning of the eighties of the last century. 'Combine all the four main characters [of the novel],' Dostoyevsky wrote to Katkov, the reactionary editor of The Moscow Herald, in which the novel was being serialized, 'and you will get a picture, reduced perhaps to a thousandth degree, of our contemporary educated Russia: that is why I regard my task as so important.' And in further letters to Katkov, he defined Ivan Karamazov's rebellion as 'the synthesis of our modern Russian anarchism', or, in other words, the Russian revolutionary movement of his day. 'The modern negationist,' he wrote to Katkov, 'declares himself openly in favour of the devil's advice and maintains that it is more likely to result in man's happiness than the teachings of Christ. To our foolish but terrible Russian socialism (for our youth is mixed up in it) it is a directive and, it seems, a very powerful one: the loaves of bread, the Tower of Babel (that is, the future reign of socialism) and the complete enslavement of the freedom of conscience – that is what the desperate negationist is striving to achieve. The difference is,' Dostoyevsky continues, 'that our socialists (and they are not only the hole-and-corner nihilists) are conscious Jesuits and liars who do not admit that their ideal is the ideal of the coercion of the human conscience and the reduction of mankind to the level of cattle. While my socialist (Ivan Karamazov) is a sincere man who frankly admits that he agrees with the views of the Grand Inquisitor and that Christianity seems to have raised man much higher than his actual position entitles him. The question I should like to put to them is, in a nutshell, this: "Do you despise or do you respect mankind, you – its future saviours?" '

In another letter Dostoyevsky quite openly declares that his main task in writing The Brothers Karamazov was the defeat of 'anarchism', which he considered to be his 'civic duty'.

Dostoyevsky's personal involvement in the social and political life of his country becomes even more evident in the last chapters of his novel in which he attacks the newly formed courts and trial by jury. Dostoyevsky shared the opinion of Pobedonostsev, the reactionary Procurator of the Holy Synod, whom he is known to have consulted on the various aspects of his novel, about the newfangled trials by jury as 'the talking shop of lawyers as a result of which the most terrible crimes, indubitable murders, and other grave felonies remain unpunished'. He was present at the famous trial in 1878 of Vera Zasulich, the twenty-seven-year-old terrorist, who was acquitted by the jury of her attempt on the life of the Petersburg Governor-General. Her acquittal was followed by a concerted attack on trial by jury by the conservative press, an attack in which Dostoyevsky joined. In fact, he went so far as to reproduce many of the incidents of the trial of Vera Zasulich in the trial of Mitya Karamazov. Thus, Mitya's trial for murder, we are told, 'had become known all over Russia', and, in spite of the fact that it was quite an ordinary, sordid case of murder without any political implications whatsoever, it had caused such 'an immense shock' that all sorts of 'distinguished personages' with 'stars on their frock-coats' (as at the trial of Vera Zasulich) travelled from Petersburg to Skotoprigonyevsk, the remote provincial town, which Dostoyevsky had given such an unsavoury name (the English equivalent of it would be Pigsty). The presence of many fashionable ladies at the trial was another of the features Dostoyevsky copied from the trial of the terrorist girl. But more significant still are Dostoyevsky's descriptions of the presiding judge, the public prosecutor, and the counsel for the defence, all of whom were recognizable copies of the judge, prosecutor, and defending counsel of Vera Zasulich. Dostoyevsky made his intention of satirizing the new trials by jury quite clear in a letter to Pobedonostsev in which he drew the Procurator's attention to the September issue of The Russian Herald.

'In this September issue,' he wrote, 'will be a description of a trial, of our public prosecutors and lawyers – and all this will be shown up in a special light.'

Equally characteristic of Dostoyevsky's methods as a novelist is the great pains he took to check up on the sources of the different incidents in his novel. In one of his letters to Pobedonostsev he underlines the fact that in one of the most important 'books' of his novel, Pro and Contra ('blasphemy and the refutation of blasphemy'), 'I have not betrayed the principles of realism even in so abstract a subject.' He tells Katkov that he had sought the advice of two public prosecutors in Petersburg before he wrote the description of Mitya's trial, and had checked up on 'the medical condition' of Ivan with medical specialists and the details of Father Zossima's burial with members of the Holy Synod. Smerdyakov's song in the chapter 'Smerdyakov with a Guitar', he wrote to Katkov, 'was not composed by me, but written down in Moscow. I heard it forty years ago. It was composed by some Moscow shop-assistants and passed on to the footmen. It had never been written down by our collectors of folk-songs and it appears in my novel for the first time.' The legend about the onion had also been written down by Dostoyevsky. 'I ask you particularly,' he wrote to Katkov, 'to go through the proofs of the legend very carefully. This gem was written down by me from the words of a peasant woman and quite certainly written down for the first time.' The stories of the maltreatment of children, too, were taken from actual life. 'Everything my hero (Ivan) relates in the text I am sending you,' he wrote to Katkov, 'is based on actual facts. All the incidents about the children actually happened and were published in the papers, and I can show you where – nothing has been invented by me. The general who hunted down the child with his hounds and the whole of that incident is an actual occurrence published last winter in the Archives, I believe, and republished in many newspapers.'

Dostoyevsky took particular care about the episode with the children, which he quite seriously intended to provide a solution to the political strife in Russia and which peters out so disastrously in the epilogue. 'In your letter,' he wrote to a correspondent on 28 March 1878, 'I was particularly struck by the fact that you love children, that you spent a great deal of your time with them and that even now you are so often with them. And so I would like to ask you a great favour: I am soon to begin a new novel in which children are to take part, and particularly children between the ages of seven and fifteen. There will be many children. I am studying them and *have been studying them all my life. I am very fond of them and I have some myself. But the observations of a man like you would be invaluable to me. And so please write to me everything you know* about children. (*Incidents, habits, replies, words, sayings, traits of character, attitude to their families, their faith, their misdeeds and innocence; nature and teacher, Latin, etc., etc., in short, everything you know.*) *You will help me very much and I shall be very grateful to you. . . .*' For his chapters about the children Dostoyevsky also studied the works of Pestalozzi and Froebel, and read the articles on schools by Leo Tolstoy.

It was by these means that Dostoyevsky sought to deepen and widen the realistic features of his novel (realism, as can be gathered from Mitya's use of this term, was one of the most popular literary slogans of that period). In the creation of his characters, however, Dostoyevsky departed from the cruder forms of realism by which he sought to give authenticity to the various incidents in his novel. His aim as a creative writer, he declared in his diary, was 'to find the man in man. I am called a psychologist,' Dostoyevsky writes. 'It is not true. I am only a realist in the highest sense of the word, that is to say, I depict all the depths of the human soul.' There was a curious dichotomy in Dostoyevsky's nature; in his journalistic works, and especially in his Diary of a Writer, he expressed views and opinions which for sheer crudity and lack of vision can hardly be paralleled in the case of any other great writer, whereas in his creative works, and especially in The Brothers Karamazov, he achieves a profundity of thought that surpasses anything written in his or, indeed, any other time. He needed what he himself called 'inspiration' to overcome his petty resentment against his political enemies, his racial prejudices, and more particularly his hatred of his more successful literary rivals. In the Legend of the Grand Inquisitor, which Dostoyevsky himself characterized as 'the culminating point of my literary activity', he launched an indirect attack on socialism by making Ivan accept what he considered to be the ultimate policies of the Catholic Church. 'By the stones and the loaves of bread,' Dostoyevsky himself commented, 'I meant our present social problems. Present-day socialism in Europe and in our country as well sets Christ aside and is first of all concerned about bread. It appeals to science and maintains that the cause of all human misfortune is poverty, the struggle for existence and the wrong kind of environment.' But actually the Legend of the Grand Inquisitor transcends the political divisions of mankind and presents the problem of the human predicament in its universal aspect. Again, however controversial Dostoyevsky's idea of expiation of sin *through suffering may appear, it is fully justified when he puts it into the mouth of Dmitry Karamazov.*

It is through the fullest possible integration of idea and character that Dostoyevsky achieves his greatest triumph not only as a creative artist, but also as a profound and fearless thinker. Indeed, the paradox of Dostoyevsky as a writer is that he puts the case against what he himself stands for much stronger than the case for his own ideas and convictions. Father Zossima's pious platitudes are never as convincing as Ivan's 'blasphemies'. Even in Father Zossima's case, his ideas of Christian morality catch fire only when Dostoyevsky gives them a fictional form, as in Father Zossima's account of his dying brother's conversion, his duel, and the story of the mysterious visitor. In this lack of consistency between Dostoyevsky the creative writer and Dostoyevsky the man lies the great tragedy of his life, and it is this perhaps more than anything else that accounts for his irritable and suspicious temperament, which was such a trial even to his closest friends. After his triumphant speech at the unveiling of the memorial to Pushkin in Moscow in June 1880, he remarked sadly: 'The main thing about me they don't understand. They extol me for not being satisfied with the present political condition of our country, but they don't see that I am showing them the way to the church.'

In The Brothers Karamazov, *too, Dostoyevsky saw the solution of Russian troubles in the Greek Orthodox Church, but that is not why his novel is recognized as the greatest achievement of his genius. It is in the universal human drama that its greatness lies, and not in Dostoyevsky's ill-contrived attempt to transform Russia into a huge monastery.*

D. M.

To the Reader

IN beginning the biography of my hero, Alexey Fyodorovich Karamazov, I find myself in some difficulty. What I mean is that though I call Alexey Karamazov my hero, I know perfectly well that he is not by any means a great man, and for this reason I can foresee all sorts of inevitable questions, such as: What is so remarkable about Alexey Karamazov that you should have chosen him for your hero? What exactly has he done? Who knows of him and what is he known for? Why should I, your reader, waste my time studying the facts of his life?

The last question is the most vital one, for all I can say in reply to it is that perhaps you will find it out for yourself from the novel. But what if after reading the novel you do not? What if you do not agree that my Alexey Karamazov is in any way remarkable? I am saying this because unhappily it may turn out to be so. He is remarkable so far as I am concerned, but I doubt very much whether I shall be able to prove it to my readers. The trouble is that though, in a way, he is a man of action, he is so only in a vague sort of way, in a way that is not quite clear. Still, it would be strange to demand clarity from people at a time like ours. One thing, though, is beyond question: he is a strange, almost eccentric sort of man. But strangeness and eccentricity are more likely to give a man a bad name than a claim to attention, especially when everyone today seems eager to reduce personality to a common denominator and find some sort of sense amid the general confusion of ideas. An eccentric, on the other hand, is mostly a personality and an exception. Isn't that so?

Now, if you don't agree with my last statement and reply, It is not so, or, It is not always so, I might feel happier about the importance of my hero. For far from 'always' being a personality and an exception, an eccentric sometimes, on the contrary, expresses the very sum and substance of a certain period while the other people of the same period for some reason or other do not seem to belong to it, just as though they had been cast up by the tide.

I wouldn't have indulged in these highly uninteresting and obscure explanations, but would have begun simply without an introduction: if they like it, they'll read it as it is; but the trouble is that while I am dealing with one biography, I have two novels on my hands. The main novel is the second one – it deals with the activity of my hero in our own day, I mean, at this very moment. The action of the first novel, on the other hand, takes place thirteen years ago and is not really a novel but just a chapter out of my hero's adolescence. It is quite impossible for me to dispense with the first novel because without it a great deal in the second novel would be unintelligible. But this fact makes my original difficulty much more complicated: if I, the biographer, find that even one novel would be too much for such a modest and unheroic hero, then why on earth do I come out with two novels, and what is more: how do I explain such arrogance on my part?

Quite at a loss to find an answer to these questions, the best thing I can do is to leave them without an answer. No doubt the perspicacious reader has long ago guessed that that is exactly what I have been driving at and cannot help being vexed with me for wasting words and precious time. To this I can truthfully say that I wasted words and precious time first out of courtesy and, secondly, out of cunning: I have, so to speak, warned you in good time. As a matter of fact, I am glad that my novel has been split into two stories in spite of the fact that it really forms one whole; for having acquainted himself with the first story, the reader will be able to decide for himself whether it is worth his while to begin the second. No one, of course, is forced to do anything, and the reader can, if he likes, close the book after reading two pages of the first story and never open it again. But there are conscientious readers who will insist on reading to the end so as not to prejudice their impartial judgement. Such, for instance, are all Russian critics. Confronted with people of this sort I should feel easier in my mind if I told them that, in spite of their conscientiousness, I am only too glad to provide them with an excuse to give up reading the novel after the first episode. Well, that's all I have to say in my introduction. I quite agree that it is unnecessary, but as it is already written, it may as well remain.

And now to business.

THE BROTHERS
KARAMAZOV

Verily, verily, I say unto you,
Except a corn of wheat fall into the ground
and die, it abideth alone : but if it die,
it bringeth forth much fruit.

ST JOHN XII. 24

PART ONE

BOOK ONE: THE HISTORY OF A FAMILY

I

Fyodor Pavlovich Karamazov

ALEXEY FYODOROVICH KARAMAZOV WAS THE THIRD SON OF Fyodor Pavlovich Karamazov, a landowner of our district, who became notorious in his own day (and is still remembered among us) because of his tragic and mysterious death, which occurred exactly thirteen years ago and which I shall relate in its proper place. For the present all I shall say about this 'landowner' (as we used to call him, though he hardly ever lived on his estate) is that he was a strange sort of individual, yet one that is met with pretty frequently, the sort of man who is not only worthless and depraved, but also muddle-headed – though one of those muddle-headed men who know very well how to bring off their far from honest business deals and, it would seem, nothing else. Fyodor Karamazov, for instance, began with next to nothing. He was a very small landowner, who always contrived to get himself invited to dinner and persistently aspired to the role of sponger. And yet at his death it was found that he left as much as a hundred thousand roubles in hard cash. And at the same time he continued all his life to be one of the most muddle-headed and preposterous fellows of our district. I repeat: it was not stupidity, for most of these preposterous fellows are rather clever and cunning, but sheer muddle-headedness, and of a special national kind at that.

He was married twice and had three sons – the eldest Dmitry by his first wife, and the other two, Ivan and Alexey, by his second. His first wife belonged to the fairly rich old aristocratic family of the Miusovs, who were also landowners in our district. How exactly it came about that a girl with a dowry, a beautiful girl too, one of those girls of character and intelligence who are often to be found in this generation and were not uncommon in the last, could have married such a poor specimen of a man, as he was called by everyone, I won't even try to explain. Why, I knew a young girl of the last 'romantic' generation who had for several years been consumed by an enigmatic passion for a certain gentleman whom she could have married at any time without any trouble at all, but who, after inventing all sorts of insurmountable difficulties, in the end threw herself one stormy night from a high cliff into a fairly deep and rapid river and was drowned out of sheer caprice, simply because she wanted to be like Shakespeare's Ophelia. Indeed, had the cliff, which she had discovered long before and which had become her favourite spot, not been so picturesque and had there been a prosaic flat river bank instead, she would perhaps never have committed suicide at all. This is a true story, and I should not be surprised if during the last two or three generations there were not a few similar or identical occurrences. In the same way, Adelaida Miusov's action was, no doubt, a reflection of other people's ideas and the impulse of a mind cribbed and confined. She may have wanted to show her feminine independence, to challenge the social conventions and the tyranny of her class and her family, and an accommodating imagination persuaded her, let us say, only for a brief moment, that Fyodor Karamazov, in spite of his status as a sponger, was one of the bravest and wittiest men of that progressively improving epoch, while as a matter of fact he was nothing but an ill-natured clown. The affair acquired still greater piquancy from the fact that it involved an elopement, and this greatly appealed to Adelaida. As for Fyodor Karamazov, he was at the time very much disposed towards enterprises of this kind by his social position, for he passionately desired to make a career for himself by fair means or foul; and to insinuate himself into a good family and get a dowry was a very attractive proposition. As for love, there does not seem to have been any of it at all – neither on the part of the bride nor on his part, in spite of Adelaida's good looks. So that this was perhaps the only case of its kind in the life of Fyodor Karamazov, a most licentious man all his life, who was ready at a moment's notice to run after any petticoat at the slightest sign of encouragement. And yet this woman alone aroused no sexual desire in him whatever.

Immediately after her elopement Adelaida realized in a flash that she felt nothing but contempt for her husband. The results of the marriage consequently became apparent with extraordinary rapidity. In spite of the fact that her family got reconciled to her marriage fairly soon and gave the runaway bride her dowry, husband and wife began to lead a cat and dog existence and there were everlasting rows between them. It was said that during their quarrels the young wife showed much more generosity and high-mindedness than her husband, who, as is now known, cheated her out of all her money to the amount of twenty-five thousand roubles as soon as she had received it, so that after that she never saw a farthing of all those thousands. In addition, he tried very hard to transfer the little estate and the fairly substantial town house, which were also part of her dowry, to his own name by the drawing up of a deed of gift. He would most certainly have succeeded in his attempt merely, as it were, because of the contempt and disgust which he constantly aroused in her by his shameless solicitations and importunities, and also because she was so sick and tired of him that she would have done anything to be left in peace. Fortunately, however, Adelaida's family intervened and restrained the swindler. It is known for a fact that there were frequent fights between husband and wife, but according to the stories current in our town it was not Karamazov but Adelaida who did the beating, for she was a short-tempered lady, fearless, impatient, dark-complexioned, endowed with extraordinary physical strength. At last she left the house and ran away with an impoverished and destitute teacher, a graduate of a religious seminar, leaving the three-year-old Mitya to be looked after by her husband. Karamazov at once turned his household into a regular harem and took to giving disorderly drinking-parties; in between these orgies he used to drive almost all over the province, complaining tearfully to all and sundry of Adelaida for having left him and going into details that any husband should have been thoroughly ashamed to give about his married life. He seemed, indeed, to be pleased and even flattered to play the ridiculous part of an injured husband before the whole world, and went into lurid details of the injuries he had suffered. 'One would think you'd got a promotion,' the scoffers used to say to him, 'you seem so pleased in spite of your great distress.' Many even added that he was glad to appear once more in his role of a clown and that, to provoke even

stronger outbursts of laughter, he pretended not to notice his ludi-
crous position. But who knows, perhaps he did it simply because he
was rather naïve at heart. At last he succeeded in discovering the
whereabouts of his runaway wife. The poor woman, it seems, was in
Petersburg, where she had gone with her seminarist and where she
had plunged headlong into a life of complete emancipation. Karamazov at once got busy and began to make preparations to go to Petersburg. Why? That, of course, he did not know himself. And he would
perhaps really have gone; but, having made up his mind to go, he at
once felt himself fully entitled to indulge in a most unrestrained drinking orgy so as to get the courage he needed for the journey. And just
at that time his wife's family received the news of her death in Petersburg. She seems to have died suddenly in some attic, according to one
version, of typhus, and another, of starvation. Karamazov learnt of
his wife's death when he was drunk and, it is said, rushed out into
the street, and, raising his hands to heaven in his joy, began shouting:
'Lord, now lettest thou thy servant depart in peace!' According to
others, he sobbed aloud like a little child, so much so that, it is said,
people were sorry to look at him in spite of the disgust he inspired.
Quite likely both versions are true, that is to say, that he rejoiced at
his release and wept for her who had given him his freedom – at one
and the same time. In the majority of cases, people, even evil-doers,
are much more naïve and artless than we generally assume. As,
indeed, we are ourselves.

2

He Turns Out His Eldest Son

IT is, of course, not difficult to imagine the sort of father such a man
would be and what upbringing he would give his children. As a
father, he was exactly what one might expect him to be, that is to say,
he completely abandoned the child of his first marriage, not out of
malice, nor because of any injured matrimonial feelings, but simply
because he completely forgot about his existence. While he was bor-
ing everyone with his complaints and tears and turning his home into
a sink of corruption, Grigory Kutuzov, a faithful servant of the family,

took the three-year-old Mitya under his care; if he had not done so at the time, there would not have been anyone to change the child's shirt. Besides, as it happened, the little boy's relations on his mother's side seemed at first also to have forgotten him. His grandfather, that is, Mr Miusov himself, Adelaida's father, was no longer alive; his widow, Mitya's grandmother, had moved to Moscow where she fell seriously ill, while Adelaida's sisters had all married, so that Mitya had to remain for almost a year under Grigory's care and live with him in the servants' cottage. However, if his father had remembered him (and he could not really have been entirely unaware of his existence), he would have sent him back to the cottage, for the child would still have interfered with his debaucheries. Just at that time, however, Peter Miusov, a cousin of Mitya's mother, happened to return from Paris. Afterwards he spent many years abroad, but just then he was still quite a young man, but one who, unlike the rest of the Miusovs, was highly cultured. He had lived in Petersburg and abroad and was, besides, all his life a European *par excellence*, and towards the end of his life a liberal of the forties and the fifties. In the course of his career he had come into contact with many of the most liberal men of his time, both in Russia and abroad. He had known both Proudhon and Bakunin personally and, towards the end of his wanderings, was particularly fond of recalling and describing the three days of the Paris Revolution of February 1848, hinting that he had almost taken part in the fighting on the barricades himself. That was one of the most delightful memories of his youth. He was a man of independent means, owning, according to the old way of reckoning, about a thousand serfs. His splendid estate was on the very outskirts of our small town and bordered on the lands of our famous monastery. Against this, while still a very young man, he began, as soon as he came into his inheritance, an interminable lawsuit about the fishing rights in the river or the wood-cutting rights in the forest, I am not sure which, but he conceived it his duty as a citizen and a man of culture to start an action in the courts against 'the clericals'. Having heard all about Adelaida, whom, of course, he remembered and to whom at one time he had even felt attracted, and learning about Mitya's existence, he took a hand in the affair in spite of all his youthful indignation and his contempt for Karamazov. It was on this occasion that he made Karamazov's acquaintance for the first time.

He told him bluntly that he would like to be responsible for the child's upbringing. Long afterwards he used to recount as a characteristic trait that when he mentioned Mitya to Karamazov, the latter looked for some time as though he did not understand what child he was talking about and even seemed surprised to learn that he had a little son somewhere in his house. If Miusov's story was somewhat exaggerated, there was still something in it that rang true. But all through his life, as a matter of fact, Karamazov liked to dissemble, to play some unexpected part before you, sometimes, moreover, without the slightest need for it, indeed even to his direct disadvantage, as, for instance, in the present case. This trait, however, is characteristic of a great many people, some of them very clever people, too, and not only of a man like Karamazov. Miusov threw himself warmly into this business and was even appointed (jointly with Karamazov) the guardian of the child, for after all there was a small estate, a house, and some land left by his mother. Mitya did, in fact, go to live with his mother's cousin, but having no family of his own, Miusov, after settling his affairs and making sure of the revenues from his estates, made haste to return to Paris, where he intended to spend a long time, and left the boy in the charge of one of his cousins, an old lady living in Moscow. It so happened that, having settled permanently in Paris, he, too, forgot all about the child, especially when the February Revolution broke out, which had made such a strong impression on his mind and which he could never forget for the rest of his life. The Moscow lady died and Mitya was taken in charge by one of her married daughters. It would seem that after that he changed his home for a fourth time. I shall not dilate on that now, particularly as I shall have to tell a great deal of Karamazov's first-born later on, but confine myself now to the most essential facts about him without which I could not even start my novel.

To begin with, Mitya was the only one of Karamazov's three sons who grew up in the belief that he, at any rate, possessed some property and that when he was of age he would be independent. He spent a turbulent boyhood and youth: he did not finish his course at the secondary school, entered a military college, was stationed in the Caucasus, promoted to a higher rank, fought a duel, reduced to the ranks, again obtained promotion, led a riotous life and spent, comparatively speaking, a great deal of money. He did not begin to receive money from his father until he came of age and till then ran into debt. He got to know and saw his father for the first time only after coming of age when he arrived in our town for the sole purpose of clearing up their misunderstanding about his property. Apparently he did not like his father even then; he did not stay long with him, but left in a hurry, having managed to obtain a certain sum of money from him and entering into some sort of agreement with him about the future receipt of revenues from his estate, an estimate of the value of which (a highly interesting fact that) he was quite unable to obtain from his father on that occasion. Karamazov noticed from the very first moment of his meeting with his eldest son (and this too must be kept in mind) that Mitya had an exaggerated and quite wrong idea of the value of his property. Karamazov, for reasons of his own, was very well satisfied with this. He came to the conclusion that the young man was thoughtless, violent, passionate, impatient, dissipated, and that, if he were given some money occasionally, he would at once be satisfied, though only for a short time, of course. It was this that Karamazov began to exploit, that is to say, he would fob him off with small sums of money, which he sent him from time to time. In the end Mitya, having lost patience, made an appearance in our town four years later in order to come to a final settlement with his father. It was then that to his great astonishment he suddenly discovered that he had absolutely nothing left, that it was quite impossible to say how much money he had received from his father, that what he had received from him already exceeded the value of his property and that he was probably even in debt to him; that because of certain transactions into which he had entered at certain specified dates of his own free will he had no right to demand anything more, and so on and so forth. The young man was stunned, suspected his father of lying and deceiving him, was almost beside himself and really seemed to have gone out of his mind. It was this circumstance that led to the catastrophe, the account of which forms the subject of my first introductory novel, or rather the external side of it. But before I pass on to this novel, I must say something of Karamazov's other two sons, Mitya's brothers, and of their origin.

3

Second Marriage and Other Children

HAVING got his four-year-old Mitya off his hands, Karamazov very
soon married a second time. His second marriage lasted eight years.
He took his second wife, Sophia Ivanovna, who was also a very young
woman, from another province where he had gone on some small
contracting business with some Jew as his partner. Though Karamazov
drank and led a disorderly and debauched life, he never neglected
investing his capital and was always successful in managing his
affairs, though, of course, almost always in a rather mean and shabby
way. Sophia was an 'orphan child', the daughter of some obscure
deacon, who had been left without relations since her early childhood.
She grew up in the wealthy house of her benefactress, her instructor,
and her tormentor – an aristocratic lady, the widow of General
Vorokhov. I do not know the details, I have only heard that the poor
adopted girl, a meek, inoffensive, gentle creature, was once cut down
after she had attempted to hang herself from a nail in a box-room –
so hard did she find it to put up with the caprices and constant
reproofs of this apparently far from ill-natured old woman who had
become an insufferable, mean, and tyrannical woman through sheer
idleness. Karamazov made her a proposal of marriage, inquiries were
made about him, and he was sent packing; and it was then that, as in
his first marriage, he suggested an elopement to the orphan girl. It is
very likely that she too would not have married him for anything in
the world, if she had found out a little more about him in good time.
But it all happened in another province; and, besides, what could a
sixteen-year-old girl be expected to know, except perhaps that she'd
sooner throw herself into the river than remain with her benefactress.
So it was that the poor girl exchanged a benefactress for a benefactor.
This time Karamazov did not get a penny, for the general's widow
was furious, gave them nothing and would have nothing more to do
with them. But he had not counted on getting anything: he was greatly
attracted by the remarkable beauty of the innocent young girl and,
chiefly, by her air of innocence which made a powerful impression
on a voluptuary like him, who till then had been a depraved admirer

of only the coarser kind of feminine beauty. 'Those sweet innocent eyes cut my heart like a knife at the time,' he used to say afterwards, sniggering loathsomely as was his wont. However, in such a lecherous man that, too, might have been only a sensual attraction. Having taken her without any money, he did not stand on ceremony with her, and taking advantage of the fact that she was, as it were, 'guilty' towards him and that he had practically 'cut her down', as well as of her phenomenal meekness and lamb-like timidity, he did not hesitate to trample on the ordinary decencies of married life. Women of the streets used to come to his house while his wife was there, and they would have wild parties. To show what actually used to happen, I may mention that the servant Grigory Kutuzov, a gloomy, stupid and obstinate moralist, who had hated his former mistress, this time took his new mistress's side, defended her and quarrelled with Karamazov because of her in a manner that was hardly permissible from a servant, and one day he even broke up the party and threw all the hussies out of the house. Later on the unhappy young woman, terrorized since her childhood, contracted one of those women's nervous diseases which are most often found in the country among village women, who are called 'shriekers' because of it. This illness, accompanied as it was by terrible fits of hysteria, at times deprived her of her reason. Yet she bore Karamazov two sons, Ivan and Alexey, the first in the first year of marriage, and the second three years later. When she died, little Alexey was in his fourth year, and though it may seem strange, I know that he remembered his mother all his life, but of course as though in a dream. After her death, almost exactly the same thing happened to the two boys as to their eldest brother Mitya: they were completely forgotten and abandoned by their father and found themselves in the charge of the same Grigory and they also lived in his cottage. It was there that they were found by the tyrannical old widow of the general, who had brought up their mother. She was still alive, and all that time, all those eight years, could not forget the injury done her. About her 'Sophia's' mode of life during those eight years, she had the most exact information from confidential sources, and learning how ill she was and in what hideous surroundings she lived, she declared aloud to her poor relations: 'It serves her right. It's God's punishment on her for her ingratitude.'

Exactly three months after Sophia's death, the old lady made an appearance in our town and went straight to Karamazov's house. She only stayed about half an hour in our town, but she did a great deal. It was in the evening. Karamazov, whom she had not seen during all those eight years, came out to her drunk. It is said that as soon as she saw him, she instantly, without any more ado, slapped his face twice with all the force at her command, and pulled him up and down three times by the tuft of his hair. Then, without another word, she went straight to the two boys at the cottage. Noticing at the first glance that they were unwashed and that their linen was dirty, she promptly slapped Grigory's face, too, and told him that she was taking them away with her. She took them out of the cottage just as they were, wrapped a rug round them, put them into her carriage, and carried them off to her town. Grigory bore the blow like a devoted slave, without uttering a rude word to her. When he saw the old lady off to the carriage, he bowed low to her, saying impressively that God would reward her for looking after the orphans. 'You're an oaf for all that!' the general's widow shouted to him as she drove away. Thinking it over, Karamazov came to the conclusion that it was a good thing and did not afterwards refuse his formal consent on any point to his children's being educated by the general's widow. As for the slaps she had given him, he himself spread the story all over town.

It so happened that soon after this the general's widow, too, died, but in her will she left the boys a thousand roubles each 'for their education', stipulating, however, that while all that money should be spent on them, it should be made to last until they came of age, because even so small a sum was too much for such children, but if anyone felt more generous let him give more, and so on. I have not read the will myself, but I heard that there was something queer of this sort and that it was rather eccentrically expressed. The principal heir of the old lady, Yefim Petrovich Polenov, Marshal of Nobility of the province, however, turned out to be an honest man. After an exchange of letters with Karamazov, he realized at once that he could extract no money from him for the education of his children (though Karamazov never directly refused, but always kept putting off in such cases, sometimes, indeed, becoming effusively sentimental). He, therefore, took a personal interest in the orphaned children and became particularly fond of the younger, Alexey, so much so that the boy lived at his house for a long time and grew up as a member of his family. I should like to ask the reader to note this from the very beginning. And if the young people were indebted for their upbringing and education to any man, that man was Mr Polenov, one of the most honourable and humane men one is ever likely to meet. He kept the thousand roubles the general's widow had left each of the two boys intact so that by the time they came of age it had doubled by the accumulation of interest. He educated them at his own expense and, needless to say, spent far more than one thousand on each of them. For the time being I shall again not enter into a detailed description of their boyhood and adolescence, but will merely indicate a few of the more important circumstances. Of the elder, Ivan, however, I will only say that he grew into a rather morose young man, who was always withdrawn into himself. He was far from timid, but it seems that already by the age of ten he had become aware that they were living among strangers and on other people's charity, that their father was a man of whom one ought to be ashamed to talk, and so on. This boy began to show very early, almost in infancy (so at least it was said), quite an extraordinarily brilliant aptitude for learning. I don't know all the particulars, but for some reason or other he left Yefim Polenov's family when he was barely thirteen, entered a Moscow secondary school, boarding at the house of an experienced and famous pedagogue, a childhood friend of Polenov's. Ivan himself used to declare afterwards that it all happened because of the 'enthusiasm for good works' of Polenov, who was carried away by the idea that a boy of such brilliant abilities had to be educated by a brilliant tutor. However, neither Polenov nor the brilliant tutor was living when, after finishing school, the young man entered the university. As Polenov had failed to make the necessary provisions for the two boys and as, owing to the unavoidable formalities and delays so customary in Russia, the money they had inherited from the general's widow, which had increased from one to two thousand roubles, had not been immediately available, the young man was very hard up indeed during his first two years at the university and was forced to earn his own living all that time as well as carry on with his studies. It should be noted that at the time he did not even attempt to enter into a correspondence with his father – perhaps out of pride, out of contempt for him and, perhaps, too, out of a commonsense reflection which told him that he would never obtain any real assistance, however small, from his father. Be that as it may, the young man was not in any way discouraged and, in spite of everything, succeeded in getting work, at first by giving lessons at sixpence an hour and then by selling short 'stories' of street incidents to different newspapers under the signature of 'Eyewitness'. These 'stories', it was said, were always so interestingly and pungently written that they were soon in great demand, and in this respect alone the young man showed his practical and intellectual superiority over that large, indigent and unhappy section of our students of both sexes who live from hand to mouth and who, in our capital cities, are always in and out of the editorial offices of different newspapers and journals, unable to think of anything better than the constant repetition of one and the same request for translations from the French or for copying out articles. Having got an entry into the editorial offices, Ivan never lost touch with them, and during his last years at the university he began to publish brilliant reviews of books on various specialized subjects, so that he became well known even in literary circles. It was, however, only quite recently that he happened to have suddenly succeeded in attracting the special attention of a much wider public, so that a rather large number of people at once noticed and remembered him. That was a rather interesting incident. Having graduated from the university and preparing to leave for abroad on his two thousand roubles, Ivan published in one of the leading newspapers a strange article, which attracted the attention even of non-specialists, and, what was so extraordinary, on a subject on which he was apparently not an expert, since he had taken his degree in natural sciences. The article dealt with the question of ecclesiastical courts which was being widely debated at the time. After discussing several opinions which had already been published on this subject, he went on to express his own view. What was so striking about his article was its tone and its extraordinarily surprising conclusion. And yet many churchmen were convinced that its author was on their side. But quite unexpectedly not only secularists but even atheists expressed their agreement with his views. In the end several shrewd persons decided that the whole thing was nothing but an impertinent practical joke. I mention this incident especially because this article eventually found its way into our famous monastery, where they were greatly interested in the question of ecclesiastical courts which had arisen just then, and, having found its way there, it produced general bewilderment. On learning the name of the author, they were also interested in the fact that he was a native of our town and the son of 'that Karamazov'. And just then the author himself made a sudden appearance among us.

Why Ivan Karamazov had arrived in our town just then was a question that I remember rather worried me at the time. This so fateful visit which led to so many consequences remained a mystery to me long afterwards and, indeed, almost always. In view of every-thing, it seemed strange that a young man, so learned, so proud, and seemingly so cautious, should suddenly take up his residence in so disreputable a house and with a father who had ignored him all his life, who neither knew nor remembered him, who, if his son had ever asked him for money, would never have given him any under any circumstances. For he was always afraid that his sons Ivan and Alexey might one day come and ask him for money. And now the young man took up residence in the house of such a father, lived with him for one month and then for another, and both of them seemed to be getting on marvellously together. This last fact seemed particularly astonishing not only to me but to many others. Peter Miusov, of whom I have already spoken, a distant relative of Fyodor Karamazov by his first marriage, happened just then to be spending some time on his estate in the vicinity of our town, having arrived from Paris, where he had settled permanently. I remember that it was he who was most of all impressed, when he had made the acquaintance of the young man. Ivan interested him exceedingly and he sometimes engaged, not without inner pangs, in furious intellectual arguments with him. 'He's proud,' he used to say to us at the time about him, 'he'll always be able to earn his living, he has money even now, he can afford to go abroad – so what is he after here? Everyone can see that he hasn't come to his father for money, for his father would never give him any. He doesn't like drinking and whoring, and yet the old man can't do without him – so well are they getting on together!' And it was true. The young man's influence over his father was quite evident; the old man seemed even to obey him at times, though occasionally he still was extremely and even maliciously per-verse; sometimes he even began to behave more decently. . . .

It only became known afterwards that one of the reasons for Ivan's arrival was that his elder brother Mitya had asked him to intercede with their father on his behalf. Ivan had met his brother for the first time almost at the same time and during that very visit, but before his arrival from Moscow he had entered into correspondence with him about an important matter that concerned Mitya more than himself. What it was the reader will learn in full detail in due course. All the same, even when I found out what this special business was, Ivan still seemed an enigmatic figure to me and his arrival in our town remained a mystery.

I may add here that Ivan was at the time trying to mediate between his father and his elder brother, who was just then at daggers drawn with his father and even instituted formal legal proceedings against him.

That family, I repeat, met for the first time just then and some of its members saw each other for the first time in their lives. Only the youngest son Alexey had lived in our town for the past year and had thus arrived there before his brothers. It is about Alexey that I find it most difficult to speak in this introductory story before bringing him on to the stage in my novel. But I'm afraid I shall have to give some preliminary description of him, too, to explain at least one very strange fact, namely, the fact that I am forced to introduce my future hero to the reader in the very first scene of my novel wearing the cassock of a novice. Yes, indeed, he had been living for the past year in our monastery and was apparently getting ready to take his vows and to spend the rest of his life there.

4

The Third Son Alyosha

HE was only twenty years old then (his brother Ivan was in his twenty-fourth year and their eldest brother Dmitry in his twenty-eighth). First of all let me say that this young man, Alyosha, was not at all a fanatic and, at least in my opinion, not even a mystic. Let me make myself absolutely clear from the very beginning: he was simply a precocious lover of humanity, and if he took up the monastic way of life it was only because at the time it alone appealed powerfully to his imagination and showed him, as it were, the ideal way of an escape for his soul struggling to emerge from the darkness of worldly wicked- ness to the light of love. And this way of life appealed so strongly to him only because just then he had met, as he thought, an extraordin- ary being, Zossima, the famous elder in our monastery, to whom he grew attached with all the warmth of the first love of his unquench- ably ardent heart. Still, I do not deny that he was very strange even then, having been so, indeed, from his cradle. I have, incidentally, already mentioned the fact that, though only in his fourth year when his mother died, he remembered her all his life – her face, her caresses, 'just as though she were standing alive before me'. Such memories, as everyone knows, may be retained from an even earlier age, even from the age of two, but merely appear all through life like shafts of light out of the darkness, like a tiny corner torn out of a huge picture which has all faded and disappeared except for that tiny corner. So it was with him: all he remembered was an evening, a quiet summer evening, an open window, the slanting rays of the setting sun (it was the slanting rays that he remembered most of all), an icon in the corner of the room, a lighted lamp in front of it, and on her knees before the icon his mother, sobbing as though in hysterics, with screams and shrieks, snatching him up in her arms, hugging him to her breast so tightly that it hurt, and praying for him to the Virgin, holding him out in both arms to the icon as though under the Virgin's protection, and suddenly a nurse runs in and snatches him from her in terror. There you have the picture! At that moment Alyosha remem- bered his mother's face, too: he used to say that as far as he could remember it was frenzied but beautiful. But there were very few people, indeed, with whom he would share this memory. In his child- hood and adolescence he was not effusive and he did not even like to talk a great deal, but it was not from mistrustfulness, nor from shy- ness or from morose unsociability; quite the contrary, it was from something else, from a sort of inner preoccupation, a preoccupation that concerned only himself and had nothing to do with anyone else, but so important to him that he seemed to forget others because of it. But he loved people: all his life he seemed to have complete faith in people, and yet no one ever took him for a simpleton or a naïve person. There was something in him that told you and indeed con- vinced you (and it was so all through his life afterwards) that he did not want to set himself up as a judge of people, that he would not like to assume the role of one who condemned or, in fact, to condemn anyone for anything. It also seemed that he tolerated everything without in the least passing judgement, though often grieving bitterly. Indeed, he went so far as not to be surprised or frightened by anything anyone did, and that even as a child. Arriving at the age of twenty at his father's house, which was a veritable den of the filthiest vice, he, chaste and pure as he was, simply withdrew in silence when it was unbearable to look on, but without the slightest sign of contempt for, or condemnation of, anyone. His father, on the other hand, having been a sponger once and, therefore, a morbidly suspicious man who was quick to take offence, had met him at first mistrustfully and sullenly ('He's much too silent and thinks too much', he thought) but finished up by constantly hugging and kissing him before a fortnight was out, with drunken tears, it is true, and with tipsy sentimentality, but it was evident that he had grown to love him sincerely and deeply, in a way no man like him could ever, of course, have been expected to love anyone.

But then, everyone loved this young man wherever he made an appearance, and that had been so from the earliest days of his childhood. When he entered the house of his benefactor and patron Yefim Polenov, everyone in that household grew so attached to him that they treated him as one of the family. And yet he had entered that household at such a tender age that it was quite impossible to suspect the child of possessing any calculating duplicity or pushfulness or any skill in ingratiating himself into anyone's favour or any knowledge of how to make oneself liked. So that his gift of arousing a special kind of love in people was, as it were, inherent in his very nature, artless and spontaneous. It was the same at school, and yet it would seem that he was one of those children who arouse the distrust of their schoolmates and are sometimes laughed at and even hated. He would, for instance, often fall into a reverie and he seemed to shun the company of others. Even as a little boy he liked to retire into some corner and read a book, and yet his schoolmates grew so fond of him that he could be described without fear of contradiction as a general favourite all the while he was at school. He was seldom playful or even merry, but one look at him was sufficient to make people realize that there was not a trace of moroseness in him, that, on the contrary, he was serene and even-tempered. He never attempted to show off before children of his own age. Perhaps that was why he was never afraid of anyone, and yet his schoolfellows at once realized that he was not at all proud of his fearlessness, but gave the impression of someone who had no idea that he was brave and fearless. He never bore a grudge against anyone. It often happened that an hour later he would reply to the boy who had offended him or speak to him with as trustful and serene an expression as though nothing had happened between them. And he did so without any indication that he had accidentally forgotten or deliberately forgiven the insult; it was simply that he did not think of it as an insult, and it was this that appealed so strongly to the children and made them like him. There was only one trait of his character which invariably aroused in all his schoolmates from the lowest to the highest form the desire to pull his leg, though not out of malice but because it amused them. This was his absurd and morbid modesty and chastity. He could not bear to hear certain words and certain conversations about women. These 'words' and 'conversations' are unhappily impossible to eradicate in schools. Boys who are pure in heart and soul, almost children, often like to talk in class in whispers and even aloud of things, pictures, or images of which even soldiers would hesitate to speak; moreover, soldiers do not know or understand a great deal of what is familiar to quite young children of our educated and higher classes of society. There is as yet no moral depravity, nor any real, corrupt, inner cynicism, but there is the appearance of it, and it is this kind of cynicism that they often consider as something refined, subtle, daring, and even worthy of imitation. Seeing that Alyosha Karamazov stopped his ears with his fingers every time they talked about 'that', they sometimes deliberately crowded round him, pulled his hands away from his ears by force and shouted obscenities into both ears, while he struggled to free himself, lay down on the floor, tried to hide his face, and he did all this without uttering a word, without quarrelling, bearing their taunts in silence. In the end, however, they left him alone and no longer teased him for being 'a silly little girl', and not only that, but they were genuinely sorry for him because of it. Incidentally, he was always one of the best pupils in the class, but was never singled out as the top boy of the form.

After Yefim Polenov's death Alyosha spent another two years at the secondary school. Almost immediately after his death, the inconsolable widow went for a long visit to Italy with her whole household, consisting entirely of women. Alyosha went to live in the house of two ladies, distant relatives of Yefim Polenov, whom he had never seen before, and he did not know himself on what terms. Another very characteristic trait of his character was that he never cared at whose expense he was living. In that respect he was in complete contrast to his elder brother Ivan, who had experienced extreme want during the first two years at the university and had had to earn his own living and who from his earliest childhood had resented the fact that he was entirely dependent on the charity of his benefactor. But this strange trait in Alyosha's character could not apparently be too severely condemned. For anyone who had only the slightest acquaintance with him was immediately convinced, whenever this question arose, that Alyosha was one of those young men who in a way resembled saintly fools and who, if they suddenly came into possession of a large sum of money, would not hesitate to give it away at the first demand either to some charity or perhaps simply to the first clever swindler who happened to ask for it. And, generally speaking, he did not seem to know the value of money, though not, of course, in a literal sense. When he was given pocket money, which he never asked for himself, he either kept it for weeks not knowing what to do with it, or was so very careless with it that it was gone in no time. Peter Miusov, who was very sensitive where money and bourgeois honesty were concerned, delivered himself of the following aphorism after he had got to know Alyosha better some years later: 'Here you have perhaps the only man in the world who, if he were left alone without a penny in a strange city of a million inhabitants, would never die of exposure or hunger because he would be instantly fed and given some job, and if not, he would find a job himself, and that would cost him no effort or humiliation, nor would he be a burden to his employers but, on the contrary, they would probably consider it a pleasure.'

He did not finish his studies at school. A year before the end of his course, he suddenly told the ladies with whom he lived that he was going to his father about a certain matter which had just happened to enter his head. The ladies, who were very fond of him, were unwilling to let him go. The journey was not an expensive one and the ladies refused to let him pawn his watch, a parting gift of his benefactor's family before they went abroad, but provided him liberally with money and even with a new suit of clothes and linen. But he returned half of their money to them, declaring that he had made up his mind to travel third class. On arriving in our little town, he at first made no direct answer to his father's question why he had come before finishing his studies at school, but was, I am told, quite unusually pensive. Soon it was discovered that he was trying to find his mother's grave. He had even confessed himself at the time that that was really why he had come. But it is doubtful whether that was the only reason for his visit. It is more probable that he did not know himself and could not possibly explain what it was exactly that seemed suddenly to rise up in his soul and draw him irresistibly towards a new, unknown, but inevitable, path. His father could not show him where his second wife was buried because he had never bothered to visit her grave after her coffin had been covered over with earth, and it had been so long ago that he had entirely forgotten where it was. . . .

A word about Karamazov. He had been living only a short time in our town before the arrival of his sons. Three or four years after the death of his second wife he had gone to the south of Russia and finally turned up in Odessa where he spent several years. At first he made the acquaintance, in his own words, of 'a lot of dirty, low-down Jews', but ended up by being received not only by 'dirty' but also by 'highly respectable' Jews. It can be reliably assumed that it was during that period of his life that he had acquired a special knack for making money and amassing capital. He returned finally to our little town only about three years before Alyosha's arrival. His former acquaintances found him terribly aged, though he was not by any means such an old man. He carried himself not so much with more dignity than before as with more arrogance. The former clown, for instance, showed an insolent predilection for making others appear as clowns. His behaviour with women was not just indecent as it had been, but somehow disgusting. Soon he opened many new public houses in the district. It was evident that he was worth perhaps a hundred thousand roubles or only a very little less. Many people of our town and district were not slow to borrow money from him – on the best possible security, of course. Of late he had somehow grown to look bloated. He seemed to have lost his balance and his self-control, he had grown rather inconsequential, beginning one thing and finishing another, letting his thoughts wander from one project to another, and was more and more often drunk. Had it not been for his servant Grigory, who had also grown quite old by that time and who sometimes looked after him almost like a nurse, Karamazov would perhaps not have escaped serious trouble. Alyosha's arrival seemed to have had a sobering effect on him even from the moral point of view, as though something had awakened in this prematurely aged man that had long been smothered in his soul. 'Do you know, my boy,' he often used to say to Alyosha, looking intently at him, 'that you're like her, the "shrieker", I mean?' That was what he called his dead wife, Alyosha's mother. It was Grigory who at last showed the 'shrieker's' grave to Alyosha. He took him to our town cemetery and in a remote corner of it showed him a cheap but decently kept grave with a cast-iron gravestone which bore the inscription of the name, social position, age, and date of death of the deceased. Below were even engraved four lines of ancient verse which is usually found on middle-class tombs. Surprisingly, this tombstone turned out to have been put up by Grigory. It was he who had put it up on the grave of the poor 'shrieker' at his own expense, after Karamazov, whom he had often annoyed by reminding him of the grave, had at last gone to Odessa, dismissing both the grave and all his memories. Alyosha did not show any particular emotion at his mother's grave; he merely listened to Grigory's sober and sensible account of the erection of the tombstone, stood there for some time with a bowed head, and walked away without uttering a word. Since then he had not visited the cemetery for, perhaps, the whole of the year. But this small episode had also had an effect on Karamazov – and a very original one, too. He suddenly took a thousand roubles to our monastery and ordered requiem masses for the soul of his wife, but not for the second, Alyosha's mother, the 'shrieker', but for the first, Adelaida, who used to beat him. In the evening of the same day he got drunk and abused the monks to Alyosha. He himself was far from religious; the man had probably never put a penny candle before an icon. Such individuals have very strange outbursts of sudden feelings and sudden thoughts.

I have already mentioned that he had grown very bloated. By

that time his face bore unmistakable traces of the sort of life he had led. In addition to the long fleshy bags under his little eyes, which were always insolent, suspicious, and sardonic, in addition to the multitude of deep wrinkles on his fat little face, there hung under his sharp chin a large Adam's apple, fleshy and longish like a little purse, which gave him a sort of revoltingly sensual appearance. Add to that a long, cruel, and sensual mouth with full lips, between which could be seen stumps of black and almost decayed teeth. He sputtered every time he began to speak. However, he liked to make fun of his own face himself, though he was apparently well satisfied with it. He used particularly to point to his nose, which was not very large but very thin and conspicuously aquiline: 'A regular Roman nose,' he used to say, 'and together with my Adam's apple a real face of an ancient Roman patrician of the decadent period.' He seemed proud of it.

It was shortly after finding his mother's grave that Alyosha suddenly told his father that he wanted to enter the monastery and that the monks were willing to receive him as a novice. He explained that it was his fervent wish and that he was asking his solemn consent as his father. The old man already knew that the elder Zossima, who was seeking salvation in the hermitage of our monastery, had made a special impression on his 'gentle boy'.

'That elder,' he said, having listened to Alyosha thoughtfully and in silence and not in the least surprised at his request, 'is, of course, one of their most honest monks. H'm – so that's where you want to be, my gentle boy!' He was half drunk, and suddenly smiled his slow half-tipsy smile, which was not without cunning and drunken craftiness. 'Well, you know, my boy, I had a feeling you'd finish up by doing something like that. You believe me, don't you? That's what you always intended to do, isn't it? I'm sure of that. Well, why not? You've got your own two thousand – there's your dowry, and I'll never leave you in the lurch, my boy. Why, I'll pay what's necessary for you there, if they ask me for it. And if they don't ask, why go begging them to accept my money? Isn't that so? Why, you spend money like a canary – two grains a week. H'm. There's a certain monastery, you know, with a cluster of houses at the bottom of the hill in which, as everyone knows, the 'monastery wives', as they are called, live, thirty wives in all, I should think. . . . I've been there, and you know, it's interesting, in its own way, of course, I mean just to relieve the monotony, you understand. The only awful thing about it is the terrible Russian patriotism of these fellows – not a single Frenchwoman among them, and they could have had them, for they have pots of money. I suppose, when they get to hear of it, they'll be coming along. Well, here there's nothing of the kind. No monastery wives, just two hundred monks. Everything above board. They keep their fasts. True enough. . . . H'm. . . . So you want to go to the monks, do you? You know, I really am sorry for you, Alyosha. You may not believe it, my boy, but I've grown very fond of you. . . . Still, I suppose it's all for the best: you'll pray for us, sinners that we are, for we have sinned quite a lot here, haven't we? I've always wondered who would ever pray for me. Does such a man exist in the world? My dear boy, I'm awfully stupid about such things. You do believe me, don't you? Awfully. You see, stupid as I am about these things, I keep thinking, thinking, not very often, of course, but I do all the same. Why, I say to myself, the devils will surely not forget to drag me down with hooks to their place when I die. Well, then, so I think to myself – hooks? Where do they get their hooks from? What are they made of? Iron? Where do they forge them? They've got some sort of workshop there, have they? You see, in your monastery the monks are quite certain that, for instance, there's a ceiling in hell. Now, I'm quite willing to believe in hell, but only if it has no ceiling – it makes it much more refined, more enlightened, more Lutheran-like, that is. But actually it doesn't make much difference whether hell has a ceiling or not, does it now? And yet the whole damned business depends on that alone! For if there is no ceiling, there can be no hooks. And if there are no hooks, the whole thing's a fake, which again is unlikely, for who would then drag me down with hooks? And if they don't drag me down, what's going to happen then? Where's justice in the world? *Il faudrait les inventer* – the hooks, I mean. Just for me. For me alone. For if you only knew, Alyosha, what a shameless wretch I am!'

'But there are no hooks there,' said Alyosha, gazing gently and seriously at his father.

'I see, I see, only shadows of hooks. I know. I know. This is how a Frenchman described hell: *J'ai vu l'ombre d'un cocher qui avec l'ombre d'une brosse frottait l'ombre d'une carrosse.* But how do you know there are no hooks, my boy? When you've been with the monks, you'll sing another tune. However, go by all means, get at the truth there and come and tell me: I daresay it will be easier going to the other world if you know for certain what it's like there. Besides, it is more seemly for you to live with the monks than here with a drunken old man and those young sluts. . . . Though, like an angel, nothing can touch you. Well, perhaps nothing will touch you there, either. You see, that's why I'm letting you go – that's what I hope for. You've got your head screwed on the right way. You're enthusiastic now, but you'll get over it – you'll be cured and come back to me. And I'll be waiting for you: for, you see, my dear boy, I feel that you're the only man in the world who hasn't condemned me – I feel it, you know. I can't help feeling it!'

And he even began to blubber. He was sentimental. He was wicked and sentimental.

5

Elders

SOME of my readers may imagine that my young man was a sickly, ecstatic, poorly developed character, a pale dreamer, a weak and emaciated little creature. On the contrary, at the time Alyosha was a well-built, red-cheeked, clear-eyed boy of nineteen, looking a picture of health. He was very handsome, too, slender, of medium height, with dark-brown hair, a regular, though a little elongated, oval face, a pair of wide-set sparkling, dark grey eyes, very thoughtful and apparently very self-composed. It may be said that red cheeks are not incompatible with fanaticism or mysticism; but I can't help feeling that, if anything, Alyosha was more of a realist than anyone. Oh, of course, in the monastery he fully believed in miracles, but in my opinion miracles will never confound a realist. It is not miracles that make a realist turn to religion. A true realist, if he is an unbeliever, will always find the strength and the ability not to believe in a miracle, and if faced with a miracle as an undeniable fact, he will sooner disbelieve his own senses than admit the fact. And if he does admit it, he will admit it as a natural fact hitherto unknown to him.

In a realist faith does not arise from a miracle, but the miracle from faith. Just because of his realism, a realist, once he believes, must admit a miracle. The apostle Thomas said that he would not believe till he saw, and when he saw, he said: 'My Lord and my God!' Was it a miracle that made him believe? Most probably not, but he believed only because he wanted to believe, and maybe he already fully believed in his innermost heart even when he said, 'Except I shall see, I will not believe.'

It will be said perhaps that Alyosha was dull-witted, undeveloped, that he had not completed his studies, and so on. That he did not complete his studies is true, but to say that he was dull-witted and stupid would be a great injustice. I shall simply repeat what I have said above: he entered upon this path solely because it alone caught his imagination and presented him all at once with an ideal way of escape for his soul from darkness to light. Add to that that he was to a certain extent a young man of our own times, that is, honest by nature, demanding truth, seeking it, believing in it, and, believing in it, demanding to serve it with all the strength of his soul, yearning for an immediate act of heroism and wishing to sacrifice everything, even life itself, for that act of heroism. Though, unhappily, these youths do not understand that the sacrifice of one's life is in most cases perhaps the easiest of all sacrifices, and that to sacrifice, for instance, five or six years of their life, full of youthful fervour, to hard and difficult study, if only to increase tenfold their powers of serving truth so as to be able to carry out the great work they have set their hearts on carrying out – that such a sacrifice is very often almost beyond the strength of many of them. Alyosha merely chose a path leading in the opposite direction to that of all the others, but with the same ardent desire for swift achievement. The moment he thought seriously about it he was overcome by the conviction of the existence of immortality and God, and he quite naturally said to himself: 'I want to live for immortality, and I won't accept any compromise.' Similarly, if he had decided that there was no immortality and no God, he would at once have become an atheist and a Socialist (for Socialism is not only the labour question, or the question of the so-called fourth estate, but above all an atheistic question, the question of the modern integration of atheism, the question of the Tower of Babel which is deliberately being erected without God, not for the sake of reaching heaven from earth, but for the sake of bringing heaven down to earth). It seemed strange and impossible to Alyosha to go on living as before. It is written: 'If thou wilt be perfect, go and sell all that thou hast . . . and come and follow me.' So Alyosha said to himself: 'I cannot give up two roubles instead of "all that thou hast" or just go to morning mass instead of "come and follow me".' Perhaps among the memories of his childhood he also preserved the memory of the monastery near our town where his mother may have taken him to morning mass. Perhaps the slanting rays of the setting sun reflected in the icon to which his mother, the poor 'shrieker', had held him up, had also something to do with it. He had arrived in our town looking thoughtful, and perhaps he wished only to see whether to give up all he had or only two roubles – and in the monastery he met this elder. . . .

This elder was, as I have explained above, the elder Zossima; but I have first to say a few words here about what 'elders' are in our monasteries and it is unfortunate that I don't feel sufficiently competent or expert to do so. I will try, however, to give a superficial account of it in a few words. To begin with, competent experts assert that elders and the institution of elders made an appearance in our country and in our monasteries quite recently, not more than a hundred years ago, while in the Orthodox East, and especially in Sinai and on Mount Athos, they have existed for over a thousand years. It is said that the institution of elders existed in Russia, too, in ancient times, or at any rate that it most certainly ought to have existed, but that owing to the troubled times in Russia, the Tartar rule, the civil wars, the interruption of our former relations with the East after the fall of Constantinople, this institution fell into decay and the elders ceased to exist. It was revived in our country towards the end of the last century by one of the great ascetics (as he was called) Paissy Velichkovsky and his disciples, but today, even after a hundred years, they are to be found only in a very few monasteries, and are sometimes even persecuted as an unheard-of innovation in Russia. It flourished especially in Russia in the famous Kozelsky monastery. When and how it was introduced into our monastery I cannot say, but there has already been a third succession of elders there. Zossima was one of the last, but he was ill and almost dying, and they did not even know who was to take his place. It was an important question for our monastery because until then it had not been renowned for anything in particular; it had no relics of saints, no wonder-working icons, nor, indeed, any glorious traditions connected with our history, nor was it known for any particularly great services to our country. It had flourished and its fame had spread all over Russia solely because of its elders, and crowds of pilgrims flocked to our monastery for thousands of miles from every corner of Russia to see and hear them. What, then, is an elder? An elder is a man who takes your soul and your will into his soul and will. Having chosen your elder, you renounce your will and yield it to him in complete sub-mission and complete self-abnegation. This novitiate, this terrible discipline is accepted voluntarily by the man who consecrates himself to this life in the hope that after a long novitiate he will attain to such a degree of self-mastery and self-conquest that at last he will, after a life of obedience, achieve complete freedom, that is to say, freedom from himself, and so escape the fate of those who have lived their whole lives without finding themselves in themselves. This invention, that is to say, the institution of elders, is not based on any theory, but has evolved in the East from a practice that today goes back over a thousand years. The obligations due to an elder have nothing to do with the ordinary 'obedience', which has always existed in our Russian monasteries. The elder's disciples must always be ready to make confession to him, and there must be an indissoluble bond between the elder and his followers. It is said, for instance, that in the early days of Christianity one such novice, who had failed to carry out a command imposed upon him by his elder, left his monas-tery in Syria and went to Egypt. There, after a long series of great exploits, he was found worthy at last of suffering torture and a mar-tyr's death for his faith. But when the church, already regarding him as a saint, was burying his body, the coffin, at the deacon's intoning, 'Depart, all ye unbaptized', broke away from its place and was cast out of the church, and this took place three times. And it was only then that they found out that this holy martyr had broken the vow of obedience and left his elder and that he could not therefore be forgiven without the elder's absolution, in spite of his great exploits. It was only after the elder, who had been summoned, had given him absolution from his vow of obedience that his burial could take place. Of course, all this is only an old legend, but here is something that happened quite recently: a Russian monk of our own day, who was seeking salvation on Mount Athos, was suddenly told by his elder to leave Athos, which he had grown to love greatly as a holy place and a haven of rest, and go first to Jerusalem to worship at the Holy Places, and then return to the north of Siberia. 'Your place is there and not here,' the elder told him. Cast down with grief, the astonished monk went to the Oecumenical Patriarch at Constantinople and begged him to release him from his vow of obedience. But the Oecumenical Patriarch replied that not only was he unable to release him, but that there was not, and could not be, on earth a power which could release him from his vow, once exacted by an elder, except the elder who had exacted it from him. Thus, the elders are in certain cases endowed with incredibly boundless authority. That is why the institution of elders at first met with something very like persecution in many of our monasteries. And yet the elders were immediately highly esteemed by the common people. Ordinary people as well as great aristocrats, for instance, flocked to the elders of our monastery, so that, prostrating themselves before them, they could confess their doubts, their sins, and their sufferings, and ask for counsel and admonition. Seeing this, the opponents of the elders cried that, in addition to other transgressions, the sacrament of the confession was being arbitrarily and frivolously degraded here, though the continual baring of their souls to the elder by the novice or the layman had nothing whatever to do with the sacrament. In the end, however, the institution of elders survived and is gradually taking root in Russian monasteries. It is, of course, true that this instrument of the moral regeneration of man from slavery to freedom and to moral perfectibility, which has stood the test of a thousand years, may be turned into a double-edged weapon, so that it may lead some man not to humility and complete self-mastery, but, on the contrary, to the most satanic pride, that is to say, to slavery and not to freedom.

The elder Zossima was sixty-five and came of a family of landowners. At some time in his early youth he had been in the army and served in the Caucasus as an officer. He had, no doubt, impressed Alyosha by some special quality of his soul. Alyosha lived in the cell of the elder, who was very fond of him and allowed him to stay with him. It should be noted that Alyosha, while living in the monastery, was in no way bound; he was completely free to go where he pleased and be away even for days on end. If he wore his cassock it was voluntarily, so as not to appear different from anyone else in the monastery. But, of course, he liked to do so. Perhaps the power and the fame which constantly surrounded the elder exercised a great influence on Alyosha's youthful imagination. It was said by many people about the elder Zossima that, by permitting everyone for so many years to come to bare their hearts and beg his advice and healing words, he had absorbed so many secrets, sorrows, and avowals into his soul that in the end he had acquired so fine a perception that he could tell at the first glance from the face of a stranger what he came for, what he wanted, and what kind of torment racked his conscience. Indeed, he sometimes astounded, confounded, and almost frightened his visitor by this knowledge of his secret before he had even had time to utter a word. But for all that Alyosha almost always noticed that many, almost all, who went for the first time to have a private talk with the elder, entered his cell in fear and trepidation, but almost always came out looking bright and happy, and that even the gloomiest face was transformed into a happy one. Alyosha was also greatly struck by the fact that the elder was not at all stern; on the contrary, he was almost always cheerful in his manner. The monks used to say about him that he invariably showed a greater attachment to those who were more sinful and that the more greatly a man had sinned the more he loved him. There were some among the monks, even up to the end of the elder's life, who hated and envied him, but they were becoming fewer in number and were silent, though some of them included quite well-known and important persons in the monastery, as, for instance, one of the oldest monks, who was greatly esteemed for his vows of silence and for the strictness with which he kept his fasts. But in spite of it all the overwhelming majority were undoubtedly on Father Zossima's side, and many of them loved him with all their hearts, warmly and sincerely; some were, indeed, almost fanatically devoted to him. These openly declared, though not in a very loud voice, that he was a saint, that there could be no doubt about it, and anticipating his impending death, expected instantaneous miracles. They hoped that the deceased would confer great glory on the monastery in the most immediate future. Alyosha, too, had absolute faith in the miraculous powers of the elder, as he had absolute faith in the story of the coffin that flew out of the church. He saw many who came with sick children or grown-up relatives and besought the elder to lay his hands upon them and offer up a prayer over them, return very soon afterwards, and some even the next day, and fall weeping on their knees before the elder, thanking him for healing their sick. Whether they had actually been healed or whether it was only a natural improvement in their health was a question that did not exist for Alyosha, for he fully believed in the spiritual powers of his teacher, whose fame he considered almost his own triumph. But his heart thrilled especially and he looked positively radiant when the elder came out to the crowd of pilgrims from the common people who were waiting for his appearance at the gates of the hermitage and who had flocked from all over Russia purposely to see the elder and obtain his blessing. They prostrated themselves before him, wept, kissed his feet, kissed the ground on which he stood, cried out to him in loud voices, the women holding up their children to him and leading sick 'shriekers'. The elder spoke to them, read a brief prayer over them, blessed and dismissed them. More recently he sometimes became so weak from his attacks of illness that he was scarcely able to leave his cell; and the pilgrims sometimes waited in the monastery several days for him to come out. Alyosha never asked himself why they loved him so much, or why they prostrated themselves before him and wept with emotion merely at the sight of his face. Oh, he realized full well that for the humble soul of the Russian of humble origin, worn out by toil and grief and, above all, by everlasting injustice and everlasting sin, both his own and the world's, there was no greater need and comfort than to find some holy shrine or person, to fall down before him and worship him: 'If there is sin, injustice, and temptation among us, then there is at any rate someone somewhere on earth who is holier and superior; he has the truth, he knows the truth, which means that it is not dead on earth and will therefore come to us, too, one day, and rule all over the earth, as it was promised.' Alyosha knew that the common people felt and even thought just like that. He understood it. But that the elder Zossima was this very saint and this custodian of God's truth in the eyes of the people – of that he had no doubt whatever, any more than the weeping peasants and their sick wives who held out their children to the elder. The conviction that after his death the elder would confer extraordinary glory upon the monastery took, perhaps, even deeper root in Alyosha's soul than in anyone else's in the monastery. Indeed, all during the last few months a sort of deep, ardent, inner ecstasy burned more and more fiercely in his heart. He was not at all troubled by the fact that this elder stood before him as a solitary example: 'It doesn't matter, he is holy, his heart contains the secret of a renewal for all, the power which will finally establish truth on earth, and all will be holy, and will love each other, and there will be no more rich nor poor, exalted nor humbled, but all men will be as the children of God and the real kingdom of Christ will come.' That was what Alyosha dreamt in his heart.

The arrival of his two brothers, whom he had not known at all till then, seemed to make a most powerful impression on Alyosha. He made friends with his half-brother Dmitry more quickly and more intimately (though he arrived later) than with his brother Ivan. He was very anxious to get to know his brother Ivan, but though Ivan had lived with his father for two months and though they had seen each other quite frequently, they did not seem to become intimate: taciturn himself, Alyosha seemed to be expecting something and to be ashamed of something, while his brother Ivan, though Alyosha had noticed at first that he looked intently and curiously at him, seemed soon to have lost all interest in him. Alyosha noticed it with some embarrassment. He ascribed his brother's indifference to the disparity in their ages and, especially, in their education. But Alyosha thought of something else: Ivan's lack of curiosity and sympathy with him might have arisen from some cause unknown to him. He could not help feeling for some reason that Ivan was preoccupied with something private and important, that he was striving towards some goal, perhaps difficult to attain, so that he had no thought to spare for Alyosha, and that that was the only reason why he paid no attention to him. Alyosha also wondered whether his brother, a learned atheist, did not feel a sort of contempt for him, a silly novice. He knew for a fact that his brother was an atheist. He could not take offence at his contempt, if, indeed, it existed, but all the same he waited with a sort of uneasy embarrassment, which he did not understand himself, for the time when his brother would want to become better acquainted with him. Dmitry spoke with the utmost respect of Ivan. He used to talk of him with a sort of special feeling. From him

Alyosha learned all the details of the important business which more recently had formed such a remarkably close bond between the two elder brothers. Dmitry's enthusiastic opinions of his brother Ivan were the more striking in Alyosha's eyes, since, compared to Ivan, his brother Dmitry was almost uneducated, and the two of them, put next to each other, seemed to present such a striking contrast both in personality and character that one could hardly think of two men who were more unlike each other.

It was at this time that the meeting, or rather the gathering, of all the members of this ill-assorted family took place in the elder's cell, a meeting which was to have a tremendous influence on Alyosha. As a matter of fact, the pretext for this meeting was not genuine. It was just at that time that the disagreements between Dmitry and his father about the inheritance and financial dealings had apparently reached a crisis. Their relationship had become intolerably strained. It was apparently Karamazov who first jokingly suggested that they should all meet in the elder Zossima's cell and, without actually resorting to his arbitration, somehow come to some sort of decent agreement, particularly as the dignified presence of the elder might inspire respect and lead to a reconciliation. Dmitry, who had never been at the elder's and had never even seen him, quite naturally jumped to the conclusion that his father was somehow trying to intimidate him with the elder; but as he secretly reproached himself for many particularly sharp outbursts in his arguments with his father recently, he accepted the challenge. It must be noted, incidentally, that, unlike Ivan, he did not live with his father, but by himself at the other end of the town. It so happened that Peter Miusov, who was at the time living on his estate near our town, jumped at this suggestion of Karamazov's. A liberal of the forties and fifties, a free-thinker and an atheist, he took a great interest in this affair, perhaps because he was bored, or, again, perhaps from a taste for light entertainment. He suddenly felt like having a look at the monastery and the 'saint'. As his old quarrels with the monastery still continued and his lawsuit with it about the boundaries of their land, the rights of tree-cutting in some woods and fishing in the stream, etc., still dragged on, he hastened to make use of it under the pretext of coming to an understanding with the Father Superior and finding some way of putting an end to their differences to their mutual satisfaction.

A visitor who came with such good intentions could, of course, expect to be received in the monastery with more attention and more courtesy than one who came out of mere curiosity. In view of all these considerations, the monastery authorities no doubt put pressure upon the elder, who had hardly left his cell of late and who refused to receive even ordinary visitors because of his illness. In the end the elder agreed to see them, and the day was fixed. 'Who has set me up to arbitrate between them?' was all he said with a smile to Alyosha.

When he heard of the meeting, Alyosha was greatly perturbed. If any one of these contending and disputing parties could regard this interview seriously, it would undoubtedly be only his brother Dmitry; the others would come only from frivolous motives, which might even be insulting to the elder – that Alyosha realized very well. His brother Ivan and Miusov would come out of curiosity, perhaps of the crudest kind, and his father perhaps to act like a clown and make some disgraceful scene. Oh, though he never uttered a word, Alyosha knew his father fairly thoroughly. I repeat, the boy was not at all simple-minded as people took him to be. He was waiting for the appointed day with a heavy heart. He was at bottom undoubtedly very anxious to see all these family disagreements come to an end somehow or other. Nevertheless, his greatest anxiety concerned the elder; he trembled for him and for his reputation, he dreaded that he might be offended, fearing particularly Miusov's refined and polite sneers and the supercilious reticences of the learned Ivan – so at least it seemed to him. He even wanted to take the risk of warning the elder and telling him something about the persons who might come to see him, but, on thinking it over, he said nothing. All he did was to send word the day before the meeting to his brother Dmitry, through a friend, that he was very fond of him and expected him to keep his promise. Dmitry was puzzled, for he could not remember promising him anything, but he replied by letter that he would do his utmost to control himself in the face of 'baseness' and though he had a profound respect for the elder and for his brother Ivan, he was convinced that the meeting was either a trap or an unworthy farce. 'All the same, I'd rather bite out my tongue than be lacking in respect for the saintly man whom you revere so much,' Dmitry concluded his short letter. It brought little comfort to Alyosha.

BOOK TWO: AN INAUSPICIOUS MEETING

I

They Arrive at the Monastery

IT WAS A BEAUTIFUL, WARM, SUNNY DAY AT THE END OF August. The meeting with the elder had been arranged to take place at about half past eleven immediately after late mass. Our visitors, however, did not put in an appearance at the church, but arrived at the end of the service. They drove up in two carriages; in the first, an elegant barouche drawn by two fine horses, was Peter Miusov with a distant relative of his, a young man of twenty, by the name of Peter Kalganov. This young man was about to enter the university, though Miusov, with whom he was for some reason staying at the time, was trying to persuade him to go abroad with him, in order to enter the university of Zürich or Jena, and take his degree there. The young man was still undecided. He was thoughtful and seemingly abstracted. He had a pleasant face, was of sturdy build, and rather tall. Occasionally there was a strangely fixed look in his eyes: like all abstracted people, he sometimes stared at you for a long time without seeing you. He was taciturn and rather awkward, but at times, though only when he was alone with someone, he would suddenly become very talkative, impetuous, and ready to burst out laughing at the slightest provocation, sometimes hardly knowing himself what he was laughing at. But his animation disappeared as quickly and as suddenly as it appeared. He was always well and even immaculately dressed; he had an independent income and expectations of much more. He was a good friend of Alyosha's.

Karamazov with his beloved son Ivan drove up in a very ancient, jolting but roomy carriage, drawn by a pair of old pinkish-grey horses, which lagged a long way behind Miusov's carriage. Dmitry had been informed the day before of the time of the meeting, but he was late. The visitors left their carriages at the inn by the monastery wall and entered the monastery gates on foot. With the exception of Karamazov, none of the three visitors had apparently ever seen a monastery, and Miusov had probably not been to church for thirty years. He gazed around him with some curiosity, not devoid of a certain affectation of ease. But, observant though he was, he found nothing to interest him within the precincts of the monastery, except perhaps the church and the domestic buildings, which were very ordinary anyway. The last of the worshippers were leaving the church, baring their heads and crossing themselves. Among the peasants were people belonging to the higher strata of society, two or three ladies and one very old general; they were all staying at the inn. The beggars at once surrounded our visitors, but no one gave them anything. Only Peter Kalganov took a ten-copeck piece out of his purse and, looking terribly nervous and embarrassed, goodness only knows why, hurriedly put it into the hands of a woman, adding quickly: 'Share it out among you.' None of his companions said anything to him about it, so that there was no reason at all for his embarrassment; but, perceiving this, he was even more embarrassed.

One thing was queer, though: they should, as a matter of fact, have been expected and perhaps received with a certain show of respect: one of them had quite recently made a donation of a thousand roubles and the other was one of the richest landowners of our district and, so to speak, a most cultured man, upon whom they were all in a way dependent, since their rights of fishing in the stream might be jeopardized as a result of some unforeseen decision of the court. And yet no official person met them. Miusov gazed abstractedly at the gravestones near the church and was about to remark that the graves must have cost a pretty penny to the relatives of the deceased for the right of burial in such a 'holy' place, but he said nothing: his habitual 'liberal' irony was turning almost into anger.

'Damn it, there doesn't seem to be anyone one could ask in this stupid place,' he muttered suddenly, as though speaking to himself. 'We'll have to do something, for time's getting on.'

Suddenly an elderly, bald-headed man with ingratiating eyes, wearing a bulky summer overcoat, walked up to them. Raising his hat and with a honeyed lisp, he introduced himself as Maximov, a Tula landowner. He immediately did his best to direct the visitors.

'The elder Zossima,' he said, 'lives in the hermitage – in the hermitage, gentlemen – in complete seclusion – just about four hundred yards from the monastery – through the wood – the wood. . . .'

'I'm quite aware of the fact that it's through the wood, sir,' Karamazov replied. 'But we don't remember the way. It's a long time since we were here.'

'It's through this gate, sir, and straight through the wood – through the wood. Follow me, sir. Please – er – I'm going there myself. . . . Yes, sir. This way, sir, this way. . . . '

They came out of the gate and walked in the direction of the wood. Maximov, a man of about sixty, did not so much walk as run alongside, gazing at them with a nervous, almost offensive curiosity. He stared at them with eyes starting out of his head.

'You see, sir,' Miusov observed severely, 'we've come to see the elder on private business. We've, as it were, been granted an audience by "that great personage", and – er – though we're grateful to you for showing us the way, we – er – cannot ask you to come in with us.'

'I've – I've already been there. . . . *Un chevalier parfait!*' and the landowner snapped his fingers in the air.

'Who is a *chevalier*?' asked Miusov.

'The elder, sir, the elder – the splendid elder. . . . The honour and glory of the monastery. Zossima, sir! Such an elder. . . . '

His confused speech was interrupted by a very pale and haggard little monk in a cowl who overtook them. The monk, with a very courteous and profound bow, announced:

'The Father Superior, gentlemen, invites you all to dine with him after your visit to the hermitage. In his rooms at one o'clock, not later. And you, too, sir,' he turned to Maximov.

'Thank you very much,' Karamazov cried, greatly delighted with the invitation, 'I shall be very glad to! Very glad, indeed. And, you know, we have all given our word to behave ourselves here. . . . What about you, Mr Miusov? Will you come too?'

'Of course I will. Why, I've come here for the express purpose of seeing all their customs. The only thing that bothers me is that I shall have to share your company, Mr Karamazov. . . . '

'Well, I can't see Dmitry anywhere. . . . '

'I hope he doesn't turn up. That would be splendid. You don't suppose I like all this disgusting business of yours, do you? And with you here, too? So we'll come to dinner,' he addressed the little monk. 'Will you please go and thank the Father Superior?'

'No, sir,' replied the monk, 'it's my duty to conduct you to the elder.'

'Well,' Maximov twittered, 'in that case I'll go to the Father Superior – I mean, I may as well, mayn't I?'

'The Father Superior,' the monk said hesitantly, 'is busy just now, but, of course, just as you like, sir.'

'A most tiresome old fellow,' Miusov observed in a loud voice after Maximov had run back to the monastery.

'Reminds me of von Sohn,' Karamazov said suddenly.

'You would say that! Why does he remind you of von Sohn? Have you ever seen von Sohn?'

'I've seen his photograph. Not by his features, but by something I can't explain. The very spit of von Sohn. I can always tell from the face.'

'Well, I daresay. You're an expert on that. But, look here, Mr Karamazov, you've just said yourself that we'd given our word to behave ourselves. Remember? I'm telling you – control yourself! For, if you start playing the fool, I've no intention of being dragged down to your level. You see the sort of man he is,' he turned to the monk. 'I'm afraid to visit decent people with him.'

A thin, quiet little smile appeared on the pale, bloodless lips of the little monk, a smile that was not without a touch of cunning, but he made no reply and it was all too evident that he said nothing out of a sense of his own dignity. Miusov frowned more than ever.

'Oh, to blazes with them all!' it flashed through his mind. 'An outward appearance carefully cultivated through the ages, but really nothing but nonsense and charlatanism.'

'Here's the hermitage!' cried Karamazov. 'We've arrived! The gates are shut.'

And he began crossing himself fervently before the images of the saints painted above and on the sides of the gates.

'When in Rome do as the Romans do,' he observed. 'There are altogether twenty-five saints seeking salvation in this hermitage, looking at one another and eating cabbage soup. What is so remarkable, though, is that no woman is allowed to enter these gates. And that's quite true, you know. But,' he suddenly addressed the monk, 'I've heard that the elder receives ladies. He does, doesn't he?'

'There are peasant women here, too, now. There, sitting on the ground near the wooden veranda. They're waiting. And for ladies two little rooms have been built on top of the veranda but outside the hermitage wall. You can see the windows up there. The elder goes to see them by an inner passage when he feels well enough. But, you see, it's still outside the wall of the hermitage. There's one lady waiting there now with her sick daughter. Mrs Khokhlakov, a Kharkov landowner. I expect he must have promised to come out to her, though lately he's been so weak that he's hardly gone out even to the common people.'

'Oh, so there is a secret passage from the hermitage to the ladies! Please, holy Father, don't think I'm suggesting anything. I'm just making a statement of fact. You know, on Mount Athos – you've heard of it, haven't you? – not only women but any creatures of the female sex are not allowed – no hens, no turkey hens, no calves. . . . '

'Look here, sir,' Miusov interjected, 'I shall go back and leave you here alone, and they'll chuck you out when I'm gone. I'm warning you.'

'I'm not interfering with you, Mr Miusov, am I? Look,' Karamazov cried suddenly, stepping inside the wall of the hermitage, 'look in what a vale of roses they live!'

And, indeed, though there were no roses now, there were a great many rare and beautiful autumn flowers growing wherever there was the least room for them to be planted. It was obvious that they were tended by a skilful hand. There were flower-beds also inside the walls of the churchyard and between the graves. The wooden, one-storied little house, with its porch in front of the entrance, where the elder lived also had flowers planted all round it.

'And was it like this in the time of the last elder Varsonofy?' asked Karamazov, as he mounted the front steps. 'I'm told he didn't like beautiful things and that he would sometimes jump to his feet and beat even lady visitors with a stick.'

'The elder Varsonofy did indeed seem a little strange sometimes,' replied the monk, 'but people tell all sorts of silly tales about him. He never beat anyone with a stick, though. And now, gentlemen,' he concluded, 'if you will kindly wait a minute, I'll announce you.'

'For the last time, sir, remember your promise,' Miusov managed to mutter once more. 'Do you hear? Behave yourself, or you'll be sorry.'

'Now I wonder why you're in such a state of excitement,' Karamazov observed sarcastically. 'You're not worried about your sins, are you? I'm told he can tell by a man's eyes what's at the back of his mind. And how seriously you take them – you, a Parisian and a man of progressive views! I'm surprised at you – indeed I am!'

But Miusov had no time to reply to this sarcastic remark. They were asked to come in. He walked in somewhat irritated.

'Well,' it flashed through his mind, 'I know perfectly well what's going to happen now. I'm angry, I'll start arguing, I'll get excited and – lower myself and my ideas.'

2

The Old Clown

THEY entered the room almost at the same moment as the elder, who came out of his bedroom as soon as they appeared. There were two monks from the hermitage waiting for the elder in his cell: one of them the Father Librarian and the other – Father Paissy, a sick man, though not old, and, it was said, a great scholar. Besides them, there stood waiting in a corner (he remained there standing all through the interview) a young man of about twenty-two, wearing ordinary dress, a seminarist and a future theologian, who for some reason was enjoying the patronage of the monastery and the monks. He was rather tall, fresh-complexioned, with prominent cheek-bones, and clever, observant, narrow brown eyes. His face wore an expression of absolute reverence, but decorous and without a trace of fawning. He did not even greet the visitors with a bow, not being of the same social standing as they, but in a subordinate and dependent position.

The elder Zossima came out accompanied by a novice and by Alyosha. The monks rose and greeted him with a very low bow, touching the floor with their fingers. Then they went up to him for his blessing and kissed his hand. Having blessed them, the elder replied with as low a bow, also touching the floor with his fingers, and asked each of them for his blessing. The whole ceremony was performed very gravely and not at all like an everyday rite, but almost with a show of feeling. It seemed to Miusov, however, that it was all done deliberately in order to impress them. He stood in front of the other visitors. He should – and he had considered it carefully the day before – out of ordinary politeness and in spite of his own ideas on the subject (since it was the custom there) have gone up to the elder to receive his blessing, even if he did not kiss his hand. But, seeing all this bowing and kissing of the two monks, he changed his mind in a moment. Looking very grave, he made a rather deep and dignified bow, as is customary in high society, and retired to a chair. Karamazov did the same, but this time mimicking Miusov like a monkey. Ivan bowed very gravely and politely, but also kept his hands at his sides, while Kalganov was so embarrassed that he did not bow at all. The elder dropped his hand, which he had raised to bless them, and, bowing to them once again, asked them to be seated. The blood rushed to Alyosha's cheeks; he felt ashamed. His worst expectations were coming true.

The elder sat down on a mahogany leather sofa of a very old-fashioned design and asked his visitors, all except the two monks, to sit down along the opposite wall, all four in a row on four mahogany chairs covered with badly worn black leather. The monks sat down on either side of the room, one by the door and the other by the window. The seminarist, the novice, and Alyosha remained standing. The whole cell was far from large and had a sort of uninspiring look. The furniture and everything in it was crude and of poor quality; there was nothing in it that was not absolutely necessary. There were two pots of flowers on the window-sill and a great number of icons in the corner, one of them of the Virgin, very large and painted long before the schism in the Orthodox Church. A lamp was burning in front of it. Beside it were two other icons in shining settings and, near them, carved cherubim, porcelain eggs, a Catholic ivory cross with a Mater Dolorosa embracing it, and a few foreign engravings of the paintings of the great Italian masters of past centuries. Next to these expensive and beautiful engravings were to be seen several very crude Russian lithographs of saints, martyrs, holy men, and so on, which were sold for a few pennies at all the fairs. There were also a few engraved portraits of Russian bishops, past and present, but those were hung on the other walls. Miusov threw a cursory glance at all these 'official' adornments and then looked intently at the elder. He had a high opinion of himself as a man who could judge a person merely by looking at him. It was an excusable weakness, considering that he was fifty, an age at which an intelligent man of the world of independent means always acquires a great respect for his own judgement, sometimes, indeed, quite involuntarily.

From the very first he could not help disliking the elder. And, indeed, there was something in the elder's face that many people besides Miusov would dislike. He was a short, bent little man, with very weak legs, no more than sixty-five years old, though looking at least ten years older because of his illness. His whole face, which was very thin, was covered with small wrinkles, particularly numerous round his eyes. His eyes were not large, light-coloured, quick and shining like two bright points. He had only a few grey hairs left about his temples; his beard was small, scanty, and pointed, and his lips, which smiled frequently, were as thin as two strings; his nose was not long, but sharp, like a bird's beak.

'To all appearances a spiteful, petty, and supercilious character,' flashed through Miusov's mind. He was thoroughly dissatisfied with himself.

The striking of the clock made it easier for them to start the conversation. The cheap little wall clock with two weights struck twelve rapidly.

'Punctually to the hour,' cried Karamazov, 'and my son Dmitry isn't here yet. I apologize for him, holy elder.' (Alyosha shuddered all over at the 'holy elder'.) 'I am always punctual myself, to the minute, remembering that punctuality is the courtesy of kings. . . .'

'But, thank goodness, you're not a king,' muttered Miusov, unable to restrain himself from the very start.

'Yes, that's quite true, I'm not a king. Strange as it may seem to you, Mr Miusov, I knew it myself. Yes, sir! And, you know, I always say the wrong thing! Your reverence,' he cried with a sort of sudden inspiration, 'you see before you a clown. Yes, sir, a real clown! That's how I'd like you to look upon me. An old habit, alas! And if sometimes I talk nonsense when I shouldn't, I do it deliberately, sir, with the express intention of being amusing and agreeable. One has to be agreeable, hasn't one? Seven years ago, sir, I happened to find myself in some filthy little hole of a town. I had some business there. Wanted to found a small company with some lousy merchants.

So off we went to the police inspector, the *ispravnik*, for we had to settle something with him first and invite him to dinner. Well, sir, so out he comes to us, a fair, tall, fat, morose-looking fellow – the most dangerous individuals in such cases: it's their liver, sir, their liver. I went straight up to him with, you know, the nonchalant air of a man of the world. "Mr *Ispravnik*," I said, "won't you be, as it were, our Napravnik?" "Napravnik?" he said. "What do you mean, sir?" Well, I could see in a flash that our affair had miscarried, for there he stood looking serious and unco-operative. "I'm sorry," I said, "I wanted to make a joke to amuse the company, for Mr Napravnik," I said, "is one of our famous Russian conductors and for the harmony of our enterprise we want a sort of conductor. ..." A good and reasonable explanation, wasn't it? An apt comparison. "I'm very sorry," he said, "I'm an *ispravnik* and I won't allow puns to be made on my official position." He turned and walked away. I rushed after him. "Yes, yes," I cried, "you are an *ispravnik* and not Napravnik." "No, sir," he said, "since you said so, I am Napravnik." And, you know, our business deal fell through! I'm always like that. I'm always doing myself some injury by my politeness – always! Once, many years ago, I said to a highly influential person: "Your wife, sir, is a ticklish lady." I meant it, of course, in the sense of a highly honourable lady, a lady of high moral principles, so to speak. But he suddenly said to me in reply to my remark: "Why? Have you tickled her?" Well, sir, so I thought to myself why not be polite? "Yes, sir," I said, "I did tickle her." Well, so he gave me a proper tickling there and then. .... It happened a long time ago, so I'm not ashamed to tell the story. I'm always doing myself an injury like that!'

'You're doing it now, too!' Miusov muttered in disgust.

The elder scrutinized them both in silence.

'Am I? Well, fancy that, Mr Miusov, I've known it all the time. You see, sir, I had a feeling I was going to do so as soon as I began speaking, and, what's more, I knew that you'd be the first to remark on it. The moment I see, your reverence, that my joke isn't coming off, my cheeks begin to stick to my lower gums and it's almost as though they were contracted in a spasm. I've had it since I was a young man, when I was living on noblemen's charity and, indeed, making a living by sponging on them. I'm an inveterate clown. A born clown. Just as if I were a saintly fool, your reverence. Mind you, I freely admit that there may be an evil spirit in me, too, but if there is, it's only a small one. Had it been a bigger one, he'd have chosen different lodgings, but not yours, Mr Miusov, for your lodgings aren't big enough, either. But I make up for it by believing – I believe in God, sir. It's only lately that I've had my doubts, but now I sit and wait for words of great wisdom. I'm just like the philosopher Diderot, your reverence. I suppose you know, most holy father, that the philosopher Diderot went to see the Metropolitan Platon at the time of the Empress Catherine. As soon as he went in, he blurted out: "There is no God." To which his holiness, the great patriarch, raised his finger and said: "The madman hath said in his heart there is no God." And the philosopher threw himself down at his feet at once: "I believe," he cried, "and I will be baptized!" So they baptized him there and then. Princess Dashkov was his godmother and Potyomkin his godfather.'

'My dear sir,' Miusov, unable to restrain himself any longer, said in a shaking voice, 'this is unbearable! You know perfectly well that you're talking nonsense and that that stupid story isn't true. Why, then, are you making a fool of yourself?'

'All my life I've had a feeling that it wasn't true!' Karamazov cried with enthusiasm. 'But I'll tell you the whole truth, gentlemen. Great elder, forgive me, I invented my last story about Diderot's christening just now, this very minute, while I was talking to you. I never thought of it before. Invented it just for fun. You see, Mr Miusov, I'm making a fool of myself so that people should like me better. Still, sometimes I don't know myself why I do it. As for Diderot, I heard this "the madman hath said in his heart" scores of times from the local landowners I lived with when I was young. I heard it from your aunt, too, Mr Miusov, as a matter of fact. They're all convinced even today that the infidel Diderot went to the Metropolitan Platon to dispute about God. . . . '

Miusov got up, having not only lost patience but looking as though he did not know what he was doing. He was furious, and he felt that that made him look ridiculous. What was taking place in the cell was really something absolutely incredible. For forty or fifty years, at the time of the former elders, visitors had gathered in the same cell, but never without a feeling of the most profound reverence. Almost everyone admitted to the cell realized, as he entered it, that a great favour was being shown to him. Many fell down on their knees and did not get up during the whole visit. Many people belonging to the 'highest' ranks of society, even great scholars, or, indeed, freethinkers who came from curiosity or for some other reason, entering the cell together with other visitors or alone, thought it to be their bounden duty – all of them – to show the most profound reverence and tact during the whole of their visit, particularly as there was no question of money, but merely love and kindness on the one hand, and, on the other, penitence and an eagerness to solve some difficult spiritual question or some crisis in one's private life. So that such sudden buffoonery as that shown by Karamazov, which was so disrespectful in such a place, bewildered and amazed everyone who was present at the interview, or at least some of them. The monks, whose faces, however, did not betray any emotion, waited with earnest attention to hear what the elder would say, but were apparently ready to get up, like Miusov. Alyosha was on the verge of tears and stood with his head bowed. What seemed to him particularly strange was that his brother Ivan, on whom alone he had relied and who alone had such influence with his father that he could have stopped him, sat now quite motionless in his chair, with his eyes lowered to the ground, apparently waiting with a sort of curious interest to see how it would all end, just as if he had nothing to do with it. Alyosha could not even bring himself to look at Rakitin (the seminarist), who was also almost an intimate friend of his: he knew his thoughts, and he was the only one in the monastery who knew them.

'I'm sorry,' began Miusov, addressing the elder, 'to appear to be also taking some part in this undignified tomfoolery. The mistake I made was to believe that even a man like Mr Karamazov would realize his obligations when paying a visit to so highly esteemed a person. I did not realize that I'd have to apologize simply for having come with him. . . . '

Miusov stopped short and, utterly discomfited, was about to leave the room.

'Please, do not distress yourself, I beg you,' said the elder, rising on his feeble legs and, taking Miusov by both hands, he made him sit down again. 'Don't worry, I beg you. I ask you particularly to be my guest,' and bowing, he turned back and resumed his seat on the sofa.

'Great elder, tell me please, do I insult you by my high spirits or not?' Karamazov cried suddenly, grasping the arms of his chair with both hands, as though he were ready to jump out of it if the reply was unfavourable.

'I beg you earnestly not to disturb yourself and not to be put out,' the elder said impressively. 'Do not be disconcerted, make yourself quite at home. And, above all, do not be so ashamed of yourself, for that is at the root of it all.'

'Quite at home? You mean be my natural self? Oh, that is much, sir, too much, but I accept it – touched to the core! Though, you know, blessed father, you must not let me be my natural self – it's too great a risk! As a matter of fact, I won't go as far as that myself. I promise you this just because I'm anxious to save you from unpleasantness. Well, sir, as for the rest, it's still enveloped in a fog of uncertainty, though I daresay some people would like to say all sorts of nasty things about me. It's you, I mean, Mr Miusov. As for you, most holy being, I can only tell you that I'm overcome with ecstasy!' He got up and, raising his hands aloft, said solemnly: ' "Blessed is the womb that bare thee and the paps that gave thee suck" – the paps especially! By your remark – "Don't be so ashamed of yourself, for that is at the root of it all" – by this remark, sir, you seem to have seen right through me and read my innermost secrets. For it does seem to me every time I go to see people that I'm more contemptible than anyone else and that everyone takes me for a clown. That's why I say to myself, "All right, let me play the clown! I'm not afraid of your opinion, because you're all without exception more contemptible than I!" That's why I'm a clown, great elder. I am a clown from shame. Yes, sir, from shame! It's my sensitiveness alone that makes me kick up a row. If only I could be sure when entering a room that everyone would accept me at once as the kindest and wisest of men – Lord! what a good man I'd be then! Master,' he cried, falling suddenly on his knees, 'what am I to do to gain eternal life?'

It was difficult to decide even now whether he was joking or whether he really was deeply moved.

The elder raised his eyes at him and said with a smile:

'You've known for a long time what you have to do. You've sense enough: do not indulge in drunkenness and incontinence of speech, do not indulge in sensual pursuits and, especially, in the love of money. Close your public houses, and if you can't close them all, close two or three at least. And most of all – do not tell lies.'

'You're referring to Diderot, aren't you?'

'No, not only to Diderot. Above all, don't lie to yourself. A man who lies to himself and who listens to his own lies gets to a point where he can't distinguish any truth in himself or in those around him, and so loses all respect for himself and for others. Having no respect for anyone, he ceases to love, and to occupy and distract himself without love he becomes a prey to his passions and gives himself up to coarse pleasures, and sinks to bestiality in his vices, and all this from continual lying to people and to himself. A man who lies to himself can be more easily offended than anyone else. For it is sometimes very pleasant to take offence, isn't it? And yet he knows that no one has offended him and that he has invented the offence himself, that he has lied just for the beauty of it, that he has exaggerated to make himself look big and important, that he has fastened on a phrase and made a mountain out of a molehill – he knows it all and yet is the first to take offence, he finds pleasure in it and feels mightily satisfied with himself, and so reaches the point of real enmity. . . . Get up, please. Sit down, I beg you. Why, all this, too, is deceitful posturing.'

'Blessed man, let me kiss your hand,' Karamazov cried, rushing up to the elder and imprinting a rapid kiss on his thin hand. 'Yes, indeed, it is pleasant to take offence. You've put it better than I've ever heard it before. Yes, indeed, I've been taking offence all my life till I glowed with pleasure, taking offence to satisfy my aesthetic feelings, for sometimes it is not only pleasant but also beautiful to be offended. That's what you, great elder, have forgotten to take into account: it is beautiful! I shall make a note of that! And I have been lying, I've indeed been lying all my life, every day and every hour. Verily, I am a lie and the father of lies! Though perhaps not the father of lies – I'm afraid I'm getting mixed-up in my texts. Let's say, the son of lies – that, too, will be enough. Only – dear angel – one may tell a lie about Diderot sometimes, mayn't one? Diderot will do no harm, but something else will. By the way, great elder, I was forgetting, but as a matter of fact I had made up my mind as far back as two years ago to find out here, I meant to come here on purpose to find out – only, please, ask Mr Miusov not to interrupt me. What I wanted to ask you is this: great Father, is the story told somewhere in the *Lives of the Saints* true, the story about some holy miracleworker, who was tortured for his faith and who, when they cut off his head at last, stood up, picked up his head and "kissing it lovingly", walked a long way, carrying it in his hands and "kissing it lovingly"? Is it true or not, upright and reverend Fathers?'

'No, it's not true,' said the elder.

'There's nothing of the kind in the *Lives of the Saints*,' said the Father Librarian. 'What saint do you say the story is told of?'

'I'm afraid I don't know what saint. Haven't the faintest idea. I've been deceived. I was told about it. I heard it, and do you know who told it? Mr Miusov here who was so angry about Diderot just now. It was he who told the story.'

'I never told you it. I never speak to you at all.'

'It's true you did not tell me, but you told it when I was there. It was over three years ago. I mentioned it because you undermined my faith, sir, by that funny story. You knew nothing about that, but I returned home with my faith shaken and since then I've been getting more and more shaken in it. Yes, sir, you were the cause of my great fall! That, sir, is not just Diderot!'

Karamazov got excited and assumed a pathetic expression, though it was perfectly clear to everyone that he was play-acting again. But Miusov was deeply hurt all the same.

'What nonsense,' he muttered. 'It's all nonsense. I may have really said something of the kind some time or other . . . but not to you. I was told it myself. I heard it in Paris from a Frenchman. He said it was read at morning mass in our churches. He was a great scholar. Made a special study of Russian statistics. He had lived in Russia a long time. . . . I've not read the *Lives of the Saints* myself and – er – I'm not going to read it. . . . All sorts of things are said at dinner. . . . We were having dinner at the time. . . .'

'Yes, you were having dinner and I lost my faith!' Karamazov taunted him.

'What do I care about your faith!' Miusov shouted, but he suddenly checked himself and said with contempt: 'You literally defile everything you touch.'

The elder suddenly got up from his seat.

'Excuse me, gentlemen, for leaving you for a few minutes,' he said, addressing all his visitors. 'But I have people waiting for me who arrived before you. And you, sir,' he turned to Karamazov with a cheerful face, 'would do well not to tell lies all the same.'

He walked towards the door. Alyosha and the novice rushed after him to help him down the stairs. Alyosha was choking. He was glad to get away, but he was glad, too, that the elder was cheerful and not offended. The elder went in the direction of the veranda to bless those who were waiting for him. But Karamazov insisted on stopping him at the door of the cell.

'Most blessed man,' he cried with feeling, 'allow me to kiss your hand once more! Yes, sir, one can talk to you, one can get on with you. Do you think I always tell lies and play the clown like that? Well, sir, I want you to know that I was acting like that all the time on purpose so as to try you. I've been watching you carefully all the time to see whether one could get on with you. Whether there was room for my humility beside your pride. Let me hand you a certificate of honour: it is possible to get on with you. Now I shall hold my peace. I shan't say another word. I'm going to sit in my chair and hold my peace. It's your turn, Mr Miusov, to speak now. You're the most important person left here now – for ten minutes. . . .'

3

Devout Peasant Women

ABOUT twenty peasant women crowded all this time near the wooden veranda built on to the outer side of the hermitage wall. They had been told that the elder would at last be coming out and they had gathered in expectation. The two ladies, Mrs Khokhlakov and her daughter, who had also been waiting for the elder, came out on the veranda, but in the part set aside for gentlewomen. Mrs Khokhlakov, a rich woman who was always dressed with taste, was still quite young and very good-looking, a little pale, with very vivacious and almost black eyes. She was not more than thirty-three and had been a widow for five years. Her fourteen-year-old daughter suffered from paralysis of the legs. The poor girl had not been able to walk for the last six months and she was pushed about in a long, comfortable wheel-chair. She had a charming face, a little thin from illness, but gay. There was a mischievous gleam in her big dark eyes with their long lashes. Her mother had been intending to take her abroad ever since the spring, but they had been detained all summer by business connected with their estate. They had been staying in our town for a week, more on business than devotion, but had already paid one visit to the elder three days before. Now they had suddenly arrived again, though they knew that the elder was hardly able to receive anyone, and requested earnestly to be granted 'the happiness of seeing the great healer once more'. In expectation of the appearance of the elder, the mother sat on a chair near her daughter's wheel-chair, and two paces away from her stood an old monk, who did not belong to our monastery but was a visitor from a remote, little-known monastery in the north. He, too, wished to receive the elder's blessing. But, on appearing on the veranda, the elder at first went straight to the peasant women, who crowded round the three front steps leading to the low veranda. The elder stood on the top step, put on his stole, and began to bless the women who clustered round him. They pulled a 'shrieker' towards him by both hands. As soon as she caught sight of him, the sick woman suddenly began hiccuping, squealing in an absurd fashion, and trembling all over as though in a fit of convulsions. Putting the stole on her head, the elder read a short prayer over her, and she at once fell silent and calmed down. I do not know how it is now, but as a child I often happened to see and hear these 'shriekers' in the villages and monasteries. They were brought to morning mass, they squealed and barked like dogs so that they could be heard all over the church, but when the Host was carried in and they were led up to it, their 'raving' stopped at once and the sick women grew quiet for a time. As a child, I was greatly struck and amazed by it. But then I was told in reply to my questions by some landowners, and especially by my town teachers, that it was all a sham and staged to avoid work, and that it could be easily eradicated by suitable severity; and various amusing stories were told to prove it. But later on I learnt with astonishment from specialists that there was no question of any sham about it, that it was a terrible illness that afflicted women, apparently mostly in Russia, which bore witness to the hard life of our village women, an illness which was caused by exhausting work shortly after difficult, abnormal labour without medical assistance; it was caused, besides, by hopeless misery, beatings, etc., which some women are unable to endure in spite of the prevalence of such ill-treatment. The strange and instantaneous cure of the raving and struggling woman as soon as she is led up to the Host, which had been explained to me as shamming and, moreover, as a trick played on the people by the 'clericals', was also probably due to most natural causes. For the women who took the 'shrieker' up to the Host and, above all, the sick woman herself sincerely believed, as an undeniable truth, that the evil spirit who had taken possession of her could not stand it if she was taken up to the Host and made to bow down before it. And that was why it always happened (and, indeed, had to happen) that the nervous and, of course, mentally ill woman always suffered a violent shock at the moment when she bowed down to the Host, a shock caused by the expectation of the certain miracle of healing and by her implicit faith in its taking place. And it did take place, if only for a moment. It took place in exactly the same way now as soon as the elder covered the sick woman with his stole.

Many of the women who had crowded round him were so thrilled and moved by the sensational cure that they burst into tears; others strove to kiss the hem of the elder's robe, while still others started keening. He blessed them all, and spoke to some of them. The 'shrieker' he knew already, for she had been brought from a nearby village only five miles from the monastery and had been taken to see him several times before.

'And here's one from a long way off,' he said, pointing to a woman who was still quite young, but thin and worn out, with a face that was not so much sunburnt as blackened. She was kneeling and staring motionless at the elder. There was almost a frenzied look in her eyes.

'From a long way off, Father, from a long way off,' the woman said in a sing-song voice, swaying her head regularly to and fro and resting her cheek on her hand. 'Two hundred miles from here – a long way, Father, a long way.'

She spoke as though she were keening. There is among the

peasants a silent and long-enduring sorrow. It withdraws into itself and is still. But there is also a sorrow that has reached the limit of endurance: it will then burst out in tears and from that moment break out into keening. This is especially so with women. But it is not easier to bear than a silent sorrow. The keening soothes it only by embittering and lacerating the heart still more. Such sorrow does not desire consolation and feeds upon the sense of its hopelessness. The keening is merely an expression of the constant need to reopen the wound.

'You're of the artisan class, aren't you?' the elder continued, looking curiously at her.

'We're townspeople, Father, townspeople. We were peasants before, but we're townspeople now – we live in the town. I've come to see you, Father. We heard about you, Father. Aye, we heard about you. I've just buried my little son, and I've come to pray to God. Been in three monasteries, I have, and they told me to go and see you, love, at this monastery. And so I've come. I was in church here yesterday, and today I've come to you.'

'What is it you're weeping for?'

'I'm sorry for my little boy, Father. He was three years old – three years in another three months he would have been. I'm grieving for my little boy, Father, for my little darling boy – the last I had left. We had four, Nikita and I, four children, but not one of them is alive, Father, not one of them, not one. I buried the first three, I wasn't very sorry for them, I wasn't, but this last one I buried and I can't forget him. He seems to be standing before me now – he never leaves me. He has dried up my soul. I keep looking at his little things, his little shirt or his little boots, and I wail. I lay out all that's left of him, every little thing. I look at them and wail. I say to my husband, to Nikita, let me go, husband, I'd like to go on a pilgrimage. He's a driver, Father. We're not poor people, Father. We're our own masters. It's all our own, the horses and the carriage. But what do we want it all now for? My Nikita has taken to drinking without me, I'm sure he has, he used to before: I had only to turn my back, and he'd weaken. But now I'm no longer thinking of him. It's over two months since I left home. I've forgotten everything, I have, and I don't want to remember. And what will my life with him be like now? I've done with him, I have. I've done with them all. I don't want to see my house and my things again. I hope I'll never see them again!'

'Now listen to me, Mother,' said the elder. 'Once, a long time ago, a great saint saw a woman like you in a church. She was weeping for her little infant child, her only one, whom God had also taken. "Don't you know," said the saint to her, "how bold and fearless these little ones are before the throne of the Lord? There's none bolder or more fearless than they in the Kingdom of Heaven: Thou, O Lord, hast given us life, they say to God, and no sooner had we looked upon it than thou didst take it away. And so boldly and fearlessly do they ask and demand an explanation that God gives them at once the rank of angels. And therefore," said the saint, "you, too, Mother, rejoice and do not weep, for your little one is now with the Lord in the company of his angels." That's what the saint said to the weeping mother in the olden days. And he was a great saint and he would not have told her an untruth. Know, then, you too, Mother, that your little one is most assuredly standing now before the throne of the Lord, and is rejoicing and happy, and praying to God for you. And, therefore, weep not, but rejoice.'

The woman listened to him with a bowed head, her cheek resting on her hand. She heaved a deep sigh.

'My Nikita, too, tried to comfort me with the same words as you, Father. "Don't be foolish," he says, "what are you crying for? Our son is now with the Lord God for certain and is singing with the angels." He said that to me, but he cried himself. I could see that he cried like me. "I know that, dear husband," I says to him. "Where else could he be if not with the Lord God. Only he isn't with us here, is he? He isn't sitting beside us now as he used to before, is he?" Oh, if only I could look at him just once, if only I could have a look at him once again! I wouldn't go up to him. I wouldn't say a word. I would just keep quiet in a corner, only to see him for one little minute, to hear him playing in the yard. He used to come to me and call in his little voice, "Mum, where are you?" Oh, if only I could see him walk across the room on his darling little feet just once, only once. I remember hearing the patter of his little feet as he rushed up to me again and again, shouting and laughing. If only I could hear it again – I'd recognize it as soon as I heard it! But he's gone, Father, he's gone and I shall never hear him again. Here's his little belt, but he's no longer here, and I shall never, never see or hear him now!'

She drew out of her bosom her boy's little embroidered belt and as soon as she looked at it she began shaking with sobs, covering her eyes with her fingers through which the tears suddenly flowed in a stream.

'Behold,' the elder said, ' "Rachel weeping for her children refused to be comforted for her children, because they were not," and such is the lot bestowed upon you, mothers, on earth. And do not be comforted. There's no need for you to be comforted. Be not comforted but weep, and every time you weep be sure to remember that your little son is one of the angels of the Lord, that he looks down on you and sees you and rejoices in your tears and points them out to God. And for a long, long time you will go on weeping as all mothers have done since time immemorial, but in the end your weeping will turn into quiet joy and your bitter tears will be only the tears of quiet, tender joy, purifying the heart and saving it from sin. I shall mention your little boy in my prayers. What was his name?'

'Alexey, Father.'

'A sweet name. After Alexey the man of God?'

'Of God, Father, of God. Alexey the man of God.'

'He was a great saint! I shall mention him in my prayers, Mother, I shall. And I shall mention your sorrow in my prayers, too, and your husband that he may live and prosper. Only you should not have left your husband. You must go back to him and look after him. Your little boy will look down on you and, seeing that you've forsaken his father, he will weep over you both: why do you destroy his bliss? For, don't forget, he's living, he's living, for the soul lives for ever, and though he is no longer in the house, he's always there unseen beside you. How do you expect him to come home if you say you hate your house? To whom is he to go, if he won't find you, his father and mother, together? You see him in your dreams now and you grieve, but if you go back he will send you sweet dreams. Go to your husband, Mother, go back to him today.'

'I will, Father, I will do as you say. You've touched my heart. Nikita, dear Nikita, you're waiting for me, my darling!' the woman began keening, but the elder had already turned away to a very old woman, dressed like a townswoman and not like a pilgrim. It could be seen from her eyes that she had come on some business and that she had something to tell him. She said she was the widow of a non-commissioned officer and lived in our town. Her son Vassily served in the army commissariat, but had gone to Irkutsk in Siberia. He had written twice from there, but now she had had no letter from him for over a year. She had made inquiries about him, but she really did not know where to inquire.

'Only the other day Stepanida Bedryagina – she's a rich merchant's wife – said to me, why don't you go and give your son's name to the priest and he'll mention it in his prayers in church just as if he was dead. His soul, she said, will pine for you and he'll write you a letter. It's quite true, she said, what I'm telling you. It's been tried many times. Only I'm not so sure, Father. Tell me, please, is it true or not, and would it be the right thing to do?'

'Don't think of it. You ought to be ashamed to ask me such a question. And indeed how is it possible for a mother of all people to pray for the peace of a living soul? It's a great sin, a sin akin to sorcery, and it is forgiven only because of your ignorance. You had better pray to the Holy Virgin, our swift intermediary and helper, to grant him health and that she may forgive you for your wrong ideas. And let me tell you this, too, Prokhorovna: your son will either soon come back to you or he will be sure to send you a letter. I want you to know this. Go now and don't worry any more. Your son is alive, I tell you.'

'May the good Lord reward you, Father. You bring us good tidings and you pray for all of us and for our sins. . . .'

But the elder had already noticed in the crowd the two burning eyes of a wasted, consumptive-looking, though quite young peasant woman, fixed upon him. She gazed at him in silence. Her eyes were beseeching him for something, but she seemed to be afraid to draw nearer.

'What's your trouble, my dear?'

'Give me absolution, dear Father,' she said quietly and unhurriedly and, kneeling, she bowed down at his feet. 'I have sinned, dear Father. I'm afraid of my sin.'

The elder sat down on the lower step. The woman approached him without rising from her knees.

'I've been a widow for over two years,' she began in a half-whisper, with a kind of shudder. 'My married life was hard, my husband was an old man and he used to beat me mercilessly. He lay ill and, looking at him, I couldn't help thinking what would happen to me if he got well and got up again. And that's when the thought came to me. . . .'

'Wait,' said the elder and put his ear close to her lips.

The woman went on in a soft whisper so that it was almost impossible to catch anything. She was soon finished.

'Over two years ago?' asked the elder.

'Over two years ago, Father. At first I didn't think about it, but now I've begun to be ill and I'm very worried. . . .'

'Have you come from far?'

'Over three hundred miles from here.'

'Have you told it to the priest at confession?'

'I have. Twice I've confessed it.'

'Have you been admitted to Communion?'

'Yes, Father. But I'm afraid. I'm afraid to die.'

'Do not be afraid of anything. Do not ever be afraid. And don't worry. So long as you remain sincerely penitent, God will forgive you everything. There's no sin, and there can be no sin in the whole world which God will not forgive to those who are truly repentant. Why, man cannot commit so great a sin as to exhaust the infinite love of God. Or can there be a sin that would exceed the love of God? Only you must never forget to think continually of repentance, but dismiss your fear altogether. Believe that God loves you in a way you cannot even conceive of. He loves you in spite of your sin and in your sin. And there's more joy in heaven over one sinner that repents than over ten righteous men. This was said a long time ago. So go and do not be afraid. Do not be upset by people and do not be angry if you're wronged. Forgive your dead husband in your heart, however badly he treated you. Be truly reconciled to him. If you are sorry for what you did, then you must love. And if you love, you are of God. . . . Everything can be atoned for, everything can be saved by love. If I, a sinner like you, have been moved by your story and am sorry for you, how much more will God be. Love is such a priceless treasure that you can redeem everything in the world by it, and expiate not only your own but other people's sins. Go and do not be afraid.'

He made the sign of the cross over her three times, took off the little icon from his neck and put it upon her. She bowed down to the ground to him in silence. He got up and looked cheerfully at a healthy peasant woman with a baby in her arms.

'From Vyshegorye, dear Father.'

'You've dragged yourself here for five miles with your baby. What do you want?'

'I've come to have a look at you, Father. I've been to see you before, or have you forgotten? You must have a bad memory, if you've forgotten me. They were saying in our village that you were ill, so I thought I'd better go and see him myself: now I see you and you're not ill at all! You'll live for another twenty years. So you will, really! And, besides, haven't you enough people praying for you? How could you be ill?'

'Thank you for everything, my dear.'

'By the way, I have something I'd like to ask you, Father. It's a small thing. I've sixty copecks here, take them and give them, dear Father, to someone poorer than me. As I was coming here, I thought to myself: I'd better give it through him. He'll know who to give it to.'

'Thank you, my dear, thank you for your kindness. I love you. I'll certainly do so. Is that your little girl in your arms?'

'Yes, Father. Lizaveta.'

'May the Lord bless you both, you and your baby Lizaveta. You've gladdened my heart, Mother. Good-bye, my dear ones, good-bye.'

He blessed them all and bowed low to them.

4

A Lady of Little Faith

WATCHING the scene of the elder's conversation with the peasant women and his blessing them, Mrs Khokhlakov shed silent tears and wiped them away with a handkerchief. She was a very sentimental society woman and a genuinely kindly one in many things. When the elder at last went up to her, she met him ecstatically.

'Oh, I've been through so much, so much while watching this moving scene. I . . .' she could not go on from excitement. 'Oh, I can see that the peasants love you, I love the peasants myself, I want to love them, and – and, besides, how can one help loving our wonderful people, so simple-minded in its greatness?'

'How is your daughter? You wanted to have another talk with me?'

'Oh, I've kept asking for it. I've prayed for it. I was prepared to go down on my knees and kneel under your windows for three days, if need be, until you let me in. We've come to you, great healer, to give full expression to our deep gratitude. You've cured my Lise, you've cured her completely, and you did it just by saying a prayer over her last Thursday and laying your hands on her. We've come to kiss those hands, to pour out our feelings and our veneration.'

'Cured her, have I? Isn't she still in her chair?'

'But her night fevers have completely vanished for the last two days, ever since Thursday,' the lady hurried on nervously. 'And what's more she feels much stronger in her legs. This morning she got up feeling well. She had slept all night. Look at her rosy cheeks, at her bright eyes. She used to be always crying, but now she laughs, she's cheerful and gay. Today she insisted on my letting her stand up, and she stood for a whole minute without any support. She has a wager with me that in a fortnight she'll be dancing a quadrille. I've called in the local doctor Herzenstube. He shrugged his shoulders and said that he was astonished and did not know what to make of it. And would you really prefer us not to disturb you, not to fly here, not to thank you? Lise, thank him – thank him!'

Lise's pretty little laughing face became suddenly serious; she raised herself in her chair as much as she could and, looking at the elder, put her hands together before him, but could not restrain herself and suddenly burst out laughing.

'I'm laughing at him, at him!' she said, pointing to Alyosha, childishly annoyed with herself for having been unable to restrain herself from laughing.

If anyone had looked at Alyosha, who was standing a step behind the elder, he would have noticed a quick flush suffusing his face. His eyes flashed and he dropped them at once.

'She has a message for you, Alexey,' the fond mother went on, suddenly addressing Alyosha and holding out her exquisitely gloved hand to him. 'How are you?'

The elder turned round and all at once looked attentively at

Alyosha, who walked up to Lise and held out his hand to her, too, with a sort of strange and awkward smile. Lise assumed an air of importance.

'Katerina sends you this through me,' she said, handing him a note. 'She asks you specially to go and see her, and as soon as possible, and not to let her down, but be quite sure to come.'

'She asks me to go and see her?' Alyosha murmured in great astonishment. 'Me see her? But why?'

He suddenly looked very worried.

'Oh, it's all because of your brother Dmitry and – all that's happened recently,' her mother explained hurriedly. 'Katerina has come to a certain decision, but – she simply has to see you about it first. Why? I'm afraid I don't know, but she asked you to go and see her as soon as possible. And you will, won't you? I know you will. Your feelings as a Christian will, I'm sure, tell you to do so.'

'I've only seen her once. . . .' Alyosha protested with the same perplexed look on his face.

'Oh, she's such a high-minded, such an incomparable creature! I mean, her suffering alone. . . . Just think what she's been through, what she must be going through now – think what awaits her now – it's all so ghastly, so ghastly. . . .'

'Very well, I'll come,' Alyosha decided after running through the very brief and enigmatic note, which, except for an earnest request to come, offered no explanation at all.

'Oh, that would be so nice and splendid of you,' Lise cried, growing suddenly very animated. 'I told mother you wouldn't come for anything because you were saving your soul. Oh, how splendid you are! I've always thought you were splendid, and I'm glad to tell you so now!'

'Lise!' her mother cried admonishingly, smiling at once though.

'You've forgotten us, too, Alexey,' she went on. 'You don't seem to want to come and see us. Yet Lise has told me twice that she's only happy when she's with you.'

Alyosha raised his downcast eyes, blushed suddenly once more and again smiled without himself knowing why. The elder, however, was no longer watching him. He had entered into a conversation with the monk who, as we mentioned before, had been waiting for him by Lise's chair. He seemed to be a monk of humble origin, that is, of the peasant class, with a narrow, unbending outlook, but a true believer and, in his own way, stubborn. He introduced himself as coming from the far north, from Obdorsk, from Saint Sylvester, a poor monastery, consisting only of nine monks. The elder blessed him and invited him to come to his cell whenever he wished.

'How do you presume to do such things?' the monk asked suddenly, pointing solemnly and impressively at Lise. He was referring to her having been 'healed'.

'It's a little too soon, of course, to talk about that,' replied the elder. 'Relief is far from a complete cure and could arise from other causes. But if anything did happen, it did so by no power except by God's will. Everything is from God. Come and see me, Father,' he added, 'but I'm afraid I can't see visitors at just any time. I'm ill, and I know that my days are numbered.'

'Oh, no, no,' cried Mrs Khokhlakov, 'God will never take you away from us – you'll live a long, long time yet. And what's wrong with you? You look so well, so cheerful, and happy!'

'I feel much better today, but I know it's only for a moment. I thoroughly understand my illness now. And thank you for saying that I look cheerful. You couldn't have said anything that would have made me so happy. For men are made for happiness, and he who is completely happy has a right to say to himself: I've carried out God's sacred will on earth. All the righteous, all the saints, all the martyrs were happy people.'

'Oh, how splendidly you talk,' cried Mrs Khokhlakov. 'What brave and lofty words. You say something and it seems to pierce one through and through. And yet – happiness, happiness – where is it? Who can say that he's truly happy? Oh, since you've been so kind as to let us see you again today, please let me tell you what I couldn't say last time, what I dared not say. Let me tell you all I am suffering from and have been suffering for so long, so long! I am suffering, I'm sorry, but I am, I am!' And she put her hands together before him, carried away by some ardent, uncontrollable feeling.

'From what specially?'

'I'm suffering from – from lack of faith.'

'Lack of faith in God?'

'Oh, no, no! I dare not even think of that! But life after death – it's such a mystery! And there's no one, absolutely no one, who can solve it. Listen, you are a healer, you're an expert on the human soul. I have no right, of course, to expect you to believe me entirely, but I give you my solemn word that I'm saying this not because I haven't thought it over carefully, but because this idea of a future life upsets me so much that it positively hurts me. It frightens and horrifies me. ... And I don't know whom to turn to – I haven't dared to all my life. ... And now I dare to turn to you. ... Oh dear, what will you think of me now?' She clasped her hands.

'Don't worry about what I think,' replied the elder. 'I quite believe in the sincerity of your anguish.'

'Oh, I *am* so grateful to you! You see, I close my eyes and think: if everyone has faith, then where does it come from? And then I hear people say that it all arose at first from fear of the terrible manifestations of nature, and that there's nothing in it all. Well, I say to myself, I've been believing all my life, but what if I die and there's nothing at all and all that will happen is that, as one writer put it, "burdock will be growing on my grave"? It's awful! How, how am I to get back my faith? Mind you, I believed only when I was a little girl, mechanically, without thinking of anything. ... But how, how am I to prove it? That's why I've come now to throw myself at your feet and ask you about it. If I miss this opportunity too now, I won't be able to get an answer for the rest of my life. How is one to prove it? How is one to be convinced? Oh, poor me! Everyone around me, almost everyone, doesn't seem to care one bit, no one worries about it now, and I'm the only one who can't stand it. It's dreadful – dreadful!'

'I daresay it is. But it's something one cannot prove. One can be convinced of it, though.'

'How? In what way?'

'By the experience of active love. Strive to love your neighbours actively and indefatigably. And the nearer you come to achieving this love, the more convinced you will become of the existence of God and the immortality of your soul. If you reach the point of complete selflessness in your love of your neighbours, you will most certainly regain your faith and no doubt can possibly enter your soul. This has been proved. This is certain.'

'Active love? That's another problem and what a problem – what a problem! You see: I love humanity so much that – would you believe it? – I sometimes dream of giving up all, all I have, leaving Lise and becoming a hospital nurse. I close my eyes, I think and dream, and at those moments I feel full of indomitable strength. No wounds, no festering sores could frighten me then. I could clean and bandage them with my own hands. I could nurse the sufferers and be ready to kiss their sores. . . . '

'That, too, is a great deal and it is well that you should be dreaming about that and not about something else. I shouldn't be surprised if by chance you really did do some good deed.'

'Yes, but how long do you think I could endure such a life?' the lady continued heatedly and almost frenziedly. 'That's the most important question! That's my most agonizing question. I close my eyes and ask myself: how long would you be able to bear such a life? And what if the patient, whose sores you're washing, does not at once show how grateful he is to you, but, on the contrary, begins to torment you with his whims, without noticing or valuing your charitable services? What if he should start shouting at you, demanding something from you rudely or even complaining to your superiors (as often happens when people are in great pain) – what then? Will you still go on loving him? And, you know, I came with horror to the conclusion that if there were anything that could instantly damp the ardour of my "active" love of humanity, it would be ingratitude. In short, I can work only if I'm paid. I demand payment at once. I mean I want to be praised and paid for love with love. Otherwise, I'm incapable of loving anyone.'

She was in a paroxysm of the most genuine self-castigation and, having finished, she looked with defiant determination at the elder.

'That's exactly the same sort of thing a doctor told me a long time ago,' observed the elder. 'He was an elderly and undoubtedly clever man. He spoke to me as frankly as you, though in jest, but in mournful jest. "I love humanity," he said, "but I can't help being surprised at myself: the more I love humanity in general, the less I love men in particular, I mean, separately, as separate individuals. In my dreams," he said, "I am very often passionately determined to serve humanity, and I might quite likely have sacrificed my life for my fellow-creatures, if for some reason it had been suddenly demanded of me, and yet I'm quite incapable of living with anyone in one room for two days together, and I know that from experience. As soon as anyone comes close to me, his personality begins to oppress my vanity and restrict my freedom. I'm capable of hating the best men in twenty-four hours: one because he sits too long over his dinner, another because he has a cold in the head and keeps on blowing his nose. I become an enemy of people the moment they come close to me. But, on the other hand, it invariably happened that the more I hated men individually, the more ardent became my love for humanity at large." '

'But what's to be done? What is one to do in such a case? Should one give way to despair?'

'No, for it is enough that you are distressed about it. Do what you can and it will be put to your account. And you've done a great deal already, since you've been able to know yourself so deeply and so sincerely. But if you've spoken to me so sincerely now simply to be commended by me for your truthfulness, as you have just been, then it goes without saying that you will achieve nothing in your attempts at active love. It will all remain a dream and your whole life will flash by like a phantom. In that case, you will of course forget all about the future life and in the end you will somehow or other find peace by yourself.'

'You've crushed me! Only now, at this very moment, as you spoke, I realized that I was really only waiting for you to commend my sincerity when I told you that I could not bear ingratitude. You've shown me the sort of person I am, you've seen through me, you've explained me to myself!'

'Do you mean what you say? Well, now after such a confession I believe that you are sincere and good at heart. If you do not achieve happiness, you must always remember that you are on the right path and try not to stray from it. Above all, run from lies, any lies, and especially from self-deception. Watch over your lies and examine them every hour, every minute. Avoid, too, a feeling of aversion towards others and towards yourself: what seems to you bad in yourself is purified by the very fact that you've noticed it in yourself. Avoid fear, too, though fear is only the consequence of every sort of lie. Never be afraid of your own cowardliness in attaining love, and do not be too much afraid of your bad actions, either. I'm sorry I cannot say anything more comforting to you, for, compared with romantic love, active love is something severe and terrifying. Romantic love yearns for an immediate act of heroism that can be achieved rapidly and that everyone can see. This sort of love really reaches a point where a man will even sacrifice his life provided his ordeal doesn't last long and is over quickly just as though it took place on a stage, and provided all are looking on and applauding. But active love means hard work and tenacity, and for some people it is, perhaps, a whole science. But I predict that at the very moment when you will realize with horror that, far from getting nearer to your goal, you are, in spite of all your efforts, actually further away from it than ever, I predict that at that very moment you will suddenly attain your goal and will behold clearly the miraculous power of the Lord who has all the time been loving and mysteriously guiding you. I'm sorry, but I can't stay longer with you. They're waiting for me. Good-bye.'

The lady was weeping.

'Lise, Lise, please, bless her – bless her!' she cried, suddenly coming to life.

'She doesn't deserve to be loved,' the elder said jokingly. 'I've seen her misbehaving all the time. Why have you been laughing at Alexey all the time?'

Lise had, as a matter of fact, been doing just that all the time. She had noticed long ago, since their last meeting, in fact, that Alyosha was shy with her and tried not to look at her, and that amused her immensely. She waited intently to catch his eye: unable to endure her fixed stare, Alyosha from time to time threw a quick glance at her himself, as though drawn by some irresistible force, and at once she smiled triumphantly straight into his face. Alyosha was thrown into confusion and was annoyed even more. At last he turned away from her altogether and hid behind the elder's back. A few minutes later, drawn by the same irresistible force, he turned again to see whether she was looking at him or not. He saw Lise, almost hanging out of her chair, looking at him sideways and breathlessly waiting for him to look at her. Catching his glance, she burst out laughing so loudly that even the elder could not resist saying to her: 'Why do you embarrass him so much, you naughty girl?'

Lise suddenly and quite unexpectedly blushed, her eyes flashed, her face assumed a very serious expression and she said nervously, speaking very fast in a warmly indignant and complaining voice:

'And why has he forgotten everything? He used to carry me in his arms when I was a little girl. We used to play together. Why, he used to come to us and teach me to read. Didn't you know that? Two years ago, when he took leave of us, he said that he would never forget me and that we should remain friends for ever and ever! And now he's suddenly afraid of me. I'm not going to eat him, am I? Why does he refuse to come near me? Why doesn't he want to talk to me? Why doesn't he want to come and see us? Don't you let him? You see, we know that he goes everywhere. I can't invite him, can I? He should have been the first to remember, if he hadn't forgotten. But no! He's saving his soul now, if you please! Why have you put that long cassock on him? ... If he runs, he'll fall down....'

And unable to restrain herself, she covered her face with her hands and shook terribly and uncontrollably with her prolonged, nervous, and inaudible laughter. The elder listened to her with a smile and blessed her tenderly; but when she began kissing his hand, she suddenly pressed it to her eyes and burst into tears.

'Don't be angry with me. I'm a silly and worthless girl and – and Alyosha is probably right, quite right, in not wanting to come to see such a ridiculous girl.'

'I will certainly send him,' the elder said firmly.

5

It Will Be! It Will Be!

THE elder was absent from his cell for about twenty-five minutes. It was half-past twelve and Dmitry Karamazov, on whose behalf they had all met there, had still not arrived. But they seemed almost to have forgotten about him, and when the elder entered the cell again he found his visitors engaged in a very animated conversation. Ivan and the two monks took a leading part in it. Miusov, too, joined in the conversation, and apparently with great warmth, but he was unlucky again: no one paid much attention to him and, indeed, they almost ignored his remarks, which merely increased his ever-growing irritability. He had, in fact, had several furious arguments with Ivan before and he could not endure his opponent's somewhat casual attitude towards him without losing his temper. 'Before at least,' he thought to himself, 'I've always been in the van of every progressive movement in Europe, but this new generation simply ignores us.' Karamazov, who had given his solemn word to sit still and be quiet, had actually been quiet for a short time, though he kept watching his neighbour Miusov with a sardonic little smile and was quite obviously pleased to see him so irritated. He had long been meaning to pay him back for something or other and he did not wish to let the opportunity slip now. At last he could restrain himself no longer and, bending over Miusov's shoulder, he taunted him again in an undertone:

'You didn't go away after my "lovingly kissing", did you? You did consent to remain in such indecent company, didn't you? You know why? Because you felt insulted and humiliated and you remained to show what a clever fellow you were and get your own back. Now you won't go before showing what a clever fellow you are.'

'You again? I'll leave now just to show you.'

'You'll be the last, the last of all to go!' Karamazov taunted him again.

That was almost at the moment of the elder's return.

The discussion stopped for a moment, but the elder, who had resumed his seat, looked round at everyone as though cordially inviting them to go on. Alyosha, who had come to know every expression of the elder's face, saw clearly that he was terribly tired and that it required an effort to stay with them. During the latter stages of his illness he had been subject to fainting fits from exhaustion. Now his face was almost covered by the same kind of pallor as before a fainting fit. His lips went white. But he evidently did not want to dismiss the company; he seemed to have some reason for it. But what? Alyosha watched him closely.

'We're discussing this gentleman's most interesting article,' Father Joseph, the librarian, said, addressing the elder and pointing to Ivan. 'There's a great number of new ideas in it, but they seem to cut both ways. I'm referring to the article on the scope of the rights of ecclesiastical courts in dealing with social problems, which Mr Karamazov published in a periodical in reply to an ecclesiastical authority who had written a book dealing with the same question.'

'I'm afraid I haven't read your article, but I have heard of it,' said the elder, looking sharply and intently at Ivan.

'His point of view is extremely interesting,' continued the Father Librarian. 'It seems that in dealing with the question of ecclesiastical courts he is against the separation of Church and State.'

'That's interesting,' remarked the elder. 'In what sense, though?' he asked Ivan.

Ivan, at last, answered, but not, as Alyosha had feared, with condescending politeness, but modestly and restrainedly, with true courtesy and apparently without any mental reservations.

'I start from the proposition that this overlapping of the elements, that is to say, of the essential principles underlying Church and State, taken separately, will of course go on for ever, in spite of the fact that it is impossible and that it will never be brought into a normal, nor indeed into any reconcilable relationship, because its very basis is false. In my view a compromise between Church and State in such questions as, for example, court jurisdiction, is by its very nature impossible. The ecclesiastic to whom I replied maintained that the Church occupied a well-defined place in the State. But I maintained that, on the contrary, the Church ought to contain the whole State and not occupy only a corner in it, and that if this is for some reason impossible now, it ought most certainly to be set up as the direct and chief aim of the entire future development of Christian society.'

'Quite right!' Father Paissy, the learned monk who had kept silent till then, said firmly and fervently.

'The purest Ultramontanism!' cried Miusov, crossing his legs impatiently.

'Ah, but we have no mountains!' cried Father Joseph and, turning to the elder, continued: 'He answers the following "fundamental and essential" propositions of his opponent who, mark you, is an ecclesiastic: first, that "no alliance of social organizations can or ought to arrogate to itself the power to dispose of the civil and political rights of its members"; secondly, that "criminal and civil jurisdiction must not belong to the Church and is not compatible with its nature both as an institution vested with divine authority and as a body of men established for the pursuit of religious aims", and finally, thirdly, that "the Church is a kingdom not of this world".'

'A most unworthy play on words for an ecclesiastic!' Father Paissy could not refrain from interrupting again. 'I've read the book you discussed in your article,' he added, turning to Ivan, 'and I was astonished at its ecclesiastic author for maintaining that "the Church is a kingdom not of this world". If it is not of this world, then it cannot exist on earth at all. In the Holy Gospels the words "not of this world" are not used in that sense. You cannot play about with such words. Our Lord Jesus Christ came for the sole purpose of setting up the Church upon earth. The Kingdom of Heaven, of course, is not of this world, but in Heaven; but you enter Heaven only through the Church which has been founded and established on earth. Therefore, irreligious ambiguities in this sense are unpardonable and highly improper. The Church is, in truth, a Kingdom, and has been ordained to rule and at the end will undoubtedly become a Kingdom on earth – for which, indeed, we have a divine promise.'

He fell silent suddenly, as though restraining himself. Having listened to him respectfully and attentively, Ivan went on with the utmost composure and, as before, good-humouredly and readily, addressing himself to the elder:

'The whole idea of my article is that in ancient times, during the first three centuries of Christianity, Christianity existed on earth as a Church and only as a Church. But when the pagan Roman State expressed the desire to become Christian, it necessarily came to pass that, having become Christian, it merely included the Church as part of the State, but itself continued to be a pagan State as before in nearly all its administrative functions. This, as a matter of fact, was bound to happen. But there remained in Rome, as a State, a great deal of the pagan wisdom and civilization, for instance, the very fundamental principles and aims of the State. On the other hand, Christ's Church, having entered the State, doubtless could not give up any of its fundamental principles, the rock on which it stands, and could only pursue its own aims, which had been once and for all firmly established and revealed to it by God himself, such as, for instance, to turn the whole world and, therefore, also the ancient pagan State, into a Church. In this way (that is, with regard to the future) it is not the Church that ought to seek for itself a definite place in the State like "any other social organization" or like "an organization of men for religious purposes" (as my opponent, the author of the book we're discussing, describes the Church), but, on the contrary, every

State on earth must eventually be entirely transformed into a Church, and become nothing but a Church, renouncing those of its aims which are incompatible with the principles of the Church. All this will in no way lower its prestige or deprive it of its honour and glory as a great State, nor of the glory of its rulers, but will merely turn it away from the false, still pagan and mistaken path to the right and true path which alone leads to the eternal goal. That is why the author of *The Foundations of Ecclesiastical Courts* would have been right if, in trying to discover and lay down these foundations, he regarded them as a temporary compromise, still necessary in our sinful and far from perfect times, and no more than that. But the moment the author of these foundations takes it upon himself to declare that the foundations he lays down now, some of which have just been enumerated by Father Joseph, are elemental, firmly established, and eternal, he is going against the Church and its eternal and firmly established vocation. That is the gist of my article, a fair and full summary of it.'

'Which, to put it briefly, means,' Father Paissy began again, emphasizing every word, 'that according to certain theories, which have become all too clearly understood in our nineteenth century, the Church must be transformed into a State, just as though it were evolving from a lower into a higher form, so as to disappear into it, making place for science, the spirit of the age, and civilization. If, however, it refuses to do so and offers resistance, it is allotted only a little corner in the State and that, too, under supervision – and this is to be everywhere in our modern European States in our time. But according to our Russian conceptions and hopes, it is not the Church that ought to be turned into a State, as from a lower to a higher form, but, on the contrary, the State ought to end by being worthy to become only the Church and nothing else. And so it will be, it will be!'

'Well, sir,' said Miusov with a smile, recrossing his legs, 'I must say you've reassured me somewhat now. As far as I can make out, all this seems to be the realization of some ideal, infinitely remote, at the second coming of Christ. That is as may be. A beautiful utopian dream of the disappearance of wars, diplomacy, banks, etc. Something like Socialism, I suppose. For a moment I really thought that all this was serious, and that the Church would *now*, for instance, try criminal cases and pass sentences of flogging and penal servitude and, for all I know, even sentences of death.'

'Why, if we had only ecclesiastical courts now,' Ivan said imperturbably and without batting an eyelid, 'the Church would never pass sentences of penal servitude or death. Crime and the idea of crime would undoubtedly have undergone a change in that case, gradually, of course, not suddenly and at once, but I daresay in a very short time. . . .'

'Are you serious?' asked Miusov, glancing at him sharply.

'If everything became the Church,' Ivan went on, 'the Church would excommunicate the disobedient and the criminal and not cut off their heads. Where, I ask you, would the excommunicated go to? Why, he would have to renounce the company not only of men, as now, but also of Christ. For by his crime he would have transgressed not only against men but also against Christ's Church. This, strictly speaking, is so even now, but it is not officially so, and our criminal today very often strikes a bargain with his conscience. "It's true I've stolen, but I'm not transgressing against the Church. I am no enemy of Christ" – that's what our criminals quite often say today. But when the Church takes the place of the State, he will find it difficult to say this, unless, of course, he denies the authority of the Church on earth: "All are mistaken, all have deviated from the right path, all belong to a false Church, I alone, a thief and a murderer, am the true Christian Church." This is a very difficult thing to say to oneself. It requires very unusual conditions, a rare combination of unusual circumstances. Now, on the other hand, consider the views on crime of the Church itself: should it not undergo a change from our almost pagan views of today, and from the automatic cutting off of an infected limb, as is done today for the preservation of society, be transformed fully, and not falsely, into the idea of the regeneration of man, his reformation and salvation?'

'What exactly do you mean?' Miusov interrupted. 'I fail to understand again. This seems to be another kind of dream. Something shapeless, something beyond comprehension. What do you mean by excommunication? I suspect you're simply pulling our leg, sir.'

'But actually it is the same thing today,' said the elder suddenly, and all turned to him at once. 'If we had no Christ's Church now, there would be no way of stopping the criminal from committing his crimes and no real punishment for them afterwards. I mean, of course, real punishment and not the automatic punishment which you, sir, have just mentioned and which in the majority of cases only exacerbates the heart, while real punishment, the only effective one, resides in the awareness of one's own conscience and inspires fear and brings peace to the soul.'

'How is that, may I ask?' Miusov inquired with lively curiosity.

'It's like this,' began the elder. 'All these sentences of hard labour in Siberian prisons, and formerly with flogging, too, do not reform anyone and, what's more, scarcely deter even one criminal, and, far from diminishing, the number of crimes are steadily increasing. You have to admit that. It therefore follows that society is not in the least protected, for though a harmful member is cut off automatically and exiled to some remote spot just to get rid of him, another criminal takes his place at once, and often two, perhaps. If anything does protect society even today and indeed reforms the criminal himself and brings about his regeneration, it is, again, only the law of Christ, which reveals itself in the awareness of one's own conscience. Only by recognizing his own guilt as a son of a Christian society, that is, of the Church, does the criminal recognize his guilt towards society itself, that is, towards the Church. The criminal today, therefore, is capable of recognizing his guilt only towards the Church, and not towards the State. So that if society exercised its jurisdiction as a Church, it would know how to return the ex-communicated evil-doer to the bosom of the Church. But now the Church, deprived of her powers of jurisdiction and enjoying only the rights of moral condemnation, refuses to have anything to do with the infliction of real punishment. She does not excommunicate. She merely does not refuse to give the criminal her motherly ex-hortations. Moreover, she does her best to preserve Christian com-munion with him: she admits him to Church services, to the holy sacrament, gives him alms, and treats him more like an enslaved than a guilty person. And what would happen to a criminal, O Lord, if Christian society, that is, the Church, cast him out just as the civil law casts him out and cuts him off? What would happen if the Church punished him by excommunication immediately after the laws of the State had punished him? Why, there could be no greater despair, at least for a Russian criminal, for Russian criminals still have faith. However, who knows? Perhaps a most terrible thing would happen then – the despairing heart of the criminal would lose its faith, and what then? But the Church, like a tender and loving mother, refuses to have anything to do with punishment herself, for the man found guilty by the courts is severely punished already, and there must be somebody to take pity on him. But the chief reason why the Church refuses to have anything to do with punishment is that the judgement of the Church is the only one that contains the truth and therefore cannot assume actual or moral responsibility for any other judgement, not even as a temporary compromise. There can be no question of striking any sort of bargain here. A foreign criminal, I understand, rarely repents, for the most modern social theories confirm him in the idea that his crime is not a crime but only an act of rebellion against an unjustly oppressive force. Society cuts him off in an absolutely automatic fashion by a force that triumphs over him, and accompanies this excommunication with hatred (so, at least, they say about themselves in Europe) – with hatred and the most complete indifference and oblivion about his subsequent fate, as their brother. All this, consequently, happens without the slightest pity on the part of the Church, for in many cases there are no more Churches left there at all, but only clergymen and magnificent church buildings, the Churches themselves having long ago striven to pass from their lower form as a Church into the higher form as a State, so as to disappear in it completely. This is, at any rate, the case in Lutheran countries, I believe. In Rome, of course, a State has been proclaimed instead of a Church for the last thousand years. And that is why the criminal himself no longer recognizes himself as a member of the Church and, having been excommunicated, sinks into despair. And if he does return to society, it is often with such hatred that society itself seems instinctively to excommunicate him. You can judge for yourselves how it all must end. In many cases, it would seem, it is the same with us; but the whole point is that, in addition to the established civil courts, we have also the Church, which never loses contact with the criminal as a dear and still precious son. Besides, there still exists and is preserved, though only in thought, the judgement of the Church, inactive though it is now, but still living for the future, though only in people's minds, and is, no doubt, recognized by the criminal himself instinctively in his soul. What has just been said here now is also true, namely that if ecclesiastical courts were to be really set up and the jurisdiction of the Church were really to be established in full force, or, in other words, if the whole of society were to be transformed into the Church, then the judgement of the Church would not only influence the reformation of the criminal, as it never does now, but perhaps also the number of crimes themselves would diminish to a quite unbelievable extent. Nor is there any doubt that the Church itself would understand the potential criminal and his potential crime from now, in many cases quite differently and would know how to bring back the excommunicated, prevent crimes, and regenerate the fallen. It is true,' the elder smiled, 'that Christian society is not yet ready and is only kept in existence because of the seven righteous men, but as their number never decreases it will remain stable in expectation of its complete transformation from a society almost pagan in its organization into a single universal and sovereign Church. This will be, it will be, even though at the end of time, for this alone has been ordained to come to pass! And one should not be troubled about times and fixed dates, for the secret of times and fixed dates is in the wisdom of God and in his foresight and his love. And what may seem still far off according to man's reckoning, may by God's predestination be close at hand and on the very eve of its appearance. And this will be, it will be!'

'It will be! It will be!' Father Paissy echoed reverently and sternly.

'Curious, extremely curious!' Miusov said, not so much with heat as with a sort of concealed indignation.

'What strikes you as so curious?' Father Joseph inquired cautiously.

'But, good Lord,' cried Miusov, as though suddenly losing his self-control completely, 'what are you talking about? The State is to be abolished on earth and the Church is to be raised to the position of the State! Why, it's no longer Ultramontanism, it's arch-Ultramontanism! It's more than Pope Gregory the Seventh dreamed of!'

'You've got it all wrong, sir,' Father Paissy said severely. 'It is not the Church that is transformed into the State. Please understand that. That is Rome and its dream. That is the third temptation of the devil. On the contrary, the State is transformed into the Church, it rises to it and becomes a Church all over the world – which is the complete opposite of Ultramontanism and Rome and your interpretation of it, and is only the great predetermined destiny of the Orthodox Church on earth. This star will shine in the East!'

Miusov was impressively silent. His whole figure expressed extraordinary personal dignity. A supercilious and condescending smile appeared on his lips. Alyosha watched it all with a fast beating heart. The whole conversation stirred him most powerfully. He cast a cursory glance at Rakitin, who was standing motionless in his former place at the door, listening and watching attentively, though with downcast eyes. But Alyosha guessed from the high colour in his cheeks that Rakitin was no less excited than he; Alyosha knew what was the cause of his excitement.

'Allow me, gentlemen, to tell you a little anecdote,' said Miusov suddenly with an impressive and a sort of specially dignified air. 'A few years ago in Paris, soon after the December revolution, I happened to meet a most interesting man at the house of an extremely important member of the government, an acquaintance of mine on whom I happened to be paying a call at the time. This individual was not just an ordinary detective, but the chief of a whole lot of security agents – a rather influential post in its way. Taking advantage of this chance meeting and being very curious to learn something of his work, I entered into a conversation with him. He had come to that house not as a guest but as a subordinate official (he had brought his latest official report with him), and seeing how well I was received by his chief, he was so good as to speak to me with some frankness – up to a point, of course; I mean he was polite rather than frank, as Frenchmen know how to be polite, particularly as he saw that I was a foreigner. But I understood him thoroughly. The subject of our conversation was the socialist revolutionaries who were, incidentally, persecuted at the time. Leaving out the main point of our conversation, I shall quote only one highly interesting remark that gentleman blurted out to me. "We are not particularly afraid," he said, "of all these socialists-anarchists, atheists, and revolutionaries; we are keeping an eye on them and all their moves are known to us. But there are several peculiar men among them, though only a few: these believe in God – they are Christians and at the same time Socialists. It is these we fear most of all. They are terrible people. A Christian Socialist is much more terrible than a Socialist who is an atheist."

These words struck me at the time, too, but now I couldn't help remembering them here for some reason, gentlemen.'

'You are applying them to us and you regard us as Socialists, don't you?' Father Paissy asked straight out, without beating about the bush.

But before Miusov had time to think of an answer, the door opened and Dmitry Karamazov, who had been so late in making an appearance, came in. They had, as a matter of fact, given up expecting him, and indeed his sudden appearance caused some surprise at first.

6

Why Does Such a Man Live?

DMITRY KARAMAZOV, a young man of twenty-eight, of medium height and pleasant appearance, looked much older than his age. He was muscular and one could see that he had considerable physical strength; and yet his face did not seem to be that of a healthy man. His face was thin, his cheeks hollow, and his complexion unhealthily sallow. There was apparent a hard, stubborn, but also somehow rather evasive look in his large, protruding dark eyes. Even when he was excited and talking irritably, his eyes did not seem to obey his inward mood and expressed something else, which sometimes had little to do with what was taking place at the time. 'It's hard to tell what he's thinking,' those who talked to him sometimes declared. Some people, who saw something pensive and sullen in his eyes, were occasionally taken aback by his unexpected laughter, which showed that his thoughts were gay and playful just at the time when he looked so gloomy. However, the somewhat sickly expression of his face at that moment was perhaps not difficult to explain: they all knew or had heard of the extremely restless and 'dissipated' life in which he had been indulging more recently in our town; his extreme irritation in his quarrels with his father about the money he claimed the latter owed him was also generally known. There were a number of stories already current in our town about it. It is true that he was irritable by nature, 'of an unstable and unbalanced mind', as our justice of the peace, Semyon Kachalnikov, characteristically described him at some public function. He came in impeccably and fashionably dressed, his frock-coat buttoned, wearing black gloves and carrying a top-hat. As an army man who had recently resigned his commission, he wore a moustache and for the time being only shaved his beard. His dark brown hair was cut short and combed somehow forward on his temples. He walked with the long, firm stride of the professional soldier. He stopped for a moment on the threshold and, with a quick glance at the company, went straight up to the elder, guessing him to be the host. He made him a low bow and asked his blessing. The elder got up and blessed him; Dmitry kissed his hand respectfully.

'I'm very sorry to have kept you waiting so long, sir,' he said with extraordinary excitement, almost with irritation. 'But Smerdyakov, the servant sent by my father, told me twice in reply to my repeated questions about the time of the appointment that it was for one o'clock. Now I suddenly learn —'

'Don't worry,' the elder interrupted him. 'It doesn't matter. You are a little late, but it's of no consequence. . . . '

'Thank you very much, sir. I could expect no less from your kindness.'

Having rapped out his apology, Dmitry bowed once more, then suddenly turning towards his father, made him, too, a similarly low and respectful bow. It was obvious that he had carefully considered this bow beforehand, and quite sincerely thought it to be almost his duty to make it and express his respect and good intentions by it. Karamazov, though taken by surprise, rose to the occasion in his own way: in reply to Dmitry's bow, he jumped up from his armchair and made his son a bow as low in return. His face suddenly assumed a grave and solemn expression, which, however, made him look absolutely vicious. After bowing silently to the rest of the company, Dmitry went up to the window with his long and firm strides, sat down on the only vacant chair, not far from Father Paissy, and, bending forward, at once prepared to listen to the interrupted conversation.

Dmitry's entrance had taken no more than two minutes and the conversation could not but be resumed. But this time Mr Miusov did not think it necessary to reply to Father Paissy's pressing and almost irritable question.

'Allow me to decline to discuss this subject,' he said with an air of well-bred casualness. 'It is I'm afraid a tricky subject, anyhow. Mr Ivan Karamazov, you see, is smiling at us. I suppose he must have something interesting to say about that, too. You'd better ask him.'

'I've nothing much to say,' replied Ivan at once, 'except to make a little remark about the curious fact that European liberals in general and our own liberal dilettanti in particular, have often, and for some time past, been mixing up the final results of Socialism with those of Christianity. This absurd conclusion is of course very characteristic of them. However, it is not only the liberals and the dilettanti who confuse Socialism with Christianity. In many cases the police – the foreign police, of course – do the same. Your Paris story is very characteristic, Mr Miusov.'

'I should again like to ask your permission, gentlemen, to drop the subject,' Miusov repeated. 'I will tell you instead another anecdote, a very interesting and most characteristic anecdote about Mr Ivan Karamazov himself. Only five days ago, at a certain social gathering, consisting mostly of ladies, he solemnly declared during an argument that there was absolutely nothing in the whole world to make men love their fellow-men, that there was no law in nature that man should love mankind, and that if love did exist on earth, it was not because of any natural law but solely because men believed in immortality. He added in parenthesis that all natural law consisted of that belief, and that if you were to destroy the belief in immortality in mankind, not only love but every living force on which the continuation of all life in the world depended, would dry up at once. Moreover, there would be nothing immoral then, everything would be permitted, even cannibalism. But that is not all: he wound up with the assertion that for every individual, like myself, for instance, who does not believe in God or in his own immortality, the moral laws of nature must at once be changed into the exact opposite of the former religious laws, and that self-interest, even if it were to lead to crime, must not only be permitted but even recognized as the necessary, the most rational, and practically the most honourable motive for a man in his position. From this paradox, gentlemen, you can conclude what sort of ideas our dear eccentric and paradoxical fellow has been propounding and, no doubt, will go on propounding in future.'

'One moment,' Dmitry suddenly cried unexpectedly, 'did you say, "Crime must not only be permitted, but even be recognized as the most necessary and the most intelligent result of the position of every unbeliever?" Is that so or not?'

'It is so,' said Father Paissy.

'I'll remember that!'

Having said this, Dmitry fell silent as suddenly as he had burst into the conversation. They all looked at him with curiosity.

'Is this really your opinion of what would happen if people lost their faith in the immortality of their souls?' the elder suddenly asked Ivan.

'Yes, that was my contention. There is no virtue if there's no immortality.'

'If that is what you believe you are either blessed or most unhappy!'

'Why unhappy?' asked Ivan with a smile.

'Because you most probably do not yourself believe in the immortality of your soul, nor even in what you've written about the Church and the Church question.'

'Perhaps you are right! . . . But all the same I wasn't altogether joking, either,' Ivan suddenly made this strange confession, though, it is true, he blushed quickly.

'You were not altogether joking – that's true. You still can't find the right answer to this question and you're very worried about it. But even a martyr sometimes likes to amuse himself with his despair, just out of despair. You, too, in your despair, are for the time being amusing yourself with magazine articles and discussions in society without believing in your arguments and smiling bitterly at them with an ache in your heart. . . . You have not made up your mind what answer to give to that question and therein lies your great grief, for the question urgently demands an answer.'

'But is it possible for me to make up my mind?' Ivan continued to ask his strange questions, looking at the elder with the same enigmatic smile. 'Can I answer it in the affirmative?'

'If you can't answer it in the affirmative, you will never be able to answer it in the negative. You know that peculiarity of your heart yourself – and all its agony is due to that alone. But thank the Creator who has given you a superior heart capable of such agony, "to mind high things and to seek high things, forasmuch as our dwelling is in heaven". God grant that your heart's answer will find you still on earth, and may God bless your path!'

The elder raised his hand and was about to make the sign of the cross over Ivan from his seat. But Ivan suddenly got up, went up to him, received his blessing and, kissing his hand, returned to his place in silence. He looked resolute and earnest. This action and all the preceding conversation with the elder, which was so unexpected of Ivan, seemed to impress everyone by its air of mystery and even by a certain solemnity, so that they all fell silent for a minute, and Alyosha looked almost frightened. But Miusov suddenly shrugged his shoulders, and at that very moment Karamazov jumped up from his chair.

'Most divine and most holy elder,' he cried, pointing at Ivan, 'this is my son, the flesh of my flesh, the dearest one of my flesh! This is, so to speak, my most respectful Karl Moor, while this son of mine, Dmitry, who has just come in, and against whom I am seeking justice from you, is the most disrespectful Franz Moor, both from Schiller's *Robbers*, which, I suppose, makes me the *Regierender Graf von Moor*! Judge and save us! We need not only your prayers, but also your prophecies.'

'Speak without fooling and don't begin by insulting the members of your family,' the elder replied in a weak, exhausted voice.

He was clearly getting more and more tired and his strength was perceptibly failing.

'A disgraceful comedy which I foresaw when I was coming here!' cried Dmitry indignantly, also jumping up from his seat. 'I'm sorry, Reverend Father,' he addressed the elder, 'I'm an uneducated man and I don't even know how to address you, but you've been deceived and you've been too good-natured in letting us meet here. All my father wants is a public scandal. He has his own reasons for it. He always has his reasons. But I think I know why —'

'They all accuse me, all of them!' Karamazov cried in his turn. 'Mr Miusov, too, has accused me. Yes, sir, you have, you have!' He suddenly turned to Miusov, though the latter was not thinking of interrupting him. 'I'm accused of hiding my children's money in my boots, taking the same amount from each of them. But, tell me, sir, isn't there a court of law? They'll count it up for you there, Dmitry, from your own receipts, your letters, and your agreements – how much you had, how much you squandered, and how much you

have left! Why does Mr Miusov refuse to arbitrate? Dmitry is not a
stranger to him. Why, because they are all against me. As for
Dmitry, he actually owes me money, and not just a few roubles,
either, but several thousand, sir! And I have all the documents to
prove it! The whole town is in an uproar with his debaucheries!
And where he served before, he had to pay a thousand or two for
seducing respectable girls. We know all about that, sir,' he turned to
his eldest son, 'all the most secret details of it, and I can prove it, sir!
Most holy father, I know it sounds incredible, but he has turned the
head of a most honourable young girl, a girl of good family and
substantial fortune, the daughter of his superior officer, a gallant
colonel, a man who has deserved well of his country, who has
received the Order of St Anne with crossed swords. He compromised
the girl by a proposal of marriage, and now she is here, an orphan,
his fiancée, and yet before her very eyes he is running after a siren
in our town. But though this siren has lived, if I may say so, out of
wedlock with a highly respectable man, she is of an independent
character, an unassailable fortress to everybody, just as if she were a
lawfully married wife, for she's virtuous, sir – yes, holy fathers, she's
virtuous! And Dmitry wants to open this fortress with a golden key,
and that's why he's trying to bully me now, to fleece me of my money,
and in the meantime he has spent thousands on this siren already. He's
constantly borrowing money for that, and who do you think from?
Shall I tell them, Mitya?'

'Shut up!' cried Dmitry. 'Wait till I'm gone. Don't you dare to
besmirch the good name of a most honourable girl in my presence!
The very fact that you've had the effrontery to mention her is an
insult to her. . . . I won't permit it!'

He was gasping for breath.

'Mitya, Mitya,' cried Karamazov weakly, squeezing out a tear,
'does a father's blessing mean nothing to you? And what if I should
put a curse on you? What then?'

'You shameless hypocrite!' Dmitry bawled furiously.

'That's what he calls his father – his father! How do you think
he would treat others? Gentlemen, just listen to this: there's a poor
but honourable man living here, a retired army captain, a man
burdened with a large family, who got into trouble and was dismissed the service, but there was no public scandal, no court martial.

He left the army without a stain on his character. And three weeks ago, my son Dmitry seized him by the beard in a pub, dragged him out into the street and beat him mercilessly in public, and all because I employ him as my agent in a little business of mine.'

'It's a damned lie!' Dmitry cried, trembling all over with rage. 'It may appear to be true, but when you examine it closely it's a lie. Father, I don't justify my actions. Yes, I confess it publicly: I behaved like a brute to that captain and I'm sorry for it now and I loathe myself for my brutal anger. But this captain of yours, this agent of yours, went to the lady whom you've just called a siren and suggested to her in your name that she should take the promissory notes I had given you and sue me for the money. Your idea was to have me put away in jail if I kept pestering you to give me an account of my property. And now you're reproaching me for being in love with that girl, while it was you yourself who suggested to her that she should get me to fall in love with her. Why, she told me so herself. She said so to my face, laughing at you! And you want to put me in jail only because you're jealous, because you've begun pursuing that woman with your love, and I know all about it, and again she laughed – do you hear? – she laughed at you as she told me about it. So that's the sort of a man he is, holy fathers, that's the father who reproaches his dissolute son! Gentlemen, forgive my anger, but I had a feeling that this cunning old man would bring you together here to create a public scandal. I came here to forgive him if he held out his hand to me: I was ready to forgive and to ask forgiveness! But as he has just this minute insulted not only me, but also a most honourable young lady, whose name I dare not take in vain out of a feeling of reverence for her, I've decided to show up his game in public, though he is my father! ...'

He could not go on. His eyes flashed and he breathed with difficulty. But everyone in the cell looked perturbed. They all, except the elder, got up from their seats uneasily. The monks looked stern, but waited to see what the elder would do. The elder, however, sat looking very pale, though not from agitation, but because he felt too weak and ill. An imploring smile played on his lips; from time to time he raised his hand as though wishing to stop the two raving men and, of course, one gesture from him would have been enough to end the scene; but he seemed to be waiting for something himself and watched them closely, as though trying to understand something that was not quite clear to him. At last Peter Miusov felt completely humiliated and disgraced.

'We are all to blame for this scandalous scene,' he said warmly, 'and yet on my way here I did not foresee it, though I knew perfectly well with whom I had to deal. We must stop it at once. I assure you, your reverence, that I had no real knowledge of all the details that have come to light here. I was loath to believe them and it's only now I've got to know about them for the first time. . . . A father is jealous of his son because of a disreputable woman, and himself plots with that creature to put his son in prison. And it is in such company that I've been forced to come here! I was deceived. I want to make it clear to you all that I was as much deceived as anyone.'

'Dmitry,' Karamazov suddenly yelled in an unnatural voice, 'if you were not my son, I'd have challenged you to a duel this very minute . . . with pistols, sir, and at a distance of three paces – yes, sir, across a handkerchief – across a handkerchief, sir!' he concluded, stamping his feet.

There are moments in the life of old liars who have been play-acting all their lives when they are so carried away by the part they're playing that they really do weep and tremble with excitement, in spite of the fact that at that very moment (or a second later) they could have whispered to themselves: 'You're lying, you shameless old fool! Now, too, you're just acting a part in spite of all your "sacred" wrath and the "sacred" moment of your wrath.'

Dmitry frowned threateningly and looked at his father with indescribable contempt.

'I thought,' he said in a kind of quiet and restrained voice, 'I thought that I'd come home with my sweetheart, my future wife, to look after him in his old age, and all I see is a dissolute voluptuary and a most contemptible clown!'

'I challenge you, sir!' the old wretch yelled again, gasping for breath and spluttering with each word he uttered. 'As for you, sir,' he turned to Miusov, 'I want you to know that there has perhaps never been a woman in your family more high-minded and more honest – do you hear, sir? – more honest than the woman you had the effrontery just now to call a creature! And you, Dmitry, have jilted your fiancée for that "creature", so that you must be perfectly clear in your mind that your fiancée is not fit to lick her boots – that's the sort of "creature" she is!'

'Shame!' Father Joseph could not refrain from exclaiming.

'It's a shame and a disgrace!' Kalganov, who had been silent all the time, suddenly cried in his boyish voice, trembling with agitation and reddening to the roots of his hair.

'Why does such a man live?' Dmitry growled in a hollow voice, almost beside himself with rage, raising his shoulders so much that he appeared almost hunch-backed. 'Tell me, can he be allowed to defile the earth by his existence?' he asked, glancing at each of them in turn and pointing to the old man.

He spoke slowly and emphatically.

'Listen, listen, monks, to the parricide!' Karamazov cried, rushing suddenly upon Father Joseph. 'That's the answer to your "shame", sir! Why shame? This "creature", this "disreputable woman", gentlemen, is perhaps holier than all of you who are seeking salvation in this monastery. She may have fallen in her youth, a victim of her environment, but she "loved much", and Christ himself forgave the woman who "loved much".'

'Christ did not forgive for that kind of love,' escaped impatiently from the gentle Father Joseph.

'Yes, for that kind of love, monks, for that very same kind of love! You're seeking salvation here by eating cabbage soup and you think you're righteous men! You eat gudgeons, a gudgeon a day, and you think you can buy God with gudgeons.'

'It's intolerable! Intolerable!' they cried from all corners of the cell.

But this scandalous scene came to an end in a most unexpected way. The elder suddenly rose from his seat. Alyosha, who had almost completely lost his head with anxiety for him and everyone else, was just in time, however, to support him by the arm. The elder stepped in the direction of Dmitry and, reaching him, went down on his knees before him. Alyosha at first thought that he had sunk down from weakness, but that was not so. Having knelt, the elder prostrated himself at Dmitry's feet with full, conscious deliberation and even touched the ground with his forehead. Alyosha was so amazed that he failed to support him when he rose again. A faint smile played on his lips.

'Forgive me! Forgive me all of you!' he said, bowing to his guests on all sides.

Dmitry stood still for a few seconds as though thunderstruck: the elder had bowed down to him – what was it all about? At last he cried: 'Oh, Lord!' and, covering his face with his hands, rushed out of the room. All the guests hurried out of the room in a crowd after him and in their confusion did not even take leave or bow to their host. Only the monks went up to the elder again for a blessing.

'What did he mean by kneeling at his feet?' Karamazov, who had grown quiet of a sudden for some reason, tried to reopen the conversation, without, however, daring to address anybody in particular. 'Is it symbolic of something or what?'

They were all leaving the hermitage at that moment.

'I can't answer for madmen or for a madhouse,' Miusov at once replied angrily, 'but I'm glad to say I shall rid myself of your company, and, believe me, sir, for good. Where's that monk?'

'That monk', that is to say, the monk who had invited them to dinner with the Father Superior, did not keep them waiting. He met the visitors as soon as they came down the steps from the elder's cell, as though he had been waiting for them all the time.

'Do me a favour, Father, and convey my deepest respects to the Father Superior and apologize personally for me, Miusov, to his reverence and tell him that owing to unforeseen circumstances I regret to be unable to be present at his table, much as I should like to,' Miusov said irritably to the monk.

'The unforeseen circumstance is, of course, myself!' Karamazov at once broke in. 'You see, Father, Mr Miusov doesn't want to remain in the same company as I, or he would come at once. And you will go, sir. Yes, sir, go to the Father Superior and – I hope you enjoy your meal! It is I who am declining and not you. Home, home, home – I'll eat at home, for I don't feel I could eat anything here, Mr Miusov, dear relative of mine!'

'I'm not your relative, sir. I've never been your relative, you contemptible man.'

'I said it on purpose to make you mad, for I know you refuse to acknowledge our relationship, though you are my relative, however much you try to shuffle out of it. I can prove it by the church calendar. I'll send a carriage for you, Ivan. You can stay if you like. As for you, Mr Miusov, good manners demand that you should go to the Father Superior. You have to apologize to him for our high jinks.'

'But is it true you're going home? You're not lying, are you?'

'My dear sir, do you really think I'd dare to lie after what's happened? Sorry, gentlemen, I was carried away! And, besides, I'm deeply shocked and ashamed, too! Gentlemen, one man has the heart of Alexander of Macedon and the other the heart of a little lap-dog. Afraid mine is like a lap-dog's. Lost my nerve! And, really, how can I go to dinner after such an escapade? Bolt the monastery sauces? I'm sorry, but I can't do it. I'm too ashamed!'

'What if he deceives us, damn him?' Miusov stopped, wondering and watching the retreating clown with a perplexed look.

Karamazov turned round and, noticing that Miusov was watching him, blew him a kiss.

'Are you coming to the Father Superior?' Miusov asked Ivan abruptly.

'Why not? Besides, the Father Superior specially invited me yesterday.'

'Unhappily, I really do feel almost obliged to go to this confounded dinner,' Miusov went on in the same tone of bitter irritability, without paying the slightest attention to the monk who could hear him. 'I suppose we ought to apologize for the disturbance we've made here and explain that it wasn't our fault. . . . What do you think?'

'Yes, we'd better explain that it wasn't our fault. Besides, father won't be there,' observed Ivan.

'Your father! That would have been the absolute limit! Oh, confound this dinner!'

And yet they all went. The little monk listened and kept quiet. Only once on their way through the wood did he observe that the Father Superior had been waiting a long time and that they were more than half an hour late. He received no answer. Miusov glanced at Ivan with hatred.

'Going to the dinner, damn him, as though nothing had happened!' he thought. 'A face of brass and the conscience of a Karamazov.'

7

A Seminarist-Careerist

ALYOSHA took his elder to the little bedroom and made him sit down on the bed. It was a very small room furnished with the bare necessities; the bed was a narrow iron one with a strip of felt instead of a mattress. In the corner by the icons was a lectern with a cross and the Gospel lying on it. The elder sank exhausted on the bed; his eyes glittered and he breathed with difficulty. Having sat down, he looked intently at Alyosha as though considering something.

'Go, my dear boy, go to the Father Superior,' he said. 'Porfiry will look after me. Hurry, you're wanted there. Go and wait at table.'

'Please, let me stay here,' Alyosha said in an imploring voice.

'They need you more there. There's no peace there. You'll wait and be useful. If the evil spirits arise, you can say a prayer. And remember, my son (the elder liked to call him that), that this is not the place for you in the future. Remember that, my boy. As soon as it is God's will to call me to him, leave the monastery. Leave it for good.'

Alyosha gave a start.

'What's the matter? For the time being this is not the place for you. I bless you for great service in the world. There is still a long road before you. And you'll have to take a wife, too. You will have to go through it all, before you come back again. There will be much for you to do. But I have no doubts about you and that is why I am sending you into the world. Christ is with you. Do not abandon him and he will not abandon you. You will know great sorrow and in that sorrow you will be happy. This is my last message to you: in sorrow seek happiness. Work, work unceasingly. Remember my words from now on, for though I shall talk to you again, not only my days, but my hours are numbered.'

Alyosha's face again showed great emotion. The corners of his lips trembled.

'Why are you crying again?' the elder said, with a gentle smile.

'Let laymen bid farewell to their dying with tears. Here we rejoice over the father who is departing. We rejoice and pray for him. Leave me, please. I must pray. Go and make haste. Be near your brothers. And not near one of them only, but near both.'

The elder raised his hand to bless him. It was impossible to protest, though Alyosha wanted very much to stay. He also wanted to ask the elder – and, indeed, the question was almost on the tip of his tongue – what was the significance of that deep bow to his brother Dmitry. But he dared not ask it. He knew that if the elder had thought fit, he would have explained it without being asked. But it did not seem to be his will. The bow had made a tremendous impression on Alyosha: he believed blindly that there was a mysterious meaning in it. Mysterious and perhaps also terrible. When he walked out of the hermitage to reach the monastery in time for dinner (only to wait at table, of course), his heart suddenly contracted painfully and he stopped dead: he seemed to hear again the elder's words foretelling his fast-approaching end. What the elder foretold, and with such exactness, too, must beyond all doubt come to pass. Alyosha believed that implicitly. But how could he be left without him? How could he go on without seeing and hearing him? And where would he go? He had told him not to cry and to leave the monastery. Dear God! It was long since Alyosha had felt such anguish. He hurried along through the wood which divided the monastery from the hermitage and, unable to bear the thoughts which oppressed him so heavily, he began looking at the age-old pines at either side of the path. He had not far to go – about five hundred yards, no more. At that hour he hardly expected to meet anyone, but at the first turn of the path he suddenly noticed Rakitin, who seemed to be waiting for someone.

'You're not waiting for me, are you?' Alyosha asked as he came up to him.

'Yes, I am,' Rakitin grinned. 'You're in a hurry to get to the Father Superior. I know. He's giving a dinner. Since he entertained the bishop and General Pakhatov, there has been no such dinner. I shan't be there, but you go and hand round the sauces. Tell me one thing, though, Alexey: what is the meaning of all this? That's what I wanted to ask you.'

'The meaning of what?'

'That business of prostrating himself before your brother Dmitry? Knocked his forehead on the ground, he did!'

'You mean, Father Zossima?'

'Yes, Father Zossima.'

'His forehead?'

'Oh, I see, I've been speaking disrespectfully! All right, so I have. Anyway, what is it all about?'

'I don't know what it means, Misha.'

'I knew he would not explain it to you. There is, of course, nothing extraordinary about it. Just the usual well-meant nonsense. But there was some purpose in the trick. Now all the sanctimonious fools in the town will talk about it and spread it all over the province, asking each other what is the meaning of it. If you ask me, the old man is a sharp one: he smells crime. Your house stinks of it.'

'What sort of crime?'

Rakitin was obviously eager to tell him something.

'It will be in your family – this crime will. It will happen between your dear brothers and that very rich father of yours. That's why Father Zossima knocked his head on the floor. Just in case it happens. Then, when it does happen, people will be saying, "Ah, that's exactly what the holy elder foretold – it was a prophecy!" Though I'm hanged if I can see what knocking his head on the floor has to do with prophesying. Not at all, they'll say, the whole thing was symbolic, an allegory, and the devil knows what! They'll trumpet it all over the place and they will remember it: Aha, he predicted the crime and marked the criminal. It's always like that with saintly fools: they cross themselves at the sight of a pub and throw stones at a church. Your elder is like that too: he drives the righteous out with a stick and bows down before a murderer.'

'What crime? What murderer? What are you talking about?'

Alyosha stopped dead; Rakitin stopped, too.

'What murderer? Don't you know? I bet you've thought of it yourself already. That's jolly interesting, though. Look here, Alyosha, you always tell the truth, though you never like to commit yourself. Tell me, have you thought of it or not? Answer.'

'I have thought of it,' Alyosha replied softly.

Even Rakitin was taken back.

'What are you saying? Have you really thought of it, too?' he cried.

'I – I haven't actually thought of it,' Alyosha murmured. 'You see, as soon as you began talking about it so strangely, I couldn't help feeling that I'd thought about it myself.'

'See? And how well you've put it! So it was while looking at your father and at Mitya, that darling brother of yours, today, that you thought of a crime, was it? So I'm not mistaken, am I?'

'But wait, wait a minute!' Alyosha interrupted him uneasily. 'What has made you see it all? And why does it interest you so much? That's what I'd like to know.'

'Two separate but natural questions. Let me answer each of them in turn. Why do I see it? I shouldn't have seen any of it, if I hadn't suddenly understood your brother Dmitry today. Seen through and through him all at once. Grasped his whole character from one significant little point. There's a point beyond which these very honourable but voluptuous people must not pass. Otherwise – otherwise he won't hesitate to stick a knife into his own father. And his dear old father is a drunkard and an intemperate old rake, who never knows where to stop, so they won't be able to restrain themselves and bang! into the ditch the two of them.'

'No, Misha, no, if that's all, you've reassured me. It will never come to that.'

'Then why are you trembling all over? Do you know what? Your Mitya may be honest (he's stupid, but honest) but he's a sensualist. That's the definition and the inner essence of him. It's from his father that he has inherited his disgusting sensuality. Why, I can't help marvelling at you, Alyosha: how is it you're still a virgin? You, too, are a Karamazov, aren't you? And in your family sensuality has reached a point where it becomes a devouring fever. So these three sensualists are now constantly watching each other – with a knife stuck in the leg of their boots. They're knocking their heads together, the three of them, and, for all I know, you may be the fourth.'

'You're mistaken about that woman. Dmitry – despises her,' Alyosha said, with a sort of shudder.

'Grushenka, you mean? No sir, he doesn't despise her. If he really has openly jilted his fiancée for her, then he does not despise her. There's something here, my dear chap, that you can't understand yet. You see, if a man falls in love with some beautiful woman, with a woman's body, or even with just one part of her body (only a sensualist can understand that), he'll sacrifice his own children for her, he'll sell his father and mother, and his country, too. If he's honest, he'll go and steal, if he is gentle, he'll kill, if he is faithful, he'll deceive. Pushkin, the singer of women's beautiful feet, sang in praise of women's feet in his verses; others do not sing their praises but cannot look calmly at women's feet. But, then, it's not only their feet. . . . In this business, my dear chap, contempt is no help, even if he did despise Grushenka. He despises her, but he can't tear himself away from her.'

'I understand that,' Alyosha suddenly blurted out.

'Do you? Well, I suppose you do understand it all right if you blurt it out at the first word,' Rakitin said spitefully. 'You see, you've blurted it out without thinking. It just escaped you against your will. Well, your confession is all the more valuable. So it's a familiar subject to you, is it? You've thought about it already, of sensuality, I mean. Oh, you virgin! You are a quiet chap, Alyosha, you're a saint. I agree. But quiet as you are, one can't tell what you haven't thought about, or what you don't know already, can one? A virgin and already plumbed such depths! I've been watching you for a long time. You're a Karamazov yourself, a full-blown Karamazov – breed and natural selection do mean something then. A sensualist after your father and a saintly fool after your mother. Why do you tremble? It's true what I'm saying, isn't it? Do you know what? Grushenka said to me, "Bring him to me (she meant you) and I'll pull his cassock off his back!" She kept begging me : "Bring him! Bring him!" I just couldn't help wondering why she should be so interested in you. You know, she's quite an extraordinary woman, too!'

'Give her my regards and tell her that I won't come,' Alyosha said with a wry smile. 'Finish what you were going to say, Mikhail. I'll tell you what I think afterwards.'

'What is there more to say? It's all clear. All this, my dear chap, is an old story. If you, too, are a sensualist at heart, then what is your brother Ivan? He, too, is a Karamazov, isn't he? That's what the Karamazov problem boils down to – sensualists, money-grubbers, and saintly fools! Your brother Ivan is writing theological articles at present as a joke and for some unknown idiotic reason, for he himself is an atheist, and this Ivan, this brother of yours, himself admits that what he is doing is mean and despicable. In addition, he's trying to get Mitya's fiancée for himself, and in this, I believe, he'll succeed. Why, he'll get her with Mitya's consent, because Mitya is letting him have her himself, just to get rid of her and go to Grushenka as quickly as possible. And, mark you, he does it all in spite of his high-mindedness and disinterestedness. It's people like that who're the most fatal of all! I'm hanged if I know what to make of you after that: he admits his own mean actions and goes on doing them! Now, listen: that old wretch of your father is now in Mitya's way. For the old goat has suddenly gone crazy about Grushenka. His mouth waters the moment he looks at her. He raised such a hullabaloo in the cell just now only because of her, only because Miusov dared call her a "loose creature". He's head over ears in love with her. At first he employed her at a salary in some shady business deals of his and in his pubs, and now he suddenly realizes what a lovely creature she is and he's worked himself up into a state of raging fury, keeps making her all sorts of offers, not honourable ones, of course. Well, so father and son are going to run into each other on that slippery path. Meanwhile, Grushenka does not seem to be particularly keen on either of them. For the time being she's sitting on the fence and teasing both of them. She's trying to make up her mind which of the two could be more useful to her, for though she could grab a lot of money from the old man, she knows he won't marry her and may even end up by turning stingy and tightening his purse-strings. In that case, Mitya, too, has his value. He has no money, but he's quite capable of marrying her. Yes, sir, he's capable of marrying her! Of jilting his fiancée, a girl of rare beauty, a rich noblewoman and the daughter of a colonel, and of marrying Grushenka, a former mistress of the mayor Samsonov, a lousy old merchant, a debauched peasant. And this may quite well lead to one of them committing a crime. That's what your brother Ivan is waiting for. If that happens, he'll be in clover: he'll get Katerina, for whom he is pining away, and get hold of her dowry of sixty thousand. To a small man who has not a penny to bless himself with this is not so bad for a beginning. And, mind you, far from hurting Mitya's feelings, he'll be doing him a great favour. For I know for a fact that last week Mitya, who had got drunk in a pub with some gipsy girls, was shouting that he did not deserve to marry a girl like Katerina but that his brother Ivan did deserve to marry her.

And Katerina, of course, will not in the end refuse such a fascinating fellow as Ivan, for even now she's already hesitating between the two of them. And what is so marvellous about this Ivan of yours that you should all be so taken with him? Why, he's laughing at you! He's in clover and having a jolly good time at your expense!'

'How do you know all this?' Alyosha asked suddenly, sharply, and frowning. 'Why are you so sure of it?'

'And why are you asking me now and why are you so afraid of my answer? It shows that you know yourself I'm speaking the truth.'

'You don't like Ivan. Ivan would not be tempted by money.'

'Wouldn't he? And what about Katerina? She's very beautiful, isn't she? It's not only the money, though sixty thousand isn't to be sneezed at.'

'Ivan has higher things in mind. Ivan wouldn't be tempted by any amount of money. It's not money or security that he is after. Perhaps it's suffering he is after.'

'What nonsense is this? Oh you – aristocrats!'

'Oh, Misha, his is a stormy spirit. His mind is in bondage. He's obsessed by a great, unsolved problem. He's one of those who don't want millions, but a solution of their problem.'

'Plagiarism, my dear chap. You're trying to paraphrase one of your elder's sayings. Hell, what a riddle Ivan has set you!' Rakitin cried with undisguised malice. He even changed countenance and his lips twitched. 'And the riddle is a stupid one. You can guess it easily. Use your brains and you'll understand. His article is absurd and ridiculous. You've heard his stupid theory, haven't you? "If there is no immortality of the soul, there is no virtue, which means that everything is permitted." (And dear old Mitya, you remember, cried out: "I'll remember that!") An attractive theory for scoundrels. . . . Sorry. I'm being abusive – that's silly. It's not a theory for scoundrels, but for bragging schoolboys with their "profound, unsolved problems". He's a dirty little boaster, but what it all comes to is that "on the one hand, we cannot but admit, and, on the other, we cannot but confess". His whole theory is nothing but a dirty trick! Mankind will find in itself the strength to live for virtue even without believing in the immortality of the soul! It will find it in love for freedom, equality, fraternity. . . .'

Rakitin grew excited and could scarcely contain himself. But, as though remembering something, he suddenly stopped short.

'Well, that's enough,' he said, smiling even more wryly than before. 'What are you laughing at? You think I'm a vulgar fool?'

'No, it never occurred to me to think you were a vulgar fool. You're clever, but – let's drop it, it was silly of me to laugh. I realize that you're capable of getting excited about it, Misha. From your excitement I guessed that you were not indifferent to Katerina yourself. You see, my dear fellow, I suspected it long ago. That's why you don't like my brother Ivan. You're jealous of him, aren't you?'

'Am I jealous of her money, too? Why not say it?'

'No, I won't say anything about money. I'm not going to insult you.'

'I believe it, since you say so, but to hell with you all and your brother Ivan! You won't understand that one can dislike him very much quite apart from Katerina. And, damn it all, why should I like him? Doesn't he do me the honour of abusing me himself? Why, then, haven't I got the right to abuse him?'

'I've never heard him say anything good or bad about you. He doesn't speak of you at all.'

'But I heard that the day before yesterday he was reviling me for all he was worth at Katerina's – that's how much he really is interested in your humble servant. And who is jealous of whom after that I don't know, old man. He was so good as to express the opinion that if I hadn't made up my mind to take up the career of an archimandrite in the very near future and become a monk, I would quite certainly go to Petersburg and become a contributor to a periodical, and quite certainly as a literary critic, and write for ten years and in the end transfer the ownership of the periodical to myself. Then I'd go on editing it and quite certainly in a liberal and atheistic spirit with a Socialist tendency, with ever such a tiny gloss of Socialism, keeping my ear to the ground, or, in other words, actually having a foot in both camps and hoodwinking the fools. The whole purpose of my career, according to your brother, is not to allow my Socialist tendency to prevent me from putting my subscribers' money into the bank and investing it at the first opportunity with the advice of some Jew, till I have enough capital to build a large house in Petersburg, transfer my editorial offices to it and let out the other stories to tenants. He has even chosen the place for it: by the New Stone Bridge across the Neva, which they say is being planned to connect the Liteyny Avenue with the Vyborg suburb. . . .'

'But, Misha, that's just what will happen, you know, every word of it!' cried Alyosha suddenly, unable to restrain himself and laughing gaily.

'So you too, sir, are getting sarcastic, are you?'

'No, no, I'm joking. I'm sorry. I've something else on my mind. But, tell me, who could possibly have given you all those details? Who could you have heard them from? You couldn't have been at Katerina's yourself when he was talking about you, could you?'

'I wasn't there, but your brother Dmitry was, and I heard him tell it with my own ears. Well, as a matter of fact, if you must know, he did not tell it me, but I overheard it, by sheer accident, of course, because I was in Grushenka's bedroom at the time and could not leave while Dmitry was in the next room.'

'Oh, yes, I forgot. She's a relative of yours, isn't she?'

'A relative? Grushenka a relative of mine?' Rakitin cried suddenly, flushing all over. 'Have you gone off your head? There must be something wrong with your brains.'

'Why? Isn't she a relative of yours? I heard she was.'

'Where can you have heard it? Oh, you Karamazovs! Giving yourselves airs as though you were great noblemen of ancient lineage, while as a matter of fact your father used to rush about playing the fool at other men's tables, and was given some job in the kitchen as a favour. All right, I may be only the son of a priest and a louse compared with you noblemen, but don't you insult me so lightheartedly and so wantonly. I too have a sense of honour, sir. I couldn't be a relative of Grushenka, a street walker, please understand that!'

Rakitin was beside himself with rage.

'I'm awfully sorry, I had no idea – and, besides, why a street walker? Is she – that kind of woman?' Alyosha said, suddenly blushing. 'I repeat I heard that she was a relative of yours. You often go to see her, and you told me yourself that you're not having an affair with her. You see, I never thought that you of all people despised her so much! Does she really deserve it?'

'If I visit her, I must have some good reason for it, mustn't I? That should be enough for you. As for being her relative, I daresay your brother or even your father is much more likely to make her your relative than mine. Well, here we are. You'd better go to the kitchen. Good Lord, what's up here? What's this? Are we late? They couldn't possibly have finished their dinner so soon! Or have the Karamazovs been up to something again? I'm sure they have. Here's your father and there's Ivan running after him. They've rushed out of the Father Superior's. And there's Father Isidore shouting something to them from the front steps. And your father, too, is shouting and waving his arms. Swearing, I suppose. Ah, there's Miusov, too, driving away in his carriage. He's driving off, you see. And there's the landowner Maximov running – why, there must have been a real brawl. So there's been no dinner! They haven't given the Father Superior a beating, have they? Or have they, perhaps, been given a beating themselves? It would serve them right!'

Rakitin was not exclaiming without good reason. There really had been a scandalous, unheard of, and unexpected scene. It all happened 'on the spur of the moment'.

8

A Scandalous Scene

WHEN Miusov and Ivan Karamazov were entering the Father Superior's room, Miusov, like the highly respectable and refined gentleman that he was, went rapidly through a highly refined process of a certain kind: he felt ashamed of being angry. He could not help feeling that he really ought to have had so little respect for a worthless wretch like old Karamazov that he should not have lost his temper in the elder's cell and so forgotten himself as he had done. 'The monks at least cannot be blamed for anything,' he decided suddenly, as he mounted the steps to the Father Superior's rooms. 'If here too there are decent people (I believe Father Nikolai, the Father Superior, is himself a nobleman), then why not be nice, kind, and courteous with them? . . . I won't argue, I shall do my best to agree with them, I shall win them over by being polite to them – and – after all, I'll show them that I have nothing to do with that absurd clown, that Pierrot, and have been merely taken in like the rest of them. . . .'

As for the disputed woodcutting and fishing rights (he did not know himself where the stream and the woods were exactly), he made up his mind to drop his court action against the monastery and let them have them finally, once and for all, and that very day, particularly as all that was not worth a great deal.

All these excellent intentions were strengthened when they entered the Father Superior's dining-room. The Father Superior did not really have a dining-room, for, strictly speaking, he only had two rooms, though they were much larger and more comfortable than the elder's. But the furnishings of the room were not particularly sumptuous, either: the furniture was of mahogany, covered with leather, in the old style of the twenties; the floors were not even stained, but everything was spotlessly clean, and there were many choice flowers in the windows; but the most sumptuous thing in the room at that moment was naturally the sumptuously laid table, though, of course, even that was comparatively speaking: the table-cloth was clean, the silver was brightly polished; three kinds of wonderfully baked bread, two bottles of wine, two bottles of excellent monastery mead, and a large glass jug of monastery *kvas*, famous throughout the neighbourhood. There was no vodka at all. Rakitin related afterwards that this time it was a five-course dinner: fish, soup of sterlets served with fish patties; then boiled fish excellently prepared in a special way; then salmon cutlets, ice cream and stewed fruits and, finally, a fruit jelly. All this Rakitin sniffed out, for he could not resist the temptation to have a special look into the Father Superior's kitchen, where he also had his connexions. He had connexions everywhere and had a spy everywhere. He had a very restless and envious disposition. He was perfectly well aware of his considerable abilities, but he exaggerated them painfully in his self-conceit. He knew for certain that he would become a public figure of some sort, but Alyosha, who was greatly attached to him, was worried by the fact that his friend Rakitin was dishonest and did not seem to be in the least conscious of it himself. On the contrary, he considered himself to be a man of the utmost integrity because he knew that he would not steal money lying on a table. No one, let alone Alyosha, could do anything about that.

Rakitin, a person of little importance, could not be invited to the dinner, but Father Joseph and Father Paissy and another monk were invited. They were already waiting for the Father Superior in the dining-room when Miusov, Kalganov, and Ivan Karamazov arrived. Maximov was there, too, waiting in a far corner of the room. The Father Superior stepped into the middle of the room to welcome his guests. He was a tall, spare, but still very vigorous old man, with black hair streaked with grey and a long, grave, pious face. He exchanged bows with his guests in silence, but this time they all went up to him for his blessing. Miusov even went so far as to try to kiss his hand, but the Father Superior snatched it away in time, and the attempt miscarried. Ivan Karamazov and Kalganov, on the other hand, went through the full ceremony, that is to say, they gave the Father Superior's hand a resounding kiss as simple-hearted peasants might have done.

'We must offer you our most humble apologies, your reverence,' began Miusov with a wide, courteous smile, but still in a dignified and respectful tone of voice, 'for having arrived without Mr Karamazov, whom I believe you have also invited. I'm sorry to say he felt obliged to decline your hospitality, and for a good reason. Carried away by his unfortunate feud with his son, he uttered certain words in the cell of the reverend Father Zossima which were – er – hardly to the point. I – I mean, they were quite unseemly as – er – I believe' (he shot a glance at the monks) 'your reverence has been informed already. And, therefore, realizing that he had been at fault and being sincerely sorry and unable to overcome his feeling of shame, he asked us, that is to say, his son Ivan and myself, to convey his sincere apologies to you and to tell you how very distressed and sorry he is not to be able to come. In short, he hopes and desires to make amends for everything later and asks your blessing and begs you to forget what has taken place.'

Miusov fell silent. As he uttered the last words of his tirade, he felt so satisfied with himself that not a trace of his former irritation remained. He again fully and sincerely loved mankind.

The Father Superior listened to him with dignity and, with a slight inclination of his head, said in reply: 'I am very sorry he cannot be here. Perhaps he'd have learnt to love us at our table as we love him. Pray, gentlemen, be seated.'

But first he turned to the icon and began to say grace aloud. All bowed their heads reverently, and Maximov bent forward zealously, putting his hands together with special fervour.

And it was at that moment that Karamazov played his last prank. It must be observed that he had really intended to go home, realizing how impossible it was to go to dine with the Father Superior as if nothing had happened after his disgraceful behaviour in the elder's cell. Not that he was so very much ashamed of himself or blamed himself; quite the contrary, perhaps; but he still felt that it would be unseemly to go to dinner. But as soon as his rickety carriage had driven up to the front steps of the inn and he was about to get into it, he suddenly stopped short. He remembered his own words at the elder's: 'It does indeed seem to me every time I go to see people that I am more contemptible than anyone else and that everyone takes me for a clown – so that's why I say to myself, all right, let me play the clown, because you're all without exception more stupid and more contemptible than I.' He wanted to revenge himself on everyone for his own filthy tricks. At that moment he suddenly recalled how a long time before he had once been asked: 'Why do you hate that man so much?' And, in a fit of his clownish shamelessness, he had replied: 'I'll tell you why. It's true he has done nothing to me, but I played him a dirty trick, and as soon as I had done it I at once hated him for it.' Recalling it now, he gave a quiet and malicious chuckle as he hesitated for a moment. His eyes flashed and even his lips quivered. 'Having started, I may as well finish it,' he suddenly decided. His innermost feeling at that moment could be expressed in the following words: 'I couldn't possibly regain my lost reputation now, so let me be as beastly to them as I can: I don't care a hang, so there!' He told the driver to wait, while he returned with rapid steps to the monastery and went straight to the Father Superior's. He still did not quite know what he was going to do, but he knew that he could not control himself and that at the slightest provocation he might be driven to do something utterly abominable, but only that and certainly not anything criminal or something for which he could be convicted in a court of law. When it came to that, he knew how to control himself, and he was often surprised at himself for being able to do so. He appeared in the Father Superior's dining-room exactly at the moment when the prayer was over and they all moved to the table. Stopping in the doorway, he glanced at the company and gave his protracted, impudent, and malicious chuckle, looking them all boldly in the face.

'And they thought I'd gone, but here I am!' he cried in a loud voice.

For a moment they all looked straight at him without uttering a word, and suddenly they all felt that something revolting and grotesque was about to happen, something that was sure to end in a scandalous scene. Miusov at once passed from the most good-humoured mood to the most fierce. Everything that had died down and subsided in his heart at once revived and rose to the surface.

'No, that I can't stand!' he cried. 'I simply can't and – I absolutely can't!'

The blood rushed to his face. He even stammered, but he was beyond worrying about his style and snatched up his hat.

'What is it he can't stand?' cried Karamazov. 'He absolutely can't, he simply can't! Your reverence, may I come in or not? Will you receive me as one of your guests?'

'You are welcome with all my heart,' replied the Father Superior. 'Gentlemen,' he added, 'I appeal to you with all my heart and soul to give up your temporary feuds and unite in love and harmony as relatives should, with a prayer to God at our humble table. . . .'

'No, no, it's impossible!' Miusov cried, beside himself.

'Well, if Mr Miusov finds it impossible, then I find it impossible, too, and I won't stay. That's what I came for. From now on I shall always be with Mr Miusov: if you go away, sir, I will go away, too, if you stay, I will stay. You've hurt his feelings very badly, your reverence, by mentioning family harmony, for he refuses to recognize me as his relation. That's right, von Sohn, isn't it? That's von Sohn standing there! How do you do, von Sohn?'

'Are you addressing me, sir?' muttered Maximov in surprise.

'Of course, you,' cried Karamazov. 'Who else do you think? The Father Superior couldn't be von Sohn, could he?'

'But I'm not von Sohn, sir. I'm Maximov.'

'Oh no, sir, you are von Sohn. Do you know what von Sohn is, your reverence? It was a famous murder case: he was killed in a house of ill-fame – that's what you call those places, I believe – he was killed and robbed and, in spite of his venerable age, he was shoved into a box, nailed down and sent labelled in a luggage van from Petersburg to Moscow. And when they were nailing him down, the harlots sang songs and played the psaltery, I mean, the pianoforte. So this gentleman here is that very same von Sohn. He has risen from the dead. Isn't that so, von Sohn?'

'What's all this? What on earth—?' voices were heard from the group of monks.

'Come, let's go!' cried Miusov, addressing Kalganov.

'No, sir, one moment, please!' Karamazov broke in shrilly, taking another step into the room. 'Let me finish. There in the cell I was put to shame for having behaved disrespectfully by shouting about gudgeons. Mr Miusov, my relation, likes to have *plus de noblesse que de sincérité* in his words, whereas I, on the contrary, like *plus de sincérité que de noblesse* in my words – and to hell with *noblesse*. That's right, isn't it, von Sohn? Excuse me, your reverence, but though I'm a clown and play the clown, I am a knight in shining armour, and I want to speak out. Yes, sir, I'm a knight in shining armour and Mr Miusov is a man of morbid sensitivity and nothing more. I came here today perhaps to have a look round and to speak out. My son Alexey is saving his soul here. I am his father. I care for his future and, indeed, it is my duty to care for it. I've been listening and playing a part but I've also been quietly observing things, and now I'd like to give you the last act of the performance. How are things with us? Well, sir, with us, if anything falls down, it just lies there for ever. With us if a thing has once fallen down, then it must lie there for ever. But that's not as it should be! I want to get up. Holy fathers, I'm indignant with you. Confession is a great sacrament, which I revere and before which I'm ready to prostrate myself, but there, in the elder's cell, everyone suddenly goes down on his knees and confesses aloud. Is it permitted to confess aloud? The holy fathers of the Church laid it down that a confession should be whispered in the priest's ear. Only then does your confession become a sacrament, and so it has been since ancient times. For how else can I explain to him before everyone that I, for instance, did this and that – I mean to say, this and that, you understand, don't you? You see, sometimes it's improper even to say it. Why, it's really scandalous! No, Fathers, for all I know you may even start practising flagellation in your monastery here. . . . I shall write to the Holy Synod about it at the first opportunity, and I shall take my son, Alexey, home. . . .'

Here it must be observed that Karamazov had heard all sorts of disreputable stories about the goings-on in monasteries. All sorts of malicious rumours had been current at one time, and they had even reached the bishop (not only about our monastery, but about other monasteries where the institution of elders had been established), to the effect that too much respect was paid to the elders, even to the detriment of the authority of the Father Superior, and that, among other things, the elders were abusing the sacrament of confession, etc., etc. Absurd charges which at the time died down of themselves both in our town and everywhere else. But the foolish devil, who had caught up Karamazov and was carrying him along on his nerves deeper and deeper into the pit of dishonour, prompted him to repeat the old accusation, of which he did not understand a single word himself. And he could not express it intelligently, particularly as this time no one had been kneeling and confessing aloud in the elder's cell, so that he could not possibly have seen anything of the kind and was merely repeating old rumours and slanders, which he only vaguely remembered. But having uttered his stupid accusation, he at once felt that he had been talking absurd nonsense, and he suddenly wanted to prove to his audience, and most of all to himself, that he had not been talking nonsense. And though he knew perfectly well that with each word he spoke he would be adding more and more absurdities, he was unable to restrain himself and plunged headlong, regardless of consequences.

'How despicable!' cried Miusov.

'Forgive me,' the Father Superior said suddenly, 'but it was said of old, "Many have begun speaking against me and saying many evil things, and, hearing it, I said to myself: it is the medicine of our Lord Jesus and he hath sent it to heal my vain soul." And therefore we humbly thank you, our dear guest!'

And he bowed low to Karamazov.

'Tut-tut-tut! Sanctimonious old phrases! Old phrases and old gestures! Old lies and conventional obeisances! We know all about these bows! "A kiss on the lips and a dagger in the heart", as in Schiller's *Robbers*. I don't like falsehood, Fathers. I want truth. But truth is not to be found in gudgeons, and I proclaimed it! Fathers, why do you fast? Why do you expect a reward in heaven for it? Why, for a reward like that I, too, will go and fast! No, holy monk, first be virtuous in life, be useful to society, without shutting yourself up in a monastery at somebody else's expense and without expecting rewards from up there – you'll find that a little harder. I can talk sense, too, Father Superior. Let's see what we have here,' he said, going up to the table. 'Old port wine, Médoc bottled by the Brothers Yeliseyev – well, well, Fathers! That doesn't look like gudgeons, does it? Look at the lovely bottles the fathers have put on the table – heh-heh-heh! And who has supplied you with it all? The toiling Russian peasant bringing you the farthings earned by his horny hands, wresting them from his family and the requirements of the State! Why, Holy Fathers, you suck the blood of the people!'

'That's quite unworthy of you!' said Father Joseph.

Father Paissy kept obstinately silent. Miusov rushed from the room, and Kalganov after him.

'Well, Fathers, I will follow Mr Miusov! I shall never come to see you again. You may beg me on your bended knees, but I shan't come. I sent you a thousand roubles, so your eyes are popping out of your heads again, heh-heh-heh! No, I won't give you another penny. I'm taking my revenge for my past, for my humiliation.' He thumped the table with his fist in a paroxysm of simulated feeling. 'This monastery has meant a lot in my life. I have shed bitter tears for it! You used to set my wife, the shrieker, against me. You cursed me with bell, book, and candle. You spread stories about me all over the district. Enough, Fathers, this is the age of liberalism, the age of steamers and railways. Not a thousand, not a hundred roubles, not a hundred copecks will you get out of me!'

It must be observed again that our monastery had never meant anything in particular in his life and he had never shed bitter tears for it. But he was so carried away by his simulated tears that for a moment he almost believed it himself; indeed, he nearly wept, so moved was he; but at the same moment he felt that it was time to beat a retreat.

In reply to his malicious lies, the Father Superior bowed his head and said again impressively: 'It is written again: "Suffer circumspectly and gladly the dishonour that befalleth thee, and be not confounded and hate not him who dishonoureth thee." We shall do likewise.'

'Tut-tut-tut! Considering thyself – and the rest of the balderdash! Consider yourselves, Fathers, and I'll be off. And I'm taking my son Alexey away from here for good by my authority as his father. Ivan, most dutiful son of mine, permit me to order you to follow me! Von Sohn, what do you want to stay here for? Come along with me now to the town. You'll have a good time there. It's only about a mile from here. Instead of lenten oil, I'll give you sucking-pig with stuffing. We'll have dinner. I'll get out the brandy, then a liqueur – I've got wild raspberry liqueur. Come on, von Sohn, don't miss your chance!'

He went out, shouting and gesticulating. It was at that moment that Rakitin saw him and pointed him out to Alyosha.

'Alexey,' his father shouted from a distance, catching sight of him, 'come home today for good, and bring your pillow and mattress, too! Mind I don't catch you here again!'

Alyosha stopped dead, observing the scene intently and in silence. In the meantime Karamazov got into the carriage. Ivan was about to get in after him in grim silence, without even turning round to say good-bye to Alyosha. But at this point a grotesque and almost incredible scene took place which gave the finishing touch to the episode. Maximov suddenly appeared at the step of the carriage. He ran up, panting, afraid of being late. Rakitin and Alyosha saw him running. He was in such a hurry that in his impatience he put his foot on the step on which Ivan's left foot was still resting and, clutching the box, was about to jump in.

'I'm coming too! I'm coming, too!' he cried, dancing about and laughing with bursts of gay, staccato laughter and a blissful look on his face, ready for anything. 'Take me, too!'

'There, didn't I say that he was von Sohn!' Karamazov cried delightedly. 'That he is the real von Sohn risen from the dead? But how did you manage to tear yourself away? What did you do there, you wicked old von Sohn, and how could you of all people get away from the dinner? One would have to have a face of brass to do that. I have one, but I must say I'm surprised at your impudence, old man! Come on, jump in. Let him, Ivan. We'll have fun. He can lie down somewhere at our feet. You will, won't you, von Sohn? Or shall we find room for him on the box with the driver? Jump on to the box, von Sohn!'

But Ivan, who had already taken his place in the carriage, without uttering a word, gave Maximov a violent push in the chest, which sent him flying three yards. If he did not fall, it was only by accident.

'Drive on!' Ivan shouted angrily to the coachman.

'What's the matter with you? What's the matter? Why did you push him away?' Karamazov broke out, but the carriage had already driven away.

Ivan made no answer.

'Good Lord, man,' Karamazov said again after two minutes, looking askance at his darling son, 'the visit to the monastery was your idea, wasn't it? You suggested it. You approved it. So why are you so angry now?'

'Stop talking nonsense,' Ivan snapped sternly. 'Have a bit of a rest now.'

Karamazov was silent again for two minutes.

'It would be nice to have a glass of brandy now,' he observed sententiously.

But Ivan made no answer.

'You'll have some, too, when we get home.'

Ivan was still silent.

Karamazov waited another two minutes:

'I'll take Alyosha away from the monastery all the same, much as you may not like it, most respectful Karl von Moor.'

Ivan shrugged his shoulders contemptuously and, turning away, began staring at the road. They did not speak again all the way home.

BOOK THREE: THE SENSUALISTS

I

In the Servants' Cottage

FYODOR KARAMAZOV'S house was some distance from the centre of the town, but it was not quite on its outskirts, either. It was rather old, but of a pleasant exterior: it was a one-storied house with an attic, painted grey and with a red iron roof. It was spacious and snug and there was no reason why it should not last for a long time yet. It had all sorts of box-rooms, hidden passages, and unexpected staircases. There were rats in it, but Karamazov was not altogether cross with them: 'Anyway,' he used to say, 'one does not feel so bored in the evenings when one is left alone.' And it was indeed his habit to send the servants away to the cottage for the night and shut himself up alone in the house. The cottage was in the yard. It was a large and solid building; Karamazov had his kitchen there, though there was a kitchen in the house; he disliked the smell of cooking, and the dishes were carried across the yard in winter and summer. The house was built for a large family, and there was room in it for five times as many people, masters and servants. But at the time of our story only Karamazov and Ivan lived in it, and in the cottage there were only three servants: old Grigory, his old wife Marfa, and the servant Smerdyakov, who was still a young man. We shall have to say a few more words about these three servants. We have already said enough about old Grigory Kutuzov. He was a resolute and steadfast man, going stubbornly and undeviatingly to his goal, if this goal for some reason (often a surprisingly illogical one) appeared to him as an immutable truth. He was, generally speaking, honest and incorruptible. His wife Marfa, though she submitted to him absolutely all her life, nagged him terribly. After the liberation of the serfs, for instance, she kept asking him to leave Karamazov, settle in Moscow and start a small business there (they had some money of their own); but Grigory decided then once and for all that the woman was talking nonsense, 'because every woman is dishonourable', and that they ought not to leave their old master, whatever he might be, because that was 'their duty'.

'Do you understand what duty means?' he asked Marfa.

'I understand what duty means, Grigory,' Marfa replied firmly, 'but why it is our duty to stay here I shall never understand.'

'You don't have to understand, but it shall be so. Hold your tongue in future.'

And so it was: they did not go away, and Karamazov gave them a small salary and paid it regularly. Grigory knew, besides, that he had an indisputable influence on his master. He felt it and it was quite true: Karamazov, a cunning and obstinate clown, a man who had a very determined character 'in certain things in life', as he put it, was, to his own surprise, rather weak in some other 'things in life'. And he knew himself in which. He knew it and was afraid of many things. In some things in life one had always to keep a sharp look-out, and that was difficult without a trustworthy servant, and Grigory was a trustworthy servant. It even happened that Karamazov had been in danger of being thrashed, and that soundly, too, many times in the course of his life, and Grigory had always come to his rescue, though every time he gave him a lecture afterwards. But blows alone would not have frightened Karamazov: there were more serious cases, very intricate and complicated ones, when Karamazov himself would not have been able to explain why all of a sudden he quite unaccountably felt that at that very moment he was in great need of the presence of a trustworthy and devoted servant. Those were almost painful cases: a most licentious man and, in his lust, as cruel as a vicious insect, Karamazov, when drunk, sometimes felt suddenly overwhelmed by irrational terror and moral shock which had an almost physical effect on him. 'At those moments,' he used to say sometimes, 'my heart is in my mouth.' It was then that he liked to have near him, though not in the same room but in the cottage, a man who was faithful and as firm as a rock, who was not at all licentious like himself, who, though he had seen the sort of debaucheries that were going on and knew all the secrets, tolerated it all out of a sense of loyalty, did not object to it, and, above all, did not reproach him or threaten him with anything, either in this world or the next; and who, in case of need, would have protected him – from whom? From someone unknown, but terrible and dangerous. What he wanted was the presence of *another* man, an old and tried friend, upon whom he should be able to call in his sick moments in order to look at his face, or perhaps exchange a few words, a few quite irrelevant words; and if that man did not protest and was not angry, he felt easier in his mind, and if he was angry, well, then it just made him feel more melancholy. It even happened (though rather rarely) that Karamazov went at night to the cottage to wake Grigory and ask him to come to the house for a moment. Grigory came, and Karamazov would start talking about the most trivial things and would send him back soon, sometimes even with a sarcastic or jesting remark, while he would go to bed with a curse and sleep the sleep of the just. Something of the kind happened to Karamazov after the arrival of Alyosha, too. Alyosha 'touched him to the quick' by 'living with him, seeing everything and condemning nothing'. What is more, he had brought with him something Karamazov had never experienced before: a total absence of contempt for him, the old man, whom, on the contrary, he treated with invariable kindness and with perfectly natural and single-minded devotion, which he so little deserved. All this was a complete surprise for the old profligate, who had lived apart from his family; it was entirely unexpected to a man like him, who till then only liked everything that was 'rotten'. After Alyosha had gone, he confessed to himself that he understood something he had hitherto not wished to understand.

I have mentioned already at the beginning of my story that Grigory hated Karamazov's first wife Adelaida, the mother of his first son, Dmitry, and how, on the other hand, he protected Sophia, the shrieker, from his master and from everyone who happened to speak ill or flippantly about her. His sympathy for the unhappy woman had become something sacred to him, so that twenty years later he would not tolerate any disparaging remark about her from anyone and would at once challenge the offender. Outwardly Grigory was cold, dignified, and taciturn. He delivered himself of weighty and trenchant words and never expressed himself in a frivolous manner. In the same way it was impossible to tell at the first glance whether he loved his meek and submissive wife or not, and yet he did love her and she of course knew it. Marfa, indeed, was far from stupid, and was probably much more intelligent than her husband, at least much shrewder in worldly affairs, and yet she gave in to him meekly and without protest and unquestionably respected him as her spiritual superior. The remarkable thing was that both of them spoke very little to each other all through their lives and only about the most necessary daily affairs. Grigory, dignified and majestic, always thought over all his affairs and troubles alone, so that Marfa had long realized that he did not require her advice. She felt that her husband valued her silence and took it as a sign of her intelligence. He had never beaten her, except once, and that, too, only a little. Once during the first year of Karamazov's marriage to Adelaida, the village girls and women, who were still serfs at the time, were collected before the country house to sing and dance. They began with 'In the Green Meadows', when Marfa, who was still a young woman at the time, leapt forward in front of the choir, and went off into the 'Russian' dance, which she danced in quite a special way, not as the village women used to dance it, but as she had danced it when she was a serf girl at the private theatre of the rich Miusovs, where the actors were taught to dance by a dancing master from Moscow. Grigory saw how his wife pranced through the dance and an hour later, at home in his cottage, taught her a lesson, dragging her about by the hair a little. This was the first and last time that he chastised her, and, besides, Marfa had forsworn dancing ever since.

God had not blessed them with children. They had one child, but it died. Grigory was very fond of children, and did not conceal it; that is to say, he was not ashamed to show it. When Adelaida had run away he took charge of Dmitry, who was three at the time, and looked after him for almost a year, combing his hair and washing him himself in a tub. Afterwards he had taken care of Ivan and Alyosha, for which he had his face slapped; but I have already related all that. His own child made him happy only in anticipation of his birth, while his wife was pregnant. When it was born, it struck his heart with grief and horror. For the boy had six fingers. When he saw it, Grigory was so crushed that he not only kept silent till the day of the christening, but used to go away to the garden to be quiet. It was spring and he spent three days digging in the kitchen-garden. On the third day the child was to be christened; but by that time Grigory came to a decision. Going into the cottage, where the clergy, the guests and, finally, Karamazov himself, who had appeared personally in his rôle as godfather, had all gathered, he suddenly declared that the child 'ought not to be christened at all'. He had announced it quietly, without any explanation, letting his words escape him slowly and gazing dully and intently at the priest.

'Why ever not?' the priest asked with good-humoured surprise.

'Because,' muttered Grigory, 'it's a dragon, sir.'

'A dragon? What sort of a dragon?'

'It's a confusion of nature,' he muttered, though rather vaguely, but very firmly, evidently not wishing to dilate on the matter.

They laughed, and the poor baby was of course christened. Grigory prayed earnestly at the font, but did not change his opinion of the new-born child. He did not interfere, however, but he never looked at the sickly child during the fortnight that it lived and did not even wish to notice it, keeping away from the cottage most of the time. But when at the end of the fortnight the baby died of thrush, he laid him in his little coffin himself, gazing at him with deep anguish, and when his little shallow grave was filled up, he went down on his knees and prostrated himself before it. Since then he had never once mentioned his child; neither did his wife Marfa speak of her baby in his presence, and when she did happen to talk to someone about 'her darling child', she did so in a whisper, even though Grigory was not present. According to Marfa, Grigory had been occupied with 'religious matters' ever since the burial, mostly reading the *Lives of the Saints* in silence and when he was alone, always putting on his large, round, silver spectacles. He seldom read aloud, except perhaps in Lent. He was fond of the Book of Job, got hold of a copy of the sayings and sermons of 'our God-bearing Father Isaac the Syrian', which he read religiously for many years, without understanding scarcely a word of it, but perhaps prizing and loving it all the more for that. More recently he had begun to listen to, and show a great interest in, the doctrines of the flagellants, taking advantage of the presence of some members of that sect in the neighbourhood. He was visibly impressed, but did not think it worth while adopting the new faith. His assiduous reading of the 'religious' tracts lent an even greater gravity to his face.

Perhaps he was inclined to mysticism. And, as though by design, the appearance in the world of his six-fingered child and its death coincided with another very strange, unexpected, and quite exceptional event which, as he himself put it afterwards, had left 'an indelible mark' on his soul. It so happened that on the very night of the funeral Marfa was awakened by what seemed to her to be the cries of a new-born baby. She got frightened and woke her husband. He listened and said that it sounded to him more like someone groaning, 'a woman perhaps'. He got up and dressed; it was a rather warm May night. As he went outside, he distinctly heard the groans coming from the garden. But the garden was locked up for the night and one could not get into it except from the yard, for it was surrounded by a strong high fence. Grigory went back into the cottage, lighted a lantern, took the garden key and, taking no notice of the hysterical fears of his wife, who was assuring him that it was a baby crying and that she was sure it was her own baby crying and calling to her, went out into the garden without uttering a word. There he realized at once that the groaning was coming from their bath-house, near the garden gate, and that it was indeed a woman who was groaning. When he opened the door of the bath-house, he saw a sight which completely dumbfounded him: the idiot girl who wandered about the streets and was known all over the town as Stinking Lizaveta (Lizaveta Smerdyashchaya), had broken into the bath-house and had just given birth to a child. Her baby lay beside her and she lay dying beside it. She said nothing, for she had never been able to speak, anyway. But all this must be explained in a separate chapter.

2

Stinking Lizaveta

THERE was one special circumstance here which deeply shocked Grigory, having finally strengthened an unpleasant and revolting suspicion he had had for some time. Lizaveta Smerdyashchaya was an undersized girl 'just under five feet', as many pious old women of our town touchingly described her after her death. She was twenty and her healthy, broad, red face bore an expression of complete idiocy; she had a fixed and unpleasant look in her eyes, though it was meek enough. She walked about barefoot all her life, in winter as well as in summer, wearing only a hempen shift. Her very thick, almost black hair, curling like lamb's wool, formed a kind of huge cap on her head. It was, besides, always matted with mud, and had

leaves, splinters of wood, and shavings clinging to it, for she always
slept on the ground and in the dirt. Her father Ilya was a homeless,
sickly artisan, who had lost all his money and was perpetually drunk.
He had been living for many years as a workman with some well-to-
do tradesmen, also artisans of our town. Lizaveta's mother had long
been dead. Ilya, always ill and in a bad temper, used to beat Lizaveta
unmercifully whenever she came home. But she came home very
rarely because she used to be fed by everybody in the town as a
saintly fool. Ilya's employers, Ilya himself, and many other com-
passionate people in the town, especially merchants and merchants'
wives, tried many times to clothe Lizaveta more decently, and towards winter always put a sheepskin and boots on her; but, although
she let them put everything on her without protest, she used to go
away, preferably to the cathedral porch, and take off everything she
had been given – kerchief, skirt, sheepskin, or boots – and leave it
there and walk away barefoot and in her shift as before. It happened
on one occasion that our new provincial governor, on his tour of
inspection of our town, caught sight of Lizaveta and was deeply hurt
in his tenderest feelings. Though he realized that she was a 'saintly
fool', as indeed he was officially informed, he insisted on pointing
out that for a young girl to wander about the streets in nothing but
her shift was a breach of the proprieties and that it must not happen
again. But the governor departed, and Lizaveta was left as she was.
At last her father died, and she became even dearer to all the pious
people in our town as an orphan. Indeed, everyone seemed to like
her and even the boys in the streets did not tease or molest her, and
the boys of our town, especially the schoolboys, are a mischievous lot.
She would walk into strange houses and no one drove her out; on
the contrary, everyone tried to be nice to her and give her a penny.
If she were given a penny, she would take it and at once drop it into
some alms-box in a church or outside the prison. If she were given a
roll or bun in the market, she would go away and give it to the first
child she came across, or else stop one of the richest ladies in our town
and hand it to her; and the ladies were very pleased to accept it. She
herself lived only on black bread and water. If she went into an
expensive shop and sat down there, the proprietors took no notice
of her, though there were costly goods and money lying about, for
they knew that even if they put thousands of roubles before her and

forgot all about it, she would not take a penny. She very rarely went to church, and slept either in a church porch or, climbing over some wattle fence (we have a great number of wattle instead of wooden fences in our town even today), in a kitchen-garden. She used to make an appearance 'at home', that is, in the house of her late father's employers, about once a week, and in winter every day, but only at night, and slept in the hall or the cowshed. People were amazed that she could survive such a life, but she was used to it; though she was so small, she had an incredibly strong constitution. Some people in our town maintained that she did all this from pride, but somehow it did not make sense: she could not speak a single word and only from time to time did she utter an inarticulate grunt – what sort of pride was that? Now it happened – ever so long ago – that one bright and warm night in September (it was full moon) a company of drunken gentlemen of our town, about five or six gay bucks, were returning in high spirits home from the club by the 'back way' at what to us provincials seemed a rather late hour. There was a wattle fence at either side of the narrow lane, behind which were the kitchen-gardens of the adjacent houses; the lane led out on to the little bridge across the long, stinking puddle which it was our custom to call a stream. At the wattle fence, among the nettles and burdocks, our gentlemen caught sight of Lizaveta asleep. The merry bucks stood over her, laughing uproariously, and began cracking jokes of a quite unprintable character. It suddenly occurred to one young gentleman to put a highly whimsical question on an absurd subject: 'Could anyone,' he asked, 'regard such an animal as a woman, just now, for instance,' and so on. They all decided with lordly disdain that it was impossible. But Karamazov happened to be among the company and he at once volunteered the opinion that it was possible to regard her as a woman, very much so, indeed, and that there was something piquant about it, and so on and so forth. It is true that at that time he seemed extremely anxious to play the part of a clown. He liked to thrust himself forward and entertain the gentlemen, pretending all the time, of course, to be their equal, though, in fact, acting in their company in a manner that befitted a country yokel rather than a gentleman. Just then he had received the news of his first wife's death and, with a crape upon his hat, drank and behaved in such an unseemly fashion that many people in our town, even the most licentious ones, were nauseated at the sight of him. The whole crowd of course laughed at this startling opinion, and one of them even tried to egg him on to act upon it, but the rest began expressing their disgust in even stronger terms, though still with the utmost hilarity, and at last they went on their way. Afterwards Karamazov swore that he had gone with them; perhaps it was so, no one knows for certain and no one ever knew. But five or six months later everyone in town was discussing with sincere and intense indignation the fact that Lizaveta was pregnant and kept asking each other who was the man who had wronged her. It was then that a strange rumour spread through the town that the scoundrel was no other than Fyodor Karamazov. Where did this rumour spring from? Of that company of drunken gentlemen only one was left in our town by that time, an elderly and respected State Councillor, who was the father of grown-up daughters and who most certainly would not have spread such a rumour even if there had been anything in it; the rest, about five men, had all left the town. But rumour pointed straight at Fyodor Karamazov and persisted in pointing at him. Karamazov, of course, was not very much upset by it: he would not have troubled to answer the allegations made against him by some merchants or artisans. He was very proud in those days and never spoke to anyone except to his own circle of civil servants and noblemen whom he entertained so well. It was just at that time that Grigory stood up for his master energetically and not only defended him with the utmost vigour against all these slanders, but also abused and quarrelled with his accusers and forced many people to change their minds. 'It's the hussy's own fault,' he used to say emphatically, and her seducer was none other than 'Karp the Jemmy' (that was the name of a dangerous convict, well known to all of us, who had escaped from prison just then and had been living in hiding in our town). This conjecture seemed plausible enough, for the memory of Karp was still fresh in everyone's mind, and he was remembered so well because he had been loitering about the streets during those autumn nights and had robbed three people. But this affair and all these rumours did not alienate the sympathy of the townspeople from the poor idiot girl, who was taken care of and looked after more than ever. Mrs Kondratyev, a well-to-do merchant's widow, took all the necessary steps at the end of April to keep

Lizaveta at her house and make sure that she was not let out until after the confinement. They kept a constant watch over her, but, in spite of their vigilance, Lizaveta stole away from Mrs Kondratyev's in the evening of the very last day and found her way into Karamazov's kitchen-garden. How she managed in her condition to climb over the strong, high fence remained a mystery. Some said that she had been 'lifted over' by somebody, and others that she was 'lifted over' by some supernatural power. It is more probable, however, that it all happened in a very natural, though perhaps tricky way, and that Lizaveta, who was used to climbing over fences to spend the night in other people's kitchen-gardens, somehow or other managed to clamber over Karamazov's fence, and, in spite of her condition, to jump down into the garden, though, it is true, not without injuring herself. Grigory rushed to Marfa and sent her to look after Lizaveta, while he ran to fetch an old midwife who, fortunately, lived close by. The child was saved, but Lizaveta died at dawn. Grigory took the baby, brought it home, told his wife to sit down and put it on her lap, right against her breast. 'A child of God,' he said, 'an orphan is everyone's kin, and yours and mine all the more. Our little baby has sent us him, and he has been born of the devil's son and a holy innocent. Feed him and weep no more.' So Marfa brought up the child. He was christened and given the name of Pavel, and as for his patronymic, everyone began to call him quite naturally Fyodorovich. Fyodor Karamazov raised no objections and even found it all very amusing, though he continued to deny it all vehemently. The people in our town were pleased that he had taken care of the foundling. Later on, Karamazov found a surname for the child: he called him Smerdyakov, after the surname of his mother, Lizaveta Smerdyashchaya. It was this Smerdyakov who became Karamazov's second servant and lived, at the time our story begins, in the cottage together with Grigory and Marfa. He was employed as a cook. I should really say something more about him, but I am ashamed to keep my reader's attention occupied with common servants too long, and I am therefore going back to my story in the hope that all the relevant facts about Smerdyakov will somehow or other emerge in the course of it.

3

The Confession of an Ardent Heart in Verse

AFTER hearing the order his father shouted to him from the carriage after he had left the monastery, Alyosha remained standing for some time in great perplexity. Not that he stood still in one place for long – he was not in the habit of doing that. On the contrary, in spite of his great uneasiness, he managed to go at once to the Father Superior's kitchen to find out what his father had been up to upstairs. Then he set off for the town in the hope that on the way he would somehow or other be able to solve the problem that was troubling him. Let me say at once: he was not at all afraid of his father's shouts or his order to return home with his 'pillows and mattress'. He realized very well that the order to return home, shouted in so ostentatious a way, was given 'in a moment of passion' and, as it were, for the sheer beauty of it – just like the tradesman in our town who, when recently celebrating his nameday, not wisely but too well, had got angry at not being given more vodka and suddenly began in the presence of his guests to smash up his own crockery, to tear up his own and his wife's clothes, and, finally, to break his windows, and all for the sheer beauty of it, and the same thing, of course, had happened now to his father. Next day, of course, the drunken tradesman became sober and was sorry for the broken cups and saucers. Alyosha knew that his father would let him go back to the monastery next day or, indeed, even that very day. He was, besides, sure that while his father might hurt anyone's feelings, he would be loath to hurt his. Alyosha was convinced that no one in the world would ever wish to hurt him; indeed, that no one ever could hurt him. That he regarded as an axiom that could be accepted once and for all without argument, and that was why he went on his way without any misgivings.

But at that moment he was vaguely obsessed by another fear, a fear of quite a different kind, and all the more agonizing since he could not define it himself. It was the fear of a woman, namely Katerina, who, in the note handed to him by Mrs Khokhlakov, had so urgently besought him to go and see her about something. This request and the necessity of going there immediately aroused a strangely poignant feeling in his heart, and all the morning, as the hours passed, this feeling grew into a more and more intensely aching pain in spite of the scenes and adventures in the monastery, and now at the Father Superior's, etc. etc., which followed so closely upon each other. He was not afraid because he did not know what she was going to talk to him about and what answers he would have to give her. And it was not the woman in her that he was afraid of: of course, he knew little of women, but all the same he had spent all his life, from early childhood till he entered the monastery, entirely with women. He was afraid of that woman alone; he was afraid of Katerina. He had been afraid of her ever since he first saw her. He had only seen her once or twice, or perhaps three times, and had even exchanged a few words with her once by chance. He remembered her as a beautiful, proud, and imperious girl. Yet it was not her beauty that troubled him, but something else. And it was just the inexplicable nature of his fear that increased the fear itself. The girl's aims were of the noblest – he knew that: she was trying to save his brother Dmitry, who had treated her badly, and she was doing so out of sheer magnanimity. And yet, in spite of the fact that he could not but appreciate these beautiful and magnanimous feelings of hers, a chill ran down his spine the nearer he drew to her house.

He realized that he would not find his brother Ivan, who was on such intimate terms with her, at her house: Ivan was most certainly now with his father. And he was even more certain that Dmitry would not be there either, and he had a pretty good idea why. So they would have their talk in private. He wanted very much to go and see his brother Dmitry before that fateful talk. Without showing him the letter, he could have a few words with him. But Dmitry lived far away and he, too, was sure to be out now. After standing still for a minute, he at last came to a final decision. Crossing himself with accustomed rapidity and at once smiling at something, he walked resolutely in the direction of the house of the young lady he was so much afraid of.

He knew her house. But if he went by the High Street, then across the square and so on, it would be rather a long way round. Our little town is very scattered and the distances between streets are rather long. Besides, his father was expecting him. Perhaps he had not yet forgotten his order and he might be in a temper and, therefore,

Alyosha had to hurry to be in time in both places. As a result of all these considerations he decided to take a short cut, for he knew all the byways in our little town like the back of his hand. To go by the back-way meant avoiding the streets, walking along deserted lanes between fences, and sometimes even climbing over fences and walking through people's back-yards, where, however, everyone knew him and greeted him. In this way he could reach the High Street in half the time. In one place he had to pass very near his father's house, past the garden adjoining his father's, belonging to a tumble-down little house with four windows. The owner of this house, as Alyosha knew, was a bed-ridden old tradeswoman, who lived with her daughter, a 'civilized' parlour-maid who had till recently been employed in Petersburg in generals' homes, but had returned home because of her mother's illness about a year ago and who liked to show off her smart dresses. The old woman and her daughter, however, had fallen upon evil days and had to go every day to Karamazov's kitchen for soup and bread, which Marfa gave them readily enough. But though coming for the soup, the old woman's daughter had not sold a single one of her dresses, one of which even had a long train. Alyosha had learnt this quite by chance, of course, from his friend Rakitin, who knew absolutely everything that was going on in their town, and naturally at once dismissed it from his mind. But as he came alongside their neighbours' garden, he suddenly remembered the dress with the train and, quickly raising his downcast head, bowed in thought, suddenly came across someone he never thought of meeting there.

In the garden, on the other side of the wattle fence, stood his brother Dmitry, perched on something and leaning over the fence. He was gesticulating violently, trying to attract Alyosha's attention and apparently afraid not only to call out but to utter a single word for fear of being heard. Alyosha at once ran up to the fence.

'It's a good thing you looked up or I would have had to call you,' Dmitry whispered to him joyfully and rapidly. 'Climb over here! Quick! Oh, I'm so glad you've come! I was just thinking of you. . . .'

Alyosha was delighted, too, and was only wondering how to climb over the fence. But Mitya caught hold of his arm with his powerful hand and helped him to jump over. Tucking up his cassock, Alyosha jumped over with the agility of a bare-legged street urchin.

'Well done! Come along now!' Mitya cried in an enthusiastic whisper.

'Where?' Alyosha, too, said in a whisper, looking round and finding himself in a deserted garden in which there was no one except themselves. The garden was not very large, but the little house was at least fifty yards away. 'But there's no one here, so why do you whisper?'

'Why do I whisper? Damn it,' Dmitry suddenly cried in a loud voice, 'why *do* I whisper? You see how a chap can get all muddled up. I'm here in secret and am keeping a secret. I'll explain everything in a minute, but, knowing it's a secret, I suddenly began talking like a conspirator and whispering like a fool, when there's no need for it. Come on! Over there. Not a word till then. Oh, I could kiss you!

> Glory to the All-Highest in excelsis,
> Glory to the All-Highest in me!

I was just repeating that, sitting here, before you came. ....'

The garden was about three acres in extent, but it was planted with trees only along the four fences – apple-trees, maples, lime-trees, and birches. The middle of the garden consisted of a grass patch which provided several hundredweights of hay every summer. It was let out for a few roubles in spring. There were also beds of raspberries, gooseberries, and blackcurrants along the fences; the vegetable beds were near the house, but they had only been planted recently.

Dmitry took his visitor to one of the remotest corners of the garden farthest from the house. There amid the thickly planted lime-trees and old blackcurrant bushes, elder, guelder-rose and lilac, stood an old tumble-down green summer-house, its latticed walls blackened and sagging with age, but with a roof that was still intact and could give shelter from rain. The summer-house was built goodness only knows when, at least fifty years before, according to popular belief, by a retired Lieutenant-Colonel, a certain Alexander von Schmidt, who had owned the house. But it was all decayed, the floor was rotting, the floorboards were loose, and the woodwork was musty. There was a green table in the summer-house fixed in the ground, and round it were green wooden benches on which it was still possible to sit. Alyosha at once noticed his brother's excited state, but as he entered the summer-house he saw half a bottle of brandy and a glass on the table.

'Brandy!' Mitya burst out laughing. 'I daresay you're already saying to yourself: "He's drinking again!" Do not believe what you see—

> Do not believe the foolish, lying crowd,
> Cast aside your doubts. . . .

I'm not tippling, I'm only "indulging myself a little", as that swine of a Rakitin of yours says. He'll be a State Councillor one day and he'll keep on saying, "I'm indulging myself a little". Sit down. I'd like to press you to my bosom, Alyosha, my lad, and crush you against it, for in the whole world I actually – ac-tu-al-ly (understand this! understand this!) love no one but you!'

He uttered the last words almost in a sort of frenzy.

'No one but you, and one other person, a slut I've fallen in love with to my own undoing. But to fall in love doesn't mean to love. One can fall in love with a woman and hate her at the same time. Remember that! For the time being I'm talking cheerfully! Sit down. Here at the table. I'll sit beside you and look at you and go on talking. You'll keep quiet and I'll go on talking, for the appointed hour has come. Still, you know, I think it might be more advisable to keep our voices down because here – here – you never know who may be listening. I'll explain everything – I told you: the continuation follows. Why do you think I was dying to see you all these days? Why was I longing to see you just now? (It's five days since I cast anchor here.) All these days? Because it's to you alone I'm going to tell everything, because I have to, because it's you I need, because tomorrow I'm going to take a header from the clouds, because tomorrow my life is ending and beginning. Have you ever felt, have you ever dreamt what it is like falling from a mountain into a chasm? Well, that's how I'm falling now, but not in a dream. And I'm not a bit afraid, and don't you be afraid, either. I mean, I *am* afraid, but I love it. I mean, I don't love it, but I feel excited. . . . Oh, to hell with it. It's all one to me, whatever it is! A strong spirit, a weak spirit, a womanish spirit – whatever it is! Let us praise nature: see how bright the sun is, how clear the sky, how green the leaves – it's still like summer, four o'clock in the afternoon, everything so still! Where were you going?'

'I was going to see father, but I meant to go and see Katerina first.'

'Going to see her and father! Good Lord, what a coincidence! Why, who do you think I was waiting for, what was it I wanted, yearned, hungered, and thirsted for so much with every fibre of my soul and every curvature of my ribs? Why, to send you to father and then to Katerina with a message from me and so finish with her and with father. To send an angel. I could have sent anyone, but I had to send an angel. And here you are on your way to her and to father.'

'Did you really mean to send me?' Alyosha could not help asking with a pained expression on his face.

'Wait! You knew it, didn't you? I can see you understood it all straight away. But not a word – not a word now. Don't be sorry for me and don't cry!'

Dmitry got up, pondered, and put a finger to his forehead: 'She's asked you to call on her herself, hasn't she? She's written you a letter or something and that's why you were going to her. You wouldn't have gone otherwise, would you?'

'Here's her note,' said Alyosha, taking it out of his pocket.

Mitya quickly glanced through it.

'And you went the back-way? Ye gods, I thank you for sending him the back-way so that I could catch him like the old fool of a fisherman caught the golden fish in the fairy-tale. Listen, Alyosha, listen, my dear fellow. Now I mean to tell you everything. For I have to tell someone. I simply have to. I've told it to an angel in heaven already, but I have to tell it to an angel on earth, too. You are an angel on earth. You'll hear, you'll judge, and you'll forgive. . . . For what I need is that someone higher should forgive. Listen: if two people suddenly break away from everything earthly and go off on some wonderful adventure, or at least one of them does, and before going off or perishing, he comes to someone and says, Do this or that for me – something no one is ever asked to do by anyone except on one's death-bed – would the other one refuse if – if he's a friend or a brother?'

'I'll do it, but tell me what it is, and tell me quickly,' said Alyosha.

'Quickly. . . . Mmm. . . . Don't be in a hurry, Alyosha: you're in a hurry and you're worried. There's no need to hurry now. Now the world has struck out along a new road. Oh, Alyosha, what a pity you've never had any idea of what ecstasy means! But why am I

saying this to you? You of all people don't know what it means?
What a silly ass I am! I say:

> Be noble, O man!

Whose verse is this?'

Alyosha decided to wait. He realized that all his business was perhaps really here. Mitya pondered for a minute, his elbows propped
up on the table and his head resting on his hand. Both were silent.

'Alyosha,' said Mitya, 'you alone will not laugh! I should like to
begin my confession with – with Schiller's Hymn to Joy. *An die
Freude*. But I don't know German. All I know is *An die Freude*. Don't
think I'm just jabbering away because I'm drunk. I'm not at all drunk.
Brandy is brandy, but I need two bottles to make me drunk.

> And Silenus, red of face,
> Upon his stumbling ass —

You see, I haven't drunk a quarter of a bottle and I'm not Silenus.
I'm not Silenus but I am *silen*, I'm strong because I've made a
decision that is final and irrevocable. Forgive the pun. You must
forgive me a lot today, let alone a pun. Don't worry, I'm not spin-
ning it out. I'm talking sense and I'll come to the point in a minute.
I'm not going to keep you in suspense. Wait, how does it go? ...'

He raised his head, thought a moment and suddenly began to recite
ecstatically:

> Timid, naked in his den
> Hid the savage troglodyte,
> Over plains there wandered men
> Spreading ruin to all in sight.
> The hunter with his spear and arrow
> Through the forests made his way ...
> Woe to any who in sorrow
> Were cast upon that shore – a prey!

> From the Olympian heights has flown
> Mother Ceres swift to find
> Her dear lost Proserpine, her own:
> Bare and waste the land unkind,
> Nothing there to ease and cherish,
> No temple there to gods above,
> No harvest of field nor burden lavish
> Of vine to grace the feast of love.

> Nothing but the blood of wretches
> Steams from altars crude and bad,
> Nothing but the flesh of corpses
> Greets the eyes of Ceres sad.
> Sunk in deepest degradation,
> Vileness everywhere displayed,
> Foulness meets her woeful vision,
> Men their loathsomeness parade!

Mitya suddenly burst into sobs. He seized Alyosha by the hand.

'My friend, my friend, in degradation, in degradation even now. Man has to suffer a fearful lot on earth. There's a fearful lot of calamities for him there. Don't think that I'm just a boor of an officer who does nothing but drink brandy and leads a life of lust and depravity. I scarcely think of anything but of this degraded man, if only I'm not deceiving myself. Would to God I was not deceiving myself or showing off just now. For, you see, I think of that man because I'm such a man myself.

> That from the worst unto the better
> Man his soul may raise up high,
> He must join his ancient mother,
> Mother earth his best ally.

But the trouble is, you see, how am I to enter into an alliance with earth for ever? I don't kiss the earth, I don't cut open her bosom – so what am I to become: a peasant or a shepherd? I go on and on and I don't know whether I shall find myself amidst stench and shame or light and joy. That's the trouble, old man, for everything in the world is a mystery! And every time I happened to plunge into the very depths of the most shameless debauchery (and that was the only thing that did happen to me), I always read that poem about Ceres and man. Did it reform me? Never! For I am a Karamazov. For if I am to precipitate myself into the abyss, I shall do so without a moment's reflection, head over heels, and indeed I shall be glad to fall in such a degrading attitude and consider it beautiful for a man like me. And it is at this very moment of shame and disgrace that I suddenly begin to intone this hymn. Let me be damned, let me be vile and base, but let me kiss the hem of the garment in which my God is clad; let me be running after the devil at that very moment,

but I am still thy son, O Lord, and I love thee, and I feel the joy
without which the world cannot be and exist.

> The soul of all creation
> Blessed joy eternal fills,
> The secret force of fermentation
> With fire the cup of life instils;
> It lures sweet grasses to the light,
> And from the far-off outer spaces,
> Beyond the ken of furthest sight,
> Suns come out and take their places.

> At the breast of bounteous Nature
> Everything that breathes is glad;
> All nations, all creatures seek her pleasure,
> She gives to man a friend when sad;
> She gives the juice of grapes and garlands,
> And lust in lowly insect fires,
> But up above the angel stands
> In sight of God – his joy admires.

But enough of poetry! I've shed tears, so please, do let me cry. It
may be foolishness at which everyone will laugh, but not you. Your
eyes are shining too. Enough of poetry. I want to tell you now about
the 'insect', about the insect God has endowed with lust.

> And lust in lowly insect fires!

I am that insect, old man, and this has been said of me specially. And
all of us Karamazovs are the same kind of insect, and that insect
lives in you, too, my angel, and raises storms in your blood. I mean
storms, for lust is a storm – worse than a storm! Beauty is a fearful
and terrifying thing! Fearful because it is indefinable, and it cannot
be defined because God sets us nothing but riddles. Here the shores
meet, here all contradictions live side by side. I'm a very uneducated
fellow, old man, but I've thought a lot about it. There's a fearful lot
of mysteries! Too many riddles oppress man on earth. Solve them as
you can, but see that you don't get hurt in the process. Beauty! It
makes me mad to think that a man of great heart and high intelligence
should begin with the ideal of Madonna and end with the ideal of
Sodom. What is more terrible is that a man with the ideal of Sodom
already in his soul does not renounce the ideal of Madonna, and it

sets his heart ablaze, and it is truly, truly ablaze, as in the days of his youth and innocence. Yes, man is wide, too wide, indeed. I would narrow him. I'm hanged if I know what he really is! What appears shameful to the mind, is sheer beauty to the heart. Is there beauty in Sodom? Believe me, for the great majority of people it *is* in Sodom and nowhere else – did you know that secret or not? The awful thing is that beauty is not only a terrible, but also a mysterious, thing. There God and the devil are fighting for mastery, and the battlefield is the heart of man. Still, one can only talk of one's own pain. Listen, now to business.'

4

The Confession of an Ardent Heart in Anecdotes

'I LED a riotous life there. Father said this morning that I had spent several thousand roubles in seducing young girls. It's a filthy delusion. I never did anything of the sort, and if anything did happen, I didn't need any money just for *that*. With me money is an accessory, a fever of the heart, the background. Today it's a society woman, tomorrow a woman of the streets takes her place. I give them both a good time. I throw money about by the handful, music, noise, gypsy girls. If necessary, I give her money too, for they all take it. They take it with avidity. That I must admit. And they're pleased and grateful, too. Young society women have been in love with me, not all of them, but some – some; but I always liked the back streets, the deserted, dark back lanes, behind the square – there you find real, true adventures, real, genuine surprises – gold nuggets in the dirt. I'm speaking allegorically, old man. In the filthy little town I lived in there were no such back streets, but there were moral ones. If you were like me, you'd understand what it means. I loved vice and I loved the feeling of shame that vice gave me. I loved cruelty: am I not a bug, am I not a vicious insect? I told you – I'm a Karamazov! Once we went on a picnic – the whole town practically, in seven *troikas*. In the dark, in winter, in the sledge I began squeezing a young girl's hand, and forced her to kiss me. She was the daughter of a civil servant, a poor, sweet, gentle, meek child. She let me, she let me do much in the dark. She thought, poor thing, that next day I'd come and propose to her (you see, they thought a lot of me there as an eligible young man). But I never exchanged a single word with her after that. Never a word for five months. I could see how her eyes followed me about from a corner of the room at a dance (we were always having dances). I saw them glowing – glowing with gentle indignation. But this game only amused the insect's lust I nurtured inside me. Five months later she married a civil servant and left the town – angry and still perhaps in love with me. Now they live happily. Mind you, I told no one about it. I did nothing that might injure her reputation. I may have low desires and I may love low things, but I'm not dishonourable. You're blushing, your eyes flashed. Well, you've had enough of this filth, I think. And all this, understand, is only a beginning, it's only, as it were, Paul de Kock flowers, though the cruel insect was already growing – growing stronger and stronger in my soul. Here, old man, you have a whole album of reminiscences. May God bless them, the sweet darlings. I never liked to quarrel when breaking off a relationship with a woman. And I never betrayed any of them, never did anything to injure their reputations. But enough of that. You don't think I asked you to come here just to tell you all this nonsense? No, I've a much more interesting thing to tell you. But don't be surprised that I'm not ashamed before you, that, indeed, I'm even glad to tell you all about it.'

'You say that because I blushed,' Alyosha observed suddenly. 'I did not blush at what you were telling me, nor at what you've done. I blushed because I'm the same as you.'

'You? You're putting it on a bit, aren't you?'

'Not a bit,' Alyosha said warmly. (The idea had obviously occurred to him long before.) 'The steps are the same. I'm on the lowest one, and you're above, somewhere on the thirteenth. That's how I look upon it. It's one and the same thing. Absolutely similar. Anyone who has put his foot on the bottom step is bound to go up to the top one.'

'So you think one shouldn't put a foot on it at all, do you?'

'Anyone who can help it – shouldn't.'

'And can you?'

'I don't think so.'

'Not another word, Alyosha, not another word, old man. I'd like to kiss your hand, I'm so touched. That clever she-devil Grushenka is quite an expert on men and she told me once that she'd eat you up one day.... Sorry – sorry.... From these filthy abominations, from this field befouled by flies, let us pass on to my tragedy, also a field befouled by flies, I mean, by every kind of vileness. You see, the point is that though that beastly old man talked a lot of nonsense about the seduction of innocent girls, there actually was something of the sort in my tragedy, though it only happened once, and even then it didn't come off. The old man, who has reproached me with these cock-and-bull stories, doesn't know about this one – for I've never told anyone about it, you're the first I'm telling it to, with the exception of Ivan, of course, for Ivan knows everything. He knew about it long before you. But Ivan is as silent as the grave.'

'Ivan – silent as the grave?'

'Yes.'

Alyosha listened very attentively.

'You see, though a lieutenant in the battalion of the line regiment in which I served, I was really under constant supervision, just as though I were a convict. But in the little town where we were stationed I was very well received. I flung money about, everyone thought I was rich, and I thought so myself. Yet I must have pleased them in some other way, too. Though they shook their heads, they really liked me. But my commanding officer, a Lieutenant-Colonel – an old man – took a sudden dislike to me. He kept finding fault with me. But I had powerful friends and, besides, the whole town was on my side, and he couldn't do much to me! I was to blame myself, for I deliberately refused to treat him with proper respect. I was proud. This obstinate old man, who was not a bad sort at all and, indeed, a most kindly and hospitable fellow, had been married twice, and both his wives were dead. The first one seems to have been of humble origin and she left him a rather plain daughter. When I joined the regiment she was a young woman of four and twenty, and she lived with her father and aunt, a sister of her late mother. The aunt was meekness and simplicity itself, and her niece, the colonel's eldest daughter, was simple but pert. Talking of that girl, I'd like to put in a good word for her – I've never, old man, known a more charming character than that girl. Agafya her name was. She wasn't too bad-looking, either. A typical Russian girl: tall, plump, with a full figure. Her eyes were beautiful, but her face was perhaps a little coarse. She was not particularly keen on getting married, though two men had proposed to her. She refused them, but lost none of her gaiety. I became intimate with her – not in the sense this is usually understood. No, there was nothing of the kind there. I mean we were just good friends. You see, I often became intimate with women without making love to them, just in a friendly way. I used to say quite shockingly frank things to her, but she only laughed. Many women like frankness – make a note of that, and she was, besides, a young girl, which made it all the more amusing. And another thing. You could not possibly call her a young lady. She and her aunt lived in her father's house, but they seemed to put themselves in a humiliating position of their own accord, refusing to consider themselves on an equal footing with the rest of society. Everyone liked her and everyone was in need of her help, for she was an excellent dressmaker: she had a talent for it, but she demanded no payment for her services, she did everything out of kindness, but when people gave her money, she did not refuse it. But the Lieutenant-Colonel was quite a different kettle of fish! The Lieutenant-Colonel was one of the most prominent personalities in our town. He lived on a grand scale, entertained the whole town, gave dinners and dances. When I arrived and joined the battalion, it was common talk in the town that his second daughter, a girl of great beauty, would soon arrive from Petersburg, where she had just finished at a most fashionable boarding-school. This second daughter is Katerina, and she was the child of the Lieutenant-Colonel's second wife, who came from an aristocratic family. She was the daughter of a rich general, though I know for a fact that she did not bring the Lieutenant-Colonel any money, either. She came of a good family, and that was all. She may have had some hopes of inheriting money, but had not a penny in hard cash. And yet when the young lady arrived (on a visit, and not to stay), the whole town seemed to come to life. Our most aristocratic ladies – the wives of two generals and one colonel – and the rest after them at once showed a great interest in her. All took her up, gave entertainments in her honour, and she became the queen of the balls, picnics, and the *tableaux vivants* given in aid of some distressed governesses. I showed no interest. I carried on with my debaucheries. In fact, I had just done something so utterly disgraceful that the whole town was talking about it. One evening at the battery commander's I saw her sizing me up with her eyes, but I didn't go up to her – not interested! I went up to her only a few days later, also at a party. I said a few words to her, but she barely glanced at me. Compressed her lips scornfully. "Ah," I said to myself, "you wait! I'll get my own back one day!" I was an awful boor at the time when faced with a situation like this, and I was aware of it myself. What I felt was that "dear Katya" was not a silly little schoolgirl, but a person of character, a proud girl of high moral principles and, what's more, a person of intellect and education, while I had neither the one nor the other. You think I wanted to propose to her? Not a bit of it. I just wanted to revenge myself on her for not realizing what a fine fellow I was. Meanwhile, I went on leading a life of riotous dissipation and in the end the Lieutenant-Colonel put me under arrest for three days. It was just then that father sent me six thousand roubles in return for a formal renunciation of all my claims upon him, that is to say, for a written acknowledge-ment that we were "quits" and that I would not demand a penny more from him. I didn't understand a thing then. . . . You see, old man, up to the day of my arrival here, up to the last few days and perhaps, indeed, up to today, I didn't understand anything of my financial disputes with father. But to hell with it. We'll discuss it later. At the time, having received the money, I suddenly received a most inter-esting piece of news from a friend of mine, who was a most trust-worthy fellow. It seemed that the authorities were dissatisfied with our Lieutenant-Colonel, that they suspected him of irregularities, in short, that his enemies were preparing a little treat for him. And, to be sure, the commander of the division arrived and hauled him properly over the coals. Then, shortly afterwards, he was asked to resign. I won't go into the details of how it all happened. He cer-tainly had enemies, but all of a sudden there was an unmistakable coolness in the town towards him and his family, and everyone seemed suddenly to desert him. It was then that I played my first trick on Katerina. I met Agafya, with whom I'd always kept up a friendship, and said to her: "Do you know your father is short of four thousand five hundred roubles of government money?" "What do you mean? Why do you say that? The general was here not long ago and all the money was there." "It was there then, but it isn't there now." She was terribly upset: "Don't frighten me, please," she said. "Who told you that?" "Don't worry," I said, "I shan't tell anyone. You know perfectly well that in a matter of this kind I'm as silent as the grave. But I'd like to add, just in case, that when they demand the four thousand five hundred roubles from your father and he hasn't got them, then to prevent him facing a court-martial and being reduced to the ranks in his old age, he'd better send your educated young lady to me in secret. I've just had money sent me and I may let her have four thousand, and I swear to keep the whole thing a dead secret." "Oh," she said, "what a cad you are!" (She actually said that.) "What a horrible cad you are! How dare you!" She went away terribly indignant, and I shouted after her again that the secret would remain sacred and inviolate. The two silly women, I mean Agafya and her aunt, I may as well tell you at once, behaved like perfect angels all through this business. They really adored that proud girl Katya, humbled themselves before her, and waited on her as if they were her maids. . . . Only Agafya told her all about it, I mean, about our conversation. I found it out for certain afterwards. She didn't conceal anything, which, of course, was what I wanted.

'Suddenly the new Major arrived to take over the battalion, which he did. The old Lieutenant-Colonel suddenly fell sick, took to his bed, didn't leave his house for two days, and didn't hand over the government money. Our Dr Kravchenko assured everybody that he really was ill. But this is what I knew confidentially for a fact, and I had known it for a long time: during the past four years the money, every time after the authorities had been through the accounts, used to disappear for a time. The Lieutenant-Colonel used to lend it to a merchant of our town, an old widower by the name of Trifonov, a man with a big beard and gold spectacles, whom he trusted implicitly. Trifonov used to go to the fair, do some business there and on his return immediately return the whole sum to the Lieutenant-Colonel, bringing with him a present from the fair and with the present the interest on the loan. Only this time (I learnt all about it quite by accident from Trifonov's slobbering young son and heir, one of the most dissolute young scamps the world has ever seen), this time, I say, Trifonov, on coming back from the fair, did not return anything. The Lieutenant-Colonel rushed to his house, but all the reply he got from him was: "I've never received any money from you, and couldn't possibly have received any." So there our

Lieutenant-Colonel sat in his house, with a towel round his head, while the three of them kept putting ice to it. Suddenly an orderly arrived with the book and the order to hand over the battalion's money immediately, within two hours. He signed the book – I saw his signature in the book afterwards – got up, said that he was going to put on his uniform, rushed into his bedroom, took down his double-barrelled shot-gun, loaded it, rammed in a service bullet, took off his boot from his right foot, pressed the gun against his breast, and began feeling for the trigger with his foot. But Agafya remembered what I had told her and, suspecting what her father might do, stole up to his bedroom and was just in time to see what he was up to. She rushed into the room, seized him from behind, threw her arms round him, the gun went off and the bullet hit the ceiling. No one was hurt. The others ran in, took away the gun, and held him by the arms. . . . All this I learnt afterwards to the last detail. I was at home at the time, dusk was falling, and I was just about to go out. I had dressed, combed my hair, put some scent on my handkerchief, taken my cap, when suddenly the door opened and there before me, in my own lodgings, stood Katerina.

'Strange things do happen sometimes: no one had seen her in the street and no one had noticed her entering my lodgings, so that no one knew of it in our town. I rented my flat from two widows of civil servants, two ancient old ladies who waited on me. The two old girls had a great respect for me, they did everything I told them and, at my request, they were afterwards as silent as two posts. Of course, I grasped the situation at once. She came in and looked straight at me, her dark eyes gazing resolutely, even defiantly, but I could see from her lips and the lines round her mouth that she was far from resolute.

' "My sister told me that you'd give us four thousand five hundred roubles if I came for them – if I came alone. I have come. . . . Give me the money!" she said, but she broke down, her breath failed her, she was frightened, her voice gave out, and the corners of her mouth and the lines round it quivered. Alyosha, are you listening to me or are you asleep?'

'Mitya,' Alyosha said in agitation, 'I know you will tell me the whole truth.'

'I was going to. If I'm to tell you the whole truth, then this is how it all happened – I'm not going to spare myself. My first thought was – a Karamazov one. Once, old man, I was bitten by a centipede and was laid up for a fortnight with a high temperature; so now, too, I suddenly felt as though I had been bitten in the heart by a centipede – a noxious insect, understand? I looked her up and down. You've seen her, haven't you? She's beautiful, isn't she? But she was beautiful in a different way then. At that moment she was beautiful because she was noble, and I was a cad. Because she was standing then in all the grandeur of her sacrifice for her father and I was a bug! And she was *entirely* dependent on me, a cad and bug, dependent upon me altogether, body and soul. That was her position. I tell you frankly: that idea, the idea of a centipede, possessed my heart so much that it almost stopped beating with suspense. It seemed that there could be no question of any struggle: I simply had to act like a bug, like a vicious tarantula, without a spark of pity. . . . For a moment I felt breathless. . . . Listen. Next morning, of course, I should have gone to ask for her hand so as to end it all, as it were, in a most honourable way, so that no one should or could know anything about it. For though I'm a man of low desires, I'm honourable. But just at that very second someone seemed suddenly to whisper in my ear: "Why, a girl like that, when you come to propose to her tomorrow, will not even come out to see you, but will order the coachman to kick you out of the yard. Defame me all over the town – I'm not afraid of you!" I glanced at the girl, my voice had not deceived me. I should be kicked out. I could tell that from her face. I was furious. I felt like playing her a filthy, swinish trick, the sort of trick some low merchant might have played on her: to look at her with a sneer and, as she stood before me, bowl her over with the tone of voice that only some dirty shopkeeper knows how to use: "The four thousand, madam? Why, madam, I was only joking! Really, madam, you've been too credulous to count on it. Now, two hundred I might let you have with pleasure and gladly too. But four thousand, my dear young lady, is a bit too much to throw away on such frippery, don't you think? I'm afraid you've put yourself to unnecessary trouble."

'You see, I shouldn't have got anything out of it, for she would have run away, but it would have been an infernally sweet revenge and it would have been worth all the trouble it caused me. I knew I should have howled with remorse all the rest of my life, but just then I felt that if I could bring myself to say that, it would be worth it! I tell you this sort of thing never happened to me with any woman before, not with one. I mean that I should look at her at such a moment with hatred – and I swear to you I looked at her just then for three or five seconds with terrible hatred – with the sort of hatred that's only a hair's-breadth removed from love, from the most insane love! I went up to the window and pressed my forehead against the frozen pane. I can still remember that the ice burned my forehead like fire. I did not detain her long, don't worry. I turned round, went up to the table, opened the drawer, and got out a five per cent letter of credit for five thousand roubles which had not been filled in (I kept it in my French dictionary). I showed it to her in silence, folded it, gave it to her, opened the door into the passage for her myself and, taking a step back, made her a deep bow, a most respectful bow – believe me! She gave a violent start, looked at me for a second, turned terribly pale – she was as white as a sheet, I tell you, and, suddenly, also without uttering a word, not impulsively, but very gently somehow, she bowed deeply, quietly, and went down on her knees at my feet – with her head touching the floor – not the sort of thing you would expect a girl from a finishing school to do, but in the true Russian fashion! She jumped up and ran away. When she ran out, I was wearing my sword – I drew it and was about to stab myself to death with it – I don't know why. It would have been damn silly, of course, but I expect it was in the ecstasy of the moment. Do you realize that one might kill oneself in certain moments of ecstasy? But I didn't kill myself. I only kissed the sword and put it back into the scabbard – which I suppose I needn't have told you. And indeed I can't help feeling that in telling you about all these inner struggles of mine, I've exaggerated a little in order to show you what a fine fellow I am. But, all right, let it be like that and to hell with all those who pry into the human heart! So much for the "incident" with Katerina. So now Ivan knows about it and you – no one else!'

Dmitry got up and took a step or two in his excitement, took out his handkerchief, mopped his brow, then sat down again, but not in the same place as before, but on the bench opposite, along the other wall, so that Alyosha had to turn round completely to face him.

5

The Confession of an Ardent Heart:
Head over Heels

'NOW,' said Alyosha, 'I know the first half of this business.'

'You understand the first half – that was a drama and it took place then, in that town. The second half is a tragedy and it will take place here.'

'So far I can't understand anything of the second half,' said Alyosha.

'And I? Do you think I understand it?'

'Wait, Dmitry. There's one important question here. Tell me, you are her fiancé, you still are her fiancé, aren't you?'

'I did not become her fiancé at once, but only three months after that incident at my lodgings. On the next day after it had happened I told myself that the incident was closed, over and done with, and that there would be no sequel. To propose to her after that seemed to me a low-down thing to do. For her part, she did not communicate with me by a single word for the rest of the six weeks she remained in our town. Except, indeed, for one thing: the day after her visit their maid slipped into my room and, without uttering a word, handed me an envelope. It was addressed to me. I opened it and found the change from the letter of credit for five thousand. All they needed was four thousand five hundred, but they had to spend more than two hundred roubles to cash it. She therefore sent me back, I believe, only two hundred and sixty roubles. I don't remember exactly, but there was only the money in the envelope. No note, no explanation. Not a word. I searched for a pencil mark on the envelope – n-nothing! All right, so I went on a spree with the rest of my money and the new Major was forced in the end to reprimand me. Well, the Lieutenant-Colonel handed over the battalion's money – without trouble and to everyone's surprise, for no one believed that he had the whole sum intact. He handed it over and fell ill, took to his bed, spent about three weeks there, then softening of the brain suddenly set in, and five days later he was dead. He was buried with military honours, for his resignation had not yet taken effect. Soon after the funeral, Katerina with her sister and aunt left for Moscow. And it was only before they left, on the very day of their departure (I had not seen them and did not see them off), that I received a little note, on fine blue paper, with only one pencilled line: "I'll write to you. Wait. K." And that was all.

'Let me explain it to you in two words. In Moscow their affairs took a turn for the better with lightning rapidity and with the un-expectedness of an Arabian tale. The General's widow, their relative, suddenly lost her two heiresses, her two nieces who were next of kin – both died of smallpox in the same week. The grief-stricken old lady welcomed Katya with open arms just as though she were her own daughter, her star of salvation, and at once changed her will in her favour. But that was in the future; in the meantime, she gave her eighty thousand roubles for her dowry, to do with as she liked. A hysterical old girl. I had a good look at her afterwards in Moscow. Anyway, suddenly I received four thousand five hundred roubles by post. I was bewildered, of course. Struck dumb with surprise. Three days later the promised letter arrived. I've still got it. I always carry it about on me and I shall die with it – do you want me to show it to you? Yes, you must read it. She proposed to me. She herself made me a proposal of marriage: "I am madly in love with you," she wrote. "I don't care if you don't love me. It makes no difference, only be my husband. Don't be afraid, I'm not going to be in your way. I shall be your furniture, I shall be the carpet under your feet. . . . I want to love you always. I want to save you from yourself. . . ." Alyosha, I'm not worthy to paraphrase those lines in my own foul words and in my own vile tone of voice, always in the vile tone I could never get rid of! That letter touched me to the quick, as it still does, even today, for you don't think I'm happy now, that I'm happy today, do you? I wrote her an answer at once (I could not possibly go to Moscow just then). I wrote it with tears. One thing I shall always be ashamed of: I mentioned that she was a rich girl now, a girl with a dowry, and that I was just a coarse, ignorant pauper – I mentioned money! I should have kept it to myself, but it slipped out. Then I wrote at once to Ivan in Moscow and explained every-thing to him, as much as I could in a letter – a letter of six pages it was – and I sent Ivan to her. What are you looking at me like that for? Yes, of course, Ivan fell in love with her. He is still in love with her. I know that. In your opinion, in the opinion of the world, I did a silly thing, but perhaps that silly thing may save us all now! Good Lord, don't you see what a lot she thinks of him, how she respects him? Can she, comparing the two of us, possibly love a man like me, and particularly after all that's happened between us?'

'I'm quite sure that she does love a man like you and not a man like him.'

'She loves her own virtue and not me,' Dmitry blurted out involuntarily and almost spitefully.

He laughed, but a moment later his eyes flashed, he blushed all over and struck the table violently with his fist.

'I swear, Alyosha,' he cried with sincere and terrible anger at himself, 'you may believe me or not, but as God is holy and as Christ is our Lord, I swear that though I sneered at her higher feelings just now, I know that I'm a million times more worthless in spirit than she, and that these better feelings of hers are as sincere as an angel's in heaven! That's the tragedy of it, I mean, that I know that for certain. What does it matter if a man declaims a little? Am I not declaiming? But I am sincere. I'm sincere! As for Ivan, I quite understand how he must be cursing nature now, and with his intellect too! To whom has preference been given – to what? It has been given to a monster, who even here, when already engaged and when the eyes of everyone are fixed on him, can't refrain from his debaucheries – and that before the very eyes of his own fiancée, before his fiancée. And a man like me is preferred, and he is rejected. And why? Because a girl wants to throw her life and her future away out of gratitude! Ridiculous! I've never said anything of the kind to Ivan. Neither did Ivan of course say a word of it to me. He never so much as hinted at it. But destiny will be accomplished, and the deserving man will occupy his rightful place and the undeserving one will vanish into his back-alley for ever – into his filthy back-alley, into his beloved back-alley, a fitting place for him, and will perish there in filth and stench of his own free will, and like it. I'm afraid I've been talking rather wildly, my words seem to have all grown threadbare, I seem to be uttering them at random, but as I've decided, so it will be. I'll rot away in the back-alley, and she will marry Ivan.'

'Wait, Dmitry,' Alyosha interrupted again with great uneasiness, 'you've still not explained one thing to me: you are her fiancé, aren't you? You're still engaged to her. So how can you break off your engagement if she, your fiancée, doesn't want to?'

'I am her official fiancé. We were formally engaged. It all happened in Moscow, after my arrival. We had a full-dress engagement, with icons, in the grandest possible style. The general's widow gave us her blessing and actually congratulated Katya. "You've chosen well," she told her. "I can see through him." And – would you believe it? – she didn't like Ivan at all and was not nice to him. I had long talks with Katya in Moscow. I told her all about myself, honourably, exactly, sincerely. She listened to everything –

> There was sweet confusion,
> There were tender words —

As a matter of fact, there were proud words, too. She made me promise her solemnly to reform. I gave my promise. And now —'

'Now what?'

'And now I called you and dragged you over here today – this very day – remember that! – to send you – this very day – to Katerina and —'

'What?'

'Tell her that I shall never come to see her again. Tell her I sent you to say good-bye to her from me.'

'But is it possible?'

'Why, the reason I'm sending you to her is that it is impossible. For I can't very well tell her that myself, can I?'

'And where will you go?'

'To the back-alley.'

'You mean to Grushenka!' Alyosha exclaimed sorrowfully, clasping his hands. 'Could Rakitin really have told the truth? And I thought you'd just been to see her a few times and that it was all over now.'

'A fiancé to visit a woman like her? Is that possible? And engaged to a girl like Katerina and before the eyes of the whole world? I've still got a sense of honour, haven't I? As soon as I began visiting Grushenka, I ceased to be engaged to Katerina. I've ceased to be an honest man. I realize that all right. What are you glaring at me for? You see, at first I went to beat her. For I knew then and I know now for a fact that the captain, father's agent, had given Grushenka my

promissory note so that she could summons me. This was done to
make me give up bothering father. They wanted to frighten me.
So I went off to Grushenka to give her a beating. I had seen her a
few times before, but only in passing. There's nothing particularly
striking about her. I knew about her old merchant – he's ill and bed-
ridden now, but I suspect he'll leave her a tidy sum all the same.
I also knew that she liked to make money by lending it at
extortionate rates of interest, that she was a pitiless, cunning she-
devil. I went to beat hell out of her and I stayed there. A thunder-
storm broke, a plague struck, I got infected and I'm still infected,
and I know that all's over and done with and that there'll never be
anything more for me. The wheel has come full circle. That's
how things are with me. And, as though on purpose, I just happened
to have three thousand roubles in my pocket just then. A beggar
like me, too! I went with her to Mokroye, about twenty miles from
here. Got gipsies there, champagne, made all the peasants drunk on
champagne, all the women and girls, too, threw thousands away.
Three days later I was stripped to the bone, but still as proud as can
be. Do you perhaps think the proud fellow got anything out of it?
Not a chance. She never let me come near her. I tell you it's those
damned curves of hers. That she-devil Grushenka has a kind of curve
of the body which can be detected even on her foot. You can see it
even in the little toe of her left foot. I saw it and kissed it, but that
was all – I swear! She says to me, "I'll marry you, if you like, for
you're a pauper. Promise not to beat me and to let me do anything I
like, and perhaps I'll marry you." She laughed. And she is laughing
still!'

Dmitry got up from his seat almost in a sort of fury, and all at
once looked as though he were drunk. His eyes suddenly became
bloodshot.

'And do you really want to marry her?'

'If she wants me to, I shall marry her at once, if not, I shall stay
with her just the same. I shall be the caretaker in her yard. You –
you, Alyosha,' he cried, stopping suddenly in front of his brother
and, seizing him by the shoulders, began shaking him violently, 'do
you realize, you innocent boy, that this is all a crazy dream, an impossible dream, for what we have here is tragedy! I'd like you to
know, Alexey, that I can be a base man, a man of low passions that

may only lead to ruin, but Dmitry Karamazov can never be a thief, a pickpocket, a little sneak-thief! Well, then, I'd like you to know now that I am a miserable little sneak-thief and pickpocket! For that very morning, just before I went to beat Grushenka, Katerina sent for me and asked me, in great secrecy, for she did not want anyone in our town to know anything about it for the time being (why, I don't know, I expect she had a good reason for it), to go to the county town and post three thousand roubles to Agafya in Moscow from there. It was with those three thousand in my pocket that I had gone to see Grushenka. It was this money that I took to Mokroye. Afterwards I pretended that I'd been to the town, but I didn't give her the post office receipt. I told her I had sent the money and would let her have the receipt, but I haven't done so yet – I've forgotten all about it – see? Now, tell me what do you think is to be done? Suppose you go to her today and say, "Mitya asked me to say good-bye for him." And she'd say, "And what about the money?" You might, of course, have said to her: "He is a low voluptuary, a vile creature with uncontrollable passions. He never sent your money, but spent it, because, low animal that he is, he could not restrain himself." But you might also have added: "He isn't a thief for all that. Here are your three thousand, he returns them to you, send it to Agafya yourself. All he wants me to do is to say good-bye to you from him." But now all she has to say is: "And where is the money?"'

'Mitya, you're unhappy, aren't you? But still things aren't as bad as you think. Don't give way to despair. Don't!'

'Why, you don't think I'm going to shoot myself if I don't raise the three thousand to give back to her, do you? That's the trouble, that I won't shoot myself. I haven't the strength to do so now. Afterwards, perhaps. But now I shall go to Grushenka. I don't care what happens to me!'

'And what will you do there?'

'I shall be her husband, I shall achieve the high distinction of being her spouse, and when her lover comes, I shall retire to another room. I shall clean the dirty galoshes of her boy-friends, I shall kindle her samovar, I shall run errands for her. . . .'

'Katerina will understand everything,' Alyosha suddenly said solemnly. 'She'll understand the full extent of your unhappiness and be reconciled to you. She is a highly intelligent woman. She will realize herself that no one could be more unhappy than you.'

'She won't be reconciled to everything,' Mitya grinned. 'You see, old man, there's something here that no woman can be reconciled to. Do you know what would be the best thing to do?'

'What?'

'Give her back the three thousand.'

'But where are we to get it? Look here, I've got two thousand. Ivan will give you another thousand – there's your three thousand. Take it and give it back.'

'And when are we going to get your three thousand? You're still a minor, and you know it's absolutely essential that you should go and say good-bye to her from me today, with or without the money, for I can't put it off any longer. That's the position. Tomorrow it will be too late. Too late. I'll send you to father.'

'To father?'

'Yes, to father first. Ask him for the three thousand.'

'But he won't give it, Mitya.'

'Of course not. I know he won't. Do you know the meaning of despair, Alexey?'

'I know.'

'Listen. Legally he owes me nothing. I've got everything out of him, everything. I know that. But morally he does owe me something, doesn't he? For he started with my mother's twenty-eight thousand and made a hundred thousand with it. Let him give me only three out of her twenty-eight thousand, only three, and he'll snatch my soul out of hell, and many of his sins will be forgiven him for that! And I'll be satisfied with the three thousand – I give you my solemn word – and he'll never hear of me again. I give him a last chance to be a father. Tell him that God Himself sends him this chance.'

'Mitya, he won't give it for anything.'

'I know he won't. I know it perfectly well. Now, especially. And that's not all. I know something else. Only the other day, or perhaps even yesterday, he found out for the first time *definitely* (underline definitely) that Grushenka may not really be joking and may be too glad of the chance of marrying me. He knows the sort of woman she is. He knows the cat. So how can he be expected to give me the money and so assist in bringing this about when he's madly in love with her himself? But that is not all, either. I can tell you something else. I know that five days ago he took three thousand out of the bank, changed them into hundred-rouble notes, packed them into a large envelope, sealed with five seals and tied across with a piece of red ribbon. You see I know every little detail of it! And the inscription on the envelope reads: "To my angel Grushenka, in case she decides to come." He scrawled it himself, in dead secret, and no one knows he has all that money in the house except his servant Smerdyakov, in whose honesty he believes as he believes in himself. So there he is waiting for Grushenka for the last three or four days. He hopes she will come for the envelope. He let her know about it and she has sent him word that she might come. Well, then, if she goes to the old man, I can't marry her, can I? Do you understand now why I'm sitting in hiding here and what exactly I am keeping watch for?'

'For her?'

'For her. Foma has a room in the house of these sluts here. I know him. He was a private in my battalion. He does odd jobs for them. He's their watchman at night, and in the daytime he goes shooting blackcock. That's how he earns his living. So I've taken up my quarters in his place here. Neither he nor the women of the house know my secret, I mean, that I'm keeping watch here.'

'Only Smerdyakov knows?'

'Yes, only Smerdyakov. He'll let me know if she comes to the old man.'

'Was it he who told you about the envelope?'

'Yes. It's a dead secret. Even Ivan doesn't know about the money or anything. The old man wants Ivan to go to Chermashnya for two or three days. Someone seems to be offering eight thousand for the timber of the copse there. So the old man keeps asking Ivan to help him by going and arranging the sale. It will take him two or three days. He wants it so that Grushenka can come when he's away.'

'Then he's expecting Grushenka today too?'

'No, she won't come today. There are signs. It's quite certain she won't come!' Mitya exclaimed suddenly. 'Smerdyakov thinks so too. Father's drinking now. Sitting at table with Ivan. Go on, Alexey, go and ask him for the three thousand.'

'Mitya, what's the matter with you?' Alyosha exclaimed, jumping up from his place and staring at Dmitry's frenzied face.

For a moment he thought that Dmitry had gone mad.

'What do you mean?' Dmitry replied looking intently and even solemnly at his brother. 'I'm not mad. Don't be afraid. I'm sending you to father and I know what I'm saying: I believe in a miracle.'

'In a miracle?'

'In a miracle of God's Providence. God knows my heart. He sees my despair. He sees it all. He wouldn't allow something awful to happen, would he? I believe in a miracle, Alyosha. Go.'

'I'll go. Tell me, will you wait for me here?'

'Yes. I realize it will take some time. You couldn't just go and blurt it out, could you? He's drunk now. I'll wait three, four, five, six, seven hours, but please remember you must go to Katerina today, at midnight, if necessary, *with or without the money*, and tell her that I've sent you to say good-bye to her. I want you to repeat it word for word: "He asked me to say good-bye to you." '

'Mitya, and what if Grushenka should come today, or if not today, then tomorrow or the day after tomorrow?'

'Grushenka? Why, I'd soon discover it and I'd rush into the house and prevent it. . . . '

'And if . . . '

'And if – there's going to be murder. I could not bear *that* to happen.'

'Whom will you murder?'

'The old man. I shan't murder her.'

'What are you saying, Mitya?'

'Oh, I don't know – I don't know. . . . Maybe I won't kill him, maybe I will. I'm afraid he'll become so hateful to me with that face of his at that very moment. I hate his Adam's apple, his nose, his eyes, his shameless sneer. I feel a physical aversion. That's what I'm afraid of. So I may not be able to control myself. . . . '

'I'll go, Mitya. I believe God will settle it for the best, so that nothing terrible happens.'

'And I'll sit here and wait for a miracle. But if it doesn't happen, then — '

Sunk in thought, Alyosha went to see his father.

6

Smerdyakov

HE really did find his father still at table. The table was as usual laid in the drawing-room, though there was a dining-room in the house. This drawing-room was the largest room in the house, furnished with a sort of outmoded pretentiousness. The furniture was white, very old, and upholstered in faded red silky material. On the walls between the windows there were mirrors in elaborate frames of ancient scroll-work, also white and gilt. On the walls, covered with white paper, which was cracked in places, hung two large portraits, one of some prince, who about thirty years earlier had been Governor-General of the province, and the other of some bishop, who had also been dead for many years. In the corner opposite the door were a few icons, before which a lamp was lighted at night . . . not so much from reverence as to light the room. Karamazov went to bed very late, at about three or four o'clock in the morning, and till then he used to pace the room or sit in an armchair, thinking. He had formed such a habit. He often slept quite alone in the house, sending his servants off to the cottage, but mostly Smerdyakov stayed with him at night, sleeping on a chest in the hall. When Alyosha went in, dinner was over, but coffee and jam had been served. Karamazov liked to have sweets with his cognac after dinner. Ivan was also sitting at table and drinking coffee. The servants Grigory and Smerdyakov were standing at the table. Both masters and servants seemed to be in quite extraordinarily high spirits. Karamazov was roaring with laughter; already in the hall Alyosha could hear his father's high-pitched laughter he knew so well, and at once concluded from the sound of it that his father was far from drunk, but was for the present quietly enjoying himself.

'Here he is! Here he is!' Karamazov yelled, highly delighted at seeing Alyosha. 'Come on, my boy, join us. Sit down. Have a cup of coffee – it's all right. It's lenten, but lovely and hot! I won't offer you brandy as you're keeping the fast, but you'd like some, wouldn't you? No – I'd better give you some liqueur – our excellent liqueur!

Smerdyakov, fetch it from the cupboard. It's on the second shelf to the right. Here are the keys. Be quick about it!'

Alyosha began refusing the liqueur.

'It will be served, anyway. If not for you, then for us,' Karamazov beamed. 'But wait, have you had your dinner?'

'Yes,' answered Alyosha, who as a matter of fact had had only a piece of bread and a glass of *kvas* in the Father Superior's kitchen. 'But I will have a cup of hot coffee, if I may.'

'Capital, my dear boy, capital! He'll have some coffee. Shall we warm it up? Oh no, it's still boiling. Excellent coffee. A Smerdyakov specialty. Smerdyakov's an artist at coffee and fish-pies, and fish-soup, too. Yes, indeed. Some day you must come and sample his fish-soup. Let me know beforehand. . . . But wait, wait! Didn't I tell you this morning to come home today for good with your pillows and mattress? Have you brought your mattress? Heh-heh-heh!'

'No, I haven't,' Alyosha, too, grinned.

'Oh, but you were frightened this morning, weren't you? My dear boy, you don't think I would hurt you, do you? I say, Ivan, I just can't see him looking at me like that and smiling. I can't. My belly starts shaking with laughter at him. I love him! Come, Alyosha, let's give you a father's blessing.'

Alyosha got up, but Karamazov had already changed his mind.

'No, no. I'll just make the sign of the cross over you now. So. Sit down. Well, now we've got a treat for you, and in your line, too. You're going to have a good laugh. Balaam's ass has begun talking to us, and how he talks, how he talks!'

Balaam's ass, it appeared, was the servant Smerdyakov. Though still a young man of twenty-four, he was quite extraordinarily unsociable and taciturn. Not that he was in any way shy or bashful – no, quite the reverse. He had a supercilious character and seemed to despise everyone. But it seems we simply must say a few words about him, and without delay too. He was brought up by Marfa and Grigory, but the boy grew up 'without a spark of gratitude', as Grigory expressed it, a wild boy with a furtive look. As a boy he was fond of hanging cats and burying them with ceremony. He used to dress up in a sheet, to represent a kind of surplice, and chant and swing something over the dead cat, as though it were a censer. All this he did on the quiet with the greatest secrecy. Grigory caught him once at this exercise and birched him severely. He retired to a corner and glowered at them for a week from there. 'He doesn't care for you or me, the monster,' Grigory used to say to Marfa. 'He cares for no one. Why,' he addressed Smerdyakov, 'are you a human being? No, sir, you're not a human being. You came from the bath-house slime, you did. That's what you are. . . .' As it appeared afterwards, Smerdyakov could never forgive him those words. Grigory taught him to read and write and, when he was twelve, began teaching him the Scriptures. But that came to nothing almost at once. One day, at the second or third lesson, the boy suddenly grinned.

'What are you grinning at?' asked Grigory, looking sternly at him from under his spectacles.

'Nothing, sir. God created the world on the first day and the sun, the moon and the stars on the fourth. Where did the light come from on the first day?'

Grigory was dumbfounded. The boy looked sneeringly at his teacher. There was even something supercilious in his look. Grigory could not control himself. 'That'll teach you where!' he shouted and struck the boy a violent blow across the cheek. The boy took the blow without a murmur, but hid in his corner again for a few days. It so happened that a week later he had his first epileptic fit, a disease to which he was subject all his life. When Karamazov heard of it, he seemed suddenly to change his attitude towards the boy. Before, he used to regard him with some indifference, though he never scolded him and always gave him a copeck when he met him. When in a good mood, he would sometimes send the boy something sweet from the table. But having learnt of his illness, he began to take a great interest in him. He called in a doctor to see if he could be cured, but apparently his illness was incurable. On the average, the boy had a fit once a month, but on different dates. The fits, too, varied in violence: some were light and some very severe. Karamazov gave strict orders to Grigory not to beat the boy and allowed him to visit him upstairs. He also forbade him to be taught anything for the time being. But one day, when the boy was fifteen, Karamazov noticed that he was always walking up to the bookcase and reading the titles through the glass. Karamazov had a fair number of books, over a hundred volumes, in fact, but no one had ever seen him reading one.

He at once handed the key of the bookcase to Smerdyakov. 'Read, if you like. You'll be my librarian. Instead of hanging about the yard, you'd better sit and read. Here, read this one,' and Karamazov gave him *Evenings on a Farm near Dikanka*.

The boy read it, but did not like it. He didn't once smile. On the contrary, he finished the book with a frown.

'Well?' asked Karamazov. 'Isn't it funny?'

Smerdyakov said nothing.

'Answer, you fool!'

'Not a word of it is true,' mumbled Smerdyakov with a grin.

'Well, to hell with you, then, you're a born lackey! Wait, here's Smaragdov's *Universal History*. That's all true. Read it.'

But Smerdyakov did not read even ten pages of Smaragdov. He thought it dull. And so the bookcase was shut again. Shortly afterwards Marfa and Grigory reported to Karamazov that Smerdyakov was beginning to show signs of quite extraordinary squeamishness: before having his soup, he would look for something in it with his spoon, bend over it, examine it closely, take a spoonful and hold it up to the light.

'What is it? A cockroach?' Grigory would ask.

'A fly, maybe,' Marfa would observe.

The finicky youth never answered, but he did the same with his bread, his meat and anything else he ate: he would, for instance, hold up a piece on his fork to the light, examine it as though under a microscope, and after a long period of indecision at last decide to put it into his mouth. 'A little gentleman, forsooth!' Grigory muttered, looking at him. When Karamazov heard of this new side of Smerdyakov's character, he at once decided that he ought to be a cook and sent him to Moscow to be trained. He was in training for several years and came back greatly changed in appearance. He seemed to have grown suddenly old, prematurely wrinkled, sallow-faced, and began to look like a castrate. Morally, however, he returned almost the same as he had been before his departure for Moscow: he was as unsociable as ever and felt no need for anyone's company. In Moscow, too, as we heard afterwards, he was always silent; he seemed to take extraordinarily little interest in Moscow itself, so that he learnt little of it and paid no attention to anything else. He went to the theatre once, but came back silent and dissatisfied. On the other hand, he returned to our town from Moscow well dressed, in a clean frock-coat and clean linen, brushed his clothes very methodically twice a day, and was very fond of cleaning his smart calf-boots with a special English polish so that they shone like mirrors. He turned out to be an excellent cook. Karamazov paid him a regular wage and Smerdyakov spent it almost entirely on his clothes, pomatum, scents, etc. But he seemed to despise women almost as much as men, and was grave and almost unapproachable with them. Karamazov's attitude towards him changed somewhat. For his epileptic fits had grown more frequent and during those days the meals were prepared by Marfa, which was not at all to Karamazov's liking.

'Why do you get your fits more frequently now?' he sometimes asked, looking askance at his new cook and peering into his face. 'Why don't you get married? Want me to get you a wife?'

Smerdyakov merely turned pale with vexation at these words, but said nothing in reply. Karamazov would leave him alone, dismissing him as a bad job. The important thing was that he had no doubts whatever about his honesty. He knew for certain that Smerdyakov would never take or steal anything. It happened once that Karamazov, walking across his courtyard when drunk, dropped three hundred-rouble notes he had just received in the mud. He discovered his loss only on the following day: he had scarcely begun fumbling in his pockets for them when he saw them lying on his table. How did they get there? Smerdyakov had picked them up and had brought them the previous evening. 'Well, I must say,' Karamazov snapped, 'I've never met anyone like you,' and he gave him ten roubles. It must be added that he was not only convinced of Smerdyakov's honesty, but he was also fond of him for some reason, though the fellow looked askance at him as much as at everyone else and was always silent. It was very rarely that he would start talking. If it had ever occurred to anyone at the time to ask himself, as he looked at Smerdyakov, what the fellow was interested in and what was more predominantly in his mind, he would have found it quite impossible to tell by looking at him. And yet he used sometimes to stop dead in the house, or the yard, or in the street and ponder, and he would stand still like that for as long as ten minutes. A physiognomist, looking closely at him, would have said that he did not think of anything in particular, but was just vaguely contemplating. The painter

Kramskoy has a remarkable picture, called *The Contemplator*. It depicts a forest in winter, and on the roadway in the forest a little peasant stands quite alone in a torn coat and bast-shoes. He seems to have wandered there by chance and seems to be standing there thinking, but he is not really thinking but only 'contemplating' something. If you were to nudge him, he would give a start and look at you as though he had only just woken up, but without understanding. He would, it is true, have come to life at once, but if you asked him what he was thinking of while standing there, he would most certainly not remember anything. But he would most certainly never forget the sensation he had experienced during the time of his contemplation, but would always keep it hidden away inside him. Those sensations are dear to him, and he is doubtlessly accumulating them imperceptibly and without being aware of it – why and for what purpose, he does not know, either: perhaps, having accumulated such impressions in the course of many years, he will suddenly give up everything and go on a pilgrimage to Jerusalem in search of salvation, or, perhaps, too, he will suddenly set fire to his village, and, again, perhaps he will do both the one and the other. There are many people who are given to contemplation among our peasants. And Smerdyakov was no doubt one of them and he, too, no doubt, was accumulating his impressions greedily, hardly knowing himself why.

7

The Controversy

BUT Balaam's ass suddenly broke into speech. The subject was a strange one: Grigory, while shopping at the merchant Lukyanov's that morning, had heard from the shopkeeper the story of a Russian soldier who had been stationed on the frontier in some remote part of Russia and had been taken prisoner by some Asiatics. Threatened by them with immediate and agonizing death if he did not renounce Christianity and adopt the Mohammedan faith, he refused to betray his religion, was flayed alive and died a martyr's death, praising and glorifying Christ. The story of his act of heroism had been published in the newspaper of that day. Grigory had told them about it at dinner. Karamazov always liked to laugh and talk over the dessert after dinner, if only with Grigory. This time he was in a particularly light-hearted and pleasantly expansive mood. Sipping his brandy and listening to the story, he observed that a soldier like that should be immediately canonized and his skin sent to some monastery. 'I can imagine,' he added, 'the crowds that would flock there and the money the monastery would make.' Grigory frowned, seeing that Karamazov was not at all moved by his story but, as usual, was beginning to blaspheme. At that moment Smerdyakov, who was standing at the door, suddenly grinned. Smerdyakov had often been allowed to wait at table before, though only towards the end of dinner. But since the arrival of Ivan in our town he had begun appearing at dinner almost every day.

'What are you grinning at?' asked Karamazov, noticing the grin at once and realizing, of course, that it referred to Grigory.

'You see, sir,' Smerdyakov said suddenly and unexpectedly in a loud voice, 'I can't help thinking that even though the praiseworthy act of that soldier was so very great, he'd have committed no sin if in an emergency like that he had renounced, if I may say so, sir, the name of Christ and his own baptism, so as to save his life for good deeds by which to atone in the course of years for his cowardice.'

'What do you mean he would have committed no sin?' Karamazov broke in. 'You're talking nonsense, my lad, and for that you'll go straight to hell and be roasted there like mutton.'

It was at this point that Alyosha came in. Karamazov, as we have seen, was highly delighted by his son's appearance.

'In your line, in your line!' he tittered gleefully, making Alyosha sit down and listen.

'So far as mutton is concerned, sir,' Smerdyakov observed gravely, 'that is not so, and, if I may say so, sir, there won't be nothing of that there for this and there oughtn't to be, neither, in all fairness.'

'What do you mean: in all fairness?' Karamazov cried more gaily, nudging Alyosha with his knee.

'He's a scoundrel, that's what he is, sir!' Grigory blurted out suddenly, looking Smerdyakov angrily in the face.

'Don't be in such a hurry to call me a scoundrel, Mr Kutuzov, sir,' Smerdyakov parried quietly and with the utmost composure. 'You'd better consider it carefully. For once I'm taken prisoner by the enemies of Christians who demand that I should curse the name of God and renounce holy baptism, I'm fully authorized to do so by my own reason, since there wouldn't be no sin in it at all.'

'You've said that already,' cried Karamazov. 'Don't keep on about it. Prove it!'

'Broth-brewer!' Grigory whispered contemptuously.

'You needn't be in such a hurry to call me a broth-brewer, either, Mr Kutuzov, sir, but consider it carefully for yourself before you starts calling me names. For as soon as I says to my torturers, "No, I'm not a Christian and I curse my true God," I become by God's high judgement, immediately and specially anathema, accursed and excommunicated from the Holy Church, just as if I was a heathen, so that at that very instant, sir, not only when I says them words, but just as I thinks of saying them, so that before even a quarter of a second has passed, I'm excommunicated. Isn't that so, Mr Kutuzov, sir?'

He addressed himself to Grigory with unconcealed pleasure, but he was really answering Karamazov's questions, and he realized it very well, though he deliberately pretended that Grigory had asked the questions.

'Ivan,' Karamazov cried suddenly, 'bend over, I want to whisper something to you. He's doing it all for your benefit. He wants you to praise him. Come on, praise him.'

Ivan listened very seriously to his father's rapturous communication.

'Wait, Smerdyakov, shut up for a moment,' Karamazov cried again. 'Ivan, bend over to me again.'

Ivan again bent over with the utmost gravity.

'I love you as much as Alyosha. Don't think I don't love you. More brandy?'

'Thank you,' replied Ivan.

'You're well plastered,' Ivan thought to himself, looking intently at his father. He was watching Smerdyakov with great interest.

'Anathema! You're already accursed now!' Grigory suddenly burst out. 'And how dare you argue, you scoundrel, after that, if —'

'Don't call him names, Grigory, don't call him names!' Karamazov interrupted.

'You'd better wait a little, Mr Kutuzov, sir, and listen to what

I've got to say, for I haven't finished yet. For, you see, the moment I'm accursed by God, at that very moment, at that highest moment, sir, I become entirely like a heathen, and my baptism is taken off me and is considered null and void – that is so, isn't it, sir?'

'Finish, my lad, come on, hurry up and finish,' Karamazov hurried him, taking a sip from his glass with relish.

'Well, sir, if I'm no more a Christian, then I can't be telling no lies to my torturers when they asks me whether I am a Christian or not, for God himself has stripped me of my Christianity on account of my intention alone and even before I've had time to say a word to my torturers. And if I've already been degraded, then in what manner and with what sort of justice am I to be called to account as a Christian in the next world for having denied Christ, when for my intention alone I've been stripped of my baptism even before I had denied him? If I'm no longer a Christian, I cannot possibly deny Christ, for there's nothing more left for me to deny. Who in heaven, Mr Kutuzov, sir, would hold even an infidel Tartar responsible for not having been born a Christian and who'd punish him for that, seeing as how you can't take two hides off one ox? Why, Almighty God himself, even if he did hold the Tartar responsible, when he dies, would, I think, only give him the smallest possible punishment (for it's impossible not to punish him), arguing that he can't be blamed for having been brought into the world by infidel parents. Surely, God when he has a Tartar before him can't be expected to say that he too was a Christian, can he? For that would mean that Almighty God would be telling an absolute lie. And can God, the Almighty Ruler of heaven and earth, tell a lie, even by one word, sir?'

Grigory was dumbfounded and looked at the orator with his eyes almost starting out of his head. Though he did not quite understand what was said, he did grasp something of all that farrago of nonsense and stood still like a man who has suddenly knocked his head against a wall. Karamazov emptied his glass and burst into a high-pitched laugh.

'Alyosha, Alyosha, what do you think of it, eh? Oh, you casuist! He must have been with the Jesuits somewhere, Ivan. Oh, you stinking Jesuit, who taught you? But you're talking through your hat, casuist! You're talking through your hat! Don't cry, Grigory, we'll

reduce him to dust and ashes in a moment. Tell me this, you ass:
you may be right before your torturers, but you've all the same
renounced your faith in your own mind and you say yourself that at
that very moment you become anathema and accursed. Well, then,
if once you are anathema, they won't pat you on the back for it in
hell, will they? What have you got to say to that, my fine Jesuit?'

'There can't be no doubt, sir, that I've renounced it in my mind,
but all the same there's no special sin in it, sir, and even if there was a
sin, it would be of the most ordinary kind, sir.'

'What do you mean: of the most ordinary kind, sir?'

'You lie, c-curse you!' Grigory hissed.

'Consider yourself, Mr Kutuzov, sir,' Smerdyakov went on,
gravely and imperturbably, conscious of victory, but as though trying to be fair to a defeated enemy, 'consider yourself: it is said in the
Scriptures, that if you've got as much faith as a grain of mustard and
if you tell the mountain to move into the sea, it will move without a
moment's hesitation at your first word of command. Well then, Mr
Kutuzov, sir, if I haven't got no faith and you've got so much faith
that you keep swearing at me continually, why don't you tell that
mountain to move not to the sea (for it's a long way from here to
the sea, sir) but just to the stinking little stream which runs at the
bottom of our garden, and you will see, sir, yourself at that very
moment that it won't move an inch, sir, and everything will stay
as it is and just where it is, however much you shout at it, sir. And
that means that you have no faith, sir, properly speaking, that is, but
merely keep abusing others as much as you can. And what's more,
taking into consideration the fact that no one in our time, not only
you, sir, but no one at all, from the highest person in the land to the
lowest peasant, sir, can push a mountain into the sea, except perhaps
one man in the whole world or, at most, two men, who are perhaps
saving their souls in secret somewhere in the Egyptian desert, so that
you would not be able to find them at all – if that is so, sir, if all the
rest seemingly have no faith, will God curse all the rest, that is, the
population of the entire world, except them two hermits in the
desert, and will he not forgive one of them in his well-known
mercy? And that is why I, too, hope that, having once doubted, I
shall be forgiven if I shed tears of repentance.'

'One moment!' screamed Karamazov in a transport of delight.

'So you think there are two men who can move mountains, do you? Ivan, make a note of this extraordinary fact, write it down. There you have the Russian all over!'

'You're quite right in saying that this is a characteristic feature of the people's faith,' Ivan agreed with an approving smile.

'So you agree! Well, then it must be so if even you agree! Alyosha it's true, isn't it? Russian faith is like that, isn't it?'

'No, Smerdyakov hasn't got the Russian faith at all,' Alyosha said, quietly and firmly.

'I'm not talking about his faith, I'm talking about this characteristic, about those two hermits – just about that little characteristic feature: that is Russian, isn't it?'

'Yes,' Alyosha smiled, 'that is a purely Russian characteristic.'

'Your words are worth a gold coin, you ass, and I'll let you have it today. As for the rest, you're talking through your hat. Yes, sir. You should know, you fool, that here we do not believe merely out of thoughtlessness, but because we haven't time: in the first place, we're too busy with our affairs, and, secondly, God has given us little time, only twenty-four hours in the day, so that we have scarcely time to have a good sleep, let alone repent of our sins. And you've renounced your faith before your torturers at a time when you had nothing to think of except your faith and just when you ought to have shown your faith! So that, my dear fellow, it does certainly constitute a sin. Am I right?'

'It may constitute a sin, but consider yourself, Mr Kutuzov, sir, that if it does, it only makes it easier. For, you see, sir, if just then I had truly believed as one should have believed, it would really have been sinful if I had not suffered torture for my faith and had gone over to the vile Mohammedan religion. But, in that case, there wouldn't have been no question of torture, for all I had to do was to say at that moment to the mountain: Move and crush my torturer, and it would have moved at that same moment and crushed him like a black-beetle, and I'd have gone forth just as if nothing had happened, praising and glorifying the Lord. But if at that same moment I'd tried it all and deliberately cried to the mountain: Crush my torturers, and it did not crush them, so how, tell me, shouldn't I have doubted at the time and at such a dreadful hour of great and mortal terror? Knowing, as it is, that I shouldn't attain altogether to the Kingdom of Heaven (for the mountain had not moved at my word, which can only mean that they don't think much of my faith up there and that I can't expect no great rewards in the next world), why should I let them flay me as well and to no good purpose, neither. For even if they'd torn my skin half off my back, even then the mountain wouldn't have moved at my word or at my cry. Why, at such a moment a fellow might not only doubt, but even lose his reason from fear, so that he wouldn't be able to think at all. So why should I be specially to blame if, seeing as how I shan't get no advantage nor reward here or there, at least I save my skin? And, therefore, putting my trust in God's mercy, I can only hope, sir, that one day I shall be altogether forgiven. . . . '

8

Over the Brandy

THE discussion was over, but, strange to say, Karamazov, who had been so full of high spirits, suddenly began to frown. He frowned and emptied his glass of brandy at one gulp, and that was already a glass too many.

'Get out of here, Jesuits,' he cried to the servants. 'Clear out, Smerdyakov. I'll let you have the promised sovereign today, but be off with you! Don't cry, Grigory. Go to Marfa. She'll comfort you and put you to bed. The swine won't let us sit in peace after dinner,' he suddenly snapped out vexatiously after his servants had promptly withdrawn at his word. 'Smerdyakov pokes his nose in here every time at dinner,' he added to Ivan. 'It's you he's so interested in. What have you done to make him so fond of you?'

'Absolutely nothing,' replied Ivan. 'Got it into his head that I'm a great fellow. A boor and a lackey like him! First-class material, though, when the time comes.'

'First class?'

'I suppose there will be others and better ones, but there'll be fellows like him, too. At first there will be fellows like him. The better ones will come after.'

'And when will the time come?'

'When the rocket goes up, but perhaps it will fizzle out. So far the common people are not very fond of listening to these broth-brewers.'

'There you are, my dear fellow. A Balaam's ass like that thinks and thinks, and the devil only knows what sort of ideas he'll think of in the end.'

'He'll get all sorts of ideas,' Ivan laughed.

'You see, I know very well that he can't stand me any more than he can stand anybody, and you, too, though you may think he's got it into his head that you're a "great fellow". And particularly Alyosha. He despises Alyosha. But, you see, he won't steal anything, he doesn't gossip, he holds his tongue and he won't wash our dirty linen in public. Bakes lovely fish-pies, too. But to hell with him. He isn't worth talking about, is he?'

'Of course he isn't.'

'As for the ideas he might get, the Russian peasant, generally speaking, ought to be flogged. I've always maintained it. Our peasants are rogues, they don't deserve to be pitied, and it's a good thing they're still sometimes thrashed even now. Russia is strong because she has lots of birch trees. If the forests were destroyed, Russia would perish. I'm all for clever people. We stopped flogging the peasants because we've got a little too clever, but they go on thrashing each other. And a good thing too. For "with what measure ye mete, it shall be measured to you again", or how does it go there? In short, it shall be measured. And Russia is just swinishness. My dear boy, if only you knew how I hate Russia. . . . I mean, not Russia, but all these vices – but I daresay Russia, too. *Tout cela c'est de la cochonnerie.* You know what I like? I like wit.'

'You've had another glass. You'd better stop.'

'Never mind, I'll have one more, and then another, and then I'll stop. No, wait. You've interrupted me. On passing through Mokroye I asked an old peasant about it and he said to me: "What we likes best of all, sir," he says, "is sentencing girls to be flogged and we lets the boys flog them. For, you see, sir, the girl he has flogged today the lad will marry tomorrow, so that," he says, "it suits the girls down to the ground, too, it does, sir." What do you say to these Marquis de Sades, eh? But, say what you like, it's witty. We ought to go and have a look at it, don't you think? Are you blushing,

Alyosha? Don't be bashful, my boy. A pity I didn't dine with the monks at the Father Superior's today. I'd have liked to tell them about the Mokroye girls. Don't be cross with me, Alyosha, for having offended your Father Superior. You see, my boy, I can't help feeling vexed. For if there's a God, if he exists, then of course I'm to blame and I shall have to answer for it, but if there isn't a God at all, they ought to be treated a hundred times worse, your Fathers, I mean, oughtn't they? For then chopping off their heads isn't enough punishment for them, for they impede progress. Believe me, Ivan, *that* hurts my feelings. No, you don't believe me. I can see it from your eyes. You believe the people who say that I'm nothing but a clown. Alyosha, do you think I'm nothing but a clown?'

'I don't think so.'

'And I believe you don't and that you're sincere. You look sincere and you speak sincerely. But not Ivan. Ivan is high and mighty. All the same, I'd make an end of your monastery. I'd get rid of this mystic stuff. Do away with it at one blow, all over Russia, so as to bring all the fools finally to reason. And think of the silver and gold that would flow into the mint!'

'But why get rid of it?' said Ivan.

'So that truth should prevail more quickly – that's why!'

'But if this truth were to prevail, you'd be the first to be robbed and then – liquidated.'

'Good Lord, I do believe you're right! Oh, what an ass I am!' Karamazov exclaimed, striking himself lightly upon the forehead. 'Well, in that case, your monastery may stay where it is, Alyosha. And we, clever people, will live in comfort and enjoy our brandy. You know, Ivan, I shouldn't be surprised if God hadn't arranged it all on purpose! Tell me, Ivan: is there a God or not? Wait: tell me the truth, tell me seriously! What are you laughing at again?'

'I'm laughing at your witty remark about Smerdyakov's belief in the existence of two elders who could move mountains.'

'Why? Am I like him now?'

'Yes, very.'

'Well, that means that I, too, am a Russian and I too have this Russian characteristic. And I daresay one can catch a philosopher like you also in some characteristic of your own of the same kind. And so I shall. I bet you I shall catch you out tomorrow. But tell me all the same: is there a God or not? Only, seriously, mind! I want it seriously now.'

'No, there's no God.'

'Alyosha, is there a God?'

'Yes, there is.'

'Ivan, is there immortality, I mean just of some sort, just a tiny little one?'

'No, there's no immortality, either.'

'None at all?'

'None at all.'

'You mean absolutely nothing, or is there something? Perhaps there is just something. Anything is better than nothing.'

'Absolutely nothing.'

'Alyosha, is there immortality?'

'There is.'

'God and immortality?'

'Yes, God and immortality. In God is immortality.'

'I see. More likely Ivan's right. Lord, to think how much faith and what strength man has sacrificed for nothing for that dream, and for how many thousands of years! Who could make such a fool of man? I say, Ivan, tell me for the last time and categorically: is there a God or not? I'm asking you for the last time.'

'And for the last time there isn't.'

'Who then is laughing at mankind, Ivan?'

'The devil, I suppose,' Ivan said with a grin.

'And is there a devil?'

'No, there isn't a devil, either.'

'A pity. Damn it all, what wouldn't I do to the man who first invented God! Hanging's too good for him.'

'If God hadn't been invented, there'd be no civilization.'

'Wouldn't there? You mean, without God?'

'Yes. And there would be no brandy, either. I'm afraid I shall have to take the brandy away from you all the same.'

'Wait, wait, wait, my boy! Just one more glass. I've offended Alyosha. You're not cross with me, Alyosha, are you? My darling Alyosha, dear little Alexey!'

'No, I'm not cross. I know your thoughts. Your heart is better than your head.'

'My heart is better than my head? Good Lord, and it's you who say so? Do you love Alyosha, Ivan?'

'I do.'

'Yes, love him.' (Karamazov was getting very drunk.) 'Listen, Alyosha. I was rude to your elder this morning. But I was excited. That elder has got wit. What do you think, Ivan?'

'I daresay he has.'

'Yes, he has, he has, *il y a du Piron là-dedans*. He's a Jesuit, a Russian one, that is. He's hiding his indignation at having to pretend and – and putting the garment of saintliness upon himself is too much for him, for he is an honourable man.'

'But he does believe in God.'

'Not a bit of it. Didn't you know that? Why, he tells everybody. I – I mean, not everybody, but all the intelligent people who come to see him. He told Governor Schultz quite frankly: *credo*, but I don't know in what.'

'Go on!'

'He certainly did. But I respect him. There's something Mephisto-phelian in him or rather something of *A Hero of our Time* – Arbenin, or whatever his name is – that is, you see, he's a sensualist. He is such a sensualist that I'd be afraid for my daughter or my wife if she went to confess to him. When he begins telling stories, you know.... The year before last he invited us to tea – with liqueur (the ladies send him liqueur). You should have heard him describing the old times! We split our sides laughing.... Especially how he once cured a paralysed woman. "If my legs were not bad," he said, "I'd perform a dance for you." What a man, eh? "I'm afraid," he said, "I've done a lot of copulating in my time." He got sixty thousand out of Demidov the merchant.'

'You mean, stole it?'

'Well, Demidov brought him the money as to a man who was honest. He asked him to take care of it because he expected the police to raid his place next day. So he took care of it. "You've donated it to the Church," he declared. I told him he was a scoundrel, but he said, no, he wasn't, he was merely broadminded. But I don't think it was him, after all.... It was someone else. I'm afraid I've got him muddled with someone else – er – without noticing it. Well, one more glass and I've done. Take away the bottle, Ivan. I've been talking a lot of nonsense. Why didn't you stop me, Ivan? Why didn't you tell me I was talking nonsense?'

'I knew you'd stop yourself.'

'You did not. You did it out of spite against me – out of sheer spite. You despise me. You've come to live with me and you despise me in my own house.'

'Very well, I'll go away. You've had too much brandy.'

'I begged you for Christ's sake to go to Chermashnya for a day or two, and you don't go.'

'I'll go tomorrow, if you really insist.'

'You won't. You want to keep an eye on me here. That's what you want. You're a spiteful fellow. That's why you won't go, isn't it?'

The old man just would not quieten down. He had reached that state of drunkenness when some drunkards, till then subdued, are suddenly overcome by an irresistible desire to fly into a rage and assert themselves.

'What are you staring at me for? You know what your eyes are like? Your eyes are looking at me and saying: "What a drunken rotter you are!" Your eyes are full of suspicion. Your eyes are full of contempt. . . . You've come here with some crafty plan in your mind. . . . Look at Alyosha. He, too, is looking at me, but his eyes are shining. Alyosha does not despise me. Alexey, you mustn't love Ivan. . . . '

'Don't be angry with my brother,' Alyosha suddenly said, insistently. 'Stop insulting him.'

'Oh, all right. Ugh, my head aches. Take away the brandy, Ivan. It's the third time I've told you.' He fell into thought and suddenly a cunning smile spread all over his face. 'Don't be angry with a feeble, stupid old man, Ivan. I know you don't love me, but don't be angry with me all the same. There's no reason why you should love me. You go to Chermashnya. I'll join you there myself and bring you a present. I'll show you a lovely little girl there. I've had my eye on her a long time. At present she's still running about barefoot. But don't fight shy of barefooted little girls – don't despise them – they're pearls.'

And he kissed his hand with a smack.

'So far as I'm concerned,' he went on, becoming animated all at once, as though growing sober for a minute as soon as he got on to his favourite subject, 'so far as I'm concerned – oh, you children, my dear children, my little sucking-pigs, so far as I'm concerned – there hasn't been an ugly woman in the whole of my life – that's been my rule! Can you understand that? But how could you understand it? You've still got milk and not blood flowing in your veins – you haven't hatched out yet! According to my rule, you can find in every woman something – damn it! – something extraordinarily interesting, something you won't find in any other woman. Only you must know how to find it – that's the point! That requires talent! For me ugly women do not exist: the very fact that she's a woman is half the attraction for me– but how could you understand that? Even in old maids you sometimes find something so attractive that you can't help marvelling at the damn fools who've let them grow old without noticing it! The first thing to do with barefooted girls and ugly women is to take them by surprise – that's how one should deal with them. You didn't know that, did you? They must be surprised till they're enraptured, till they're transfixed, till they're ashamed that such a gentleman should have fallen in love with such a swarthy creature. What's so wonderful is that so long as there are peasants and gentlemen in the world – and there always will be – there will also be such lovely little scullery maids and their masters – and that's all one needs for one's happiness! Wait – listen, Alyosha. I always used to surprise your mother, only it was in a different way. I never caressed her, but all at once, when the right moment came, I'd dance attendance on her, crawl on my knees before her, kiss her feet and always, always – I remember it as though it were today – I'd make her burst out into a quiet little laugh, a crisp, tinkling, soft, nervous, peculiar kind of laugh. That's the only kind of laugh she had. I knew that her attacks always began like that, that the next day she'd begin shrieking, that her present little laugh was not a sign of delight. But though deceptive, it sounded like delight. That's what it means to be able to find the typical in everything! There was that Belyavsky – a handsome fellow and rich too – who fell in love with her. He used to visit us almost every day. Suddenly, during one of his visits, he slapped my face, and in her presence too. And she – such a sheep – why, I thought she'd beat me black and blue for that blow. How she set upon me! "You've been thrashed, thrashed," she kept saying. "You've had your face slapped by him. You were trying to sell me to him," she said. "And how dared he strike you in my presence! And don't you ever dare come near me again! Go at once and challenge him to a duel! . . . " So I took her to the monastery to teach her meekness. The holy fathers read prayers over her. But I swear to you, Alyosha, I never did anything to offend my poor shrieker! Once only, perhaps, only once! It happened during the first year of our marriage. She used to pray a lot then and she was especially keen on keeping the feasts of our Lady. She used to drive me away from her then to my study. Well, I thought to myself, let's knock that mysticism out of her. "You see," I said to her, "you see your icon – there – well, look, I'm going to take it down. Now watch me. You think it's a miracle-working icon, don't you? But I'm going to spit on it in front of you and nothing will happen to me!" As soon as she heard me, good Lord, I thought she'd kill me on the spot. But she only jumped to her feet, threw up her hands, then covered her face with them, began shaking all over and fell on the floor – fell all of a heap. . . . Alyosha, Alyosha, what's the matter?'

The old man jumped up from his seat in alarm. From the moment he began talking about his mother, a gradual change came over Alyosha's face. He flushed, his eyes glowed, his lips quivered. . . . The drunken old man had gone on spluttering and noticed nothing till the very moment when something strange happened to Alyosha – exactly the same thing, in fact, as had happened to the 'shrieker' when he threatened to spit on her icon. Alyosha suddenly jumped up from his seat, exactly as his mother had done, threw up his hands, then buried his face in them and trembled all over in a sudden fit of hysteria, shaking with silent sobs. The old man was particularly struck by his extraordinary resemblance to his mother.

'Ivan, Ivan! A glass of water, quick! It's like her, exactly like her! Just as his mother was then! Spurt some water on him from your mouth. I used to do the same to her. He's upset for his mother, for his mother . . . ' he muttered to Ivan.

'But his mother was my mother, too, wasn't she?' Ivan suddenly burst out with uncontrollable anger and contempt.

His flashing eyes made the old man start. But here something very strange had happened, though perhaps it lasted only a second: the fact that Alyosha's mother was also Ivan's mother seemed to have slipped Karamazov's mind completely.

'Your mother?' he muttered, uncomprehendingly. 'What are you talking about? What mother are you.... Was she really? Why, damn it! Of course, she was your mother too! Damn it! I'm sorry, my dear fellow, I didn't know what I was saying.... This never happened to me before. I'm sorry. I was thinking, Ivan – heh-heh-heh!'

He stopped short. A broad, drunken, half-witted grin spread all over his face. And that very moment a terrible uproar broke out in the hall, violent shouts could be heard, the door was flung open and Dmitry burst into the room. The old man rushed up to Ivan in terror.

'He'll kill me? He'll kill me! Don't let him get near me, don't let him!' he screamed, clutching at the skirt of Ivan's coat.

9

The Sensualists

GRIGORY and Smerdyakov ran into the room immediately after Dmitry. They had been struggling with him in the hall, trying not to let him in (acting on the instructions given by Karamazov himself some days before). Taking advantage of the fact that after bursting into the room Dmitry had stopped dead for a moment to look round, Grigory ran round the table, closed the double doors on the opposite side of the room leading to the inner apartments, and stopped before the closed door with his hands crossed, ready, as it were, to defend the entrance to the bedroom with the last drop of his blood. Seeing that, Dmitry did not so much shout as scream and rushed at Grigory.

'So she's there! She's been hidden there! Get out of my way, you blackguard!'

He tried to pull Grigory away, but Grigory pushed him back. Beside himself with fury, Dmitry raised his hand and struck Grigory with all his might. The old man collapsed in a heap on the floor, and Dmitry, jumping over him, burst open the door. Smerdyakov remained at the other end of the drawing-room, pale and trembling and clinging to Karamazov.

'She's here,' shouted Dmitry. 'I just saw her myself turning towards the house, but I couldn't overtake her. Where is she? Where is she?'

The shout: 'She's here!' produced an astonishing effect upon Karamazov. All his terror left him.

'Hold him! Hold him!' he yelled, rushing after Dmitry.

Meanwhile Grigory had got up from the floor, but he still seemed dazed. Ivan and Alyosha rushed after their father. In the third room something was suddenly heard to fall to the floor with a crash: it was a large glass vase (an inexpensive one) on a marble pedestal which Dmitry brushed against as he ran past it.

'At him!' yelled the old man. 'Help!'

Ivan and Alyosha overtook the old man and forced him to go back to the drawing-room.

'What are you running after him for?' Ivan shouted angrily at his father. 'He really will murder you there!'

'Ivan, Alyosha, my dear boys, she must be here then. Grushenka is here. He said he saw her himself running into the house.'

He was gasping for breath. He was not expecting Grushenka that day and the sudden news that she was there drove him out of his mind. He was trembling all over. He seemed to have gone mad.

'But you've seen yourself she hasn't come!' Ivan shouted.

'She may have come by the back entrance.'

'But it's locked – the back entrance is locked, and you've got the key.'

Dmitry suddenly appeared in the drawing-room again. He had of course found the back entrance locked, and the key actually was in Karamazov's pocket. The windows of all the rooms were also closed; Grushenka could not possibly have got into the house from anywhere, nor could she have run out from anywhere.

'Hold him!' screamed Karamazov as soon as he caught sight of Dmitry. 'He's stolen my money from the bedroom!'

Breaking loose from Ivan, he again rushed at Dmitry. But Dmitry raised both his hands and suddenly seized the old man by the remaining wisps of his hair, gave a pull and flung him with a crash on the floor. He had just time to kick him two or three times in the face with his heel. The old man let out a piercing moan. Ivan, though not as strong as his brother Dmitry, flung his arms round him and dragged him away from the old man with all the force at his command.

Alyosha, too, helped him with all his feeble strength, clasping his brother round the waist.

'Madman, you've killed him!' shouted Ivan.

'Serves him right!' Dmitry cried breathlessly. 'If I haven't killed him now, I'll come back and kill him. You won't be able to protect him!'

'Dmitry, get out of here at once!' Alyosha shouted peremptorily.

'Alexey, tell me, please, you're the only one I'll believe – was she here just now or not? I saw her myself a minute ago stealing past the fence from the lane towards the house. I shouted and she ran away.'

'I swear she hasn't been here and no one expected her to come.'

'But I saw her. . . . So that she – I'll find out at once where she is. Alexey, good-bye. Don't tell the old swine about the money now. You must go to Katerina at once and tell her that I told you to bid her good-bye, bid her good-bye. Yes, bid her good-bye. Tell her that. He bids you farewell! Describe this scene to her.'

Meanwhile Ivan and Grigory had raised the old man and seated him in an arm-chair. His face was covered with blood, but he was conscious and he listened eagerly to Dmitry's shouts. He still seemed to think that Grushenka was really somewhere in the house. As he left the room, Dmitry gave him a baleful look.

'I'm not sorry to have spilt your blood!' he cried. 'Take care, old man, take care of your dreams, for I too have dreams! I curse you and disown you entirely! . . .'

He ran out of the room.

'She's here! I'm sure she's here! Smerdyakov, Smerdyakov!' the old man wheezed almost inaudibly, beckoning to Smerdyakov with a finger.

'She is not here, she isn't, you crazy old man!' Ivan shouted at him spitefully. 'Good Lord, he's fainted! Water! A towel! Be quick about it, Smerdyakov!'

Smerdyakov rushed out for water. The old man was at last undressed, taken to the bedroom and put to bed. A wet towel was wrapped round his head. Weakened by the brandy, the violent sensations and the blows, he shut his eyes and fell asleep as soon as his head touched the pillow. Ivan and Alyosha went back to the drawing-room. Smerdyakov was carrying away the pieces of the broken vase and Grigory stood at the table looking down gloomily at the floor.

'Don't you think you'd better put a wet towel round your head too and go to bed?' Alyosha said to Grigory. 'We'll look after him here. My brother must have given you a terrible blow – on the head.'

'He dared do this to me!' Grigory said gloomily and distinctly.

'He "dared" do this to father, too, not only to you,' Ivan remarked with a wry smile.

'I used to wash him in a tub and – he dared do this to me!' Grigory repeated.

'Damn it all, if I hadn't pulled him away, he'd probably have killed him. It wouldn't take much to do the old fool in,' Ivan whispered to Alyosha.

'God forbid!' cried Alyosha.

'Why?' Ivan went on in the same whisper, with a malicious grin. 'One reptile will devour another reptile, and serve them both right!'

Alyosha shuddered.

'I won't of course let him be murdered as I didn't just now. Stay here, Alyosha. I'll go out for a breath of fresh air. I've got a headache.'

Alyosha went into his father's bedroom and sat down at his bedside behind the screen for about an hour. The old man suddenly opened his eyes and gazed silently at Alyosha for a long time, evidently remembering and pondering. Suddenly there was a look of extraordinary agitation in his face.

'Alyosha,' he whispered, cautiously, 'where's Ivan?'

'He's gone out into the yard. He's got a headache. He's keeping watch over us.'

'Hand me the looking-glass. It's over there. Give it me!'

Alyosha handed him a little, round, folding looking-glass which stood on the chest of drawers. The old man examined his face in it: his nose was rather badly swollen and there was a purple bruise on his forehead over the left eyebrow.

'What does Ivan say? Alyosha, my dear, my only son, I'm afraid of Ivan. I'm more afraid of Ivan than of the other. You're the only one I'm not afraid of.'

'Don't be afraid of Ivan, either. Ivan's angry, but he'll protect you.'

'Alyosha, and what about the other? He's run off to Grushenka! My dear boy, tell me the truth: was Grushenka here just now or not?'

'No one has seen her. It's not true. She wasn't here.'

'You know, Mitya wants to marry her – he wants to marry her!'

'She won't marry him.'

'She won't, she won't, she won't, she won't, she won't marry him for anything in the world!' the old man cried, starting with joy, as though nothing more comforting could have been said to him at that moment.

In his delight he seized Alyosha's hand and pressed it firmly to his heart. Even tears glistened in his eyes.

'Take your mother's icon of the Virgin – the one I was telling you about – take it home with you. And I'll let you go back to the monastery. . . . I was joking this morning – don't be angry with me. My head aches, Alyosha. . . . Alyosha, comfort me, be a good boy, and tell me the truth.'

'Are you still harping on the same thing?' Alyosha said sorrowfully. 'Has she been here or not?'

'No, no, no, I believe you. What I want you to do is this: go to Grushenka yourself or try to see her. Find out from her as quickly as possible and find out for yourself which one of us she will have, me or him? Eh? What? Can you do it or not?'

'If I see her, I'll ask her,' Alyosha murmured, looking embarrassed.

'No, she won't tell you,' the old man interrupted. 'She's a flirt. She'll start kissing you and say that it's you she wants. She's a cheat, she's a shameless slut – no, you mustn't go to her, you mustn't!'

'And it wouldn't be nice, father. It wouldn't be nice at all.'

'Where was he sending you just now when he shouted "Go there!" as he ran out of the house?'

'To Katerina.'

'For money? To ask her for money?'

'No, not for money.'

'He has no money. Not a penny. Listen, Alyosha. I'll stay in bed tonight and think things over, and you can go now. Perhaps you will meet her. Only be sure to come and see me tomorrow morning. Be sure to. I'll tell you something important tomorrow. Will you come?'

'I will.'

'When you come, pretend to have come of your own accord to

see how I am. Don't tell anyone I asked you to come. Not a word of it to Ivan.'

'All right.'

'Good-bye, my boy. You stood up for me just now. I shall never forget that. I'll tell you something tomorrow – only I have to think it over first.'

'And how do you feel now?'

'Tomorrow, tomorrow I'll get up and go out. I'm very well, very well, very well.'

As he crossed the yard, Alyosha saw his brother Ivan sitting on a bench by the gate: he was writing something in pencil in his note-book. Alyosha told Ivan that the old man was awake and conscious, and had let him go back to spend the night in the monastery.

'Alyosha, I'd very much like to meet you tomorrow morning,' Ivan said affably, getting up from the bench.

His affability took Alyosha completely by surprise.

'I shall be at the Khokhlakovs' tomorrow,' replied Alyosha. 'I may be at Katerina's tomorrow, too, if I don't find her in now.'

'So you *are* going to Katerina's now? To "bid her a last farewell"?' Ivan suddenly smiled.

Alyosha looked embarrassed.

'I think I understood everything from his exclamations a short while ago and something of what went on before. Dmitry, I suppose, has asked you to go and see her and tell her that he – well, in short – that "he bids her a last farewell"?'

'Tell me, Ivan, what will be the outcome of this horrible situation between father and Dmitry?' Alyosha cried.

'It's impossible to say for certain. Perhaps nothing will come of it: the whole thing will just peter out. That woman is a wild animal. In any case, the old man must be kept at home and Dmitry must not be let in.'

'I'd like to ask you one more thing, Ivan: has any man a right to decide who deserves to live and who doesn't?'

'Why try to decide who deserves to live and who doesn't? This question is more often decided in men's hearts not on the basis of whether a man deserves to live or not, but on quite different grounds, on much more natural grounds, I would say. As for the right to decide – who hasn't the right to wish?'

'Not, surely, the death of another man?'

'Why not even the death of another man? Why lie to yourself when all people live like that and perhaps cannot live otherwise. Are you referring to what I said just now about two reptiles devouring each other? Let me ask you in that case: do you consider me capable, like Dmitry, of shedding the blood of that crazy fool, I mean, killing him?'

'What are you saying, Ivan? The idea never entered my head! I don't think even Dmitry —'

'Well, thanks for that, anyway,' Ivan smiled. 'I'd like you to know that I'll always protect him. But as for my wishes in this case, I reserve for myself the right to think as I please. Good-bye till to-morrow. Don't condemn me and don't look upon me as a criminal,' he added with a smile.

They shook hands warmly, as never before. Alyosha felt that his brother had taken the first step towards him and that he did so most certainly with some kind of intention.

10

Both Together

ALYOSHA left his father's house feeling more depressed and crushed in spirit than when he entered it. His thoughts, too, seemed disjointed and scattered so that he could not help feeling that he was afraid to piece them together and form a general idea from all the agonizing contradictions he had experienced that day. He was almost on the verge of despair, something which had never happened to him before. Over everything towered like a mountain the main fatal and insoluble question: what would be the end of the affair between his father and his brother Dmitry and that terrible woman? Now he had been a witness. He had been there himself and he had seen them facing each other. However, it was only his brother Dmitry who could be made unhappy, terribly unhappy: he was certainly in for some trouble. There were also apparently other people who were concerned in all this and perhaps more than Alyosha first imagined. Indeed, there seemed to be something mysterious about it all. Ivan had taken a step towards him, which Alyosha had long been wishing for. But for some unknown reason he now felt that he was frightened by this step towards a closer understanding between them. And those women? It was certainly strange: only a few hours before he had felt greatly embarrassed when he set out to visit Katerina, but now he felt no embarrassment at all; on the contrary, he was hurrying, as though expecting to find some solution to his problems at her place. And yet it was evidently more difficult now to give her his brother's message than before: the matter of the three thousand roubles was finally decided, and nothing, of course, would stop Dmitry now that he felt himself dishonoured and without hope, however great his downfall. He had, besides, asked him to describe the scene at his father's to Katerina.

It was already seven o'clock and it was getting dark when Alyosha entered the very spacious and comfortable house Katerina occupied in the High Street. Alyosha knew that she lived with two aunts. One of them, however, was only the aunt of her half-sister Agafya, the taciturn old lady who looked after the two sisters in their father's house after Katerina had returned from her boarding-school. The other aunt was a grand Moscow society woman, though in reduced circumstances. It was rumoured that both of them did everything Katerina told them and that she kept them merely as chaperons. Katerina herself did only what she was told by her benefactress, the general's widow, who had stayed in Moscow because of illness and to whom she had to write two letters a week with a full account of herself.

When Alyosha entered the hall and asked the parlour maid, who had opened the door, to announce him, the ladies in the drawing-room evidently already knew of his arrival (perhaps they had noticed him from the window), for he suddenly heard a noise, the sound of running footsteps and the rustle of skirts: two or three women, perhaps, had run out of the room. Alyosha thought it strange that he should have created such a commotion by his arrival. He was immediately shown into the drawing-room, however. It was a large room, elegantly and substantially furnished, not at all in provincial style. There were many sofas and settees, little ottomans, big and little tables; there were pictures on the walls, lamps and vases on the tables, there were lots of flowers, and there was even an aquarium by the window. Because of the twilight it was a little dark in the room. Alyosha noticed a silk shawl thrown down on a sofa, where people had evidently just been sitting, and on a table in front of the sofa were two unfinished cups of chocolate, cakes, a porcelain saucer with blue raisins, and another with sweets. Someone was being entertained. Alyosha guessed that he had interrupted visitors and frowned. But at that moment the curtain over a door was raised and Katerina came in with quick, hurrying footsteps and held out her hands to Alyosha with a joyful and rapturous smile. At the same moment a maid brought in two lighted candles and put them on a table.

'Thank God, at last you've come too! I've been simply praying to God for you to come all day! Sit down, please.'

Alyosha had been struck by Katerina's beauty even before, when Dmitry, three weeks earlier, had brought him, at Katerina's special request, for the first time to be introduced to her. During that meeting, however, they had not talked a great deal. Thinking that Alyosha was very shy, Katerina seemed anxious to spare him and had talked all the time to Dmitry. Alyosha had been silent, but he had seen through a great deal. He had been struck by the imperiousness, the proud casualness and self-assurance of the haughty girl. And his suspicion was confirmed. Alyosha felt that he had not been exaggerating. He thought her large glowing black eyes were very beautiful and suited her pale, even yellowish pale, elongated face. But there was something about those eyes and even about the lines of her exquisite lips with which his brother might well have fallen passionately in love, but which perhaps one could not love for long. He nearly expressed this thought frankly to Dmitry, when, after the visit, his brother implored him persistently not to conceal his impressions after seeing his fiancée.

'You will be happy with her, but perhaps not – serenely happy.'

'There you are, old man! Such women always remain the same. They never give in to fate. So you don't think that I shall love her for ever?'

'I don't know. Perhaps you will, but perhaps you won't be always happy with her. . . .'

Alyosha had given his opinion at the time, blushing and vexed with himself for having given in to his brother's entreaties and expressed such 'stupid' ideas. For his opinion had seemed awfully stupid to him the moment he had put it into words. Besides, he felt ashamed to express an opinion about a woman in such emphatic terms. He was even more surprised now, at the first glance at Katerina as she ran into the room, that he should feel that perhaps he had been entirely mistaken. This time her face shone with unaffected, good-natured kindliness, and genuine and fervent sincerity. Of all her former 'pride and haughtiness', which had struck him so forcibly at their first meeting, he was now aware only of her brave and generous energy and of a sort of serene and strong faith in herself. Alyosha realized at the first glance at her, from the first words she uttered, that the whole tragedy of her position in regard to the man she loved so much was no secret to her and that she probably knew everything, absolutely everything. And yet, in spite of that, there was so much brightness in her face and so much faith in the future that Alyosha suddenly felt that in some grave and premeditated way he had wronged her. He was conquered and won over at once. Besides all this, he noticed at her first words that she was in a state of great excitement, which was perhaps quite exceptional in her – an excitement that was almost indistinguishable from ecstasy.

'I was so anxious to see you because I can learn the whole truth only from you – from you and no one else!'

'I've come — ' Alyosha murmured, stammering, 'I've – he sent me. . . .'

'Oh, he sent you! I had a feeling he would! Now I know everything, everything!' exclaimed Katerina with suddenly flashing eyes. 'Wait a moment, I'd better tell you first why I wanted to see you so much. You see, I know perhaps much more than you do yourself. It is not news I'd like you to tell me. All I want you to tell me is this: I want to know your own, personal, last impression of him. All I want is that you should tell me frankly, simply and even coarsely (oh, as coarsely as you like!), what is your opinion of him and of his condition after your meeting with him today. That would be much better perhaps than if I, whom he doesn't want to see any more, had a personal explanation from him. Do you understand what I want from you? Now tell me plainly what was his message to me (I knew that he would send you to me!). Tell me every word of his message, please!'

'He asked me to say – good-bye to you and that he would never come again – but first to say good-bye.'

'Say good-bye? Was that how he put it?'

'Yes.'

'Perhaps he accidentally made a mistake in the word? Perhaps he did not use the right word?'

'No, he asked me most definitely to give this message – "to say good-bye". He asked me three times not to forget to tell you that.'

Katerina flushed.

'Please, help me now, Alexey. It is now that I require your help most. I'll tell you what I think, and you must tell me simply whether I'm right or not. Listen, please: if he had told you to say good-bye to me unreflectingly, without insisting on your repeating the exact words, without emphasizing them, then that would be the end – the end of everything! But if he particularly insisted on those words, if he asked you specially not to forget to say his good-bye to me – then he must have been in a state of excitement, perhaps beside himself. He had made his decision and was terrified of it! He was not walking away from me with a determined step, but taking a headlong leap. The emphasis on that word may have been simply bravado.'

'Yes, yes!' Alyosha agreed warmly. 'I think so myself now.'

'And if that is so, he is not lost yet! He's merely in despair and I can still save him. Wait, though. He didn't by any chance tell you anything about money – about three thousand roubles?'

'Why, of course he did, and that perhaps more than anything is making him so unhappy. He said that he had lost his honour and that he did not care what happened to him now,' Alyosha replied warmly, feeling with all his heart the dawn of a new hope and that there might really be a way of escape and salvation for his brother. 'But do you know about – that money?' he added and suddenly stopped short.

'I've known about it a long time – and I know all the particulars. I telegraphed to Moscow and I've known for some time that the money had not arrived. He hadn't sent the money, but I said nothing. Last week I found out how much he needed the money and that he still needed it. There's only one thing I want: that he should know to whom to turn and that I'm his true friend. But he doesn't want to believe that I'm his true friend. He doesn't want to know me. He looks upon me only as a woman. I've been terribly worried all this week. I wondered what I could do so that he shouldn't be ashamed before me for having spent that three thousand. What I mean is, let him be ashamed before everyone and before himself, but don't let him be ashamed before me. He tells everything to God without being ashamed, doesn't he? Why, then, doesn't he yet realize how much I'm ready to bear for his sake? Why, why doesn't he know me? How did he dare not to know me after all that has happened? I want to save him for ever. Let him forget that I'm his fiancée! And now he fears me because his honour is at stake! He was not afraid to be frank with you, was he? Why then haven't I yet deserved to be treated in the same way?'

The last words she uttered in tears: tears gushed from her eyes.

'I must tell you,' said Alyosha, too, in a trembling voice, 'what happened just now between him and my father.'

And he described the whole scene to her, told her that he had been sent for the money, that Dmitry had burst into the room, had assaulted his father, and after that had begged him specially and earnestly to go and bid her 'good-bye'. . . .

'He's gone to that woman,' Alyosha added softly.

'And do you think I won't put up with that woman? Does he think I won't? But he won't marry her,' she went on, suddenly laughing nervously. 'Could a Karamazov burn with such a passion for ever? It is passion, not love. He won't marry her because she won't marry him.'

Again Katerina suddenly smiled strangely.

'He may marry her,' said Alyosha mournfully, dropping his eyes.

'He won't marry her, I'm telling you! This girl is an angel – do you know that? Do you know that?' Katerina exclaimed suddenly with extraordinary warmth. 'She's one of the most fantastic of fantastic creatures! I know how fascinating she is, but I also know how good, how firm and noble she is. What are you looking at me like that for? Are you perhaps surprised at my words? Don't you believe me? Grushenka, my angel,' she shouted suddenly to someone, peeping into the next room, 'please come in. This is a very nice man. This is Alyosha. He knows all about our affairs. Come and meet him!'

'I've only been waiting behind the curtain for you to call me,' said a gentle, one might almost say, a sugary, feminine voice.

The curtain parted and – Grushenka herself, laughing and looking very pleased, walked up to the table. Something seemed to turn over in Alyosha. His eyes were riveted upon her and he could not take them off her. So there she was, that terrible woman, the 'wild animal', as Ivan had angrily called her half an hour before. And to look at her it would seem that a most ordinary and simple human being was standing before him – a nice, kind woman, beautiful, to be sure, but how like all other beautiful but 'ordinary' women! It was true that she was very, very good-looking indeed, a typical Russian beauty so passionately loved by many men. She was a rather tall woman, though a little shorter than Katerina, who was exceptionally tall – plump, with soft, almost inaudible movements of the body, which also seemed so delicate as to be, somehow, specially sugary, like her voice. She went up to him not as Katerina had done with a vigorous, bold step, but, on the contrary, noiselessly. Her feet made absolutely no sound on the floor. She sank softly into an arm-chair, with a soft rustle of her gorgeous black silk dress, delicately wrapping an expensive black woollen shawl round her plump, milk-white neck and ample shoulders. She was twenty-two years old and she looked exactly her age. Her face was very pale, with a pale pink tint on her cheekbones. The outline of her face seemed rather broad and her lower jaw even protruded a trifle. Her upper lip was thin, her slightly prominent lower lip was twice as full, just as though it were a little swollen. But her magnificent, abundant dark brown hair, her dark sable-like eyebrows, and her exquisite grey-blue eyes with long eye-lashes would have made the most indifferent and absent-minded person, meeting her in a crowd, on a promenade, in a crush, stop dead suddenly at the sight of her face and remember it long after. Alyosha was most of all struck by the childish, good-natured expression of her face. She had the look of a child, she expressed her delight like a child, she came up to the table 'looking delighted' and as though expecting something to happen immediately with childish, impatient and confiding curiosity. Her expression gladdened the heart – Alyosha felt that. There was something else about her, which he could not and would not know how to describe – but which he, too, must have been aware of unconsciously – that was again her soft-ness, the delicacy of her movements, the cat-like noiselessness of those movements. And yet hers was a powerful and ample body. Under her shawl could be discerned full, broad shoulders and a high, still girlish bosom. Her figure gave promise of becoming in form a Venus de Milo, but already in somewhat exaggerated proportions – one could see that. Looking at Grushenka, connoisseurs of Russian female beauty could have foretold unmistakably that this fresh, still youthful beauty would lose its harmony by the age of thirty, would spread, that her face would become puffy, that wrinkles would very rapidly appear round the eyes and on the forehead, that her complexion would grow coarse and red perhaps – in short, it was an ephemeral beauty, a beauty that does not last, which one meets so often among Russian women. Alyosha did not, of course, think of this, but though fascinated, he could not help asking himself with a sort of unpleasant feeling and as though with regret why she drawled like that and why she could not speak naturally. She did so evidently because she thought this dragging out of the words and the exaggerated and sugary modulation of syllables and sounds was attractive. That was, of course, a bad, ill-bred habit that showed bad education and a vulgar understanding, instilled in childhood, of what constitutes good manners. And yet this enunciation and intonation of words struck Alyosha as almost incredibly incongruous with the childishly ingenuous and gay expression of her face and with the soft, childishly happy radiance of her eyes. Katerina at once made her sit down in an arm-chair opposite Alyosha and kissed her rapturously a few times on her laughing lips. She seemed to be in love with her.

'This is the first time we've met,' she said to Alyosha ecstatically. 'I wanted to know her, to see her. I wanted to go to her, but no sooner had I expressed the wish to see her than she came to me. I knew we should settle everything, absolutely everything. I felt it in my heart. . . . They begged me not to take this step, but I felt that it would turn out for the best and I was not mistaken. Grushenka has explained everything to me. She has told me all her plans. She flew down here like a good angel and brought peace and joy with her. . . .'

'You were not too proud to see me, my sweet, good young lady, were you?' Grushenka drawled in her sing-song voice and with the same charming, happy smile.

'You mustn't speak to me like that, my enchantress! Too proud to see you, indeed! Let me kiss your sweet lower lip again. It looks as if it were a little swollen, well, let it be a little more swollen, and more, and more. ... Look how she laughs, Alexey. It does one's heart good to see such an angel. ...'

Alyosha blushed and a faint, imperceptible shiver kept running down his spine.

'You're so sweet to me, my dear young lady, but perhaps I don't deserve your kisses.'

'Don't deserve them! She doesn't deserve them!' Katerina cried again with the same warmth. 'Do you know, Alexey, we've got such a fantastic little head and such a wilful and proud little heart! We're noble, we're generous – you didn't know that, did you? We've only been unfortunate. We were too ready to make every sacrifice for a man who was perhaps unworthy or fickle. There was one such man, only one, also an army officer. We fell in love with him, we sacrificed everything for him – it was a long time ago, five years ago, and he has forgotten us, he has married. Now he's a widower, he has written, he's coming here – and, please, don't forget it's him alone we love, no one but him. We've loved him all our life and we love him still. He'll come and Grushenka will be happy again, for she's been so unhappy during the last five years! But who can reproach her? Who can boast of her favours? Why, only one bedridden old man – a merchant, but he was more like a father to us, he was our friend and protector. He found us then in despair, in agony, deserted by the man we loved so much – why, she was about to throw herself into the river at the time and it was that old man who saved her – he saved her!'

'You're so kind to defend me, my dear young lady. You're a little too much in a hurry about everything,' Grushenka drawled again.

'Defend you? Who are we to defend you? And have we a right to defend you? Grushenka, darling, give me your hand. Look at this charming, chubby little hand, Alexey. See it? It has brought me happiness. It has given me a new lease of life, and I'm going to kiss it, inside and outside, here, here, and here!'

And she really did kiss Grushenka's charming and perhaps a little too chubby little hand three times in a kind of rapture. Grushenka held out her hand and watched the 'dear young lady' with her charming, ringing, nervous little laugh, and she was obviously pleased to have her hand kissed like that.

'Perhaps there's a little too much enthusiasm,' it flashed through

Alyosha's mind. He blushed. All the time he felt peculiarly uneasy at heart.

'You make me feel ashamed, my dear young lady, kissing my hand like that before Mr Karamazov.'

'But you don't think I wanted to make you feel ashamed, do you?' said Katerina with some surprise. 'Oh, my dear, how little you know me!'

'But perhaps you don't quite know me, either, my dear young lady. Perhaps I'm much worse than you think. I have a wicked heart. I'm headstrong. I turned poor Dmitry's head that time just for fun.'

'But, then, you're going to save him now, aren't you? You've given me your word. You'll make him see sense. You'll tell him that you love another man, that you've loved him for a long time, a man who is now offering you his hand.'

'Oh, but I never promised you to do that. It was you who kept telling me all that. I never promised you.'

'I must have misunderstood you then,' Katerina said softly, turning a little pale. 'You promised —'

'Oh no, my darling young lady, I've promised you nothing,' Grushenka interrupted her, softly and equably, with the same gay and innocent expression. 'Now you can see at once, my dear young lady, what a bad and wilful woman I am compared with you. If I want to do something, I do it. I may have promised you something a little while ago, but now I can't help thinking: what if I should take a fancy to him again? You see, I did like Mitya very much once – I liked him for almost a whole hour. So perhaps I'll go and tell him now to stay with me from this day.... That's how inconstant I am....'

'Just now you said – you said something quite different...' Katerina whispered faintly.

'Oh, just now! You see, I'm so tender-hearted. I'm so silly. To think what he's gone through because of me! What if I should suddenly feel sorry for him when I come home – what then?'

'I never expected —'

'Oh, my dear young lady, how good and noble you are compared with me. I daresay you'll hate a silly creature like me now that you know what I'm really like. Please, give me your hand, darling young lady,' she said tenderly, and she took Katerina's hand with a kind of reverence. 'You see, my dear young lady, I'm taking your hand and I'm going to kiss it as you did mine. You've kissed mine three times, and I really ought to kiss yours three hundred times for us to be quits. Very well, I'll do it, and then let it be as God thinks fit. Perhaps I shall be your obedient slave and do my best to please you like a slave. As God thinks fit, so let it be, without any agreements and promises. What a lovely little hand you have, my dear, beautiful young lady!'

She slowly raised Katerina's hand to her lips, with the strange intention, it is true, 'to be quits' with her in kisses. Katerina did not take her hand away: she listened with timid hope to Grushenka's rather strangely expressed promise to please her 'like a slave'. She looked tensely into her eyes: in those eyes she still saw the same good-natured, confiding expression, the same serene gaiety. 'She's perhaps a little too naïve,' thought Katerina with a glimmer of hope in her heart. Meanwhile Grushenka, as though enraptured by 'the sweet hand', kept raising it slowly to her lips. But having raised it to her lips, she suddenly held it there for two or three seconds as though considering something.

'Do you know what, my sweet young lady?' she drawled suddenly in her soft and most sugary little voice, 'Do you know what? I don't think I'm going to kiss your hand after all.'

And she laughed her gay little laugh.

'As you please. . . . What's the matter with you?' asked Katerina with a sudden start.

'You see, I want you to remember always that you kissed my hand, but I didn't kiss yours.'

There was a sudden flash in her eyes. She was looking with terrible intensity at Katerina.

'You insolent creature!' Katerina cried all of a sudden and, as though suddenly realizing something, she flushed all over and jumped up from her seat. Grushenka, too, got up, but without haste.

'So I shall tell Mitya how you kissed my hand and I didn't kiss yours at all. And how he'll laugh!'

'You dirty slut! Get out!'

'What language, my dear young lady, what language! Really, you ought to be ashamed of yourself! A young lady like you didn't ought to have used such language!'

'Get out, you filthy prostitute!' screamed Katerina. Every muscle was quivering in her terribly distorted face.

'A prostitute, am I? Didn't you used to visit gentlemen in the evening for money yourself? Offered your beauty for sale, didn't you? I know all about it, you see.'

Katerina uttered a shriek and was about to rush at her, but Alyosha held her back with all his strength.

'Not another step! Not a word! Don't speak, don't answer her. She'll go away. She'll go at once.'

At that moment Katerina's two aunts ran into the room, followed by the maid. They all rushed up to her.

'I will go away,' said Grushenka, picking up her shawl from the sofa. 'Alyosha, darling, see me off home, please.'

'Go away, please, go away at once!' Alyosha besought her, clasping his hands together beseechingly before her.

'Darling Alyosha, do see me home! I've got something very, very nice to tell you on the way. I've staged this scene especially for you, Alyosha, dear. See me home, darling. You'll be glad of it afterwards.'

Alyosha turned away, wringing his hands. Grushenka rushed out of the house, laughing loudly.

Katerina had a fit of hysterics. She sobbed and shook with convulsions. They were all fussing round her.

'I warned you,' said the elder of her aunts. 'I tried to prevent you from taking this step. You're too impulsive. How could you do such a thing? You don't know what these creatures are like, and they say she's worse than any of them. You are too headstrong.'

'She's a tigress!' Katerina screamed. 'Why did you hold me back, Alexey? I'd have thrashed her within an inch of her life!'

She was quite incapable of controlling herself before Alyosha, and perhaps she didn't want to.

'She ought to be flogged in public by the hangman on a scaffold!'

Alyosha backed towards the door.

'But, good Lord,' Katerina cried suddenly with a despairing movement of the hands, 'what about him? How could he be so dishonourable, so inhuman? Why, he actually told that horrible creature what happened on that dreadful day, on that hateful, for ever hateful day! "You went there to sell your beauty, my dear young lady!" She knows all about it! Your brother is a cad, Alexey!'

Alyosha wanted to say something, but he couldn't find the right words. His heart contracted painfully.

'Please go, Alexey. I feel so ashamed, so horrid! Come tomorrow – I beg you on my knees, come tomorrow. Don't think badly of me. Please forgive me. I don't know what I'm going to do with myself now!'

Alyosha went out into the street almost staggering. He, too, felt like crying as she did. Suddenly he was overtaken by the maid.

'Miss Katerina forgot to give you this letter from Mrs Khokhlakov, sir. She's had it since dinner.'

Alyosha took the little pink envelope mechanically and almost unconsciously put it into his pocket.

I I

Another Ruined Reputation

IT was not more than a mile from the town to the monastery. Alyosha walked hurriedly along the road, which was deserted at that hour. It was almost night and too difficult to distinguish anything thirty yards ahead. There were cross-roads half-way along the road. At the cross-roads a figure loomed into sight under a solitary willow-tree. As soon as Alyosha reached the cross-roads the figure detached itself rapidly from its place, rushed at him and shouted in a fierce voice:

'Your money or your life!'

'So it's you, Mitya!' cried Alyosha in surprise, violently startled, however.

'Ha, ha, ha! You didn't expect me, did you? I wondered where to wait for you. Near her house? There are three roads leading from there and I would have missed you. At last I decided to wait for you here. You were quite certain to pass here, for there's no other way to the monastery. Well, tell me the truth. Crush me like a cockroach. But what's the matter with you?'

'Oh, nothing, Mitya. You gave me such a fright. Oh, Dmitry, this afternoon father's blood' – Alyosha began to cry, he had been on the verge of tears for a long time, but now something seemed to snap inside him. 'You nearly killed him – you cursed him – and now – here – you're making jokes – your money or your life!'

'Well, what about it? Improper, is it? Doesn't it fit the situation?'

'Why no – I merely —'

'Wait a moment. Look at the night: see what a dark night it is! Look at the clouds! What a wind has risen! I hid here under the willow, waiting for you, and suddenly – God's my witness! – I thought to myself: why go on like this? What am I waiting for? Here's a willow, I have a handkerchief, I have a shirt, I can twist them into a rope in no time, and a pair of braces too, and – no longer burden the earth, no longer dishonour it with my vile presence! And then I heard you coming and – Lord, it was as if something had dawned on me suddenly: so there is a man whom I love – there he is, that dear man, that dear little brother of mine whom I love more than anyone in the world and the only one I love! And I loved you so much, I loved you so much at that moment, that I thought: let me fall on his neck at once! Then a stupid thought struck me: Let me amuse him, let me scare him! And so I shouted like a fool: "Your money!" I'm sorry for my tomfoolery – it was stupid – as for what I really feel – that, too, is quite proper. . . . But to hell with it. Tell me what happened there? What did she say? Crush me, strike me down, don't spare me! Was she furious?'

'No, it wasn't that at all. . . . There was nothing of the kind there. There – I found them both there.'

'Both who?'

'Grushenka was at Katerina's.'

Dmitry was thunderstruck.

'Impossible!' he shouted. 'You're raving! Grushenka at her place?'

Alyosha told him all that had happened to him from the moment he entered Katerina's house. He was describing it for ten minutes. It cannot be said that he did so fluently or coherently, but he went over everything as clearly as possible, recounting the most significant words that had passed between the two young women and their feelings at the time, and describing his own feelings vividly, sometimes by a single characteristic detail. Dmitry listened in silence, staring straight at him with a look of terrible immobility, but it was clear to Alyosha that he had understood everything and had grasped every fact. But his face, as the story went on, became not so much gloomy as menacing. He knit his brows, he clenched his teeth, his immobile stare grew even more immobile, more intent, more terrible. . . . It was therefore all the more surprising when, with indescribable rapidity, his face, till then angry and fierce, suddenly changed, his compressed lips parted, and he burst into the most uncontrolled and unforced laughter. He literally shook with laughter and for a long time he could not speak for laughing.

'So she didn't kiss her hand! So she didn't kiss it! So she ran away!' he kept shouting with a sort of morbid delight, with insolent delight, one might almost have said, if his delight had not been so unaffected. 'So the other one shouted she was a tigress! Well, she is a tigress! So she should be whipped by the public hangman! Yes, yes, so she should, so she should! That's exactly what I think – she should have been – she should have been long ago! You see, old man, I don't mind her being whipped by the public hangman, but not before I get over my infatuation. I quite understand the queen of impudence – that's her all over, she's revealed herself entirely in that hand-kissing episode – the she-devil! She's the queen of all the she-devils that you can imagine in the world! She's delightful in her way! So she ran home? I'm going to – oh – I'll run to her at once! Alyosha, don't blame me. You see, I quite agree that strangling is too good for her!'

'And what about Katerina?'

'I can see her too! I can see through her. I see her as I've never done before! What we have here is a discovery of all the four continents of the world – of the five, I mean! What a thing to do! And that's the same little Katya, the little schoolgirl, who was not afraid to beard an absurd, coarse army officer in his den and risk a mortal insult because of a generous idea to save her father! But her pride, the need for taking the risk, the challenge to fate, the boundless challenge! You say her aunt tried to stop her? That aunt of hers, you know, is a despot herself. She's the sister of the general's widow in Moscow. She used to look down her nose even more than her Moscow sister, but her husband was caught stealing government money, lost everything, his estate and all, and his proud spouse had to get off her high horse and could not mount it again ever after. So she was trying to hold Katya back, but she would not listen to her. She thinks she can conquer everything, that everything must give way to her, that she had only to wish and she could bewitch Grushenka. And who is to blame if she believed so much in herself and was so proud of herself? Do you think she kissed Grushenka's hand first on purpose, with some crafty design of her own? No, she really did fall for Grushenka, or rather not for Grushenka, but for her own fantastic dream, her own crazy scheme, because, you see, it was *her* dream, it was *her* crazy scheme! Poor Alyosha, how did you get away with your life from those two females? Tucked up your cassock and ran, eh? Ha, ha, ha!'

'But, Mitya, you don't seem to have realized how much you've insulted Katerina by telling Grushenka about what happened that day. You see, Grushenka immediately flung it in her face that she had gone "to gentlemen in secret to sell her beauty". Could there be any greater insult than that, Mitya?'

Alyosha was most of all worried by the thought that his brother seemed to be pleased with Katerina's humiliation, though, of course, that could not possibly be true.

'Good Lord!' Dmitry frowned fiercely and clapped his hand to his forehead.

He had only now realized it, though Alyosha had told him about the insult and Katerina's cry: 'Your brother is a cad!'

'Yes, perhaps I did tell Grushenka about that "dreadful day", as Katya called it. Yes, I did. I did tell her. I remember it now! It was at Mokroye. I was drunk, the gispy women were singing. . . . But I was sobbing, I was sobbing then, I was on my knees, praying to Katya's image, and Grushenka understood it. She understood everything then. I remember, she cried herself. . . . Oh, damn! But it couldn't have been otherwise now, could it? Then she cried, but now – now "a dagger in the heart"! It's always like that with women.'

He dropped his eyes and sank into thought.

'Yes, I am a cad! A thorough-going cad!' he said suddenly in a gloomy voice. 'Makes no difference whether I cried or not, I'm still a cad! Tell her I accept the name if that's any consolation. Well, that's enough. Good-bye. What's the use of talking? It's not a particularly cheerful subject, is it? You go your way and I'll go mine. And I don't want to see you again except as a last resource. Good-bye, Alexey!'

He pressed Alyosha's hand warmly, and still looking down and without raising his head, as though tearing himself away, walked off in the direction of the town. Alyosha gazed after him, unable to believe that he had gone off so suddenly.

'Wait, Alexey!' cried Dmitry, suddenly turning back. 'I've another confession to make to you alone. Look at me! Look at me closely: see, here, here – a terrible disgrace is being prepared for me. (As he said 'here', Dmitry smote his chest with his fist and with so strange an expression as though the disgrace was actually lying on his chest, in some place, in a pocket perhaps, or hanging in a sewn-up bag round his neck.) You know me now: I'm a scoundrel, an acknowledged scoundrel! But know that what I may have done before or may do in the future, nothing, nothing can compare in baseness with the disgrace which I am carrying now, at this very moment, here on my breast – here – here, which is about to be carried out, but which I have the power to stop – I can stop it or I can carry it out, make a note of that! Well, then, I want you to know that I shall carry it out, that I shan't stop it. I told you everything just now, but I didn't tell you that because even I am not brazen enough to do so! I can still stop myself; if I do I can retrieve half of my lost honour tomorrow. But I won't do it. I shall carry out my despicable plan, and you can be a witness that I told you so beforehand and that I'm fully aware of what I'm doing! Death and perdition! No need to explain. You'll find it out in your own good time. The stinking back-alley and the she-devil! Good-bye. Don't pray for me. I don't deserve it. And, besides, it's unnecessary. It's quite unnecessary – I don't need it. Away! ...'

And he was suddenly gone, this time for good. Alyosha went towards the monastery. 'What does he mean by saying that I shall never see him again? What is he talking about?' The whole thing seemed utterly absurd to him. 'I shall most certainly go and see him tomorrow. I'll find him. I shall make a point of finding him. What is he talking about? ...'

*

He walked round the monastery and went straight to the hermitage through the pine-wood. The gate was opened to him, though at that hour no one was admitted. His heart trembled when he entered the elder's cell: Why, why had he gone out? Why had the elder sent him into the world? Here was peace. Here was holiness, and there was confusion, there was darkness in which one went astray at once and lost one's way.

In the cell he found the novice Porfiry and Father Paissy, who came every hour to inquire after Father Zossima, whose condition, Alyosha learnt with consternation, was getting worse and worse. This time he could not even hold his usual evening discourse with the monks. As a rule, the monks gathered in the elder's cell before retiring to bed every evening after service, and everyone confessed aloud his sins of the day, his sinful dreams, thoughts, temptations, and even the quarrels among themselves, if there had been any. Some of them confessed kneeling. The elder settled their difficulties, reconciled, exhorted, imposed penance, gave his blessing and dismissed them. It was against these 'confessions' that the opponents of the institution of elders protested, claiming that it was a profanation of the confession as a sacrament and almost a sacrilege, though it was not so. They even represented to the diocesan authorities that far from attaining a good end, such confessions actually and deliberately led to sin and temptation. It was asserted that many monks were loath to go to the elder, but went against their own will because everyone went, afraid lest they should be accused of pride and a rebellious spirit. It was said that, before going to the evening confession, some monks agreed beforehand what to say: 'I'll say that I lost my temper with you in the morning, and you confirm it', so that they would have something to say in order to get it over and done with. Alyosha knew that it really did happen sometimes. He also knew that there were monks who deeply resented the fact that, according to custom, they had first to bring their letters from home to the elder to be opened and read by him before they themselves could do so. The idea was, of course, that all this should be done freely and sincerely and without the slightest reservation, for the sake of voluntary submission and salutary guidance, but actually the whole thing sometimes turned out to be highly insincere, false, and affected. But the older and more experienced monks stood their ground, arguing that those who had come within those walls in order to obtain salvation would most certainly find all these acts of obedience and self-denial salutary and of great benefit; those, however, who protested and found it too hard to comply were no true monks, anyway, and their proper place was not in a monastery but in the world. 'One cannot protect oneself from sin and the devil neither in the world nor in church, so that there is no need to encourage sin.'

'He's grown much weaker, a drowsiness has come over him,' Paissy told Alyosha in a whisper after blessing him. 'It's difficult to rouse him. But there's no need to wake him. He was awake for five minutes, asked to send his blessing to the monks and requested the monks to say prayers for him at night. He intends to take the sacrament again in the morning. He remembered you, Alexey, and asked whether you had gone away. He was told you were in town. "That was what I blessed him for. His place is there and not here for the time being" – that was what he said about you. He remembered you lovingly, with anxiety – do you realize how greatly you've been favoured? But why did he decide that you should spend some time in the world? He must have foreseen something in your destiny! Understand, Alexey, that if you return to the world it will be to fulfil the duty imposed upon you by the elder and not for vain frivolities and worldly pleasures.'

Father Paissy went out. That the elder was dying, Alyosha did not doubt, though he might live for another day or two. Alyosha firmly and ardently resolved not to leave the monastery next day, but to remain with the elder to the end in spite of the promises he had given to his father, the Khokhlakovs, his brother, and Katerina. His heart was ablaze with love and he reproached himself bitterly for having been able to forget in town for one moment him whom he had left in the monastery on his death-bed and whom he revered more than anyone in the world. He went into the elder's little bedroom, knelt down and bowed to the ground before the sleeping old man. Father Zossima slept quietly, without stirring, breathing regularly and almost imperceptibly. His face was peaceful.

On returning to the other room, where the elder had received his guests in the morning, Alyosha, without undressing and only taking off his shoes, lay down on the hard and narrow leather sofa, on which he had always slept, every night, for a long time, bringing only a pillow. The mattress, about which his father had shouted in the morning, he had long forgotten to put under him. He merely took off his cassock and used it for a blanket. But before going to bed, he fell on his knees and prayed a long time. In his fervent prayer he did not ask God to clear up his confusion, but only craved the joyous emotion, the emotion that always came over his soul after praising and glorifying God, of which his prayer before bedtime always consisted. The joy that came over him always brought him a light and peaceful sleep. While saying his prayers now, he accidentally felt in his pocket the little pink note which Katerina's maid had handed him in the street. He was troubled, but he finished his prayer. Then after a moment's hesitation he opened the envelope. It contained a letter for him signed by Lise, Mrs Khokhlakov's young daughter, who had laughed at him in the morning in the presence of the elder.

'Dear Alexey,' she wrote, 'I am writing to you unknown to everybody, even Mother, and I know how wrong it is. But I can't live without telling you what has arisen in my heart, and this no one but us two must know for the time being. But how can I tell you what I want so much to tell you? Paper, they say, does not blush, but I can assure you that it is not true and that it is blushing now just as I am blushing now all over. Dear Alyosha, I love you. I have loved you ever since I was a little girl, since Moscow, where you were not at all as you are now, and I will love you all my life. I have chosen you with my heart, to unite with you, and to end our life together in old age. Of course, on condition that you leave the monastery. As for our age, we shall wait, as long as the law prescribes. By that time I shall certainly be well and be able to walk and dance. There can be no doubt about that.

'You see how I've thought it all out. But there is one thing I can't imagine: what you will think of me when you read this? I am always laughing and being naughty. I made you angry this morning, but I assure you that just now before I took up the pen, I prayed before the icon of the Virgin, and even now I am praying and almost crying.

'My secret is in your hands. When you come to see us tomorrow, I don't know how I shall be able to look you in the face. Oh, dear Alexey, what if I shan't be able to control myself again and burst out laughing, like a silly girl, as I did this morning when I looked at you? I'm afraid you will think me a bad girl who is only making fun of you and you won't believe my letter. And that's why I implore you, my dearest, if you have any pity for me, not to look me straight in the face when you come tomorrow, because when my eyes meet yours, I may burst out laughing, and especially as you'll be wearing your long cassock.... Even now I turn cold all over when I think of it. So that when you come in, don't look at me at all for some time, but look at Mummy or at the window....

'There, I've written you a love letter. My goodness, what have I done? Alyosha, don't despise me, and please forgive me if I've done something very bad and annoyed you. Now the secret of my reputation, which has probably been ruined for ever, is in your hands.

'I'm sure I'm going to cry today. Good-bye for now, till our *terrifying* meeting. Lise.

'P.S. Alyosha, you must, must, must come! Lise.'

Alyosha read the note in amazement, read it through twice, thought it over, and then suddenly burst into a soft, sweet laugh. He gave a start: his laugh seemed sinful to him. But a moment later he laughed again just as softly and happily. He slowly replaced the note in the envelope, crossed himself and lay down. The perturbation of his spirit suddenly passed. 'God have mercy upon all of them, save and preserve them, the unhappy and rebellious in spirit, and set them on the right path. All the ways are thine: save them according to thy ways. Thou art Love, thou wilt send joy to all!' Alyosha murmured, crossing himself and sinking into tranquil sleep.

PART TWO

BOOK FOUR: HEARTACHES

I

Father Ferapont

ALYOSHA WAS ROUSED EARLY IN THE MORNING BEFORE DAWN. The elder woke up feeling very weak, though he wished to get out of bed and sit up in an armchair. He was in full possession of his faculties; his face, though it looked very tired, was bright, almost joyous, and there was a cheerful, cordial, welcoming look in his eyes. 'Perhaps I shall not live through this day,' he said to Alyosha; then he expressed the wish to confess and take the sacrament at once. His confessor had always been Father Paissy. After the communion came the ministering of extreme unction. The senior monks assembled and the cell gradually filled up with the lesser monks of the hermitage. Meantime it was daylight. Monks began arriving also from the monastery. When the service was over, the elder wished to take leave of everyone and he kissed them all. The cell being so crowded, those who had come first went out and made room for others. Alyosha stood beside the elder who was again seated in his armchair. He spoke and taught as much as he could. Though weak, his voice was still fairly firm. 'I have been teaching you for so many years, beloved Fathers and brethren, and I've been talking aloud for so many years that I seem to have acquired the habit of talking and teaching you while I talk, so much so, indeed, dear Fathers and brethren, that it's almost harder for me to keep silent than to talk, in spite of my weakness,' he joked, gazing with deep emotion at those who crowded round him. Alyosha remembered afterwards something of what he said at that time. But though he spoke distinctly and though his voice was sufficiently firm, his speech was rather incoherent. He spoke of many things and he seemed to be anxious before the moment of death to say everything he had had no time to say in his life, and not merely for the sake of instructing them, but as though craving to share his joy and rapture with all men and all creation and pour forth his heart once more while he yet lived. . . .

'Love one another, Fathers,' the elder taught (as far as Alyosha could remember afterwards). 'Love God's people. We are not holier than the laymen because we have come here and shut ourselves up within these walls, but, on the contrary, everyone who has come here has by the very fact of his coming here acknowledged that he is worse than all the worldly and than all men and all things on earth. . . . And the longer the monk lives within the walls of his monastery, the more deeply must he be conscious of that. For otherwise he would have had no reason for coming here at all. But when he realizes that he is not only worse than all the worldly, but that he's responsible to all men for all people and all things, for all human sins, universal and individual – only then will the aim of our seclusion be achieved. For you must know, beloved, that each one of us is beyond all question responsible for all men and all things on earth, not only because of the general transgressions of the world, but each one individually for all men and every single man on this earth. This realization is the crown of a monk's way of life, and, indeed, of every man on earth. For a monk is not a different kind of man, but merely such as all men on earth ought to be. It is only then that our hearts will be moved to a love that is infinite and universal and that knows no surfeit. It is then that each of you will have the power to gain the world by love and wash away the sins of the world by his tears. . . . Each of you must keep constant watch over your heart and confess your sins to yourselves unceasingly. Be not afraid of your sins, even when you perceive them, provided there is penitence, but make no conditions with God. And I say to you especially – be not proud. Be not proud before the small, and be not proud before the great. Hate not those who reject you, who defame you, who abuse and slander you. Hate not atheists, the teachers of evil, materialists, even the most wicked of them, let alone the good ones, for there are many good ones among them, particularly in our own day. Remember them in your prayers thus: Save, O Lord, all who have no one to pray for them, and save those, too, who do not want to pray to thee. And add: It is not in my pride that I beseech thee, O Lord, for that, for I am myself viler than all men and all things. . . . Love God's people, let not strangers drive off your flock, for if you fall asleep in your sloth and censorious pride, and, worse still, in covetousness, they will come from all countries and will drive off your flock. Expound the Gospel to the people unceasingly. . . . Be not usurious. . . . Do not love silver and gold, do not hoard it. . . . Have faith and hold fast the banner. Raise it on high. . . .'

The elder, however, spoke much more disjointedly than it is stated here or than Alyosha wrote down his words afterwards. Sometimes he broke off altogether, as though husbanding his strength, his breath failing him, but he seemed to be in a kind of ecstasy. They heard him with emotion, though many wondered at his words and found them obscure. . . . Afterwards they all remembered his words. When Alyosha happened to leave the cell for a moment, he was surprised by the general excitement and the air of expectation in the crowd of monks in and near the cell. Some of them looked almost anxious and others solemn. They were all expecting some miracle to happen immediately after the elder's death. This expectation was, from one point of view, almost frivolous, but even the most austere of the monks were affected by it. Father Paissy's face was the sternest of all. Alyosha had left the cell only because he had been mysteriously summoned through a monk by Rakitin who had arrived from town with a strange letter from Mrs Khokhlakov. The letter contained a very curious and opportune piece of news. It concerned the old woman of our town, a sergeant's widow, called Prokhorovna, who the day before had come with the other devout women of the people to receive the elder's blessing. She had asked the elder whether she might order prayers for the soul of her son Vassya, who had been stationed far away in Siberia, in Irkutsk, and from whom she had had no news for over a year. But the elder had told her sternly that she must not do anything of the sort, calling such a prayer a kind of sorcery. But he then forgave her on account of her ignorance, adding 'as though reading the book of the future' (as Mrs Khokhlakov put it in her letter), in consolation that 'her son Vassya was most certainly alive, and would either come himself very shortly or write to her and that she was to go home and wait there'. 'And what do you think?' Mrs Khokhlakov added ecstatically, 'the prophecy has been fulfilled, indeed more than fulfilled.' Immediately on her return home, the old woman was handed a letter from Siberia which had been waiting for her. But that was not all: in his letter, written on the road from Yekaterinburg, Vassya informed his mother that he was returning to Russia with an official and that three weeks after the receipt of the letter he hoped 'to embrace' his mother. Mrs Khokhlakov begged Alyosha urgently and warmly to report this newly performed 'miracle of prediction' to the Father Superior and the monks: 'Everyone, everyone ought to know of it!' she exclaimed at the conclusion of her letter. Her letter had been written in great haste, and the excitement of the writer could be perceived in every line of it. But Alyosha had no longer anything to tell the monks, for all of them knew already: Rakitin, having sent the monk to Alyosha, had also commissioned him 'to inform most respectfully his reverence Father Paissy, that he, Rakitin, had something of such great importance to tell him, that he dared not put it off for a single moment and begged him humbly to forgive him for his presumption'. As the monk had told Father Paissy of Rakitin's request before he saw Alyosha, there remained nothing for Alyosha to do after reading the letter but to hand it to Father Paissy merely as a further written confirmation of the 'miracle'. And even that stern and mistrustful man, though he frowned as he read of 'the miracle', could not wholly restrain a certain inward emotion. His eyes flashed and a grave and rapt smile suddenly appeared on his lips.

'Who knows?' it seemed to escape him suddenly. 'We may see greater things yet!'

'We may see greater things yet!' the monks kept repeating around.

But Father Paissy, frowning again, asked them all not to speak of it to anyone 'till it be more fully confirmed, for there is a great deal of thoughtlessness among the worldly and, besides, the whole thing might have occurred naturally,' he added cautiously, as if to salve his conscience, but scarcely believing his own mental reservation, which his listeners very clearly perceived. The 'miracle', of course, became known immediately to the whole monastery and to many people from outside who had come for mass. But it would seem that the man who was most struck by the miracle was the visiting little monk from 'Saint Sylvester', the small monastery of Obdorsk in the far North. He had come to pay his respects to the elder the day before, and it was he who, standing beside Mrs Khokhlakov and pointing to the 'cured' daughter of that lady, asked Father Zossima with much feeling, 'How do you presume to do such things?'

As a matter of fact, he was now somewhat bewildered and almost did not know what to believe. The evening before, he had paid a visit to Father Ferapont in his cell in the hermitage, standing apart behind the apiary, and had been greatly struck by that meeting which had made quite an extraordinary and terrifying impression on him. This Father Ferapont was the aged monk, the great observer of fasts and silence, whom we have already mentioned as one of elder Zossima's opponents and, most of all, an enemy of the institution of elders which he considered a harmful and frivolous innovation. He was a very dangerous opponent in spite of the fact that, as one who had taken the vow of silence, he scarcely uttered a word to anybody. He was so dangerous chiefly because a great many monks shared his opinion and because many of the people who came to visit the monastery looked upon him as a great saint and ascetic, although they had no doubt that he was a saintly fool. But it was just the fact of his being a saintly fool that fascinated them. Father Ferapont never went to see the elder Zossima. Although he lived in the hermitage, they did not worry him unduly by their rules, just because he behaved like a saintly fool. He was seventy-five, or perhaps more, and he lived behind the hermitage apiary, in a corner of the wall, in an old, almost dilapidated wooden cell, which had been built a great many years ago, in the last century, for Father Jonah, another great observer of fasts and silence, who had lived to a hundred and five and of whose exploits many curious stories were still told in the monastery and in the neighbourhood. Father Ferapont had at last succeeded seven years before in obtaining permission to take up his quarters in the same solitary little cell. It was simply a peasant's hut, but it looked like a chapel because it contained an extraordinary number of icons with lamps perpetually burning before them – all gifts brought by people outside the monastery. Father Ferapont was supposed to look after them and keep the lamps burning. It was said (and it is quite true) that he ate no more than two pounds of bread in three days; the bee-keeper, who lived close to the apiary, brought it to him every three days, but Father Ferapont rarely spoke a word even to the bee-keeper who waited upon him. The four pounds of bread, together with the Sunday wafer, which the Father Superior regularly sent him after late mass, made up the whole of his weekly rations. The water in his jug was changed every day. He rarely appeared at mass. Those who came to do homage to him saw him sometimes kneeling in prayer all day long without looking round. If he did occasionally enter into conversation with them, he was brief, abrupt, strange, and almost always rude. On very rare occasions, however, he would talk to visitors, but mostly he would just utter one strange saying, which always greatly puzzled his visitor, and, in spite of earnest entreaties, refused to utter another word in explanation. He had no priestly rank and was only an ordinary monk. There was a very strange rumour, though only among the most ignorant people, that Father Ferapont was in communication with heavenly spirits and conversed only with them and that was why he was silent with men. The Obdorsk monk, having got as far as the apiary at the direction of the bee-keeper, who was also a very surly and taciturn monk, went to the corner where Father Ferapont's cell stood. 'He may speak to you as you are a newcomer, but perhaps you won't get a word out of him,' the bee-keeper had warned him.

The monk, as he related afterwards, approached the cell in the greatest trepidation. It was rather late in the evening. Father Ferapont was sitting this time at the door of his cell on a low bench. An old elm was rustling faintly over him. A cold evening breeze was blowing. The Obdorsk monk prostrated himself before the saintly fool and asked his blessing.

'Do you want me to prostrate myself before you, too, monk?' said Father Ferapont. 'Get up!'

The monk got up.

'Blessing, and having been blessed, sit down beside me. Where have you come from?'

What struck the poor monk most of all was the fact that Father Ferapont, in spite of his undoubtedly strict fasting and great age, still looked such a vigorous old man. He was tall, held himself erect and did not stoop, and had a thin face, but a fresh and healthy complexion. There could be little doubt that he was still very vigorous. He was of athletic build. In spite of his advanced age, he was not even quite grey, and still had thick hair and a full beard, which had once been black. His eyes were grey, large, and luminous, but so prominent that one could not help being struck by it. He spoke with a strong northern accent. He was dressed in a peasant's long, reddish coat of coarse convict cloth, as it used to be called, and had a thick rope round his waist. His neck and chest were bare. His shirt, of the coarsest linen and almost black with dirt, not having been changed for months, showed from under his coat. It was said that he wore iron chains weighing thirty pounds under his coat. On his bare feet he wore a pair of old shoes which were almost falling to pieces.

'I'm from the small Obdorsk monastery, from St Sylvester,' the visiting monk answered humbly, observing the hermit with his sharp, inquisitive, though rather frightened little eyes.

'I've been at your Sylvester's. Stayed there, I have. Is Sylvester well?' The monk hesitated.

'You're a lot of fatheads! How do you keep the fasts?'

'Our fare is regulated in accordance with the ancient monastic rules. During Lent there are no meals provided on Mondays, Wednesdays, and Fridays. On Tuesdays and Thursdays the monks have white bread, stewed fruit with honey, cloudberries or salt cabbage, and oatmeal porridge. On Saturdays white cabbage soup, pea soup with noodles, thin porridge, all with vegetable oil. On weekdays we have cabbage soup, dried fish, and porridge. From Monday till Saturday evening, during the six days in Holy Week, we have bread and water, and that, too, sparingly, and no other food is cooked; taking no food every day, if possible, but as it is ordered for the first week in Lent. On Good Friday nothing is eaten, and likewise on the Saturday nothing is eaten till three o'clock and then only a little bread and water and a cup of wine afterwards. On Holy Thursday we have something cooked without oil and we drink wine, or we have something not cooked at all. Inasmuch as it is laid down by the Laodicean Council for Holy Thursday: "It is not seemly to break your fast on the Thursday of the last week in Lent and to dishonour the whole of Lent." This is how it's done at our monastery. But,' added the monk, plucking up courage, 'what is that compared with you, Father? For you have nothing but bread and water all the year round, and even at Easter, and you consume as much bread in a week as we do in two days. Verily, such great abstinence is a wondrous thing to behold.'

'And mushrooms?' Father Ferapont asked suddenly.

'Mushrooms?' the little monk repeated in surprise.

'Aye,' replied Father Ferapont, 'I'm thinking of giving up their bread, for I don't need it at all, and going away into the woods and living on mushrooms or wild berries. They can't give up their bread here, and so they're still in bondage to the devil. Nowadays the infidels say there's no need to fast. Haughty and impious is this judgement of theirs.'

'Aye, that's true enough,' sighed the monk.

'And have you seen devils among those?' asked Father Ferapont.

'Which "those"?' the little monk inquired timidly.

'I went to the Father Superior's on Trinity Sunday last year, and haven't been there since. I saw a devil sitting in one monk's bosom. Hiding under his cassock he was, only his horns poking out. Another had one peeping out of his pocket. Such sharp eyes he had, too. Afraid of me. Aye, he was that. Still another had one in his stomach, inside his unclean belly, and another had one hanging round his neck, clutching at it, and he was carrying him about without seeing him. . . .'

'And you – you see them?' inquired the little monk.

'Aye, I see them. I see through them. As I was coming out from the Father Superior's, I saw one hiding from me behind the door. A big one he was, three feet and more in height. Had a thick, long, brown tail. Just then he got the tip of his tail in the crack of the door and, well, being no fool, I slammed the door to suddenly and pinched his tail in it. You should have heard him squealing! Began struggling, he did, but I made the sign of the cross over him three times and that was the end of him. Died on the spot, he did. Like a crushed spider. I suppose he must have rotted away by now there in the corner and is stinking the place out, but they don't see and don't smell it. Haven't been there for a year. I'm telling you this, as you're a foreigner.'

'Your words are dreadful, Father! And, great and blessed Father,' the little monk grew bolder and bolder, 'is it true – the great things they tell about you even in distant lands, I mean, that you are in constant communication with the Holy Ghost?'

'Aye, he does fly down. It happens sometimes.'

'How does he fly down? In what shape?'

'As a bird.'

'The Holy Ghost in the shape of a dove?'

'Aye, there's the Holy Ghost and there is the Holy Spirit. The Holy Spirit is different. He can appear in the shape of some other bird: sometimes as a swallow, sometimes as a goldfinch, and sometimes as a tom-tit.'

'How do you know him from an ordinary tom-tit?'

'He speaks.'

'How does he speak? In what language?'

'In human language.'

'And what does he tell you?'

'Well, today he told me that a fool would come to see me and ask me unseemly questions. You want to know a lot, monk.'

'Your words are dreadful, most blessed and most holy Father,' the monk said, shaking his head.

There was, however, a look of incredulity in his timid little eyes.

'Do you see this tree?' asked Father Ferapont after a short pause.

'I do, most blessed Father.'

'You think it's an elm, but it looks different to me.'

'What does it look like to you?' the little monk asked after a pause, in vain expectation.

'It happens at night. See those two branches? At night it is Christ holding out his arms to me and seeking me with those arms. I see it clearly and tremble. It's terrible, oh, terrible!'

'What's there so terrible about it if it's Christ himself?'

'He may snatch me up and carry me into heaven.'

'Alive?'

'In the spirit and glory of Elijah. Haven't you heard? He'll put his arms round me and take me up.'

Though after that conversation the Obdorsk monk returned to the cell he was sharing with one of the monks in great perplexity of mind, his heart was undoubtedly more with Father Ferapont than with Father Zossima. The Obdorsk monk stood first of all for fasting, and it was not strange for so great an observer of fasts as Father Ferapont 'to see marvels'. His words, of course, sounded rather absurd, but God knows what meaning lay hidden in them, and, besides, the words and actions of the saintly fools who lived by begging were a great deal stranger. As for the story of the devil's pinched tail, he was quite ready to believe it not only figuratively but literally. Indeed, it gave him great pleasure to believe it. Besides, he was greatly prejudiced against the institution of elders even before his arrival at the monastery. He had known about it only from hearsay and, like many others, regarded it definitely as a harmful innovation. But after spending a day at the monastery, he had discovered that a number of thoughtless monks who were opposed to the institution of elders were murmuring in secret. He was, besides, by nature a meddlesome and nimble-witted monk, with an insatiable curiosity about everything. That was why the great news of the fresh 'miracle' performed by the elder Zossima threw him into a state of great bewilderment. Alyosha recalled afterwards the figure of the inquisitive Obdorsk visitor darting to and fro among the groups of monks crowding inside and round the elder's cell, listening and asking questions. But he paid little attention to him at the time and only remembered everything afterwards. . . . And indeed, he had other things to think of just then, for the elder Zossima, who had felt tired again, had gone back to bed and, as he was closing his eyes, he remembered him and sent for him. Alyosha came running at once. There were only Father Paissy, Father Joseph, and the novice Porfiry in the cell at the time. The elder opened his weary eyes and, looking intently at Alyosha, suddenly asked him:

'Are your people expecting you, my son?'

Alyosha hesitated.

'Have they no need of you? Did you not promise yesterday to see some of them today?'

'I did – to my father – my brothers and – others too.'

'Well, you see. You must go. Don't grieve. I shall not die without saying my last word on earth in your presence. I shall say that word to you, my son. I shall bequeath it to you. To you, my dear son, for you love me. But now go and see those you've promised to see.'

Alyosha immediately obeyed, though it was hard for him to go. But the promise that he should hear his last word on earth and, above all, that it would be bequeathed to him filled his soul with rapture. He made haste so as to finish his business in town and be back as soon as possible. As it happened, Father Paissy, too, uttered a few parting words to him which impressed and surprised him greatly. That was when the two of them had left the elder's cell.

'Always remember, young man,' Father Paissy began at once

without any preliminary introduction, 'that secular science, having become a great force in the world, has, especially in the last century, investigated everything divine handed down to us in the sacred books. After a ruthless analysis the scholars of this world have left nothing of what was held sacred before. But they have only investigated the parts and overlooked the whole, so much so that one cannot help being astonished at their blindness. And so the whole remains standing before their eyes as firm as ever and the gates of hell shall not prevail against it. Has it not existed for nineteen centuries and does it not exist today in the inmost hearts of individual men and the masses of the people? Why, it is living in the hearts of the atheists who have destroyed everything, and is as firmly rooted there as ever! For even those who have renounced Christianity and are rebelling against it, are essentially of the same semblance as Christ, and have always been that, for so far neither their wisdom nor the ardour of their hearts has been able to create a higher ideal of man or of man's dignity than the one shown by Christ in the days of old. And any attempts that have been made resulted only in monstrosities. Remember this especially, young man, for you are being sent into the world by your dying elder. Perhaps when you recall this great day, you will not forget my words, given you as a heartfelt send-off, for you are young and the temptations of the world are very great and beyond your strength to withstand them. Well, now go, my orphan boy.'

With these words Father Paissy blessed him. As he left the monastery and thought over Father Paissy's parting words, Alyosha suddenly realized that he had found a new and unexpected friend in the monk who had been so severe and stern to him before, a new guide who loved him warmly, just as if the elder Zossima had bequeathed him to him before his death. 'Perhaps that was what had passed between them,' Alyosha reflected suddenly. The unexpected learned discourse which he had just heard – just that and not something else – merely bore witness to the warmth of Father Paissy's heart: he was in great haste to arm the young man's mind for a fight against temptations and to fence in the young soul bequeathed to him by the strongest fence he could imagine.

2

At His Father's

FIRST of all Alyosha went to see his father. As he approached the house, he remembered that the day before his father had insisted that he should enter it without being noticed by his brother Ivan. 'Why that?' Alyosha thought suddenly now. 'If father wants to tell something to me alone in secret, then why should I go in in secret? I suppose in his excitement yesterday he wanted to say something else, but did not manage to,' he decided. He was nevertheless glad when Marfa, who opened the gate to him (Grigory, it seemed, was lying ill in the cottage), told him in reply to his question that Ivan had gone out two hours before.

'And my father?'

'He's got up, sir, and is having his coffee,' Marfa replied somewhat drily.

Alyosha went in. The old man was sitting alone at the table, in his slippers and an old overcoat. He was looking through some accounts, just to pass away the time and without apparently paying much attention to them. He was quite alone in the house (Smerdyakov had also gone out to do some shopping for dinner). But it was not the accounts that interested him. Though he had got up early and done his best to keep up his spirits, he looked tired and weak. His forehead, on which huge purple bruises had come out during the night, was tied round with a red handkerchief. His nose, too, had swollen up terribly in the night, and it, too, was covered with a few small bruises, which certainly gave his whole face a peculiarly spiteful and irritable appearance. The old man was aware of it himself and he glared in an unfriendly way at Alyosha as he came in.

'The coffee's cold,' he cried brusquely. 'I'm not offering you any. I shall be having nothing but lenten fish soup myself today and I'm not inviting anyone to dinner. What have you come for?'

'To find out how you are,' said Alyosha.

'I see. But didn't I tell you myself yesterday to come? It's all a lot of nonsense. You shouldn't have bothered. I knew, though, that you'd drag yourself here at once.'

He said this in a most unfriendly way. Meanwhile he got up and looked anxiously at his nose in the looking-glass (perhaps for the fortieth time that morning). He also began adjusting the red handkerchief on his forehead more becomingly.

'A red one's better,' he remarked sententiously. 'In a white one it would have looked like a hospital. Well, what's been going on at your monastery? How's your elder?'

'He's very bad, he may die today,' replied Alyosha, but his father had never bothered to listen and had forgotten his question at once.

'Ivan's gone out,' he said suddenly. 'He's doing his damnedest to get Mitya's fiancée for himself. That's why he's staying here,' he added spitefully, making a wry face and glaring at Alyosha.

'He didn't tell you that, did he?' asked Alyosha.

'He did. Long ago. Three weeks ago, as a matter of fact. He hasn't come here, too, to get me murdered in secret, has he? He must have come for something!'

'Good heavens, why do you say such things?' Alyosha said, looking terribly embarrassed.

'It's true he doesn't ask for money, but he won't get a penny from me all the same. You see, my dear Alexey, I've made up my mind to go on living as long as possible. Don't make any mistake about that. That's why I need every penny I have. And the longer I live, the more I shall need it,' he went on, walking from one corner of the room to the other, his hands thrust in the pockets of his loose, soiled coat made of yellow summer calamanco. 'At present I'm still a man in the prime of life. I'm only fifty-five. But I'd like to go on being a man in the full sense of the word for another twenty years. When I grow old, I shall be no damn good any longer. No woman will come to me of her own accord. It's then that I shall need money. And that's why I'm saving up now more and more for myself alone, sir. Yes, dear son, make no mistake about that. I intend to carry on with my filthy kind of life to the end. Get that into your head once and for all. This filthy kind of life is sweet, sir: everyone abuses it and everyone lives it, except that they all do it surreptitiously, while I do it openly. It's because I make no bones about it that all the filthy swine are attacking me for being so simple-minded. As for your paradise, my dear sir, I want none of it. Make no mistake about that, either. Besides, your paradise is no proper place for a decent fellow, even if it does exist. In my opinion, a man falls asleep and doesn't wake up, and that's all there is to it. Order prayers for me in church, if you like. If you don't, to hell with you! That's my philosophy. Ivan spoke well here yesterday, though we were all drunk. Ivan's a boaster, and he has no real learning . . . nor any particular education, either. Keeps silent and grins at you without uttering a word. That's the only way he makes people think he's so clever.'

Alyosha listened to him in silence.

'Why won't he talk to me? And when he does talk, he gives himself airs. Your Ivan is a blackguard, sir! And I'm going to marry Grushenka any time I like. For, you see, my dear sir, a chap who has money has only to want something and he'll get it. That's what Ivan is so afraid of. He keeps watch over me to prevent me from marrying her. That's why he's egging on Mitya to marry Grushenka: he thinks he'll prevent Grushenka marrying me that way (as though I'd leave him my money, if I don't marry the slut!). Then again if Mitya marries her, Ivan will get his rich fiancée – that's what he is counting on! He's a blackguard, your Ivan is, sir!'

'How irritable you are!' said Alyosha. 'It's because of what happened yesterday. You'd better go and lie down.'

'You see,' the old man observed suddenly, as though it had occurred to him for the first time, 'you say that and I'm not angry with you, but if Ivan had said it, I'd be angry. It's only with you that I've had my good moments, for I'm a vicious man by nature.'

'You're not vicious, but warped,' said Alyosha with a smile.

'Listen, I had a good mind to have that bandit Mitya locked up today, and I'm not sure even now what I shall decide. Of course, in our modern times it's the fashion to regard honouring your father and mother as a prejudice, but I believe that legally it's not permitted even in our enlightened times to drag one's father about by the hair and kick him in the face on the floor in his own house and come and brag about murdering him – and all that, mind you, in the presence of witnesses! If I wanted to, I'd make him suffer all right. I could get him locked up for what he did yesterday.'

'So you don't want to tell the police, do you?'

'Ivan has dissuaded me. I shouldn't have taken any notice of Ivan, but there's something else to consider.' And bending over Alyosha, he went on in a confidential undertone: 'If I got the scoundrel locked up, she'd hear of it and run to him at once. But if she hears today that he has thrashed me, a feeble old man, within an inch of my life, she may give him up and come to see me. . . . That's the way we're made – we do everything contrary to what's expected of us. I know her through and through! Well, you'll have a drop of brandy, won't you? Pour yourself out a cup of cold coffee, and I'll pour a quarter of a glass of brandy in it. Makes the coffee taste twice as good.'

'No, thank you, but I'll take that roll, if I may,' said Alyosha, and taking a halfpenny French roll he put it in the pocket of his cassock. 'And you'd better not have any more brandy, either,' he suggested cautiously, peering into the old man's face.

'You're right, my boy. It merely irritates but doesn't soothe me. But, perhaps, just a little glass. . . . I'll get it out of the little cupboard. . . .'

He unlocked the 'little cupboard', poured himself out a glass, drank it, then locked the cupboard and put the key back in his pocket.

'That's enough. One glass won't kill me.'

'You see, you're a much kinder man now,' said Alyosha, smiling.

'Well, I love you even without brandy, but with blackguards, I'm a blackguard, too. Ivan isn't going to Chermashnya – why not? Because he has to spy on me. Wants to see how much I'll give Grushenka if she comes. They're all blackguards. I don't care a damn for Ivan. You see, I don't know Ivan at all. Don't know what sort of a fellow he is. Where did he spring from? He isn't our kind at all. And does he really think I'm going to leave him anything? Why, I won't make a will at all – make no mistake about that! As for Mitya, I'll crush him like a black beetle. I squash black beetles at night with my slipper: it crunches when you step on it. Your Mitya will crunch, too. *Your* Mitya, because you love him. You see, you love him, and I'm not afraid of your loving him. But if Ivan loved him, I would be afraid of it. But Ivan loves nobody. Ivan is not one of us. People like Ivan, my boy, are not like us – they're like dust driven by the wind. When the wind blows, the dust will be gone. I had a silly idea in my head yesterday when I told you to come today: I wondered if I could find out about Mitya through you. I mean if I let him have a thousand, or maybe two thousand, now, would the dirty pauper agree to get out of here altogether for five years or,

better still, for thirty-five? Without Grushenka. Give her up altogether. What do you think?'

'I – I'll ask him,' Alyosha murmured. 'If you gave him three
thousand, he might perhaps —'

'Nonsense! You needn't ask him now – no need to say anything
to him! I've changed my mind. I got that silly idea into my head
yesterday in a silly moment. I shan't give him anything. Not a damn
thing. I want my money myself,' cried the old man, waving his
hands. 'I'll crush him like a black beetle without it. Don't say anything to him or you'll be raising his hopes. And there's nothing for
you to do here, either. You can go now – go! Is that fiancée of his,
whom he has been hiding from me so carefully, going to marry him
or not? Katerina, I mean. You went to see her yesterday, didn't you?'

'She won't leave him for anything in the world.'

'Aye, it's fellows like him that these nice young ladies love – rakes
and blackguards! Rubbish – that's what these pale young ladies are,
I tell you. Of course, if – oh well, if I'd been as young as he and if I
had the looks I had then (for I was a better-looking man than he
when I was twenty-eight), I'd have made the same conquests as he.
The dirty swine! But he won't get Grushenka all the same. No, sir!
. . . I'll rub his nose in the dirt! . . .'

He got into a rage again at the last words.

'You'd better go, too,' he snapped out harshly. 'There's nothing
for you to do here today.'

Alyosha went up to say good-bye to him and kissed him on the
shoulder.

'Why did you do that?' the old man asked with some surprise.
'We'll see each other again. Or don't you think so?'

'Not at all. I did it without thinking.'

'I didn't mean anything, either. I, too, said it without thinking.
I say, I say,' he shouted after him, 'come again soon, I'll have a fish
soup for you, a special one not like today. Be sure to come! Tomorrow – you hear? – come tomorrow!'

And as soon as Alyosha had gone out of the door, he went up to
the cupboard again and knocked back another half glass of brandy.

'No more!' he muttered, clearing his throat.

He locked the cupboard again, put the key in his pocket, then went
into his bedroom, lay down exhausted on the bed and fell asleep at once.

3

He Gets Involved with Schoolboys

'THANK goodness he didn't ask me about Grushenka,' Alyosha thought in his turn as he left his father's house and turned towards Mrs Khokhlakov's, 'or I might have had to tell him about my meeting with Grushenka yesterday.' Alyosha felt painfully that since the night before the combatants had gathered new strength and that their hearts had hardened again with the coming of daylight. 'Father,' he thought, 'is exasperated and spiteful. He's hatched out some plan, too. And what about Dmitry? He also had grown more determined overnight, and, I suppose, he also is exasperated and spiteful and, no doubt, he's got some plan, too. Oh, I simply must manage to find him today!'

But Alyosha's thoughts were soon interrupted: he became involved in an incident on the way which, though apparently of no great consequence, made a great impression on him. As soon as he had walked across the square and turned to cross the bridge leading into Mikhailovsky Street, which runs parallel to the High Street but is separated from it by a ditch (our whole town is criss-crossed by ditches), he saw on the other side of the bridge a small group of young schoolboys between the ages of nine and twelve. They were going home from school with their satchels on their backs or with leather bags slung over their shoulders, some in school tunics, others in overcoats, and some even wore high boots turned over at the top, in which small boys, spoilt by well-to-do parents, particularly love to show off. The whole group was discussing something animatedly and apparently holding a consultation. Alyosha could never pass by children without feeling interested in them. That had happened to him in Moscow, too, and though he was particularly fond of children of three years old or thereabouts, he also liked children of ten and eleven. That was why, greatly worried as he now was, he felt a sudden desire to go up to the children and start a conversation with them. As he drew close, he scrutinized their rosy, animated faces and all of a sudden noticed that all the boys had one or two stones in their hands. Behind the ditch, about thirty paces from the group, another boy was standing by a fence. He, too, was a schoolboy with a bag at his side, about ten years old or perhaps less, pale, delicate-looking, and with flashing black eyes. He was watching the group of six schoolboys attentively and searchingly. They were obviously his schoolmates who had just left school with him and with whom he evidently had a feud. Alyosha went up to them, and addressing a fair, curly-headed, rosy-cheeked boy in a black tunic, observed after examining him closely:

'When I used to wear a bag like yours, I always carried it on my left side so as to be able to reach it with my right hand. You've got yours on the right side and you'll find it inconvenient to get at it.'

Without any premeditation or guile Alyosha began straight with that practical remark, and indeed a grown-up person could not begin in any other way if he wished to gain at once the confidence of a child and, especially, of a whole group of children. One must begin in a serious and practical manner so as to be on a perfectly equal footing. Alyosha understood it instinctively.

'But he's left-handed, sir,' another high-spirited, healthy-looking boy of eleven answered at once.

The other five boys stared at Alyosha in silence.

'He even throws stones with his left hand,' a third boy observed.

At that moment a stone flew into the group, grazing the left-handed boy, but missing them, though it was carefully and vigorously aimed by the boy on the other side of the ditch.

'Let him have it! Give it to him, Smurov!' they all shouted.

But Smurov (the left-handed boy) was not slow in retaliating: he threw a stone at the boy on the other side of the ditch, but missed him: the stone hit the ground. The boy on the other side of the ditch at once flung another stone at the group, aiming this time straight at Alyosha and hitting him rather painfully on the shoulder. The boy on the other side of the ditch had his pockets stuffed with stones. That could be clearly seen from the way his pockets bulged.

'He aimed at you, sir, at you, he did it on purpose,' the boys shouted, laughing. 'You're Karamazov, aren't you, sir? Come on boys, all together – fire!'

And six stones flew from the group all at once. One struck the boy on the head. He fell down, but immediately jumped to his feet and began throwing stones ferociously at the group. Both sides began exchanging shots incessantly, many of the group having their pockets full of stones as well.

'What are you doing?' cried Alyosha. 'You ought to be ashamed of yourselves! Six against one? Why, you'll kill him!'

He leapt forward to meet the flying stones and shield the boy on the other side of the ditch. Three or four boys stopped throwing stones for a moment.

'He started it, sir!' shouted a boy in a red shirt in an exasperated, childish voice. 'He's a beast! He stuck his penknife into Krasotkin in class today and drew blood, sir. Only Krasotkin didn't want to tell on him, but he must be given a good hiding.'

'But whatever for? I suppose you tease him. Don't you?'

'Look out, sir, he's hit you in the back again. He knows you, sir,' the boys shouted. 'It's at you he's throwing now, not at us. Come on, boys, all of you, at him again. Don't miss him, Smurov!'

And another exchange of stones began, and a very vicious one this time. The boy on the other side of the ditch was hit in the chest. He uttered a scream, began to cry, and ran away uphill towards Mikhailovsky Street. The boys yelled after him: 'See, he's funked it! He's running away! Bast-sponge!'

'You don't know, sir, what a rotter he is,' the boy in the tunic, who seemed to be the eldest in the group, repeated with flashing eyes. 'Killing's too good for him.'

'Why, what's wrong with him?' asked Alyosha. 'Is he a tell-tale?'

The boys looked at one another as though in derision.

'Are you going that way, too, sir? To Mikhailovsky Street?' went on the same boy. 'You'd better catch him up. You see, he's stopped again. He's waiting and looking at you.'

'He's looking at you! He's looking at you!' the boys echoed.

'You ask him if he likes a bath bast-sponge, a tattered one. Please, ask him that.'

There was a general outburst of laughter. Alyosha looked at them and they at him.

'Don't go near him, sir, he'll hurt you,' Smurov cried warningly.

'I'm not going to ask him about a bast-sponge, for I expect you must be teasing him with that. But I am going to find out from him why you hate him so much.'

'Yes, sir, find out, find out!' the boys laughed.

Alyosha crossed the bridge and went up the hill by the fence straight towards the ostracized boy.

'Look out, sir,' the boys shouted after him warningly, 'he won't be afraid of you. He'll stick a knife into you when you're not looking, just as he did into Krasotkin.'

The boy waited for him without budging. Coming up to him, Alyosha saw a boy of no more than nine years old, undersized and weakly, with a longish, pale, thin face and large dark eyes, looking vindictively at him. He was dressed in a rather threadbare old overcoat, which he had monstrously outgrown. His bare arms protruded from his sleeves. There was a large patch on the right knee of his trousers and a large hole, obviously heavily blackened with ink, on the right boot where the big toe was. Both pockets of his overcoat were bulging with stones. Alyosha stopped within two paces of him and looked at him questioningly. Realizing at once from Alyosha's eyes that he had no intention of beating him, the boy, too, dropped his defiant air and himself opened the conversation.

'I'm one and they're six, sir,' he said suddenly, with flashing eyes. 'I'll beat them all by myself.'

'I expect one of the stones must have hurt you badly,' observed Alyosha.

'And I hit Smurov on the head!' cried the boy.

'They said that you knew me and you threw a stone at me for some reason. Is it true?' asked Alyosha.

The boy looked darkly at him.

'I don't know you. Do you know me?' Alyosha went on with his interrogation.

'Leave me alone!' the boy suddenly cried irritably, without, however, stirring from his place, as though waiting for something and again with a malicious flash in his eyes.

'Very well, I'm going,' said Alyosha. 'Only I don't know you and I don't tease you. They told me how to tease you, but I don't want to tease you. Good-bye!'

'A monk in fancy trousers!' cried the boy, watching Alyosha with the same malicious and defiant look and taking up a defensive attitude, thinking that Alyosha would most certainly attack him now. But Alyosha turned back, looked at him, and walked away. But before he had gone three steps, a huge stone, the biggest one in the boy's pocket, hit him a painful blow in the back.

'So you'll hit a man from behind, will you? So they're telling the truth. You do attack people when they're not looking!' Alyosha said, turning round again.

But this time the boy, in a rage, threw a stone straight in Alyosha's face, but Alyosha managed to shield himself in time, and the stone struck him on the elbow.

'Aren't you ashamed of yourself?' Alyosha cried. 'What did I do to you?'

The boy waited defiantly and in silence, expecting that now Alyosha would most certainly attack him; seeing, however, that he made no attempt to do so even now, he grew vicious like a little wild beast: he dashed forward and flew at Alyosha himself, and before Alyosha had time to move, the vicious boy lowered his head, and seizing his left hand with both of his, bit his middle finger painfully. He dug his teeth into it and did not let go for ten seconds. Alyosha cried out with pain, trying with all his might to pull his finger away. The boy let go at last and jumped back the same distance. The finger had been badly bitten to the bone, close to the nail; it began to bleed. Alyosha took out his handkerchief and tied it firmly round his injured hand. It took him a whole minute to bandage it. The boy stood waiting all the time. At last Alyosha raised his gentle eyes and looked at him.

'All right,' he said, 'you see how badly you've bitten me, don't you? You're satisfied, aren't you? Now tell me what have I done to you?'

The boy looked at him in surprise.

'Though I don't know you at all and see you for the first time,' Alyosha went on in the same quiet tone of voice, 'it's quite impossible that I shouldn't have done something to you. You wouldn't have hurt me like that for nothing. So tell me, please, what I've done and how I've wronged you.'

Instead of answering, the boy burst out crying loudly, at the top of his voice, and suddenly ran away from Alyosha. Alyosha walked slowly after him towards Mikhailovsky Street, and for a long time he saw the little boy running in the distance, without slowing down or turning round, and probably still crying at the top of his voice.

He made up his mind to find him as soon as he had time and solve the mystery which had struck him so forcibly. Just now he had no time.

4

At the Khokhlakovs'

HE soon reached Mrs Khokhlakov's house, a beautiful, two-storied stone house, one of the best houses in our little town. Though Mrs Khokhlakov spent most of her time in another province, where she had an estate, or in Moscow, where she had a house of her own, she also owned a house in our town, inherited by her fathers and fore-fathers. The estate she owned in our district, too, was the largest of her three estates, and yet she had hitherto visited our province very rarely. She ran out to Alyosha in the hall.

'Have you received my letter about the new miracle?' she said rapidly and nervously. 'Have you? Have you?'

'Yes.'

'Did you show it to everybody? He restored the son to his mother!'

'He will die today,' said Alyosha.

'I've heard. I know. Oh, how I long to talk to you! To you or to anyone else about it all. No, to you, to you! And what a pity I can't see him again! The whole town is excited. Everyone's expecting something to happen. But now – do you know that Katerina is here now?'

'Oh, that's lucky!' cried Alyosha. 'So I'll be able to see her here. She told me yesterday not to fail to come and see her today.'

'I know everything, everything. I've heard all the details about what happened at her place yesterday and – and the dreadful trouble she had with that – that horrible creature. *C'est tragique*, and if I'd been in her place – I simply don't know what I'd have done if I'd been in her place! But your brother Dmitry, too, has behaved dis-gracefully – oh dear! I'm afraid, Alexey, I'm in a dreadful muddle. Do you know who's here? Your brother – I don't mean that dreadful brother of yours, but the other one, Ivan. He's sitting with her and talking – they're having a most important conversation. . . . Oh, if you knew what's happening between them now! It's simply awful!

It's a heartache, I tell you. It's like some frightful folk-tale which it's quite impossible to believe: they're both ruining themselves, goodness only knows why. They realize it themselves and they seem to enjoy it. I've been waiting for you! I've been longing to see you! You see, I simply can't bear it. I'll tell you all about it presently, but I've got to tell you something else now, something frightfully important – goodness me, I'd quite forgotten that it was so important. Tell me, why is Lise in hysterics? The moment she heard you coming in, she began to be hysterical.'

'It's you who're hysterical now, not me, Mother,' Lise's sweet voice was heard saying rapidly through a tiny crack of the door of one of the rooms.

The crack was very tiny and her voice, too, had a catch in it, just as though she wanted terribly to laugh, but did her utmost to suppress it. Alyosha at once noticed the little crack in the door, and Lise must have been trying to look through it at him from her wheelchair, but that he could not see.

'I shouldn't wonder, Lise, I shouldn't wonder. Your caprices will drive me into hysterics too. But then, dear Alexey, she's so ill. She's been so ill all night, feverish and moaning! I could hardly wait for the morning and Herzenstube. This Herzenstube always comes and says he can make nothing of it and that one has to wait. As soon as you approached our house, she uttered a scream, had an attack of hysterics and told me to wheel her back into her old room here. . . .'

'I had no idea he was coming, Mother, and it wasn't at all because of him that I wanted to be wheeled into this room.'

'That's not true, Lise. Julia ran to tell you that Alexey was coming. She was on the look-out for you.'

'Darling Mother, that's awfully silly of you! And if you want to make up for it and say something awfully clever, Mother dear, then you'd better tell Mr Alexey Karamazov, who has just come in, that he has shown how little clever he is by deciding to come to see us today after what happened yesterday and in spite of the fact that everyone is laughing at him.'

'Lise, you go too far and I'm afraid I shall have to be very severe with you. Who's laughing at him? I'm so glad he has come. I need him, I simply can't do without him. Oh, my dear Alexey, I'm terribly unhappy!'

'But what's the matter with you, Mother darling?'

'Oh, Lise, all these caprices of yours, your restlessness, your illness, that frightful night of fever, that frightful and everlasting Herzenstube, everlasting, everlasting – that's what's so awful! And everything, in fact, everything! And even that miracle, too! Oh, my dear Alexey, I can't tell you how that miracle has upset me, how it has shattered me! And now that tragedy in the drawing-room there, which I simply can't bear. I can't bear it, I tell you, I can't bear it. A comedy, perhaps, not a tragedy. Tell me, do you think Father Zossima will live till tomorrow? Oh dear, what is happening to me? I keep closing my eyes and I can see that it's all nonsense, a lot of nonsense!'

'I wonder if you would mind giving me a clean rag,' Alyosha interrupted suddenly, 'to bandage my finger with. I've injured it badly and it hurts me very much now.'

Alyosha unwound his bitten finger. The handkerchief was soaked with blood. Mrs Khokhlakov uttered a scream and screwed up her eyes.

'Good heavens, what a wound! This is frightful!'

But as soon as Lise saw Alyosha's finger through the crack, she flung the door wide open.

'Come in, come in here at once,' she cried, insistently and peremptorily. 'No nonsense now, please! Goodness, how could you stand there all this time without saying anything? He might have bled to death, Mother! Where did it happen? How did you do it? First of all, water, water! You must wash your wound thoroughly. Simply put it in cold water to ease the pain and keep it there, keep it there all the time. Quickly, quickly, some water, Mother, in a basin. And do hurry, Mother!' she concluded nervously.

She was terribly frightened; Alyosha's wound completely unnerved her.

'Shouldn't we send for Herzenstube, dear?' Mrs Khokhlakov cried.

'Mother, you'll be the death of me. Your Herzenstube will come and say that he can't make anything of it! Water, water! Mother, for goodness' sake, go yourself and hurry Julia. She's got stuck somewhere and she never can come quickly! But do hurry, Mother, or I shall die. . . . '

'Why, it's nothing!' cried Alyosha, alarmed at their alarm.

Julia ran in with water. Alyosha put his finger in it.

'Mother, for goodness' sake, fetch some lint, lint and that muddy caustic lotion for wounds – what do you call it? We've got some, we've got some, we've got some! You know where the bottle is, Mother. In your bedroom. In the medicine box on the right. There's a big bottle of it there and lint.'

'I'll bring everything in a minute, Lise, only, please, don't scream and don't fuss. You see how bravely Alexey bears his pain. And where did you get such a frightful wound, Alexey?'

Mrs Khokhlakov left the room hurriedly. This was all Lise was waiting for.

'First of all, answer my question,' she said rapidly to Alyosha. 'Where did you manage to get that dreadful wound? And then I shall talk to you about something quite different. Well?'

Feeling instinctively that the time before her mother's return was precious to her, Alyosha told her quickly and briefly, leaving out all the inessentials, but clearly and precisely, about his strange encounter with the schoolboys. Having heard him out, Lise threw up her hands in astonishment.

'But how could you, how could you get yourself mixed up with little schoolboys, and in that dress, too?' she cried angrily, as though she had a right to exercise her authority over him. 'Why, you're only a boy yourself after that, just a little boy, as little as can be! Still, you'd better find out what you can for me about that horrid little boy, and tell me all about it, for there's some mystery there. Now, something else. But first a question: can you, Alexey, in spite of your dreadful pain, talk about something quite unimportant, but sensibly, mind?'

'Of course I can, and, besides, I don't feel much pain now.'

'That's because your finger is in the water. It will have to be changed presently, because it will get warm. Julia, go and fetch some ice from the cellar and another basin of water. Well, now that she's gone, to business: please, dear Alexey, let me have the letter I sent you yesterday at once – at once, please, for Mother may be back directly, and I don't want her —'

'I'm awfully sorry, but I haven't got it on me.'

'That's not true. You have got it. I knew you'd say that. You've got it in that pocket. I've been regretting that silly joke all night. Please, let me have my letter back at once! Give it me!'

'I've left it at the monastery.'

'But I hope you don't think I'm a little girl, just a silly little girl, for having sent you a letter with such a stupid joke! I'm sorry for that stupid joke, but you must bring me the letter, if you really haven't got it now. Bring it today. Without fail, you hear?'

'I can't possibly bring it today, for I must go back to the monastery and I shan't be able to come and see you for two, three, or even four days, because the elder Zossima —'

'Four days? What nonsense! Listen, did you laugh at me very much?'

'I didn't laugh at you at all.'

'Why not?'

'Because I believed every word of your letter.'

'You're insulting me!'

'Not at all. As soon as I read it I thought that it would all be like that, for I have to leave the monastery as soon as Father Zossima dies. I shall then carry on with my studies, pass my exams, and when you've reached the legal age, we'll get married. I shall love you. Though I haven't had time to think about it, I don't expect I could find a better wife than you, and the elder tells me I must marry. . . .'

'But I'm a horrible cripple. I'm wheeled about in a chair!' Lise laughed, colouring.

'I'll wheel you about in a chair myself, but I'm sure you'll be well by that time.'

'But you're mad,' Lise said nervously, 'jumping to such a silly conclusion from such a joke! Oh, here's Mother – just at the right moment, too, perhaps. Mother, you're always so late! How can you be so long? Here's Julia with the ice, too!'

'Oh, Lise, don't scream – please, don't scream! Your screams drive me — What was I to do if you put the lint in another place? I've been looking and looking for it. I expect you did it on purpose.'

'But how was I to know that he'd come with his finger bitten through? If I had, I might really have done it on purpose. Darling Mother, you do say such clever things.'

'Clever or not, Lise, but must you make such a fuss about poor Alexey's finger and everything? Oh, my dear Alexey, what's worrying me is not one particular thing, not Herzenstube, but everything together. That's what I simply can't bear!'

'That's enough, Mother, enough about Herzenstube,' Lise cried with a happy laugh. 'Give me the lint quickly, Mother, and the water. This is simply a zinc lotion, Alexey. I've just remembered what it is, but it's an excellent lotion. Just fancy, Mother, he's had a fight with some boys in the street on the way here, and one boy bit his finger. Isn't he just a little boy himself, and is he fit to be married after that? For, just imagine it, Mother, he actually wants to be married! Just imagine him a married man! Isn't it laughable? Isn't it awful?'

And Lise went on laughing her thin, nervous laugh, gazing mischievously at Alyosha.

'But why should he marry, Lise? And why talk about it now? It's hardly the right occasion, dear, when – I mean, when that boy may have had rabies?'

'Goodness, Mother, do boys have rabies?'

'But why not, Lise? Don't look at me as though I'd said something stupid. Your boy might have been bitten by a mad dog and he would get mad and bite someone in turn. How beautifully she's bandaged your finger, Alexey! I should never have been able to do it. Does it still hurt?'

'Only a little.'

'And you're not afraid of water?' asked Lise.

'That will do, Lise. Perhaps I was a little hasty in talking about the boy having rabies, and you're already jumping to conclusions. The moment Katerina learnt that you were here, Alexey, she simply pounced on me. She's dying to see you. She's simply dying to see you.'

'Oh, Mother, you'd better go there alone. He can't go now, he's in such pain.'

'I'm not in pain at all,' said Alyosha. 'I'm quite fit to go there.'

'What? Are you going? So that's the sort of man you are!'

'But why not? When I've finished there, I'll come back and we can talk again as much as you like. I'd very much like to see Miss Verkhovtsev now, for I'd like to be back at the monastery as soon as I can today.'

'Take him away quickly, Mother. Don't trouble to come and see me afterwards, sir, but go straight back to your monastery – and a good riddance! I want to go to bed. I haven't slept all night!'

'Oh, Lise, you're just joking, I know, but I wish you really would go to sleep!' cried Mrs Khokhlakov.

'I don't know what I've — ,' muttered Alyosha. 'I could stay another three minutes – even five, if you like.'

'Even five! Take him away quickly, Mother! He's a monster!'

'Lise, you've gone out of your mind! Come along, Alexey. She's very capricious today and I'm afraid to irritate her. Oh, my dear Alexey, the trouble one has with nervous girls! But perhaps she really does feel sleepy. How quickly you've made her sleepy and how fortunate it is!'

'Oh, Mother, how nicely you talk! I'd like to kiss you for that, darling Mother!'

'Let me kiss you, too, Lise, dear. Listen, Alexey,' Mrs Khokhlakov said gravely and mysteriously in a rapid whisper as she went out of the room with Alyosha, 'I don't want to suggest anything to you. I don't want to lift the veil. But you'd better go in and see for yourself what's going on there. It's dreadful! It's a most fantastic comedy. You see, she loves your brother Ivan, but she does all she can to persuade herself that she loves your brother Dmitry. It's simply dreadful! I'll go in with you, and if they don't turn me out, I'll stay to the end.'

5

Heartache in the Drawing-room

BUT in the drawing-room the conversation was already coming to an end. Katerina was in a state of great excitement, though she looked determined. At the moment when Alyosha and Mrs Khokhlakov came in, Ivan was getting up to go. His face was a little pale, and Alyosha looked at him uneasily. For one of the things that puzzled him, a problem that had been worrying him for some time, was about to be solved now. It had been suggested to him several times a month before by all sorts of people that Ivan was in love with Katerina and, what's more, that Ivan really meant 'to take her away' from Mitya. Up to the last moment that seemed a monstrous insinuation to Alyosha, though it had worried him a great deal. He loved both his brothers and was afraid of just such a rivalry between them. And yet Dmitry himself had told him plainly the day before that he was even glad of Ivan's rivalry and that it would be of great help to him. Be of great help for what? To make it possible for him to marry Grushenka? But that Alyosha considered a last and most desperate step. Besides all this, Alyosha had been absolutely convinced up to the previous evening that Katerina was passionately and truly in love with Dmitry – but he had believed it only till the previous evening. Moreover, he couldn't help feeling for some reason that she could not possibly love a man like Ivan, but loved Dmitry exactly as he was, in spite of the utterly monstrous nature of such a love. But in the scene with Grushenka the night before he had seemed to be dimly aware of something else. The word 'heartache' which Mrs Khokhlakov had just used, almost made him start, because it was during the previous night, half awake at daybreak, that, as though in reply to a dream he had had, he had said aloud: 'Heartache, heartache!' He had dreamt all night of the scene at Katerina's. Now Mrs Khokhlakov's unmistakable and dogmatic assertion that Katerina loved his brother Ivan and was only deceiving herself on purpose, for the sake of some fanciful idea of her own, because of 'heartache', and tormenting herself by her imagined love for Dmitry out of some apparent feeling of gratitude – struck Alyosha very forcibly. 'Yes, perhaps what she says is quite true!' But in that case how awful Ivan's position was: Alyosha felt by some sort of instinct that a woman like Katerina had to exert her power over people, and that she could do so only with a man like Dmitry and most decidedly not with a man like Ivan. For only Dmitry could (though perhaps after a long time) submit to her at last 'for his own happiness' (which Alyosha, indeed, desired), but not Ivan. Ivan could never submit to her, and, besides, submission would not have made him happy. Alyosha had for some reason involuntarily formed such an idea about Ivan. And now all these arguments and hesitations flashed through his mind the moment he had entered the drawing-room. Another thought, too, flashed through his mind suddenly and irresistibly: 'And what if she did not love anyone, neither Ivan nor Dmitry?' I must observe that Alyosha seemed to be ashamed of his thoughts and had reproached himself for them when, during the past month, they happened to occur to him. 'What do I really know about love and about women and how can I possibly come to such conclusions?' he thought reproachfully every time such a thought or conjecture occurred to him. And yet he could not help thinking about it. He realized instinctively that, for instance, this rivalry between his two brothers was now a highly important matter upon which too many things depended. 'One reptile will devour the other reptile,' Ivan had said the day before when speaking with irritation about his father and Dmitry. So he thought Dmitry a reptile and perhaps he had been thinking him a reptile a long time! Was it since the time Ivan had met Katerina? Those words, of course, had escaped Ivan involuntarily, but that made them all the more important. If that was so, then what kind of peace could there be between them? Were there not, on the contrary, new reasons for feuds and hatreds in their family? And, above all, whom was he, Alyosha, to pity? And what could he wish each of them? He loved them both, but what could he wish for each of them among so many contradictions? One could easily lose oneself in that confusion, and Alyosha's heart could not stand uncertainty, for his love was always active. He could not love passively. When he loved someone, he at once set about helping him. But to do that he had to know what to aim at, he had to know what each of them needed and what was good for them, and having become convinced of the correctness of his aim, he would naturally help each of them. But instead of some fixed, steady purpose everything was vague and confused. 'Heart-ache' – that was the word spoken just now. But what on earth was he to make even of this heartache? He did not understand a single thing in all this confusion!

On seeing Alyosha, Katerina said quickly and joyfully to Ivan, who had already got up to go:

'One moment, please. Stay for another minute. I'd like to hear the opinion of this man whom I trust completely. Mrs Khokhlakov, please don't you go, either,' she added.

She made Alyosha sit down beside her and Mrs Khokhlakov sat down facing her beside Ivan.

'Here,' she began warmly in a voice trembling with genuine, anguished tears, which made Alyosha's heart go out to her, 'here you are all my friends, the dearest friends I have in the world. You, Alexey, were present at yesterday's – horrible scene and you saw the state I was in. You, Ivan, did not see it. He did. What he thought about me yesterday, I don't know. All I know is that if the same thing had happened now, today, I should have expressed the same sentiments as I did yesterday – the same sentiments, the same words and the same actions. You remember my actions, Alexey, don't you? You restrained me from one of them.' (She reddened as she said this and her eyes flashed.) 'I tell you, Alexey, I cannot be reconciled to anything. Listen, Alexey. I don't even know that I love *him* now. I'm sorry for him, and that's a bad sign so far as love is concerned. If I'd loved him, if I'd gone on loving him, I shouldn't perhaps have been sorry for him now. I should have hated him. . . .'

Her voice trembled and tears glistened on her eyelids. Alyosha shuddered inwardly: this girl, he thought, was truthful and sincere and – and she no longer loved Dmitry!

'Yes, yes, it is so!' Mrs Khokhlakov cried.

'Wait, my dear Mrs Khokhlakov. I haven't told you the most important thing. I haven't told you what I decided last night. I can't help feeling that this decision of mine is perhaps a terrible one – for me, but I know I shall never change it – not for anything in the world. All my life it's going to be like that. My dear, kind, generous adviser and the only friend I have in the world, Ivan Karamazov, a man who has a profound knowledge of the human heart, is entirely of my opinion and approves my decision. . . . He knows it.'

'Yes, I approve it,' Ivan said in a soft but firm voice.

'But I want Alyosha too (I'm sorry, Alexey, to have called you simply Alyosha), I want Alexey, too, to tell me now in the presence of my two friends whether I'm right or not. I feel instinctively that you, Alyosha, my dear brother (because you are my dear brother),' she repeated rapturously, seizing his cold hand with her hot one, 'I feel that your decision, your approval, will set my mind at rest, in spite of all my sufferings, because after your words I shall calm down and reconcile myself to my fate – I feel it!'

'I don't know what you're going to ask me,' Alyosha said, colouring. 'I only know that I like you and wish you more happiness at this moment than I wish myself! But, you see, I know nothing about these things,' he suddenly hastened to add for some reason.

'What is important about these things now, Alexey, is honour and duty, and I don't know what else, but something higher, something higher perhaps than duty itself. My heart tells me about this irresistible feeling and it draws me on irresistibly. However, the whole thing can be put in a few words. I've made up my mind already. Even if he marries that – that – creature,' she began solemnly, 'whom I can never, never forgive, *I shall not leave him all the same!* From this day on I shall never, never leave him!' she declared with a sort of heartache and a sort of pale, agonizing rapture. 'I don't mean, of course, that I'm going to trail after him, catch his eye every minute, torment him – oh, no! I'll go away to another town, anywhere you like, but I shall keep watch over him all my life, all my life, without ever tiring of it. And when she makes him unhappy, which she is sure to do, and very soon, too, then let him come to me and he'll find a friend, a sister. . . . Only a sister, of course, and that will always be so, but at last he'll be convinced that this sister is really *his* sister, who loves him and who has sacrificed all her life for him. I'll see to it. I shall insist that at last he shall know me as I am and tell me everything without being ashamed of it!' she cried, as though beside herself. 'I shall be his goddess, to whom he will offer up prayers – that at least he owes me for his treachery and for what I went through yesterday because of him. And let him see all through his life that in spite of the fact that he was untrue to me and betrayed me, I shall be true to him all my life and faithful to the word I gave him once. I shall – I shall be only the means of his happiness or – how shall I put it? – the instrument, the engine of his happiness, and that all my life, all my life, and let him know that beforehand all through his life! That is my decision! Ivan is entirely in agreement with me.'

She was choking. She may have wished to express her thought in a much more dignified, more skilful and more natural way, but it turned out to be too hurried and much too obvious. There was a great deal of youthful lack of self-control, a great deal of it was the result of her exasperation of the day before, of her need to hold up her head, and she was conscious of it herself. Her face suddenly seemed to become overcast and there was an angry look in her eyes. Alyosha noticed it all at once and his heart was touched with pity. And just then Ivan put in his word, too.

'I've merely expressed my opinion,' he said. 'With any other woman all this would be morbid and neurotic, but with you it isn't. Any other woman would have been wrong, but you are right.

I don't know what reason to give for it, but I can see that you're as sincere as it's possible to be, and that is why you are right. . . . '

'But that's only at this moment,' cried Mrs Khokhlakov, unable to restrain herself, though obviously not wishing to interfere, but suddenly hitting the nail on the head. 'And what is this moment? Why, it's simply yesterday's insult – that's all it is!'

'Quite true, quite true,' Ivan interrupted with a kind of sudden passion and visibly furious at being interrupted, 'quite true! With any other woman this moment would be only the result of yesterday's impression, and it would be only a moment, but with Katerina's character this moment will last all her life. What for others is only a promise, is for her an everlasting, a heavy, perhaps a grim, but an unremitting duty. And she will be sustained by this feeling of fulfilled duty! Your life, Katerina, will now be spent in a martyr-like contemplation of your own feelings, your own heroism and your own sorrow, but later on that suffering will be alleviated and your life will be transformed into sweet contemplation of a steadfast and proud design carried out once and for all, a truly proud design of its kind, desperate in any case, but which you've carried out triumphantly. And the consciousness of it will at last bring you the fullest possible satisfaction and will reconcile you to everything else. . . . '

He said it quite unmistakably with a sort of malice, obviously on purpose, and perhaps without even meaning to conceal his intention, that is to say, of saying it on purpose and derisively.

'Oh dear, it isn't like that at all!' Mrs Khokhlakov cried again.

'Tell me what you think, Alexey! I'm so anxious to know what you will say!' exclaimed Katerina, suddenly bursting into tears.

Alyosha got up from the sofa.

'It's nothing, nothing!' she went on, weeping. 'It's because I'm upset, it's because of what happened last night. But by the side of two such friends as you and your brother, I still feel strong. For I know that – that you two will never desert me.'

'I'm afraid,' Ivan said suddenly, 'that unfortunately I may have to go to Moscow tomorrow and leave you for a long time. And – er – unfortunately I can't do anything about it.'

'To Moscow – tomorrow!' Katerina cried, her whole face suddenly becoming contorted. 'But – good heavens, how fortunate that is!' she exclaimed in a completely changed voice and in a flash wiping away her tears so that not a trace of them was left.

This remarkable change in her, which greatly astonished Alyosha, took place in a flash: instead of a poor insulted girl who a moment before had been weeping as if her heart would break, there suddenly appeared a woman who was in complete control of herself and who even seemed to be extremely self-satisfied, as though she were suddenly glad of something.

'Oh,' she seemed to correct herself suddenly with the charming smile of a woman of the world, 'I don't mean it is fortunate because I must take leave of you. A friend like you can't possibly think that. On the contrary, I'm very unhappy to lose you' (she suddenly rushed up impetuously to Ivan and, seizing him by both hands, pressed them warmly). 'What is fortunate is that you will now be able to tell my aunt and my sister Agafya personally about my present situation, about the awful state I'm in now, and I hope you'll be absolutely frank with Agafya but spare my dear aunt, for I'm sure you will know best how to do it. You can't imagine how unhappy I was yesterday and this morning trying to think how to write this awful letter to them – for it's quite impossible to tell them everything in a letter. . . . But now I'll find it easy to write because you'll be there to explain everything. Oh, I'm so glad! But, please, believe me, I'm only glad of that. You yourself are of course quite indispensable to me. I'll go at once and write the letter,' she suddenly concluded, and even made to leave the room.

'And what about Alyosha?' cried Mrs Khokhlakov. 'What about Alyosha's opinion which you were so anxious to hear?'

An angry and caustic note could be heard in her voice.

'I haven't forgotten that,' said Katerina, stopping suddenly. 'And why are you so unkind to me at such a moment, Mrs Khokhlakov?' she cried with warm and bitter reproach. 'I stand by what I said. I must have his opinion and, what's more, I must have his decision! I shall do as he says. That's how much I long to hear what you have to say, Alexey, but – what's the matter with you?'

'I never thought it possible!' Alyosha suddenly cried sorrowfully. 'I couldn't have imagined it!'

'What? What?'

'He's going to Moscow and you cry that you're glad – you said that on purpose! Then you began explaining that you were not glad he was going, but that you were sorry to – to lose a friend, but that, too, you were acting on purpose – you were playing a part in a comedy – as on the stage!...'

'On the stage? What? What do you mean?' Katerina exclaimed in great astonishment, flushing all over and frowning.

'Why, however much you assure him that you're sorry to lose a friend in him, you still persist in telling him to his face that it's fortunate he is leaving,' Alyosha said, almost choking with excitement.

He was standing at the table and did not sit down.

'What are you talking about? I don't understand....'

'I hardly know myself.... It's as though I had a sudden illumination.... I know I'm putting it badly, but I'll tell you everything all the same,' Alyosha went on in the same trembling and faltering voice. 'My illumination consists in the realization that perhaps you don't love my brother Dmitry at all ... that you've never loved him from the very beginning. And Dmitry, too, perhaps doesn't love you at all and has never loved you – from the very beginning. He only respects you. I – I really don't know how I dare tell you all this now, but I must tell the truth to someone because – because no one here wishes to tell the truth....'

'What truth?' cried Katerina, and there was a hysterical note in her voice.

'This,' murmured Alyosha, as though jumping off a roof. 'Call Dmitry now – I'll fetch him – and let him come here and take you by the hand and then take Ivan by the hand and join your hands. For you're torturing Ivan only because you love him – and you torture him because, having worked yourself up into an emotional state of heartache, you imagine that you love Dmitry – but you don't love him – you've only persuaded yourself that you do....'

Alyosha broke off and was silent.

'You – you – you're a little religious halfwit – that's what you are!' Katerina suddenly snapped out, her face white and her lips contorted with anger.

Ivan suddenly burst out laughing and got up. His hat was in his hand.

'You're mistaken, my good Alyosha,' he said with an expression

Alyosha had never seen on his face before, an expression of a sort of youthful sincerity and powerful, irresistibly frank emotion. 'Katerina never cared for me! She knew all the time that I loved her, though I never said a word to her about my love – she knew, but she did not care for me. Neither have I ever been her friend – not once, not for a single day: she's a proud woman and did not need my friendship. She kept me at her side out of a constant desire for revenge. She revenged herself on me and with me for all the insults which she continually had to bear all the time from Dmitry, ever since their first meeting. For even the memory of their very first meeting remained in her heart as an insult. That's what her heart is like! All I heard from her was about her love for him. I'm going away now, but I'd like you to know, Katerina, that you really love only him. And the more insults he heaps on you, the more you love him. That is your heartache. You love him just as he is. You love him even while he insults you. If he reformed, you'd at once throw him over and fall out of love with him entirely. But you need him in order to be able to contemplate continually your great act of faithfulness and to reproach him for his unfaithfulness. And all this because of your pride. . . . Oh, there's a lot here of humiliation and humility, but it's all because of your pride. . . . I'm too young and I loved you too much. I know that I shouldn't have told you that, that it would have been more dignified of me just to leave you. It would not have been so offensive to you. But then I'm going far away and I shall never come back. It's for good. . . . I do not wish to stay beside a woman suffering from heartache. . . . However, I don't know what more I could say. I've said everything. . . . Good-bye, Katerina. You mustn't be angry with me, because I've been punished a hundred times more than you: punished by the very fact that I shall never see you again. Good-bye. I don't want your hand. You've tortured me too deliberately for me to forgive you now. I shall forgive you later, but I don't want your hand now.

Den Dank, Dame, begehr ich nicht!'
he added with a wry smile, having proved, however, quite unexpectedly that he, too, could read Schiller to be able to quote him, which Alyosha would not have believed before.

He went out of the room, without even taking leave of the hostess, Mrs Khokhlakov. Alyosha clasped his hands in dismay.

'Ivan,' he shouted after him, miserably, 'come back, Ivan! No,' he exclaimed again in a flash of grief-stricken illumination, 'he won't come back for anything now! But I – I am to blame for that. I began wrongly. Ivan spoke unfairly and spitefully. He must come here again. He must come back. He must!' Alyosha kept crying like one demented.

Katerina suddenly went into the other room.

'You've done nothing wrong, you acted beautifully, like an angel!' Mrs Khokhlakov whispered rapidly and rapturously to the grief-stricken Alyosha. 'I'll do all I can to prevent Ivan from going away.'

Her face, to Alyosha's great distress, was radiant with joy. But Katerina suddenly came back. She had two hundred-rouble notes in her hands.

'I have a great favour to ask of you,' she began, addressing herself straight to Alyosha in an apparently calm and level voice, as though nothing had really happened a moment before. 'A week ago, yes, I believe it was a week ago, Dmitry was guilty of a very hasty and unfair action, a very ugly action. There's a very low-class public house here. There he met that retired army officer, that captain your father had employed on some business of his. Losing his temper with the captain for some reason or other, Dmitry seized him by the beard and dragged him out into the street in that humiliating state, and dragged him for a long distance. I'm told that a boy, the son of this captain, who is at the school here, quite a child, saw it all and ran behind them crying and begging for his father, appealing to everyone in the street to defend him, but everyone laughed at him. I'm sorry, Alexey, but I cannot recall without indignation this disgraceful action of *his* – one of those actions which only Dmitry would be capable of in his anger and – in his passion! I cannot even tell you about it. I can't bring myself to. I cannot find the right words. I've made inquiries about the injured man and I found out that he is very poor. His surname is Snegiryov. He seems to have committed some offence in the army and been discharged. I'm afraid I can't tell you anything about it. Now he and his family, his unhappy family of sick children and a sick wife – I believe she is insane – are absolutely destitute. He's been living in this town a long time, he used to do some work as a copying clerk in some office, but now he isn't paid anything. When I saw you, I – I mean, I thought – I don't know –

I'm afraid I'm rather confused – you see, I wanted to ask you, Alexey, my dear Alexey, to go and see him. Find some excuse to go there, I mean, to that captain – oh dear, I'm so muddled – and delicately and courteously, as only you can do it' (Alyosha suddenly blushed), 'I mean as only you would know how to, give him these two hundred roubles. I'm sure he'll accept it – I mean, you'll persuade him to accept it. Or rather how am I to put it? You see, I'm not giving him the money because I want to conciliate him and keep him from going to the police (as I believe he was going to do), but just as an expression of my sympathy, of my desire to help him. From me, from me, Dmitry's fiancée, and not from Dmitry. . . . In short, you'll know how to do it. He lives in Lake Street, in the house of a Mrs Kalmykov. Do me this favour, Alexey, for heaven's sake, and now – now – I'm afraid I'm feeling a little tired. . . . Good-bye. . . . '

She turned round and again disappeared behind the door curtains so suddenly that Alyosha had no time to say anything, and he wanted to speak to her. He wanted to ask her forgiveness, to blame himself – just to say something, for his heart was full and he was unwilling to leave the room without it. But Mrs Khokhlakov seized him by the hand and led him out of the room herself. In the hall she stopped him once more as before.

'She's proud, she's struggling with herself, but she's so kind, so charming, so generous!' Mrs Khokhlakov kept exclaiming in an undertone. 'Oh, how I love her, especially when – and how glad I am of everything, simply of everything now! Dear Alexey, I don't think you knew it, but now I can tell you that all of us, her two aunts and I, I mean, simply everyone, even Lise, have been praying that she should give up your favourite Dmitry, who doesn't want to know her and doesn't love her, and marry Ivan, who is such a cultured and nice young man and who loves her more than anything in the world. You see, we've been hatching a regular plot here, and that's perhaps why I'm staying here. . . . '

'But,' Alyosha exclaimed, 'she's been crying, she's been humiliated again!'

'Do not believe a woman's tears, dear Alexey. In a case like this, I'm always against the woman and for the man.'

'Mother, you're spoiling and ruining him,' Lise's thin voice was heard again behind the door.

'No, I'm the cause of it all, I'm to blame for everything!' the disconsolate Alyosha kept repeating in a fit of agonizing shame for his outburst, and even covering his face in his shame.

'On the contrary, you acted like an angel, like an angel. I don't mind repeating it a hundred thousand times.'

'Mother, why was he acting like an angel?' Lise's thin voice was heard again.

'Seeing it all, I imagined for some reason,' Alyosha went on, as though he had not heard Lise, 'that she loved Ivan. That's why I said that stupid thing – and what's going to happen now?'

'But to whom – to whom?' cried Lise. 'Mother, I'm sure you want to kill me. I'm asking you and you don't answer.'

At this moment the parlour maid rushed in.

'Miss Katerina is ill. She's crying – she's in hysterics, she's having convulsions!'

'What's the matter?' cried Lise, with real alarm. 'Mother, I'm going to have hysterics, not her!'

'Lise, for heaven's sake, don't scream and don't upset me so. You're much too young to know everything grown-ups know. I'll come presently and tell you everything you can be told. Oh, good heavens, I'm coming, I'm coming! She's having hysterics – that's a good sign, Alexey. It's wonderful that she's having hysterics. It's just what she needs. In a case like that I'm always against women, against all these hysterical fits and tears. Julia, go and tell her that I'm coming to her. And she's only herself to blame that Ivan has gone out like that. But he won't go away. Lise, for goodness' sake, don't scream like that! Oh dear, you're not screaming at all, are you? It's me who's screaming. Forgive your mother, darling, but I'm delighted, delighted, delighted! And did you notice, my dear Alexey, how young, how young Ivan looked when he went out, when he said all that and went out? I thought he was so learned, so scholarly, and suddenly he spoke so warmly, so warmly, so frankly, just like a very young man, a very inexperienced young man. And how wonderful it all was! How wonderful, just as if it were you. . . . And he recited that German verse just like you too! But I must fly, I must fly. Do hurry up with her commission, Alexey, and come back quickly. Lise, you don't want anything, do you, darling? For goodness' sake don't keep Alexey a minute longer. He'll come back to you presently. . . . '

Mrs Khokhlakov ran off at last. Before leaving, Alyosha was about to open the door to see Lise.

'Not for anything in the world!' cried Lise. 'Not for anything in the world now! Speak through the door. Why are you an angel? That's all I want to know.'

'Because I did something terribly stupid, Lise. Good-bye.'

'Don't you dare to go away like that!' cried Lise.

'Lise, I am terribly unhappy! I'll be back presently, but I have a great, great sorrow!'

And he ran out of the room.

6

Heartache in the Cottage

HE really was very unhappy and it was something he had rarely experienced before. He had rushed in and 'put his foot in it', and in what sort of business: in a love affair! 'What do I understand of such things?' he asked himself for the hundredth time, blushing. 'How can I be expected to make sense of such an affair? Oh, shame wouldn't matter, shame is nothing but the punishment I deserve. The trouble is that I shall now be the cause of more unhappiness. . . . And the elder sent me to reconcile and bring them together. Is that the way to bring them together?' Here he again remembered how he 'joined their hands' and he again felt terribly ashamed. 'Though I did it in all sincerity, I must be more intelligent in future,' he concluded suddenly and did not even smile at his conclusion.

Katerina's commission took him to Lake Street and his brother Dmitry lived not far away, in a lane near Lake Street. Alyosha decided in any case to go and see him before the captain, though he had a feeling that he would not be in. He suspected that he would perhaps somehow deliberately try to avoid him now, but he had to find him at all costs. Time was passing and the thought of the dying elder had not left him for one moment ever since he had left the monastery.

There was, besides, one thing in Katerina's commission that interested him particularly: when she mentioned the little boy, the schoolboy who had run crying loudly beside his father, the thought had suddenly flashed through Alyosha's mind that that boy was quite certainly the schoolboy who had bitten his finger when he had been trying to find out how he had wronged him. Now Alyosha was almost sure of it, though he did not know why himself. Having become thus absorbed in another train of thought, he felt better and decided not to think of 'the trouble' he had just caused, not to torture himself with remorse, but to carry on with what he had to do regardless of the consequences. That thought restored his good spirits. At the same time, turning into the lane where his brother lived and feeling hungry, he took out the roll he had brought from his father's and ate it on the way. This fortified him.

Dmitry was out. The owners of the little house where he lived – an old carpenter, his old wife, and his son – looked at Alyosha with suspicion. 'He hasn't slept here for three nights, perhaps he's gone away somewhere,' the old man replied to Alyosha's repeated questions. Alyosha realized that he was replying in accordance with Dmitry's instructions. When he asked whether Dmitry was at Grushenka's or whether he was again hiding at Foma's (Alyosha spoke frankly of these confidential matters on purpose), all three of them looked at him with alarm. 'They must be fond of him,' thought Alyosha. 'They're on his side. That's good!'

At last he found the house of Mrs Kalmykov in Lake Street. It was a ramshackle little house, lopsided, with only three windows looking on to the street, and a filthy backyard, in the middle of which stood a solitary cow. The entrance to the house was from the yard straight into the passage and on the left of the passage lived the old landlady with an old daughter, both of them apparently deaf. In reply to his inquiry about the captain, which he had to repeat a few times, one of them at last grasped that he was asking about their lodgers, and pointed to the door of the living-room across the passage. The captain's lodging really turned out to be simply the living-room of the cottage. Alyosha took hold of the iron latch to open the door when he was suddenly struck by the unusual silence behind it. He knew, however, from what Katerina had told him that the retired captain had a family. 'They are either all asleep or they may have heard me coming in and are waiting for me to open the door; perhaps I'd better knock first,' and he knocked. An answer came, not at once, though, but after an interval of about ten seconds.

'Who's there?' someone shouted harshly in a loud and angry voice.

Alyosha opened the door and crossed the threshold. He found himself in a fairly spacious room, cluttered up with furniture and household things of all kinds. There were a number of people in it. To the left was a large Russian stove. A line with all sorts of washing was stretched across the whole room from the stove to the window on the left. Along the two walls on the left and right stood beds covered with knitted blankets. On the left one was a heap of four cotton pillows, each smaller than the other. On the right one, however, only one very small pillow could be seen. The opposite corner was screened off by a curtain or a sheet, hanging over a rope stretched across it. Behind the curtain could be seen another bed made up of a bench and a chair. A plain, square wooden table of the type found in peasants' cottages had been moved from the corner to the middle window. All the three windows, each consisting of four green, grimy little panes, let through very little light and were tightly shut, so that the room was rather stuffy and dark. On the table was a frying-pan with the remnants of fried eggs, a half-eaten piece of bread and, in addition, half a pint with the dregs of earthly cheer on the very bottom. On a chair beside the bed on the left sat a woman of genteel appearance wearing a cotton dress. Her face was very thin and sallow and her exceedingly hollow cheeks showed at once that she was ill. But Alyosha was most of all struck by the look the poor lady had given him – a questioning and at the same time very haughty look. And until the woman spoke herself and while Alyosha was explaining the reason for his visit to the captain, she kept glancing from the one to the other with the same questioning and haughty brown eyes. A rather plain-looking young girl, with thin, reddish hair and poorly, though neatly, dressed, stood by the left window near the woman. As Alyosha came in, she looked him up and down with unconcealed revulsion. There was another girl sitting by the bed on the right. She was a very pitiful little thing, a young girl of twenty, but a hunch-back, and, as Alyosha was afterwards told, with withered legs. Her crutches were beside her, in the corner between the bed and the wall. The remarkably beautiful and tender eyes of the poor girl looked at Alyosha with a kind of meek serenity. At the table, finishing the fried egg, sat a man of about five and forty, of medium height,

spare, weakly built, with reddish hair and a thin, reddish beard which
bore a striking resemblance to a bast-sponge (this comparison and
particularly the word 'bast-sponge' for some reason flashed instan-
taneously through Alyosha's mind – he recalled it afterwards). It
was evidently that same man who had shouted, 'Who's there?',
for there was no other man in the room. But when Alyosha came in,
he seemed to leap from the bench on which he was sitting at the
table and, hastily wiping his mouth with a tattered napkin, rushed
up to Alyosha.

'A monk begging for his monastery,' the young girl standing in
the left corner said in a loud voice. 'He came to the right place!'

But the man, who had run up to Alyosha, at once spun round to
her and answered her in an excited and a sort of shaky voice:

'No, madam, it's not that at all. You're wrong! May I ask you,
sir,' he suddenly turned round to Alyosha again, 'to what I owe the
honour of your visit to this – er – humble abode?'

Alyosha looked at him attentively: it was the first time he had
seen the man. There was something angular, flurried, and irritable
about him. Though he had obviously been drinking just now, he
was not drunk. His face expressed a sort of extreme arrogance and,
which was so strange, at the same time unconcealed cowardice. He
looked like a man who had for a long time been at the beck and call
of other people and had suffered a great deal, but who had suddenly
jumped to his feet and tried to assert himself. Or, better still, like a
man who wanted terribly to hit you, but who was terribly afraid
that you might hit him back. There was a sort of weak-minded
humour in his words and the inflexion of his rather shrill voice,
spiteful and timid in turn, but unable to keep it up for any length of
time and faltering continuously. His question about 'the humble
abode' he asked with protruding eyes and as though trembling all
over, and rushing up so close to Alyosha that he unconsciously recoiled a step. The man was wearing a dark, rather threadbare overcoat of some nankeen material, stained and patched. His trousers were
of a very light check material, which had not been in fashion for a
long time and which were so crumpled at the bottom that they
looked as though he had worn them as a boy and grown out of them.

'I'm – Alexey Karamazov,' Alyosha said in reply.

'That, sir, I'm perfectly well aware of,' the man at once snapped out to let him know that his identity was no secret to him. 'And I, sir, am Captain Snegiryov, sir. But I'm still anxious to know, sir, to what I owe the honour — '

'As a matter of fact, I haven't come for any special reason. I just wanted to have a word with you, if you don't mind.'

'In that case, sir, here's a chair and do me the honour of being seated. That, sir, is what they used to say in the old comedies: "do me the honour of being seated".'

And with a rapid gesture the captain seized an empty chair (a plain, deal, unupholstered chair), and put it almost in the middle of the room; then, seizing another similar chair for himself, he sat down facing Alyosha, and, as before, so close to him that their knees almost touched.

'Nikolai Ilyich Snegiryov, sir, a former captain of Russian infantry, sir, and though disgraced by his vices, still a captain, sir. I should perhaps have introduced myself as Captain Sir and not as Captain Snegiryov, for it's only during the latter half of my life that I have begun saying "sir" to people. The word, "sir", sir, one acquires only when one has come down in the world.'

'That is so,' Alyosha smiled, 'but does one acquire it voluntarily or involuntarily?'

'God knows, involuntarily. I never used to say it, all my life I never used to say "sir", but suddenly I fell and got up with "sir" on my lips. That is brought about by a higher power. I can see that you're interested in contemporary problems. But how could I have aroused your curiosity, living as I do in surroundings in which the exercise of hospitality is impossible?'

'I've come about – that business.'

'About what business?' Snegiryov interrupted impatiently.

'About that encounter of yours with my brother Dmitry,' Alyosha blurted out awkwardly.

'What encounter, sir? You don't mean *that* encounter, sir? Are you referring to the bast-sponge, the bath bast-sponge?'

This time he moved so close to Alyosha that their knees positively knocked against each other. He compressed his lips so tightly that they seemed almost to disappear.

'What bast-sponge?' murmured Alyosha.

'He's come to complain to you about me, Daddy,' cried a voice familiar to Alyosha, the voice of the schoolboy, from behind the curtain. 'It was me who bit his finger this afternoon.'

The curtain was drawn aside, and Alyosha saw his old enemy lying on the bed made up on the bench and the chair in the corner under the icons. The boy lay covered by his overcoat and an old quilt. He was evidently not well and, to judge by his burning eyes, in a fever. He looked fearlessly, and not as he had done earlier, at Alyosha, as though he wished to say: 'You won't dare touch me at home!'

'Bit his finger?' Snegiryov cried, half rising from his chair. 'Did he bite your finger, sir?'

'Yes, I'm afraid so. He was exchanging volleys of stones with the boys in the street. There were six of them against him alone. I went up to him and he threw a stone at me, then another at my head. I asked him what I had done to him, but he suddenly rushed up to me and bit my finger badly. I don't know why.'

'I shall give him a hiding at once, sir. This very minute, sir!' Snegiryov now really did jump up from his chair.

'But I'm not complaining at all. I merely told you what happened. I don't want you to give him a hiding. Besides, I believe he's ill now. . . .'

'And did you really think I'd give him a hiding, sir? That I'd take my darling boy and thrash him in front of you for your greater satisfaction? Do you want me to do it immediately, sir?' said Snegiryov, turning suddenly to Alyosha as though about to hurl himself upon him. 'I'm very sorry, sir, for your poor finger, but, before thrashing my boy, wouldn't you rather I chopped off four of my fingers in front of you with this knife for your still greater satisfaction? Four fingers, I should think, sir, should be enough to satisfy your thirst for revenge. You won't demand my fifth one, too, will you?'

He suddenly stopped short as though out of breath. Every muscle of his face jerked and trembled, and he looked with the utmost defiance at Alyosha. He seemed beside himself.

'I think I understand everything now,' Alyosha replied quietly and sadly, without getting up. 'So your little boy is a good boy. He loves his father and attacked me because I'm the brother of the man who insulted you. I understand it now,' he repeated musingly. 'But my brother Dmitry is sorry for what he did. I know that. And if he could only come to see you, or, better still, if he could meet you in the same place, he'd apologize to you before everyone – if you wish it.'

'You mean, he pulled out my beard and now he's going to apologize for it? Everything fair and square. Is that what he thinks?'

'Oh, no. Quite the contrary. He'll do anything you like and as you like.'

'So that if I, sir, should ask his lordship to go down on his knees before me in that same pub – Metropolis it's called – or in the square, he'd do so, would he?'

'Yes, he would.'

'I'm deeply moved, sir. Deeply moved. Moved to tears, sir. I feel it, sir. I do, indeed. Allow me to introduce my family: my two daughters and my son – my litter, sir. If I die, who will care for them? And while I live, sir, who but they will care for a dirty wretch like me? This great thing the good Lord has arranged for every man of my sort, sir. For it's necessary that a man of my sort, too, should have someone to care for him, sir.'

'Yes, that's quite true!' cried Alyosha.

'Oh, do stop playing the fool!' cried the girl at the window unexpectedly, turning to her father with an air of disgust and disdain. 'Some idiot comes along and you have to put us all to shame!'

'Wait a little, Varvara, let me show myself in my true colours first,' cried her father in a peremptory tone, but looking at her quite approvingly. 'That's the sort of character she has, sir,' he turned again to Alyosha.

'And in all creation there was naught
To which his blessing he would give.

'I really should have put it in the feminine: to which her blessing she would give. But now do let me introduce you to my wife, Arina Petrovna, a lady with bad legs. She's forty-three. She can move her legs, but only a little, sir. She's of humble origin, sir. Smooth your brow, madam: this is Mr Alexey Karamazov. Get up, sir,' he addressed Alyosha, taking him by the hand and pulling him up with quite unexpected force. 'You're being introduced to a lady, sir, so you have to get up. It isn't the Karamazov, Mother, who – well –

and so on, but his brother, shining bright with lowly virtues. Allow me, my dear, allow me, Mother, to kiss your hand first.'

And he kissed his wife's hand respectfully and even tenderly. The girl at the window turned her back indignantly on the scene. An expression of extraordinary tenderness suddenly came over the disdainfully questioning face of Mrs Snegiryov.

'Good afternoon, do sit down, Mr Chernomazov,' she said.

'Karamazov, Mother, Karamazov! We're of humble origin, sir,' he again whispered to Alyosha.

'Well, Karamazov, or whatever it is, but I always say Chernomazov. Sit down, please. Why has he made you get up? A lady with bad legs, says he, but I've got legs all right, only they're swollen like buckets, while I'm all wasted myself. Used to be ever so fat before, but now I'm as thin as a rake.'

'We're of humble origin, sir, of humble origin,' Snegiryov whispered again in explanation.

'Oh, Father, Father!' the hunchbacked girl, who had been silent till then, said suddenly and hid her eyes in her kerchief.

'Buffoon!' the girl at the window snapped out.

'You see the sort of news we have,' said the mother, spreading out her hands and pointing to her daughters. 'It's just like clouds coming over: the clouds pass, and again the same music. Before, when we were army folk, we had many such visitors. Comparisons are odious, my dear sir. If anyone loves someone, let him love him, I says. The deacon's wife used to visit us and, "Alexander Alexandrovich," she says, "is a most excellent man," she says, "but Nastasya Petrovna is a fiend of a woman." "Well," I says to her, "everyone to his taste," I says, "but you, my dear," I says, "may be a little thing, but you smell bad." "And you," she says, "must be kept in your place." "Oh," I says to her, "you common dirt, who have you come to teach?" "My breath," she says, "is sweet and yours is foul." "Well," I says to her, "you'd better ask the gentlemen officers whether my breath is sweet or foul." And ever since I can't get it out of my mind. A few days later I was sitting just as I'm doing now, when the general who came at Easter comes in: "Sir," I says to him, "ought not a lady to breathe fresh air?" "Why, yes," he says, "only you'd better open a window or the door because," he says, "the air here is not fresh." And they all go on like that! And why make such a fuss about my

breath? The dead smell still worse. "I'm not befouling your air,"
I says to them. "I'll order a pair of shoes and go away." My darlings,
don't blame your own mother! Nikolai, dear, haven't I done everything to please you? I've only got darling Ilya who comes home from
school and loves me. He brought me an apple yesterday. Forgive me,
my darlings, forgive your own mother, my dears, forgive a lonely
old woman. And why has my breath become so repulsive to you?'

And the poor woman burst out sobbing, her tears gushing out of
her eyes. Snegiryov dashed up to her.

'Stop crying, my dear, stop crying, darling! You're not a lonely
old woman. We all love you. We all adore you, my dear!'

And he began kissing her hands again and stroking her face tenderly
with both hands. Snatching up the table napkin, he suddenly began
wiping her tears. Alyosha fancied that he, too, had tears in his eyes.

'Well, sir,' Snegiryov suddenly turned to him fiercely, pointing
to the poor feeble-minded woman, 'seen her? Heard her?'

'I see and hear,' murmured Alyosha.

'Father, father, you're not appealing to him, are you?'

'Leave him alone, Daddy!' the boy cried suddenly, sitting up on
his bed and looking at his father with burning eyes.

'It's high time you stopped playing the clown and showing off
your silly tricks, which never lead to anything!' cried Varvara from
the corner of the room, losing her temper completely and even stamping her foot.

'You're quite right to lose your temper this time, madam, and I
shall instantly satisfy you. Put on your cap, sir,' he addressed Alyosha,
'and I'll put on mine and let's go, sir. I've something important to
tell you, but outside these walls. This girl sitting here is my daughter
Nina, sir. I'm afraid I forgot to introduce you – she's an angel
incarnate who – er – who's flown down to us mortals – if – er – you
see what I mean, sir. . . . '

'Look at him, shaking all over, as though seized with spasms,'
Varvara went on indignantly.

'And that one who's stamping her feet at me and called me a
clown, sir, is also an angel incarnate, and she was right, sir, to call
me that. Come along, sir, we must get it settled. . . . '

And seizing Alyosha by the hand, he led him out of the room into
the street.

7

And in the Open Air

'HERE the air's fresh, sir, but I'm afraid I can't say as much for the air in my castle in any sense of the word. Let's walk slowly, sir. I'd very much like to enlist your interest, sir.'

'I too, have to discuss a very important matter with you,' observed Alyosha. 'Only I don't know how to begin. . . .'

'I realize, of course, that you have some business with me, sir. You'd never have come to see me if you had no business. You didn't really come to complain about my boy, did you? That would indeed be highly improbable. By the way, about my boy, sir. I couldn't explain it to you in there, but now I can describe the scene to you. You see, sir, only a week ago my bast-sponge was much thicker. I'm referring to my beard, sir. It's my little beard they nicknamed a bast-sponge, sir. The schoolboys chiefly. Well, then, sir, so there was your brother Dmitry dragging me by my beard. Dragged me out into the square, sir, and just then the schoolboys were coming out of school and Ilyusha with them. As soon as he saw me in such a state, he rushed up to me: "Daddy," he cried, "Daddy!" He caught hold of me, flung his little arms round me, trying to free me and shouting to my assailant: "Let him go, let him go! It's my Daddy! Forgive him, sir!" Yes, indeed. "Forgive him!" he cried. He clutched at him with his hand. He kissed his hand. That same hand – yes, sir, he kissed it! I remember what his face looked like at that moment – I haven't forgotten it, sir. I shall never forget it!'

'I swear,' cried Alyosha, 'he'll apologize to you with the utmost sincerity, with absolute sincerity, even if he has to go down on his knees in that same square. . . . I shall make him do it, or he's no brother of mine!'

'Oh, I see! So that's still only a suggestion! It doesn't come from him, but only from the generosity of your own warm heart, sir! Why didn't you say so before, sir? Well, sir, in that case let me, too, tell you of your brother's highly chivalrous and soldierly generosity, for he showed it to the full at the time. After he'd left off dragging me by my bast-sponge and had set me free, he said to me: "You're an officer and I'm an officer. If you can find a decent fellow to be your second, send him to me, and I'll give you satisfaction, dirty rotter though you are!" That's what he said, sir. A truly chivalrous spirit! We went away then, Ilyusha and I, and our genealogical family tree remained forever imprinted on little Ilya's mind. No, sir, we cannot claim to be noblemen any more. Judge for yourself, sir. You've just been in our castle – what did you see there? Three ladies, sir, one a weak-minded cripple, another a hunchback cripple, and a third not crippled but too clever by half. A university woman, sir. Anxious to go back to Petersburg and look for the rights of the Russian women on the banks of the Neva. I say nothing about Ilyusha. He's only nine years old, sir. I'm all alone in the world, and if I die what will become of all of them – tell me that, sir! And if that's so, what's going to happen if I challenge him and he kills me on the spot? What will then become of them all? And if he doesn't kill me but only cripples me, it will be still worse: I shan't be able to work, but a mouth has to be fed, and who'll feed it, my mouth, that is, and who will feed all of them? Or should I send Ilyusha out to beg in the streets instead of sending him to school? So that's what challenging to a duel means to me, sir. It's a lot of silly talk, sir, and nothing else.'

'He will beg you to forgive him,' Alyosha cried again with burning eyes. 'He'll go down on his knees at your feet in the square!'

'I thought of summonsing him,' Snegiryov went on, 'but look up our code of laws, sir. Could I get much compensation from my assailant for a personal injury? And then Miss Svetlov, sir, sent for me: "Don't you dare to think of it," she shouted. "If you summons him, I'll see to it that the whole world gets to know that he beat you because of your own double-dealing, and then you'll be put on trial yourself!" And Lord only knows, sir, who was responsible for my double-dealing and at whose orders an insignificant worm like me acted – wasn't it at her own and Mr Karamazov's? "And what's more," she added, "I shall have nothing more to do with you and you'll never earn another penny from me. I shall also tell my merchant (that's what she calls her old man: my merchant), and he'll have nothing to do with you, either." Well, I think to myself, what's going to happen to me if the merchant, too, will have nothing to do with me? Who will provide me with a living then? Those two are the only ones left to me, for your father, sir, has not only stopped trusting me for quite a different reason, but he, too, wants to drag me into court, having obtained my signature to some receipts. As a result of it all, sir, I'm keeping quiet and you've seen our humble abode, haven't you? And now let me ask you: did he bite your finger badly? Ilyusha, I mean? You see, sir, I didn't want to go into it in my castle in front of him.'

'Yes, I'm afraid he did, rather. He was very angry. He was revenging himself on me as a Karamazov for you. I can see it now. But if you'd only seen how he was exchanging volleys of stones with his schoolfellows! It's very dangerous. They might kill him. They're children and stupid. A stone is thrown and somebody's head might get broken.'

'He was hit by a stone today, sir. Not on the head but on the chest, just above the heart. A big bruise, sir. He came home crying and groaning, and now he's ill.'

'And, you know, it's he who attacks them first. He's furious with them on your account. They say he stabbed a boy by the name of Krasotkin with a pen-knife the other day.'

'I've heard about that, too. It is dangerous, sir. Krasotkin is a civil servant here. I daresay there may be trouble.'

'I'd advise you,' Alyosha went on warmly, 'not to send him to school at all for a time until he quiets down and – his anger will pass.'

'His anger, sir!' Snegiryov repeated. 'That's just what it is, sir: anger! A great anger, sir, in a little creature like him. You don't know it all, sir. Let me explain this business in particular. You see, sir, after that incident all his schoolfellows began teasing him at school by calling him a bast-sponge. Schoolchildren are pitiless: singly they are angels, but together, especially at school, they're quite often pitiless. They began teasing him and this roused his spirit. An ordinary boy, a weak son, would have submitted. He would have been ashamed of his father. But Ilyusha stood up for his father – one against the lot of them. For his father, sir. For truth and justice. What he went through when he kissed your brother's hand and shouted to him: "Forgive my Daddy, forgive my Daddy!" – that only God knows, and myself, sir. And this is how our children – I don't mean yours but ours, sir, ours, the children of the despised but honourable poor, sir, learn about justice on earth even when they are only nine years old. The rich never get the chance; they will never explore such depths during the whole of their lives, but my Ilyusha, sir, grasped the whole meaning of truth at the very moment as he was kissing his hands in the square, at that very moment. That truth entered into him and crushed him forever,' Snegiryov said warmly and again as though in a frenzy, striking his right fist on his left hand, as if wishing to demonstrate how 'the truth' had crushed Ilyusha. 'That very day he lay in a fever and was delirious all night. He spoke little to me all that day. He was silent most of the time. Only I noticed that he kept looking at me from his corner, but mostly he kept turning to the window and pretending to be doing his homework. I could see, though, that his mind was not on his homework. Next day, sir, I'm afraid I got drunk, sinner that I am, to drown my sorrows, and I don't remember much. My wife, sir, started crying, too – I love my wife very much, sir – and, well, I spent my last penny on drink. Do not despise me, my dear sir: in Russia the drunkards are the most kindly people. The most kindly people in our country, sir, are the greatest drunkards. Yes, sir. Well, so there I was lying drunk and paying no attention to my little boy, and it was on that very day that the boys at school had made fun of him since morning: "Bast-sponge!" they shouted at him. "Your father was dragged out of the pub by his bast-sponge and you ran alongside asking for forgiveness." When the day after he came back from school again, I could see that he looked very pale. "What's the matter?" I asked. He did not reply. Well, sir, in my castle it's impossible to talk, for my wife and the girls interfere at once. Besides, the girls had by then got to know all about it. On the very first day, in fact. Varvara had begun grumbling already: "Buffoons, clowns, can you ever do anything sensible?" "Quite right," I said to her, "we can't do anything sensible!" That time I got away with it. In the evening, sir, I took my boy out for a walk. I used to take him out for walks every evening before tea, sir, the same way we are walking along now, from our gate to that big stone lying there alone by the wattle fence where the town pasture begins: a deserted and beautiful spot, sir. So there I was walking along with Ilyusha, his hand clasped in mine as usual: a tiny little hand, his fingers thin and cold: he suffers from a weak chest, you know. "Daddy," he says, "Daddy!" "What?" I asked. I could see his eyes flashing. "Daddy, how badly he treated you then, Daddy!" "I'm afraid," I said, "it can't be helped." "Don't make it up with him, Daddy, don't make it up. The boys at school say he's given you ten roubles for it." "No, my boy," I said, "I will never take any money from him for anything." The poor child trembled all over, took my hand in both his hands and kissed it again. "Daddy," he said, "Daddy, you must challenge him to a duel. They say at school that you're a coward and that you won't challenge him to a duel, but accepted ten roubles from him." "I'm afraid, my boy," I replied, "I can't challenge him to a duel," and I explained briefly to him what I've just told you. He listened to me and then he said: "But you shouldn't make it up with him all the same. When I grow up, I'll challenge him myself and kill him!" His eyes shone and glowed. Well, sir, I am his father and I had to tell him what was right, so I told him that it was a sin to kill a man even in a duel. "Daddy," he said, "Daddy, when I grow up I'll knock him down. I'll knock his sabre out of his hand with my own sabre. I'll hurl myself on him, throw him down, raise my sabre over him and say to him: 'I could kill you now on the spot, but I forgive you – there!'" You, you see, sir, what's been going on in his little head during the last two days. He must have been thinking of revenging himself with the sabre for a whole day and night and he must have been talking about it in his delirium at night. Yes, sir. But after that he began to come home from school badly beaten. I found out about it the day before yesterday, and you're quite right, sir: I shall not send him to that school again. When I learnt that he was standing up to his whole class and challenging them all by himself, that he'd become embittered and that his heart was full of resentment, I was frightened for him. We went out for a walk again. "Daddy," he asked, "Daddy, the rich are stronger than anybody else in the world, aren't they?" "Yes," I said, "there are no people in the world stronger than the rich." "Daddy," he said, "I'll get rich, I'll become an officer and I'll conquer everybody, and the Czar will reward me, and I'll come back here and no one will then dare to—" Then after a pause he said, his lips still trembling as before: "Daddy," he said, "what a horrid town this is, Daddy!" "Yes, darling," I said, "it isn't a very nice town." "Daddy," he said, "let's move to another town, to a nice town, where they don't know about us!" "Very well, Ilyusha," I said, "we shall as soon as I've saved up enough money." I was glad of the opportunity of distracting him from his gloomy thoughts, and we began dreaming how we would move to another town, buy a horse and cart. "We'll put Mummy and your sisters in it, cover them up, and you and I will walk beside it. I'll put you in the cart, too, now and then, and I'll walk beside, for we must take care of our horse and we can't all ride. That's how we will go." He was delighted with it, and especially that we would have a horse and cart of our own and he would ride in it. And it's a well-known fact, sir, that a Russian boy is born among horses. We chattered a long time and, "Thank God," I thought, "I've distracted and comforted him." This was the day before yesterday, in the evening, and yesterday evening everything was different again. He went to school in the morning and came back looking very gloomy, too gloomy for my peace of mind. In the evening I took him by the hand and we went out for a walk. He was silent and would not talk. It was getting windy, the sun had gone behind the clouds, there was a nip of autumn in the air, and anyway it was growing dark. We were walking along, feeling depressed both of us. "Well, my boy," I said, "let's see how we're going to get ready for the journey," thinking of how to resume our talk of the day before. He was silent. Only I felt his fingers trembling in my hand. Oh, thought I, it's bad, something new must have happened. We had reached this stone where we are now. I sat down on the stone. In the sky there were lots of kites, flapping and rustling. There must have been as many as thirty kites. For, you see, sir, it's the kite season now. "Well, Ilyusha," I said, "it's time we too got out our last year's kite. I'll mend it –where did you put it away?" My boy said nothing. He looked away, standing sideways to me. Just then the wind rose suddenly, whipping up the sand. He suddenly rushed up to me, threw his arms round my neck, and held me tight. You know, children who are silent and proud and who keep back their tears for a long time are liable to break down suddenly when in great trouble, and once they start crying, they dissolve into floods of tears. With those warm streams of tears he suddenly wetted my face. He sobbed as though in convulsions, trembling all over and clinging close to me as I sat on the stone. "Daddy," he kept crying out, "dear Daddy, how he humiliated you!" Well, sir, I burst into tears, too, and there we sat embracing each other and crying. "Daddy," he said, "Daddy!" "Ilya," I said, "my darling Ilya!" No one saw us there. No one, sir.

Only God saw it. Perhaps he'll put it on my service record. You must thank your brother, sir. No, sir, I shall not thrash my boy for your satisfaction!'

He finished again on his former note of shrill resentment. Alyosha, however, felt that he trusted him and that had there been someone else in his, Alyosha's, place, he would not have 'gone on' like that and would not have told what he had just told him. This encouraged Alyosha, who was moved almost to tears.

'Oh, how I'd like to make friends with your boy!' he exclaimed. 'If only you could arrange it. . . .'

'Why, yes, sir,' Snegiryov murmured.

'But now I must talk to you about something else, something quite different,' Alyosha went on excitedly. 'Listen, please. I've a message for you. That brother of mine, Dmitry, had also insulted his fiancée, a most high-minded girl, of whom you've probably heard. I have a right to tell you about her insult. Indeed, I must do so. For, you see, when she heard about the abominable way you'd been treated and about your unfortunate position, she commissioned me at once – this very afternoon – to offer you some assistance. But only from her alone and not from Dmitry, who had thrown her over. No, not from him and not from me, his brother, either, but from her alone! She begs you to accept her help – you've both been insulted by the same man. . . . In fact, she remembered you when she suffered a similar insult from him – an insult, that is, of equal force. It's as though a sister had come to the assistance of her brother. . . . Indeed, she asked me to persuade you to accept these two hundred roubles from her as from a sister. No one will ever know anything about it, there can be no question of any unjust gossip arising from it – I swear you must accept them, for otherwise – otherwise all men on earth must be enemies of one another! But there are brothers in the world, too. . . . You have a generous heart – you must understand that – you must!'

And Alyosha held out the two new rainbow-coloured hundred-rouble notes to him. They were both standing by the large stone just then, by the fence, and there was no one near. The notes seemed to have produced a tremendous impression on the captain: he gave a start, but at first apparently from sheer astonishment: he had never dreamt of anything of the kind and he had never expected such an outcome. Nothing could have been further from his thoughts than help from anyone – and so large a sum, too! He took the notes and for a whole minute he was almost unable to utter a word. Quite a new expression came into his face.

'Is that for me – for me? So much money – two hundred roubles! Good Lord, I haven't seen so much money for four years – dear me! And she says it's from a sister – is it true, true?'

'I swear that all I told you is the truth!' cried Alyosha.

Snegiryov coloured.

'Look here, sir, look here, if I take it, I shouldn't be acting like a scoundrel, should I? I shouldn't be a scoundrel in your eyes, sir, should I? No, sir, please, listen, listen,' he went on rapidly, touching Alyosha with both hands. 'You're persuading me to accept it by telling me that "a sister" sends it, but inside, deep inside you – you won't feel contempt for me if I take it, will you, sir?'

'No, no, of course not! I swear to you by my salvation I won't. And not a soul will ever know about it: only you, she, and I, and another lady, a great friend of hers. . . .'

'Never mind the lady! Listen, sir, listen carefully, for the time has now come when you have to listen carefully to what I have to say, because you can have no idea what these two hundred roubles mean to me,' the poor fellow went on, working himself up gradually into a kind of incoherent, almost wild enthusiasm. He seemed bewildered and spoke rapidly and hurriedly as though afraid that he would not be allowed to finish what he had to say. 'Apart from the fact that it has been honestly acquired from a highly respected "sister", sir, do you realize that now I shall be able to get medical treatment for my wife and my darling Nina – my hunchback angel – my daughter? Dr Herzenstube paid me a visit once out of the goodness of his heart and spent a whole hour examining them. "Can't make anything of it," he said, "but the mineral water which you can get at our local chemist's" (he left a prescription for it) "will certainly do her a lot of good," and he also prescribed some medicinal baths for her legs. The mineral water costs thirty copecks, and she'd have to drink forty jugs of it, perhaps. So I took the prescription and put it on the shelf under the icons, and it's still there now. And he prescribed hot baths for Nina with some kind of solution in them, twice a day, in the morning and in the evening, so where could we provide such treatment for her in that castle of ours, without a maid, without help, without a bath, and without water? Poor Nina has rheumatic pains all over. I didn't tell you that, did I? All her right side aches at night. She's in great pain and, you know, the dear angel bears it in silence so as not to trouble us. She doesn't groan so as not to waken us. We eat anything we can get, but she'll only take what's left over, what one would only give to a dog: "I'm not worth it, I'm taking it away from you, I'm a burden to you" – that's what her angelic look is meant to express. We wait on her, but she can't bear it: "I'm not worth it, not worth it, I'm a contemptible, useless cripple." Not worth it! Why, she'd obtain salvation for us all by her angelic meekness. Without her, without her gentle words, it would be hell in our house. She mollified even Varvara. And you mustn't blame Varvara, either, sir. She, too, is an angel. She, too, has been hardly done by. She came to us in the summer. She had sixteen roubles on her which she had earned by giving lessons and put away for her fares so that she could go back to Petersburg in September, that is, now. And we took her money and spent it and she has nothing to go back with now. That's how it is, sir. And she can't go back, for she works her fingers to the bone for us, for we've harnessed her like a mare. She looks after us all, mends, washes, sweeps the floor, puts her mother to bed, and her mother is capricious, her mother is tearful, her mother is insane, sir! But now I can engage a maid with this money, you understand, sir. I can afford medical treatment for my dear ones. I can send our student back to Petersburg. I can buy beef. I can get decent food for them all. Good heavens, why, it's a dream!'

Alyosha was terribly glad that he had brought so much happiness and that the poor man had consented to be made happy.

'Wait, sir, wait!' Snegiryov snatched at a new daydream that had just occurred to him and he again babbled away with frenzied rapidity. 'Do you realize that Ilyusha and I can really carry out our dream now? We'll buy a horse and a buggy, a black horse, he set his heart on a black horse, and we'll be off as we had planned the other day. I know a lawyer in the Kursk province, a very old friend of mine, and he let me know by a trustworthy person that if I were to go there he'd get me a job at his office as his clerk, and – who knows – perhaps he would too. . . . So I'd put mother and Nina in the buggy, let Ilyusha drive, and run on foot beside it, and I'd get them all there.

Why, sir, if I could only get one debt that's owing me paid up, I would be able to afford that, too!'

'You would, you would!' cried Alyosha. 'Miss Verkhovtsev will let you have more money, as much as you like. And, you know, I have money, too. Take as much as you like, as you would from a friend, from a brother. You'll pay me back afterwards. . . . You'll get rich, yes, rich! And, you know, you couldn't have thought of anything better than to move to another province! That would be the saving of you and, above all, of your boy. And, you know, you must go quickly, before the winter, before the cold, and you could write to us from there, and we will always be brothers. . . . No, it is not a dream!'

Alyosha was about to embrace him, so pleased was he. But, glancing at him, he stopped short. Snegiryov stood with outstretched neck, protruding lips, and a frenzied, pale face, his lips moving as though he were going to say something; but no sound issued from them, though he kept moving them. It was ghastly.

'What's the matter?' asked Alyosha, with a sudden start.

'You, sir. I —' Snegiryov muttered, faltering and looking at him with a strange, wild, fixed stare, like a man who had made up his mind to throw himself down a precipice, and at the same time with a strange smile on his lips. 'I, sir – you, sir —Would you like me to show you a lovely trick, sir?' he suddenly said in a rapid, firm whisper, his speech no longer faltering.

'What sort of trick?'

'A lovely trick, sir, a hocus-pocus,' Snegiryov kept whispering.

His mouth was twisted on the left side, his left eye was screwed up, and he kept staring fixedly at Alyosha, as though he were chained to him.

'But what is the matter with you?' cried Alyosha in real alarm. 'What kind of trick?'

'This kind,' Snegiryov suddenly squealed. 'Look!'

And showing him the two rainbow-coloured notes, which he had kept by one corner between thumb and forefinger during their conversation, he suddenly snatched them up in a kind of frenzy, crumpled them and squeezed them tightly in his right hand.

'See, sir, see!' he shrieked at Alyosha, pale and beside himself, and, raising his fist suddenly, he flung the two crumpled notes violently on the sand. 'You see, sir?' he shrieked again, pointing to them. 'Well, that's what I'm going to do!'

And raising his right foot, he began trampling the notes under his heel with wild fury, gasping for breath and exclaiming as he did so: 'So much for your money, sir! So much for your money! So much for your money!'

Suddenly he leapt back and drew himself up to his full height before Alyosha. His whole figure expressed indescribable pride.

'Tell those who sent you that the bast-sponge does not sell his honour!' he cried, raising his hand aloft.

Then he turned away quickly and began to run; but he had not run five yards before he turned round and blew Alyosha a kiss. He ran another five yards and turned round for the last time. But this time his face was no longer contorted with laughter. On the contrary, it was quivering all over with tears. In a tearful, faltering, choking voice he cried rapidly:

'And what would I say to my son if I took money from you for my disgrace?'

Having said it, he ran away, this time without turning back.

Alyosha looked after him with inexpressible sorrow. Oh, he understood that the poor man had not realized till the last moment that he would crumple and fling away the notes. He did not turn back once. Alyosha knew he would not. He did not want to run after him and call him, and for a very good reason. When Snegiryov was out of sight, Alyosha picked up the two notes. They were only badly crumpled, crushed and pressed into the sand, but were not damaged and even rustled like new ones when Alyosha unfolded and smoothed them out. Having done so, he folded them up, put them in his pocket and went to Katerina to report on the outcome of her commission.

I

The Engagement

MRS KHOKHLAKOV was again the first to meet Alyosha. She was in a hurry. Something important had happened: Katerina's attack of hysterics had ended in a fainting fit, followed, Mrs Khokhlakov informed him, 'by a terrible, awful weakness. She lay down, turned up her eyes and became delirious. Now she has a temperature and I've sent for Herzenstube and her aunts. The aunts are already here, but Herzenstube hasn't arrived yet. They're all sitting in her room and waiting. Something terrible is bound to happen. She's unconscious. What if it should be brain fever?'

Exclaiming this, Mrs Khokhlakov looked genuinely alarmed. 'This is serious, serious!' she added at every word, as though everything that had happened to her before was not serious. Alyosha listened to her sadly. He began telling her of his adventures, but she interrupted as soon as he had begun. She had no time to listen and she asked him to sit with Lise and to wait for her.

'Lise, my dear Alexey,' she whispered almost in his ear, 'Lise has given me a strange surprise just now, but she has also moved me deeply, and that is why I find it in my heart to forgive her for everything. Just fancy, as soon as you had gone, she began to be really sorry for having apparently laughed at you yesterday and today. But she was not really laughing. She was only joking. She was so sorry that she almost burst into tears. I couldn't help being surprised at her. She had never been sorry for anything so much before when she was laughing at me, but always made a jest of it. And, you know, she's always laughing at me. But now she's serious. Everything with her now is serious. She thinks highly of your opinion, Alexey, and try not to be offended with her or bear a grudge against her. I myself do all I can to spare her because she's such a clever girl. Don't you think so? She's been telling me just now that you were a friend of her childhood – "the truest friend of my childhood". How do you like that? The truest friend – and what about me? She had most sincere feelings about that, and even memories, but what is so remarkable are the phrases and words she uses, particularly the words which are most unexpected. You have no idea what she's going to say next and suddenly out it comes. There was, for instance, that thing she said about a pine-tree the other day. There used to be a pine-tree in our garden when she was very little. Perhaps it's still there so that there's no need to talk of it in the past tense. Pine-trees aren't people and they remain the same for a long time. "Mother," she said to me, "I've such a vivid recollection of the pine as if I pined for it." You see, "pine as if I pined". I mean, she may have expressed it differently, because I think I got it all muddled. Pine is such a silly word. But she said something so original about it that I simply can't repeat it. Besides, I can't remember it. Well, good-bye. I'm terribly upset and I shouldn't be surprised if I went out of my mind. Oh, dear Alexey, I've gone out of my mind twice in my life and I had to have medical treatment. Go to Lise and cheer her up as you always do it so charmingly. Lise,' she cried, going up to her daughter's door, 'I've brought you Alexey whose feelings you've hurt so badly. He isn't at all angry, I assure you. On the contrary, he's surprised that you should have supposed he was!'

'Thank you, Mother. Come in, Alexey.'

Alyosha went in. Lise looked somehow embarrassed and all of a sudden she blushed all over. She seemed to be ashamed of something, and, as always happens in such cases, she began talking very rapidly about something else, as though that was the only thing she was interested in at that moment.

'Mother has just told me the whole story about the two hundred roubles, Alexey, and about your commission to – to take them to that poor officer and – and she told me the terrible story of how he had been insulted and, you know, though Mother told it in such a jumbled-up way, jumping from one thing to another, I couldn't help crying when I heard it. Well, did you give him the money and how is the poor man now?'

'That's just the trouble, I didn't give it to him, and it's a long story,' replied Alyosha, as though what worried him most was that he had not handed over the money, and yet Lise was perfectly well aware that he, too, looked away and that he, too, was trying to talk about something else.

Alyosha sat down at the table and began to tell his story, but at his first words he completely lost his embarrassment and engaged Lise's interest, too. He spoke under the influence of strong emotion and of the powerful impression he had just received, and he succeeded in telling his story well and circumstantially. He had even before, as a boy in Moscow, liked to come to her and tell her what had just happened to him, what he had read or remembered of his days as a child. Sometimes they even used to daydream together and invent all sorts of stories, mostly cheerful and amusing ones. Now they seemed both to have been transported back to the old days in Moscow, two years before. Lise was very touched by his story. Alyosha knew how to describe 'little Ilya' to her with warm feeling. But when he finished telling her of the scene when the unhappy man had trampled on the money, Lise clasped her hands and exclaimed with unrestrained feeling:

'So you didn't give him the money! You let him run away without it! Oh dear, you should have run after him and overtaken him.'

'No, Lise, it's better not to have run after him,' said Alyosha, getting up from his chair and pacing the room with a worried look.

'Why better? How is it better? Now they can't afford to buy bread and they'll die of starvation!'

'They won't, because they will get the two hundred roubles in spite of everything. I'm sure he'll accept the money tomorrow. Yes, I'm quite sure of it,' Alyosha repeated, pacing the room thoughtfully. 'You see, Lise,' he went on, suddenly stopping short before her, 'I made one mistake, but that mistake, too, is for the best.'

'What mistake? And why is it for the best?'

'I'll tell you why. He is a timid man, a man of weak character. He's worn out with suffering and he's very good-natured. I keep on wondering why he should suddenly have become so offended and trampled on the money. He did it, I assure you, because up to the very last moment he did not know that he was going to trample on the notes. And I can't help feeling that there were lots of things he took offence at and – and it couldn't be otherwise in his position. . . . First of all, he resented having been so happy over the money in front of me and not having concealed it. If he'd been pleased, but not so much, if he hadn't shown it, but given himself airs, as others do when accepting money, if he'd dissembled, then he could have borne it and accepted the money. But he'd shown his joy too openly and that was why he felt so badly. Oh, Lise, he's a truthful and kindly man, and that's the whole trouble in a case like this! All the time he was talking to me his voice was so weak and feeble, and he spoke so fast, he kept chuckling in such a funny way, or he was crying – yes, he was crying, so delighted was he and – and he talked about his daughters and – and the job he hoped to get in another town. . . . But no sooner had he poured out his heart than he felt ashamed of having opened up his heart like that to me. That's why he conceived such a hatred for me at once. He's one of those awfully reserved poor people. But what he resented most of all was that he accepted me as his friend too quickly and gave in to me too soon. At first he sprang at me and tried to intimidate me, but as soon as he saw the money he began embracing me. For he did almost embrace me. He kept touching me with his hands. That was how he came to feel how humiliating it all was and it was just then that I made that mistake, that very serious mistake. You see, I suddenly told him that if he hadn't enough money to move to another town, he would be given more money, and indeed that I myself would give him as much as he liked of my own money. It was this that struck him suddenly as rather peculiar: for why should I, he thought, rush forward to help him? You know, Lise, it's awful for a man who's been through a great deal of trouble when everyone looks at him as if they were his benefactors. . . . I've been told of that. The elder told me about it. I don't know how to put it, but I've seen it often myself. Besides, you know, that's exactly how I feel, too. And the interesting thing is that though up to the last moment he did not know that he would trample on the notes, he did have a premonition of it. I'm sure of that. It's just because he had this premonition that he was so highly delighted. And yet though it's turned out so badly, it's all for the best. Indeed, I think that nothing better could have happened. . . . '

'Why, why could nothing better have happened?' Lise cried, looking in great surprise at Alyosha.

'Because, Lise, if he had taken the money and not trampled on it, he would have wept at his humiliation an hour after getting home. Yes, that would most certainly have happened. He would have wept and perhaps have come to me early tomorrow morning and flung the notes at me and trampled on them as he did today. But now he's gone off feeling very proud and triumphant, though he knows that he has "ruined" himself. Which, of course, means that there's nothing easier now than to make him accept the two hundred roubles to-morrow, because he has vindicated his honour by trampling on the money. He couldn't possibly have known when he did it that I would take him the money again tomorrow. And yet he needs the money badly. Though he may be proud today, he'll be thinking even today of what he has lost. He will be thinking of it even more at night, he will be dreaming of it, and tomorrow morning, I expect, he'll be ready to run to apologize to me. And just then I will appear and say: "You are a proud man and you've proved it. Now take the money and forgive us." Then I'm quite sure he'll take it!'

Alyosha uttered the last sentence: 'And then I'm quite sure he'll take it!' with a kind of rapture. Lise clapped her hands.

'Oh, it's true, it's true! Oh, I understand it all now so awfully well! Alyosha, how do you know all this? You're so young and you can see into people's minds. I should never have thought of it!'

'What we must do now is to convince him that he is on the same level with all of us, in spite of the fact that he's taking money from us,' Alyosha went on rapturously. 'And not only on the same level, but even on a higher level.'

'On a higher level - excellent, Alexey, but go on, go on!'

'I'm afraid I've put it rather badly. I mean, about the higher level - but it doesn't matter, because —'

'Oh, of course it doesn't matter in the least! I'm sorry, Alyosha dear. . . . You know, I hardly respected you till now. I mean, I did respect you, but on the same level, but now I shall respect you on a higher level. . . . Darling, don't be angry with me for "making puns",' she added at once with strong feeling. 'I'm an absurd little girl, but you, you — Listen, Alexey, don't you think our reasoning - I mean, yours - no, better say ours - don't you think it shows that we regard him - that unfortunate man - with contempt? I mean that we analyse his soul like this, as though from above? I mean that we're so absolutely certain that he'll accept the money. Don't you think so?'

'No, Lise, it doesn't show any contempt,' Alyosha replied firmly, as though he had been prepared for this question. 'I thought of that myself on my way here. Just think, what sort of contempt can it be if we ourselves are the same as he, if everyone is like him. For we are the same as he, you know. Not a bit better. And even if we were better, we'd be just the same in his place. I don't know about you, Lise, but I can't help feeling that in many ways I am small-minded. And he is not. On the contrary, he's very sensitive. No, Lise, there's no question of any contempt for him! You know, Lise, my elder said that one had to care for people as one would for children, and for some people as though they were patients in a hospital.'

'Oh, darling Alexey, let's care for people as we would for the sick!'

'Yes, let's, Lise. I'm willing, but I'm afraid I'm not quite ready for it. Sometimes I'm very impatient and at other times I don't seem to be able to see things. You're different.'

'Oh, I don't believe it! Alexey, I'm so happy!'

'It's nice of you to say that, Lise!'

'You're awfully nice, Alexey, but sometimes you're a bit of a prig. And yet you're not really a prig. Please, go to the door, open it gently, and see whether Mother is listening,' Lise suddenly said in a hurried, nervous whisper.

Alyosha went, opened the door a little and reported that no one was listening.

'Come here, Alexey,' Lise went on, blushing more and more, 'give me your hand – so. Listen, I have to make a great confession: I didn't write you yesterday's letter as a joke, but in earnest. . . .'

And she covered her eyes with her hand. One could see that she was greatly ashamed of this confession. Suddenly she seized his hand and kissed it impulsively three times.

'Oh, Lise,' Alyosha cried joyfully, 'that's all right then! I was quite sure that you had written it in earnest.'

'Quite sure – fancy that!' she cried, pushing away his hand without, however, releasing it, colouring terribly and laughing a little, happy laugh. 'I kissed his hand, and he says "that's all right!"'

But she was unfair to reproach him: Alyosha, too, was greatly embarrassed.

'I want you always to like me, Lise, but I don't know how to make you,' he murmured, also blushing.

'Alyosha, darling, you're cold and cheeky. How do you like that? He did me the honour of choosing me as his wife and that's enough for him! He's sure I was in earnest – really! Why, that's cheek – that's what it is!'

'Why, was it bad of me to be sure?' Alyosha laughed suddenly.

'Why no, Alyosha, it was awfully good of you,' said Lise, gazing tenderly and happily at him.

Alyosha was still standing beside her, holding her hand in his. Suddenly he bent over her and kissed her full on the mouth.

'Really Alexey! What's the matter with you?' exclaimed Lise.

Alyosha was thrown into utter confusion.

'I'm sorry if I shouldn't have. . . . Perhaps it was awfully stupid of – of me — You said I was cold, so I kissed you. Only I can see that it was stupid. . . .'

Lise laughed and hid her face in her hands.

'And in your cassock!' she cried between her bursts of laughter, but suddenly she stopped laughing and became very serious, almost stern. 'I think we'd better postpone our kisses, because we don't really know how to kiss and we shall have to wait a long time yet,' she concluded suddenly. 'You'd better tell me why you want to marry such a little fool as me, such a sickly little fool, you who are so clever, so intellectual, so observant? Oh, Alyosha, I'm awfully happy, for I don't deserve you a bit.'

'You do, Lise. I shall be leaving the monastery for good in a few days. If I go out into the world, I shall have to marry. That at least I know. He told me to marry, too. And whom could I marry better than you and – and who would marry me except you? I've been thinking about it. First of all, you've known me since childhood and, secondly, you've a great many qualities I haven't. You're a much more cheerful person than I and, what's more, you're much more innocent than I, for I've already come in contact with many, many things. Oh, you don't know, but I, too, am a Karamazov! I don't care if you laugh and joke, and at me too! On the contrary, go on laughing – I'm so glad of it. . . . But you laugh like a little girl and you think like a martyr. . . .'

'Like a martyr? How's that?'

'Yes, Lise. You see, your question whether we do not despise that unhappy man by dissecting his soul was the question of a person who has suffered a lot. I'm afraid I don't know how to put it properly, but a person to whom such questions occur is himself capable of suffering. Sitting in your invalid chair, you must have thought over many things already. . . .'

'Alyosha, give me your hand, don't take it away,' Lise said in a small voice, weak with happiness. 'Listen, Alyosha, what clothes are you going to wear when you leave your monastery? Don't laugh and don't be angry, please. It's very, very important to me.'

'I haven't thought of it yet, Lise, but I'll wear any clothes you like.'

'I'd like you to have a dark blue velvet coat, a white piqué waist-coat, and a soft grey felt hat. Tell me did you really think I didn't love you when I said I didn't mean what I wrote yesterday?'

'No, I didn't.'

'Oh, you impossible, incorrigible man!'

'You see, I suspected that – that you perhaps cared for me, but I pretended to believe you so that you – you shouldn't feel uncomfortable.'

'That makes it worse! Worse and better than everything, Alyosha. I love you awfully! Before you came I said to myself: shall I ask him for my letter? If he took it out calmly and gave it back to me (which could always be expected of him), then he doesn't love me at all, he doesn't feel anything, he is simply a stupid, good-for-nothing boy, and I am done for. But you left the letter in the monastery cell and that made me feel better. You did leave the letter behind so as not to give it back because you had a feeling that I'd ask for it, didn't you? You did, didn't you?'

'Oh, Lise, I'm afraid you're quite wrong. You see, I've got the letter on me now, and I had it on me before, too. It's in this pocket. Here it is.'

Alyosha pulled the letter out laughingly, and showed it to her at a distance.

'Only I'm not going to give it to you. Look at it from here.'

'Oh? So you told a lie, you – a monk?'

'I suppose I did,' Alyosha, too, laughed. 'I lied because I didn't want to give you back the letter. It's very dear to me,' he added suddenly with strong feeling, blushing again. 'It always will be and I shan't ever give it to anyone!'

Lise looked at him with admiration.

'Alyosha,' she murmured again, 'have a look at the door. Is Mother listening?'

'All right, Lise, I'll look. Only wouldn't it be better not to? Why suspect your mother of such meanness?'

'Meanness? What meanness? She has a right to eavesdrop on her daughter. It's not mean at all,' cried Lise, flushing. 'You may be sure, sir, that when I am a mother and have a daughter like myself, I shall most certainly be eavesdropping on her.'

'Would you really, Lise? It's wrong.'

'Goodness, what kind of meanness is it? If it had been some ordinary society gossip, I shouldn't dream of eavesdropping, for that would be mean. But if my own daughter were shut up with a young man — Listen, Alyosha, I shall be spying on you, too, after we're married, and you may as well know now that I intend to open all your letters and read them. You may as well be forewarned. . . . '

'Why, of course, if that's how —,' Alyosha murmured. 'Only it's not right.'

'Oh, what contempt! Darling Alyosha, don't let's quarrel the very first day. But I'd better be quite frank with you: it's of course very wrong to eavesdrop and, of course, I'm wrong and you're right, but I shall eavesdrop all the same.'

'By all means,' said Alyosha, laughing. 'Only you won't catch me doing anything wrong.'

'But will you do as I tell you, Alyosha? That, too, we'd better settle beforehand.'

'Very gladly, Lise. I most certainly shall, except in the most important things. If you don't agree with me in the most important things, I shall still do as my duty tells me to.'

'So you should. But I'd like you to know that I'm ready to submit to you not only in the most important things but in everything else, and I'm willing to take an oath on it now – in everything and all my life,' Lise exclaimed fervently. 'And I'll do that gladly, gladly! And what's more, I swear I shall never eavesdrop on you, never once – nor read a single letter of yours, for you're right and I'm wrong. And though I'd awfully like to eavesdrop – I know that – I shan't do it for all that because you don't consider it honourable. I shall look upon you now as my Providence. Listen, Alexey, why have you been so sad all this time – yesterday and today? I know you've had a lot of troubles and worries, but I can see that something is worrying you especially. It isn't some secret grief, is it?'

'Yes, Lise, it is,' Alyosha said sadly. 'I can see you love me, if you've guessed that.'

'What sort of grief? What is it about? Can't you tell me?' Lise asked with timid entreaty.

'I'll tell you later, Lise, later,' said Alyosha, looking embarrassed. 'If I told you now, you would not understand. Besides, I'm not sure I know how to tell you about it.'

'I know your brothers and your father are worrying you too.'

'Yes, my brothers too,' said Alyosha, as though sunk in thought.

'I don't like your brother Ivan, Alyosha,' Lise suddenly remarked.

Alyosha was somewhat surprised at that remark, but did not comment on it.

'My brothers are destroying themselves,' he went on, 'and my father, too. And they are destroying others together with themselves. What we have here is "the earth-bound Karamazov force", as Father Paissy expressed it the other day, earth-bound, unrestrained, and crude. I don't even know whether the spirit of God moves over that force. All I know is that I, too, am a Karamazov. I a monk, a monk? Am I a monk, Lise? I believe you said I was a monk a moment ago.'

'Yes, I did.'

'And yet I don't think I even believe in God.'

'You don't believe? What's the matter with you?' Lise said softly and guardedly.

But Alyosha made no answer. There was something very mysterious and very subjective in these sudden words of his, something that he perhaps did not understand himself, but that undoubtedly worried him.

'And, on top of that, my friend is passing away. The best man in the world is leaving the earth now. Oh, if only you knew, Lise, if only you knew how bound up, how closely knit I am spiritually with him! And now I shall be left alone. . . . I shall come to you, Lise. . . . In future we shall be together. . . .'

'Yes, together, together! From now on always together and for the rest of our lives! Listen, kiss me. I'll let you.'

Alyosha kissed her.

'Well, you can go now. Christ be with you' (and she made the sign of the cross over him). 'Go quickly to *him* while he is still alive. I think it was cruel of me to keep you. I shall pray for you and for him today. Alyosha, we shall be happy. Shall we be happy? Shall we?'

'I believe we shall, Lise.'

On going out of Lise's room, Alyosha did not think it necessary to go to see Mrs Khokhlakov and he went downstairs without taking leave of her. But as soon as he opened the door and began to descend the stairs, Mrs Khokhlakov suddenly appeared before him. Alyosha guessed from the first word she uttered that she had been waiting for him there on purpose.

'Alexey, this is terrible! It's all a lot of childish nonsense. It's ridiculous. I hope you won't take it into your head to dream of — It's foolishness, foolishness, nothing but foolishness!' she pounced on him.

'Only don't tell her that,' said Alyosha, 'or she'll be upset and that's bad for her.'

'I'm glad to hear a sensible word from a sensible young man. Am I to understand that you agreed with her only out of compassion for her ailing condition? Because you didn't want to make her angry by contradicting her?'

'Oh no, not at all,' Alyosha declared firmly. 'I spoke quite seriously with her.'

'Seriousness is out of place here, it's unthinkable, and, first of all, I shall never be at home to you again, and, secondly, I shall go away and take her with me. Make no mistake about that.'

'But why?' said Alyosha. 'It's still so far off. We may have to wait another sixteen months.'

'Oh, Alexey, that's quite true, of course, and I daresay in sixteen months you'll have time to quarrel a thousand times and to drift apart. But I'm so unhappy, so unhappy! Maybe it is all nonsense, but it's such a blow to me. Now I'm just like Famussov in the last scene of *The Misfortune of Being Clever*. You're Chatsky, she's Olga, and just imagine I've run on purpose to meet you on the stairs, and in the play, too, the tragedy happens on the stairs. I heard everything, I could hardly restrain myself. So that's the explanation of all the horrors of last night and of her hysterics! Love to the daughter and death to the mother. I might as well be in my grave. Now another thing and most important of all: What is the letter she's written to you? Show it to me at once, at once!'

'I'm sorry I can't. Tell me how is Katerina. I must know.'

'She's still delirious and hasn't regained consciousness yet. Her aunts are here, but they do nothing but sigh and turn up their noses at me. Herzenstube came and he was so alarmed that I didn't know what to do with him and how to calm him. I nearly sent for a doctor. I had him driven home in my carriage. And to crown it all – you and this letter! It's true all this cannot happen for a year and a half. I implore you, Alexey, in the name of all that's holy, in the name of your dying elder, to show me, her mother, this letter! If you like, you can hold it in your hand and I'll read it like that.'

'No, I won't show it to you, Mrs Khokhlakov. Even if I had her permission to show it, I wouldn't show it to you. I shall come to-morrow and if you like I shall talk many things over with you, but now – good-bye!'

And Alyosha ran downstairs and out into the street.

2

Smerdyakov with a Guitar

BESIDES, he had no time to lose. Even while he was saying good-bye to Lise a sudden idea occurred to him – an idea of how he might catch Dmitry, who was evidently hiding from him, by some clever strata-gem. It was already rather late, three o'clock in the afternoon. Alyosha was longing with all his heart to go back to the monastery to his 'great departing friend', but the necessity of seeing Dmitry outweighed every other consideration: the conviction of some im-pending terrible catastrophe was growing stronger and stronger in Alyosha's mind with every hour. What the nature of the catastrophe was and what he meant to say to his brother just then, he could not perhaps tell himself. 'Let my benefactor die without me, but at least I shall not have to reproach myself all my life with being able to prevent something and not doing so, but passing by and hurrying back home. In doing this, I'm acting in accordance with his great precept. . . . '

His plan was to catch his brother Dmitry unawares by climbing over the fence, entering the garden as he had on the day before, and concealing himself in the summer-house. 'If he isn't there,' he thought, 'I shall wait in the summer-house till the evening, if necessary, without telling Foma or the women of the house. But if, as before, he is lying in wait for Grushenka, he will most likely come to the summer-house. . . . ' Alyosha, however, did not give much thought to the details of the plan, but decided to carry it out even if it meant that he could not go back to the monastery that day.

Everything happened without hindrance: he climbed over the fence almost in the same spot as the day before and got to the summer-house without being seen. He did not want to be seen: both the women of the house and Foma (if he were there), might be on his brother's side and carry out his instructions, that is to say, refuse to let Alyosha into the garden, or warn his brother betimes that he was being sought and asked for. There was no one in the summer-house. Alyosha sat down on the same seat as on the day before and began to wait. He examined the summer-house and for some reason it looked to him more dilapidated than the day before. It seemed such a wretched place this time. The day, though, was as fine as the day before. On the table there was the circle left by his brother's glass of brandy which had evidently spilt over. Idle and futile thoughts kept drifting into his mind as always in time of tedious waiting: for instance, why, having come there, had he sat down precisely in the same place as the day before and not in another? At last he felt very depressed – depressed by anxious uncertainty. He had not been sitting there for more than a quarter of an hour when he suddenly heard the strum of a guitar somewhere very near. Some people were sitting or had only just sat down somewhere in the bushes not more than twenty yards away from him. Alyosha suddenly recalled that, after he had left his brother in the summer-house the day before, he saw, or just caught a glimpse of, an old low green garden seat on the left by the fence among the bushes. Some new arrivals must have sat down on it now. But who? A male voice suddenly began to sing in a sugary falsetto a verse from a popular song, accompanying himself on a guitar.

> My devotion to my love
> All my life I shall prove,
> Lord have mer-r-cy
> On her and me!
> On her and me!
> On her and me!

The voice ceased. It was a lackey's tenor and the fanciful way of singing was also that of a lackey. Another voice, a woman's, suddenly asked caressingly and rather timidly, but in an affected, mincing voice:

'Why haven't you been to see us for so long? Why do you always turn your back upon us?'

'Not at all,' replied a man's voice, politely, though with unmistakably firm and emphatic dignity.

It was clear that the man was the master of the situation and the woman was making advances to him. 'The man must be Smerdyakov,' thought Alyosha. 'At least the voice is his, and his lady friend must be the daughter of the house, who has come from Moscow and who wears a dress with a train and goes to Marfa for soup.'

'I'm ever so fond of poetry, especially if it rhymes,' the woman's voice continued. 'Why don't you go on?'

The voice sang again:

> For an emperor's crown I cannot,
> If my dear one but keep her health,
> Lord, have mer-r-rcy,
> On her and me!
> On her and me!
> On her and me!

'Last time it was ever so much nicer,' the woman's voice observed. 'After the crown you sang "If my dearest darling but keep her health". It was ever so much more tender. I suppose you've forgotten it today.'

'Poetry's rubbish!'

'Oh, no, I'm very fond of a nice bit of poetry.'

'If it's poetry, it's absolutely rubbish, my dear. Consider yourself: have you ever met a person who talks in rhyme? And if we all started talking in rhyme, even at the order of the authorities, how much, do you think, should we say? Poetry's of no use, my dear.'

'How clever you are!' the woman's voice was growing more and more ingratiating. 'How did you get to know so many things?'

'I could have done lots of things and I could have known lots of things, too, if I wasn't born unlucky. I'd have shot a man in a duel, I would, if he'd called me a bastard because I'm the son of that stinking idiot woman and haven't got no father. In Moscow, my dear, they used to throw it in my teeth and all because the story got round to them thanks to Grigory. Grigory rebukes me for rebelling against my birth. "You've torn apart her thighs," he says. Well, I don't know about her thighs, but I'd have let myself be killed in the womb rather than come into the world at all. They used to talk about it in the market place, they did. And your mother, a very indelicate lady your mother is, my dear, she started telling me that she used to walk about with the hair of her head in a tangled mat and that she was four feet tall and a *wee* bit over. Why say a *wee* bit, when she might have said a *little* bit, like everyone else. Wanted to move me to tears, I suppose, but them's the sort of tears you would expect from a peasant, my dear – crude peasant feelings. Aye, that's what it is. Can a Russian peasant have feelings like an educated man? He can't have no feelings, and why? Because he's ignorant, that's why. Even as a child when I heard people say "a wee bit" I felt like knocking my head against a brick wall. I hate all Russia, my dear.'

'You wouldn't have talked like that, I'm sure, if you was a handsome cadet in the army or a dashing young hussar officer. You'd have drawn your sword to defend all Russia.'

'Far from wishing to be a dashing hussar officer, my dear, I'd have liked to do away with all soldiers.'

'But who'd defend us against an enemy then?'

'There's no need to, my dear. In 1812 there was a great invasion of Russia by the French Emperor Napoleon the First, the father of the present one, and it would have been a good thing if them Frenchies had conquered us. A clever nation, my dear, would have conquered a stupid one and annexed it. Things would have been different then, my dear.'

'As if they're so much better in their country than we are! Why, I'd never dream of exchanging one of our really handsome young gentlemen for three young Englishmen,' Maria Kondratyevna said in a tender voice, no doubt accompanying her words with a most languorous glance.

'It depends who you love, my dear.'

'But you're just like a foreigner yourself. Just like a real foreign gentleman. I'm telling you that even if it makes me blush.'

'If you really want to know, my dear, our folk here and theirs there are all alike when it comes to vice. They're all rogues, except that the rogues there walk about in patent-leather boots, and our scoundrels here wallow in their filth and see nothing bad in that. The Russian peasant, my dear, must be flogged, as Mr Karamazov quite rightly said yesterday, mad though he is, and all his children.'

'But you told me yourself that you've a great respect for Mr Ivan Karamazov.'

'Well, my dear, he called me a stinking lackey. He thinks I might turn against them, but he's mistaken, my dear. If I had a tidy sum of money in my pocket, I'd have cleared out long ago. Dmitry's worse than any lackey the way he goes on. He's poor and he isn't clever. He's no damn good for anything, but everyone respects him all the same. I may be only a broth-brewer, but with a bit of luck I could open a café-restaurant in Moscow, in Petrovka, because my cooking's something special and there's no one in Moscow, except the foreigners, whose cooking's something special, too. Dmitry's as poor as a church mouse, but if he was to challenge the son of the first count in Russia, he'd fight a duel with him. But how is he better than me? For, you see, my dear, he's so much stupider than me. Think of the money he's poured down the drain without getting anything for it!'

'Oh, I think a duel is ever so nice!' Maria Kondratyevna observed suddenly.

'How so, my dear?'

'Oh, it's so thrilling and brave, especially when two dashing young army officers with pistols in their hands fire at one another for some lady. It's lovely! Oh, if only they let girls go and look, I'd love to see it.'

'It's all very well if you're the chap what's doing the shooting, but if someone else is pointing a pistol straight at your mug, you'd feel pretty silly, I can tell you. You'd run away, you would, my dear.'

'You don't mean to say you'd run away, too?'

But Smerdyakov did not deign to answer. After a short pause he struck another chord on the guitar and burst into the last couplet of the song in his reedy falsetto:

> Whatever you say,
> I shall go away,
> Be mer-r-ry and gay ...

> For the great city I'll leave,
> And shall not grieve,
> Never shall I grieve,
> Never again do I mean to grieve!

At this point something unexpected happened. Alyosha suddenly sneezed. The people on the garden seat at once fell silent. Alyosha got up and walked towards them. It was, indeed, Smerdyakov, dressed up, his hair pomaded and almost curled, and wearing patent-leather shoes. His guitar lay on the garden seat. The woman was Maria Kondratyevna, the daughter of the woman of the house, who was wearing a light blue dress with a train two yards long. She was a very young girl and she would have been quite good-looking if her face had not been a little too round and terribly freckled.

'Will my brother Dmitry be back soon?' Alyosha asked as calmly as he could.

Smerdyakov rose slowly from the seat; Maria Kondratyevna also got up.

'What makes you think I know about Mr Dmitry Karamazov's movements?' Smerdyakov replied quietly, in measured tones and with a scornful air. 'It isn't as if I was his keeper, is it?'

'Why, I simply asked you if you knew,' explained Alyosha.

'I knows nothing about his whereabouts, sir, and I don't want to know.'

'But my brother told me that it was you who let him know about all that went on in the house and promised to let him know when Miss Svetlov came.'

Smerdyakov slowly raised his eyes and looked at him imperturbably.

'And how,' he asked, looking intently at Alyosha, 'did you manage to get in here, seeing as how the gates was bolted an hour ago?'

'I came in from the lane over the fence and went straight to the summer-house. I hope,' he turned to Maria Kondratyevna, 'you don't mind. I was in a hurry to find my brother.'

'Of course we don't mind,' drawled Maria Kondratyevna, flattered by Alyosha's apology. 'For, you see, sir, Mr Dmitry Karamazov, too, often goes to the summer-house that way. We don't even know he's here, and there he's sitting in the summer-house.'

'I'm trying to find him now. I'm very anxious to see him, or to learn from you where he is now. I assure you it's a matter of the highest importance to him.'

'I'm afraid, sir, he never tells us,' Maria Kondratyevna murmured.

'Though I'm coming here to see some friends,' Smerdyakov began again, 'he's been worrying me something cruel even here by his constant questions about the master: how is he, what's going on in the house, who's coming and who's going, and what else I could tell him. Twice he even threatened to kill me.'

'Kill you?' cried Alyosha in surprise.

'It don't mean nothing, sir, to a man of his character. As you was so good as to observe yourself yesterday. If, he says to me, you let Miss Svetlov in and she spends the night here, you'll be the first to die. I'm terribly afraid of him, sir, and if I wasn't even more afraid of telling the police about him, I'd have gone and done it. God only knows, sir, what he may not do!'

'He told him the other day: I'll pound you in a mortar,' added Maria Kondratyevna.

'Well, if it's in a mortar, it may be only talk,' observed Alyosha. 'If I could meet him now, I might say something to him about it too.'

'All I can tell you, sir,' Smerdyakov seemed at last to have made up his mind to say, 'is that I'm coming here to visit my friends and neighbours. There's nothing wrong in that, is there? On the other hand, Mr Ivan Karamazov sent me early this morning to his lodgings in Lake Street, without a letter but with a message to be sure to go and dine with him at the restaurant in the square. I went but your brother was out, though it was eight o'clock. "He's been in," they told me, "but he's gone out for the whole day," those were his land-lady's very words, sir. It's just as though there was some kind of plot between them. I suppose they must be dining at the pub now, for Mr Ivan Karamazov hasn't been home to dinner, and the master had his dinner an hour ago by himself and is having his nap now. But I'd like to ask you, sir, not to say a word about me and about what I've told you to him, for he'd kill me for nothing at all.'

'My brother Ivan asked Dmitry to dine with him at an inn today?' Alyosha inquired quickly.

'Yes, sir.'

'At the "Metropolis" in the square?'

'That's right, sir.'

'That's very possible!' cried Alyosha in great excitement. 'Thank you, Smerdyakov. That's important. I'll go there at once.'

'Don't give me away, sir,' Smerdyakov called after him.

'Don't worry, I won't. I'll look into the restaurant as though by accident.'

'But where are you going?' Maria Kondratyevna cried. 'I'll open the gate for you.'

'No, it's much nearer this way. I'll climb over the fence again.'

The news about his brothers was a great shock to Alyosha. He ran to the inn. It was improper for him to go into the inn in his cassock, but he could ask for them on the stairs and call them down. But as soon as he reached the inn, one of the windows was thrown open and his brother Ivan called down to him from it.

'Alyosha, can you come up here to me or not? I shall be very grateful.'

'Of course I can, only what about my dress? . . .'

'I'm in a private room. Come up the steps to the entrance, and I'll come down to meet you.'

A minute later Alyosha was sitting beside his brother. Ivan was alone. He was having his dinner.

3

The Brothers Get Acquainted

IVAN was not, however, in a separate room. It was merely a place by the window separated from the rest of the bar by a screen, so that those sitting there could not be seen by the other people in the inn. It was the first room from the entrance with a bar along the opposite wall. Waiters were continually running to and fro in it. There was only one customer in the room, an old retired army officer who was drinking tea in a corner. But there was the usual bustle going on in the other rooms of the inn, people were calling for the waiters, beer bottles were being opened, billiard balls were clicking, the organ was droning. Alyosha knew that Ivan did not as a rule visit the inn and was not generally fond of inns. So he must have come there, he thought, to keep an appointment with Dmitry. Yet Dmitry was not there.

'Shall I order fish soup or something else for you? You don't live on tea alone, do you?' cried Ivan, evidently very pleased to have got hold of Alyosha. He had finished dinner and was drinking tea.

'Yes, let me have fish soup and tea afterwards,' said Alyosha gaily. 'I'm famished.'

'What about cherry jam? They have it here. Remember how you used to love cherry jam when you were little and living with Polenov?'

'You remember that? Let me have the jam, too. I still love it.'

Ivan rang for the waiter and ordered fish soup, tea, and jam.

'I remember everything, Alyosha. I remember you till you were eleven. I was fifteen then. There's such a difference between fifteen and eleven that brothers are never real friends at those ages. I don't even know whether I was fond of you or not. When I went away to Moscow I never even thought of you. Then, when you came to Moscow yourself, we met only once, I believe. And now I've been living here for over three months and we've scarcely exchanged a single word till now. Tomorrow I'm going away and I was thinking as I sat here how I could arrange to see you to say good-bye, and there you were passing by.'

'Did you want to see me very much?'

'Yes, very much. I want to get to know you once for all, and I want you to know me. And then to say good-bye. I think the best time to get to know people is before you part from them. I've seen how you've been looking at me during these three months. There was a sort of look of continual expectation in your eyes, and it was that I couldn't bear. That was why I've kept away from you. But in the end I learnt to respect you: this little fellow, I said to myself, has a firm hold on life. Mind you, though I'm laughing now, I'm speaking seriously. You do have a firm hold on life, haven't you? I like people who are firm like that, whatever it is they stand by, and even if they are such little boys as you. I didn't dislike your expectant look in the end; on the contrary, I grew fond of it. I believe you are fond of me for some reason, aren't you, Alyosha?'

'Yes, Ivan, I am. Dmitry says about you: Ivan is as silent as the grave, but I say about you: Ivan is a riddle. You're still a riddle to me, but something about you I already understand, and that, too, only since this morning!'

'What's that?' Ivan laughed.

'You won't be angry, will you?' Alyosha, too, laughed.

'Well?'

'I mean that you're just as young as all the other twenty-three-year-old young men. Just as young. Just a very young, fresh, and nice boy – just a young and inexperienced boy, in fact! You're not offended, are you?'

'On the contrary, you've surprised me by a coincidence!' Ivan cried gaily and warmly. 'You know after our last meeting at her place all I could think of was that I was just a young, inexperienced boy, and you seem to have guessed it now and begin with that. I was sitting here just now and do you know what I was saying to myself? I said to myself: if I didn't believe in life, if I lost faith in the woman I love, if I lost faith in the order of things, if I were convinced that everything was, on the contrary, a disorderly, damnable, and perhaps devil-ridden chaos, if I were completely overcome by all the horrors of man's disillusionment – I'd still want to live and, having once raised the cup to my lips, I wouldn't tear myself away from it till I had drained it to the dregs! However, I shall probably fling it away at thirty, even if I haven't emptied it, and turn away – where I don't know. But till I'm thirty, I know for certain that my youth will triumph over everything – every disappointment and every disgust with life. I've asked myself many times: is there in the world any despair that would overcome this frenzied and, perhaps, indecent thirst for life in me, and I've come to the conclusion that, perhaps, there isn't. But, of course, that holds true only till I'm thirty. After that I shall not want to go on myself – that's how I feel now. Some snivelling trivial moralists, poets especially, often call this thirst for life a base thing. It's to some extent a Karamazov characteristic. That's true. You, too, in spite of everything, have this thirst for life. But why is it a base thing? There's still a great deal of the centripetal force on our planet, Alyosha. I want to live and I go on living, even if it is against logic. However much I may disbelieve in the order of things, I still love the sticky little leaves that open up in the spring, I love the blue sky, I love some people, whom, you know, one loves sometimes without knowing why, I love some great human achievement, in which I've perhaps lost faith long ago, but which from old habit my heart still reveres. Here's your fish soup. Eat it. It's excellent. They know how to make it here. I want to travel in Europe, Alyosha, and I shall be going abroad from here. And yet I know very well that I'm only going to a graveyard, but it's a most precious graveyard – yes, indeed! Precious are the dead that lie there. Every stone over them speaks of such ardent life in the past, of such a passionate faith in their achievements, their truth, their struggles, and their science, that I know beforehand that I shall fall on the ground and kiss those stones and weep over them and – and at the same time deeply convinced that it's long been a graveyard and nothing more. And I shall not weep from despair, but simply because I shall be happy in my tears. I shall get drunk on my own emotion. I love the sticky little leaves of spring and the blue sky – yes, I do! It's not a matter of intellect or logic. You love it all with your inside, with your belly. You love to feel your youthful powers asserting themselves for the first time. . . . Do you understand anything of all this rigmarole, Alyosha, or don't you?' Ivan suddenly laughed.

'I understand it too well, Ivan: one longs to love with one's inside, with one's belly – yes, you put it excellently and I'm terribly glad you have such a longing for life!' cried Alyosha. 'I think everyone must love life more than anything else in the world.'

'Love life more than the meaning of it?'

'Yes, certainly. Love it regardless of logic, as you say. Yes, most certainly regardless of logic, for only then will I grasp its meaning. That's what I've been vaguely aware of for a long time. Half your work is done, Ivan: you love life. Now you must try to do the second half and you are saved.'

'So you're already saving me, though I may not be lost at all! And what does this second half of yours consist of?'

'Why, to raise up your dead who have perhaps never died at all. Well, let's have tea now – I'm glad, Ivan, that we're talking at last!'

'I see you're in a sort of inspired mood. I do like such *professions de foi* from such – novices. You're a steadfast fellow, Alexey. Is it true that you want to leave the monastery?'

'Yes, my elder sends me into the world.'

'We shall see each other, then, in the world. We shall meet before I'm thirty, before, that is, I begin to tear myself away from the cup.

Father doesn't want to tear himself away from his cup till he's seventy. He even means to hang on to it till he's eighty. He told me so himself. He's quite serious about it, though he's a clown. Stands on his sensuality as though it were a rock – though after thirty, I suppose, that is the only thing one can stand on. But it's disgusting to hold on to it till the age of seventy. It's much better till one is thirty: one could then retain "the outward show of nobility" by deceiving oneself. You haven't seen Dmitry today, have you?'

'Afraid not, but I saw Smerdyakov.'

And Alyosha told his brother rapidly and in detail of his meeting with Smerdyakov. Ivan suddenly began listening with a very preoccupied air and even asked Alyosha to repeat some of his statements.

'Only he begged me not to tell Dmitry what he had told me about him,' added Alyosha.

Ivan frowned and sank into thought.

'Are you frowning because of Smerdyakov?' asked Alyosha.

'Yes, because of him. But to hell with him. I really did want to see Dmitry, but now there's no need,' Ivan said reluctantly.

'And are you really going away so soon?'

'Yes.'

'But what about Dmitry and father? How will it all end?' Alyosha asked anxiously.

'You're still harping on it! What have I got to do with it? I am not my brother Dmitry's keeper, am I?' Ivan snapped irritably, but suddenly he smiled bitterly. 'Cain's reply to God about his murdered brother – eh? Perhaps that's what you're thinking now, aren't you? But, damn it all, I can't very well stay here to be their keeper, can I? I've finished what I had to do and I'm going away. You don't think I'm jealous of Dmitry, that I've been trying to filch his beautiful Katerina from him for the last three months, do you? Damn it, I had business of my own. I've finished it and I'm going away. I finished it just now, as you saw yourself.'

'At Katerina's?'

'Yes, and I've done with it once and for all. And, really, what is all the fuss about? What have I to do with Dmitry? It doesn't concern Dmitry at all. I had my own business to settle with Katerina. And you know yourself that Dmitry behaved as though he'd been in a plot with me. I never asked him. It was he himself who solemnly handed her over to me and gave us his blessing. The whole thing's too funny for words. Oh, Alyosha, if only you knew how happy I am now! I sat here having my dinner and, believe me, I felt like ordering some champagne to celebrate my first hour of freedom. Dear, oh dear, six months almost – and suddenly I got rid of it all at once. Why, even yesterday I never dreamt that I had only to wish and the whole thing would be over and done with!'

'Is it your love you're speaking of, Ivan?'

'My love, if you like. Yes, I fell in love with a young lady, a boarding-school miss. I had an awful time with her, and she, too, gave me an awful time. Spent hours with her . . . and now suddenly it's all over! This morning I spoke on the spur of the moment, but as soon as I got away I burst out laughing. You don't believe me? Honestly, I did. I mean every word of it.'

'Why, you seem to be happy about it even now,' observed Alyosha, looking closely at his face, which really had grown much more cheerful.

'How was I to know that I did not love her at all? Ha, ha! Well, it seems I didn't. But I did feel attracted to her! Even when I was making my speech this morning I felt attracted to her. Even now, you know, I like her awfully, and yet I don't mind leaving her a bit. You don't think I'm bragging, do you?'

'No, only perhaps that it was not love.'

'Dear Alyosha,' Ivan laughed, 'don't you get involved in arguments about love. It doesn't become you. The way you rushed in this morning! Dear me! I've forgotten to kiss you for it. . . . But what a dance she led me! It was certainly a case of incurable heartache. Oh, she knew well enough that I loved her! She loved me and not Dmitry,' Ivan insisted cheerfully. 'Dmitry was only a case of heartache. Everything I told her today was absolutely true. But, you see, the trouble is that it will take her perhaps fifteen or twenty years to realize that she didn't love Dmitry at all, that she loved only me, whom she only tortures. And I daresay she'll never realize it in spite of her lesson today. Well, it's best like that: get up and go away for good. Incidentally, how is she now? What happened there after I had gone?'

Alyosha told him about her hysterical fit and that she was apparently still unconscious and delirious.

'Mrs Khokhlakov isn't imagining it all, is she?'

'I don't think so.'

'I'll have to make inquiries. Still no one has ever died of hysterics. So she had hysterics – what does it matter? The good Lord gave hysterics to women out of love. I won't go back there. Why thrust myself upon her again?'

'But you did tell her this morning that she never loved you, didn't you?'

'I did so on purpose. Alyosha, let me order some champagne and let's drink to my freedom. Oh, if you knew how glad I am!'

'No, I don't think we'd better drink,' Alyosha said suddenly. 'Besides, I feel rather sad.'

'Yes, you've been feeling sad for some time. I noticed it long ago.'

'So you've quite made up your mind to leave tomorrow morning?'

'Tomorrow morning? I didn't say I was going to leave in the morning. Still, I might leave in the morning. You know, I dined here today only to avoid dining with the old man – I detest him so much. If it had only been him, I'd have left long ago. And why are you so worried about my going away? We've plenty of time before I go. A whole eternity of time – immortality!'

'What kind of eternity is it if you're leaving tomorrow?'

'But what does that matter to us?' Ivan laughed. 'We shall have plenty of time to talk over the things that interest us, the things we've come here to talk over, shan't we? Why do you look so surprised? Tell me: what have we come here for? To talk about Katerina's love? About the old man and Dmitry? About going abroad? About the calamitous position of Russia? About the Emperor Napoleon? Have we come for that?'

'No, not for that.'

'Very well, then. You know, therefore, what for. Others have their own subjects of conversation, and we, greenhorns, have ours. We have first of all to solve the eternal problems. That's our worry. Young Russia is talking of nothing but the eternal problems now. Now especially, for the old men have suddenly become preoccupied with practical problems. Why did you look so expectantly at me for all these three months? To ask me, "What do you believe or do you not believe at all?" That was the meaning of your glances for the last three months, my dear fellow, wasn't it?'

'I suppose it was,' Alyosha smiled. 'You're not laughing at me now, are you?'

'Me laughing at you? Why, I should hate to disappoint my little brother who'd been looking at me with such expectation for three months. Alyosha, look straight at me: am I not exactly the same little boy as you, except, of course, that you are a novice? For what have Russian boys been doing up to now? Some of them, I mean? Well, take this stinking pub, for instance. They meet here and sit in a corner for hours. They haven't known each other all their lives and when they leave the pub they won't meet again for another forty years. But, tell me, what are they going to talk about while snatching a free moment in a pub? Why, about eternal questions: is there a God, is there immortality? And those who do not believe in God? Well, those will talk about socialism and anarchism and the transformation of the whole of mankind in accordance with some new order. So, you see, they're the same damned old questions, except that they start from the other end. And thousands of the most original Russian boys do nothing nowadays but talk of eternal questions. Isn't that so?'

'Yes,' said Alyosha, looking at his brother with the same gentle and probing smile, 'to real Russians the questions whether there is a God and whether there is immortality, or, as you say, the questions that start from the other end, of course come first, and so they should.'

'Look here, Alyosha. Sometimes it isn't at all clever to be a Russian, but all the same it's impossible to imagine anything sillier than the way Russian boys spend their time now. But one Russian boy called Alyosha I'm awfully fond of.'

'How beautifully you got that in,' Alyosha laughed suddenly.

'Well, tell me what to begin with – give the order yourself – with God? Does God exist? Is that it?'

'Begin with anything you like, even "from the other end",' Alyosha said, looking searchingly at his brother. 'Didn't you declare at father's yesterday that there was no God?'

'I said that on purpose to tease you yesterday at dinner at father's and I saw how your eyes glowed. But I'm not at all averse from discussing it with you now and I mean it very seriously. I want to be friends with you, Alyosha, because I have no friend. I want to try to. Well, this may surprise you, but perhaps I accept God,' Ivan laughed. 'You didn't expect that, did you?'

'Of course I didn't, if, that is, you're not joking now.'

'Joking? They said I was joking at the elder's yesterday. You see, my dear chap, there was an old sinner in the eighteenth century who delivered himself of the statement that if there were no God, it would have been necessary to invent him: *S'il n'existait pas Dieu il faudrait l'inventer*. And, to be sure, man has invented God. And what is so strange, and what would be so marvellous, is not that God actually exists, but that such an idea – the idea of the necessity of God – should have entered the head of such a savage and vicious animal as man – so holy it is, so moving and so wise and so much does it redound to man's honour. So far as I'm concerned, I made up my mind long ago not to speculate whether man has created God or God has created man. Nor, of course, am I going to analyse all the modern axioms laid down by the Russian boys on that subject, all of them based on European hypotheses; for what is only an hypothesis there, becomes at once an axiom with a Russian boy, and not only with the boys but, I suppose, also with their professors, for Russian professors are quite often just the same Russian boys. And for this reason I'm going to disregard all the hypotheses. For what is it you and I are trying to do now? What I'm trying to do is to attempt to explain to you as quickly as possible the most important thing about me, that is to say, what sort of man I am, what I believe in and what I hope for – that's it, isn't it? And that's why I declare that I accept God plainly and simply. But there's this that has to be said: if God really exists and if he really has created the world, then, as we all know, he created it in accordance with the Euclidean geometry, and he created the human mind with the conception of only the three dimensions of space. And yet there have been and there still are mathematicians and philosophers, some of them indeed men of extraordinary genius, who doubt whether the whole universe, or, to put it more widely, all existence, was created only according to Euclidean geometry and they even dare to dream that two parallel lines which, according to Euclid, can never meet on earth, may meet somewhere in infinity. I, my dear chap, have come to the conclusion that if I can't understand even that, then how can I be expected to understand about God? I humbly admit that I have no abilities for settling such questions. I have a Euclidean, an earthly mind, and so how can I be expected to solve problems which are not of this world. And I advise you too, Alyosha, my friend, never to think about it, and least of all about whether there is a God or not. All these are problems which are entirely unsuitable to a mind created with the idea of only three dimensions. And so I accept God, and I accept him not only without reluctance, but, what's more, I accept his divine wisdom and his purpose – which are completely beyond our comprehension. I believe in the underlying order and meaning of life. I believe in the eternal harmony into which we are all supposed to merge one day. I believe in the Word to which the universe is striving and which itself was "with God" and which was God, and, well, so on and so forth, *ad infinitum*. Many words have been bandied about on this subject. So it would seem I'm on the right path – or am I? Anyway, you'd be surprised to learn, I think, that in the final result I refuse to accept this world of God's, and though I know that it exists, I absolutely refuse to admit its existence. Please understand, it is not God that I do not accept, but the world he has created. I do not accept God's world and I refuse to accept it. Let me put it another way: I'm convinced like a child that the wounds will heal and their traces will fade away, that all the offensive and comical spectacle of human contradictions will vanish like a pitiful mirage, like a horrible and odious invention of the feeble and infinitely puny Euclidean mind of man, and that in the world's finale, at the moment of eternal harmony, something so precious will happen and come to pass that it will suffice for all hearts, that it will allay all bitter resentments, that it will atone for all men's crimes, all the blood they have shed. It will suffice not only for the forgiveness but also for the justification of everything that has ever happened to men. Well, let it, let it all be and come to pass, but I don't accept it and I won't accept it! Let even the parallel lines meet and let me see them meet, myself – I shall see and I shall say that they've met, but I still won't accept it. That is the heart of the matter, so far as I'm concerned, Alyosha. That is where I stand. I'm telling you this in all seriousness. I deliberately began our talk as stupidly as I could, but I finished it with my confession, because that's all you want. You didn't want to hear about God, but only to find out what your beloved brother lived by. And I've told you.'

Ivan concluded his long tirade suddenly with a sort of special and unexpected feeling.

'And why did you begin "as stupidly as you could"?' asked Alyosha, looking thoughtfully at him.

'Why, first of all, for the sake of proving to you that I'm a Russian: Russian discussions on these subjects are all conducted as stupidly as possible. And, secondly, the stupider, the more to the point. The stupider, the clearer. Stupidity is brief and artless, but intelligence shifts and shuffles and hides itself. Intelligence is a knave, while stupidity is straightforward and honest. I've brought my argument down to my despair, and the more stupidly I presented it, the better for me.'

'Will you explain to me why you do not accept the world?' said Alyosha.

'Why, by all means. It isn't a secret. That's what I've been leading up to. My dear brother, it's not you I want to corrupt and push off the firm foundations on which you stand, it's me, perhaps, that I'd like to be healed by you,' Ivan said, smiling suddenly just like a little gentle child. Alyosha had never seen him smile like that before.

4

Rebellion

'I MUST make a confession to you,' Ivan began. 'I never could understand how one can love one's neighbours. In my view, it is one's neighbours that one can't possibly love, but only perhaps these who live far away. I read somewhere about "John the Merciful" (some saint) who, when a hungry and frozen stranger came to him and begged him to warm him, lay down with him in his bed and, putting his arms round him, began breathing into his mouth, which was festering and fetid from some awful disease. I'm convinced that he did so from heartache, from heartache that originated in a lie, for the sake of love arising from a sense of duty, for the sake of a penance he had imposed upon himself. To love a man, it's necessary that he should be hidden, for as soon as he shows his face, love is gone.'

'The elder Zossima has talked about it more than once,' observed Alyosha. 'He, too, declared that a man's face often prevented many people who were inexperienced in love from loving him. But then there's a great deal of love in mankind, almost Christ-like love, as I know myself, Ivan. . . . '

'Well, I'm afraid I don't know anything about it yet and I can't understand it, and an innumerable multitude of people are with me there. You see, the question is whether that is due to men's bad qualities or whether that is their nature. In my opinion, Christ's love for men is in a way a miracle that is impossible on earth. It is true he was a god. But we are no gods. Suppose, for instance, that I am capable of profound suffering, but no one else could ever know how much I suffer, because he is someone else and not I. Moreover, a man is rarely ready to admit that another man is suffering (as if it were some honour). Why doesn't he admit it, do you think? Because, I suppose, I have a bad smell or a stupid face, or because I once trod on his foot. Besides, there is suffering and suffering: there is humiliating suffering, which degrades me; a benefactor of mine, for instance, would not object to my being hungry, but he would not often tolerate some higher kind of suffering in me, for an idea, for instance. That he would only tolerate in exceptional cases, and even then he might look at me and suddenly realize that I haven't got the kind of face which, according to some fantastic notion of his, a man suffering for some idea ought to have. So he at once deprives me of all his benefactions, and not from an evil heart, either. Beggars, especially honourable beggars, should never show themselves in the streets, but ask for charity through the newspapers. Theoretically it is still possible to love one's neighbours, and sometimes even from a distance, but at close quarters almost never. If everything had been as on the stage, in the ballet, where, if beggars come in, they wear silken rags and tattered lace and beg for alms dancing gracefully, then it would still be possible to look at them with pleasure. But even then we might admire them but not love them. But enough of this. All I wanted is to make you see my point of view. I wanted to discuss the suffering of humanity in general, but perhaps we'd better confine ourselves to the sufferings of children. This will reduce the scope of my argument by a tenth, but I think we'd better confine our argument to the children. It's all the worse for me, of course. For, to begin with, one can love children even at close quarters and even with dirty and ugly faces (though I can't help feeling that children's faces are never ugly). Secondly, I won't talk about grown-ups because, besides being disgusting and undeserving of love, they have something to compensate them for it: they have eaten the apple and know good and evil and have become "like gods". They go on eating it still. But little children haven't eaten anything and so far are not guilty of anything. Do you love little children, Alyosha? I know you do and you will understand why I want to talk only about them now. If they, too, suffer terribly on earth, they do so, of course, for their fathers. They are punished for their fathers who have eaten the apple, but this is an argument from another world, an argument that is incomprehensible to the human heart here on earth. No innocent must suffer for another, and such innocents, too! You may be surprised at me, Alyosha, for I too love little children terribly. And note, please, that cruel men, passionate and carnal men, Karamazovs, are sometimes very fond of children. Children, while they are children, up to seven years, for instance, are very different from grown-up people: they seem to be quite different creatures with quite different natures. I knew a murderer in prison: in the course of his career he had murdered whole families in the houses he had broken into at night for the purpose of robbery, and while about it he had also murdered several children. But when he was in prison he showed a very peculiar affection for them. He used to stand by the window of his cell for hours watching the children playing in the prison yard. He trained one little boy to come up to his window and made great friends with him. You don't know why I'm telling you this, Alyosha? I'm afraid I have a headache and I'm feeling sad.'

'You speak with a strange air,' Alyosha observed uneasily, 'as though you were not quite yourself.'

'By the way, not so long ago a Bulgarian in Moscow told me,' Ivan went on, as though not bothering to listen to his brother, 'of the terrible atrocities committed all over Bulgaria by the Turks and Circassians who were afraid of a general uprising of the Slav population. They burn, kill, violate women and children, nail their prisoners' ears to fences and leave them like that till next morning when they hang them, and so on – it's impossible to imagine it all. And, indeed, people sometimes speak of man's "bestial" cruelty, but this is very unfair and insulting to the beasts: a beast can never be so cruel as a man, so ingeniously, so artistically cruel. A tiger merely gnaws and tears to pieces, that's all he knows. It would never occur to him to nail men's ears to a fence and leave them like that overnight, even if he were able to do it. These Turks, incidentally, seemed to derive a voluptuous pleasure from torturing children, cutting a child out of its mother's womb with a dagger and tossing babies up in the air and catching them on a bayonet before the eyes of their mothers. It was doing it before the eyes of their mothers that made it so enjoyable. But one incident I found particularly interesting. Imagine a baby in the arms of a trembling mother, surrounded by Turks who had just entered her house. They are having great fun: they fondle the baby, they laugh to make it laugh and they are successful: the baby laughs. At that moment the Turk points a pistol four inches from the baby's face. The boy laughs happily, stretches out his little hands to grab the pistol, when suddenly the artist pulls the trigger in the baby's face and blows his brains out. . . . Artistic, isn't it? Incidentally, I'm told the Turks are very fond of sweets.'

'Why are you telling me all this, Ivan?' asked Alyosha.

'I can't help thinking that if the devil doesn't exist and, therefore, man has created him, he has created him in his own image and likeness.'

'Just as he did God, you mean.'

'Oh, you're marvellous at "cracking the wind of the poor phrase", as Polonius says in *Hamlet*,' laughed Ivan. 'You've caught me there. All right. I'm glad. Your God is a fine one, if man created him in his own image and likeness. You asked me just now why I was telling you all this: you see, I'm a collector of certain interesting little facts and, you know, I'm jotting down and collecting from newspapers and books, from anywhere, in fact, certain jolly little anecdotes, and I've already a good collection of them. The Turks, of course, have gone into my collection, but they are, after all, foreigners. I've also got lovely stories from home. Even better than the Turkish ones. We like corporal punishment, you know. The birch and the lash mostly. It's a national custom. With us nailed ears are unthinkable, for we are Europeans, after all. But the birch and the lash are something that is our own and cannot be taken away from us. Abroad they don't seem to have corporal punishment at all now. Whether they have reformed their habits or whether they've passed special legislation prohibiting flogging – I don't know, but they've made up for it by something else, something as purely national as ours. Indeed, it's so national that it seems to be quite impossible in our country, though I believe it is taking root here too, especially since the spread of the religious movement among our aristocracy. I have a very charming brochure, translated from the French, about the execution quite recently, only five years ago, of a murderer in Geneva. The murderer, Richard, a young fellow of three and twenty, I believe, repented and was converted to the Christian faith before his execution. This Richard fellow was an illegitimate child who at the age of six was given by his parents *as a present* to some shepherds in the Swiss mountains. The shepherds brought him up to work for them. He grew up among them like a little wild animal. The shepherds taught him nothing. On the contrary, when he was seven they sent him to take the cattle out to graze in the cold and wet, hungry and in rags. And it goes without saying that they never thought about it or felt remorse, being convinced that they had every right to treat him like that, for Richard had been given to them just as a chattel and they didn't even think it necessary to feed him. Richard himself testified how in those years, like the prodigal son in the Gospel, he was so hungry that he wished he could eat the mash given to the pigs, which were fattened for sale. But he wasn't given even that and he was beaten when he stole from the pigs. And that was how he spent all his childhood and his youth, till he grew up and, having grown strong, he himself went to steal. The savage began to earn his living as a day labourer in Geneva, and what he earned he spent on drink. He lived like a brute and finished up by killing and robbing an old man. He was caught, tried, and sentenced to death. There are no sentimentalists there, you see. In prison he was immediately surrounded by pastors and members of different Christian sects, philanthropic ladies, and so on. They taught him to read and write in prison, expounded the Gospel to him, exhorted him, tried their best to persuade him, wheedled, coaxed, and pressed him till he himself at last solemnly confessed his crime. He was converted and wrote to the court himself that he was a monster and that at last it had been vouchsafed to him by God to see the light and obtain grace. Everyone in Geneva was excited about him – the whole of philanthropic and religious Geneva. Everyone who was well-bred and belonged to the higher circles of Geneva society rushed to the prison to see him. They embraced and kissed Richard: "You are our brother! Grace has descended upon you!" Richard himself just wept with emotion: "Yes, grace has descended upon me! Before in my childhood and youth I was glad of pigs' food, but now grace has descended upon me, too, and I'm dying in the Lord!" "Yes, yes, Richard, die in the Lord. You've shed blood and you must die in the Lord. Though it was not your fault that you knew not the Lord when you coveted the pigs' food and when you were beaten for stealing it (what you did was very wrong, for it is forbidden to steal), you've shed blood and you must die." And now the last day comes. Richard, weak and feeble, does nothing but cry and repeat every minute: "This is the happiest day of my life. I'm going to the Lord!" "Yes," cry the pastors, the judges, and the philanthropic ladies, "this is the happiest day of your life, for you are going to the Lord!" They all walked and drove in carriages behind the cart on which Richard was being taken to the scaffold. At last they arrived at the scaffold: "Die, brother," they cried to Richard, "die in the Lord, for His grace has descended upon you!" And so, covered with the kisses of his brothers, they dragged brother Richard on to the scaffold, placed him on the guillotine, and chopped off his head in a most brotherly fashion because grace had descended upon him too. Yes, that's characteristic. That brochure has been translated into Russian by some aristocratic Russian philanthropists of the Lutheran persuasion and sent gratis to the newspapers and other editorial offices for the enlightenment of the Russian people. The incident with Richard is so interesting because it's national. Though we may consider it absurd to cut off the head of a brother of ours because he has become our brother and because grace has descended upon him, we have, I repeat, our own national customs which are not much better. The most direct and spontaneous historic pastime we have is the infliction of pain by beating. Nekrassov has a poem about a peasant who flogs a horse about its eyes, "its gentle eyes". Who hasn't seen that? That is a truly Russian characteristic. He describes how a feeble nag, which has been pulling too heavy a load, sticks in the mud with its cart and cannot move. The peasant beats it, beats it savagely and, in the end, without realizing why he is doing it and intoxicated by the very act of beating, goes on showering heavy blows upon it. "Weak as you are, pull you must! I don't care if you die so long as you go on pulling!" The nag pulls hard but without avail, and he begins lashing the poor defenceless creature across its weeping, "gentle eyes". Beside itself with pain, it gives one tremendous pull, pulls out the cart, and off it goes, trembling all over and gasping for breath, moving sideways, with a curious sort of skipping motion, unnaturally and shamefully – it's horrible in Nekrassov. But it's only a horse and God has given us horses to be flogged. So the Tartars taught us and left us the whip as a present. But men, too, can be flogged. And there you have an educated and well-brought-up gentleman and his wife who birch their own little daughter, a child of seven – I have a full account of it. Daddy is glad that the twigs have knots, for, as he says, "it will sting more" and so he begins "stinging" his own daughter. I know for a fact that there are people who get so excited that they derive a sensual pleasure from every blow, literally a sensual pleasure, which grows progressively with every subsequent blow. They beat for a minute, five minutes, ten minutes. The more it goes on the more "stinging" do the blows become. The child screams, at last it can scream no more, it is gasping for breath. "Daddy, Daddy, dear Daddy!" The case, by some devilishly indecent chance, is finally brought to court. Counsel is engaged. The Russian people have long called an advocate – "a hired conscience". Counsel shouts in his client's defence: "It's such a simple thing, an ordinary domestic incident. A father has given a hiding to his daughter and, to our shame, it's been brought to court!" Convinced by him, the jurymen retire and bring in a verdict of not guilty. The public roars with delight that the torturer has been acquitted. Oh, what a pity I wasn't there! I'd have bawled out a proposal to found a scholarship in the name of the torturer! . . . Charming pictures. But I have still better ones about children. I've collected a great deal of facts about Russian children, Alyosha. A father and mother, "most respectable people of high social position, of good education and breeding", hated their little five-year-old daughter. You see, I repeat again most emphatically that this love of torturing children and only children is a peculiar characteristic of a great many people. All other individuals of the human species these torturers treat benevolently and mildly like educated and humane Europeans, but they are very fond of torturing children and, in a sense, this is their way of loving children. It's just the defencelessness of these little ones that tempts the torturers, the angelic trustfulness of the child, who has nowhere to go and no one to run to for protection – it is this that inflames the evil blood of the torturer. In every man, of course, a wild beast is hidden – the wild beast of irascibility, the wild beast of sensuous intoxication from the screams of the tortured victim. The wild beast let off the chain and allowed to roam free. The wild beast of diseases contracted in vice, gout, bad liver, and so on. This poor five-year-old girl was subjected to every possible torture by those educated parents. They beat her, birched her, kicked her, without themselves knowing why, till her body was covered with bruises; at last they reached the height of refinement: they shut her up all night, in the cold and frost, in the privy and because she didn't ask to get up at night (as though a child of five, sleeping its angelic, sound sleep, could be trained at her age to ask for such a thing), they smeared her face with excrement and made her eat it, and it was her mother, her mother who made her! And that mother could sleep at night, hearing the groans of the poor child locked up in that vile place! Do you realize what it means when a little creature like that, who's quite unable to understand what is happening to her, beats her little aching chest in that vile place, in the dark and cold, with her tiny fist and weeps searing, unresentful and gentle tears to "dear, kind God" to protect her? Can you understand all this absurd and horrible business, my friend and brother, you meek and humble novice? Can you understand why all this absurd and horrible business is so necessary and has been brought to pass? They tell me that without it man could not even have existed on earth, for he would not have known good and evil. But why must we know that confounded good and evil when it costs so much? Why, the whole world of knowledge isn't worth that child's tears to her "dear and kind God"! I'm not talking of the sufferings of grown-up people, for they have eaten the apple and to hell with them – let them all go to hell, but these little ones, these little ones! I'm sorry I'm torturing you, Alyosha. You're not yourself. I'll stop if you like.'

'Never mind, I want to suffer too,' murmured Alyosha.

'One more, only one more picture, and that, too, because it's so curious, so very characteristic, but mostly because I've only just read about it in some collection of Russian antiquities, in the *Archives* or *Antiquity*. I'll have to look it up, I'm afraid I've forgotten where I read it. It happened in the darkest days of serfdom, at the beginning of this century – and long live the liberator of the people! There was at the beginning of the century a General, a very rich landowner with the highest aristocratic connexions, but one of those (even then, it is true, rather an exception) who, after retiring from the army, are almost convinced that their service to the State has given them the power of life and death over their "subjects". There were such people in those days. Well, so the General went to live on his estate with its two thousand serfs, imagining himself to be God knows how big a fellow and treating his poorer neighbours as though they were his hangers-on and clowns. He had hundreds of hounds in his kennels and nearly a hundred whips – all mounted and wearing uniforms. One day, a serf-boy, a little boy of eight, threw a stone in play and hurt the paw of the General's favourite hound. "Why is my favourite dog lame?" He was told that the boy had thrown a stone at it and hurt its paw. "Oh, so it's you, is it?" said the General, looking him up and down. "Take him!" They took him. They took him away from his mother, and he spent the night in the lock-up. Early next morning the General, in full dress, went out hunting. He mounted his horse, surrounded by his hangers-on, his whips, and his huntsmen, all mounted. His house-serfs were all mustered to teach them a lesson, and in front of them all stood the child's mother. The boy was brought out of the lock-up. It was a bleak, cold, misty autumn day, a perfect day for hunting. The General ordered the boy to be undressed. The little boy was stripped naked. He shivered, panic-stricken and not daring to utter a sound. "Make him run!" ordered the General. "Run, run!" the whips shouted at him. The boy ran. "Sick him!" bawled the General, and set the whole pack of borzoi hounds on him. They hunted the child down before the eyes of his mother, and the hounds tore him to pieces! I believe the General was afterwards deprived of the right to administer his estates. Well, what was one to do with him? Shoot him? Shoot him for the satisfaction of our moral feelings? Tell me, Alyosha!'

'Shoot him!' Alyosha said softly, raising his eyes to his brother with a pale, twisted sort of smile.

'Bravo!' yelled Ivan with something like rapture. 'If you say so, then – you're a fine hermit! So that's the sort of little demon dwelling in your heart, Alyosha Karamazov!'

'What I said was absurd, but —'

'Yes, but – that's the trouble, isn't it?' cried Ivan. 'Let me tell you, novice, that absurdities are only too necessary on earth. The world is founded on absurdities and perhaps without them nothing would come to pass in it. We know a thing or two!'

'What do you know?'

'I understand nothing,' Ivan went on as though in delirium, 'and I don't want to understand anything now. I want to stick to facts. I made up my mind long ago not to understand. For if I should want to understand something, I'd instantly alter the facts and I've made up my mind to stick to the facts. . . .'

'Why are you putting me to the test?' exclaimed Alyosha, heart-brokenly. 'Will you tell me at last?'

'Of course I will tell you. That's what I was leading up to. You're dear to me. I don't want to let you go and I won't give you up to your Zossima.'

Ivan was silent for a minute and his face suddenly became very sad.

'Listen to me: I took only children to make my case clearer. I don't say anything about the other human tears with which the earth is saturated from its crust to its centre – I have narrowed my subject on purpose. I am a bug and I acknowledge in all humility that I can't understand why everything has been arranged as it is. I suppose men themselves are to blame: they were given paradise, they wanted freedom and they stole the fire from heaven, knowing perfectly well that they would become unhappy, so why should we pity them? Oh, all that my pitiful earthly Euclidean mind can grasp is that suffering exists, that no one is to blame, that effect follows cause, simply and directly, that everything flows and finds its level – but then this is only Euclidean nonsense. I know that and I refuse to live by it! What do I care that no one is to blame, that effect follows cause simply and directly and that I know it – I must have retribution or I shall destroy myself. And retribution not somewhere in the infinity of space and time, but here on earth, and so that I could see it myself. I was a believer, and I want to see for myself. And if I'm dead by that time, let them resurrect me, for if it all happens without me, it will be too unfair. Surely the reason for my suffering was not that I as well as my evil deeds and sufferings may serve as manure for some future harmony for someone else. I want to see with my own eyes the lion lie down with the lamb and the murdered man rise up and embrace his murderer. I want to be there when everyone suddenly finds out what it has all been for. All religions on earth are based on this desire, and I am a believer. But then there are the children, and what am I to do with them? That is the question I cannot answer. I repeat for the hundredth time – there are lots of questions, but I've only taken the children, for in their case it is clear beyond the shadow of a doubt what I have to say. Listen: if all have to suffer so as to buy eternal harmony by their suffering, what have the children to do with it – tell me, please? It is entirely incomprehensible why they, too, should have to suffer and why they should have to buy harmony by their sufferings. Why should they, too, be used as dung for someone's future harmony? I understand solidarity in sin among men, I understand solidarity in retribution, too, but, surely, there can be no solidarity in sin with children, and if it is really true that they share their fathers' responsibility for all their fathers' crimes, then that truth is not, of course, of this world and it's incomprehensible to me. Some humorous fellow may say that it makes no difference since a child is bound to grow up and sin, but, then, he didn't grow up: he was torn to pieces by dogs at the age of eight. Oh, Alyosha, I'm not blaspheming! I understand, of course, what a cataclysm of the universe it will be when everything in heaven and on earth blends in one hymn of praise and everything that lives and has lived cries aloud: "Thou art just, O Lord, for thy ways are revealed!" Then, indeed, the mother will embrace the torturer who had her child torn to pieces by his dogs, and all three will cry aloud: "Thou art just, O Lord!", and then, of course, the crown of knowledge will have been attained and everything will be explained. But there's the rub: for it is that I cannot accept. And while I'm on earth, I hasten to take my own measures. For, you see, Alyosha, it may really happen that if I live to that moment, or rise again to see it, I shall perhaps myself cry aloud with the rest, as I look at the mother embracing her child's torturer: "Thou art just, O Lord!" But I do not want to cry aloud then. While there's still time, I make haste to arm myself against it, and that is why I renounce higher harmony altogether. It is not worth one little tear of that tortured little girl who beat herself on the breast and prayed to her "dear, kind Lord" in the stinking privy with her unexpiated tears! It is not worth it, because her tears remained unexpiated. They must be expiated, for otherwise there can be no harmony. But how, how are you to expiate them? Is it possible? Not, surely, by their being avenged? But what do I want them avenged for? What do I want a hell for torturers for? What good can hell do if they have already been tortured to death? And what sort of harmony is it, if there is a hell? I want to forgive. I want to embrace. I don't want any more suffering. And if the sufferings of children go to make up the sum of sufferings which is necessary for the purchase of truth, then I say beforehand that the entire truth is not worth such a price. And, finally, I do not want a mother to embrace the torturer who had her child torn to pieces by his dogs! She has no right to forgive him! If she likes, she can forgive him for herself, she can forgive the torturer for the immeasurable suffering he has inflicted upon her as a mother; but she has no right to forgive him for the sufferings of her tortured child. She has no right to forgive the torturer for that, even if her child were to forgive him! And if that is so, if they have no right to forgive him, what becomes of the harmony? Is there in the whole world a being who could or would have the right to forgive? I don't want harmony. I don't want it, out of the love I bear to mankind. I want to remain with my suffering unavenged. I'd rather remain with my suffering unavenged and my indignation unappeased, *even if I were wrong*. Besides, too high a price has been placed on harmony. We cannot afford to pay so much for admission. And therefore I hasten to return my ticket of admission. And indeed, if I am an honest man, I'm bound to hand it back as soon as possible. This I am doing. It is not God that I do not accept, Alyosha. I merely most respectfully return him the ticket.'

'This is rebellion,' Alyosha said softly, dropping his eyes.

'Rebellion? I'm sorry to hear you say that,' Ivan said with feeling. 'One can't go on living in a state of rebellion, and I want to live. Tell me frankly, I appeal to you – answer me: imagine that it is you yourself who are erecting the edifice of human destiny with the aim of making men happy in the end, of giving them peace and contentment at last, but that to do that it is absolutely necessary, and indeed quite inevitable, to torture to death only one tiny creature, the little girl who beat her breast with her little fist, and to found the edifice on her unavenged tears – would you consent to be the architect on those conditions? Tell me and do not lie!'

'No, I wouldn't,' Alyosha said softly.

'And can you admit the idea that the people for whom you are building it would agree to accept their happiness at the price of the unjustly shed blood of a little tortured child and having accepted it, to remain for ever happy?'

'No, I can't admit it. Ivan,' Alyosha said suddenly with flashing eyes, 'you said just now, is there a being in the whole world who could or had the right to forgive? But there is such a being, and he can forgive everything, everyone and everything and *for everything*, because he gave his innocent blood for all and for everything. You've forgotten him, but it is on him that the edifice is founded, and it is to him that they will cry aloud: "Thou are just, O Lord, for thy ways are revealed!"'

'Oh, "the only one without sin" and his blood! No, I have not forgotten him, and indeed I could not help being surprised at you all the time for not bringing him in, for in all your arguments you usually put him forward first of all. You know, Alyosha – don't laugh, but I made up a poem about a year ago. If you can spare me another ten minutes, I'll tell you about it.'

'You wrote a poem?'

'Oh, no, I didn't write it,' Ivan laughed. 'And I've never composed two lines of poetry in my life. But I made up this poem and I remembered it. I made it up in a moment of inspiration. You will be my first reader, I mean, listener,' Ivan grinned. 'Shall I tell you or not?'

'I'd be glad to hear it,' said Alyosha.

'My poem is called "The Grand Inquisitor". It's an absurd thing, but I'd like to tell you about it.'

5

The Grand Inquisitor

'I'M afraid here, too, it's impossible to begin without an introduction, that is, a literary introduction – oh, dear,' Ivan laughed, 'what a rotten author I'd make! You see, the action of my poem takes place in the sixteenth century and in those days, as you no doubt know from your lessons at school, it was the custom in poetical works to bring heavenly powers down to earth. Not to mention Dante, in France court clerks as well as monks in monasteries performed plays in which the Madonna, the angels, the saints, Christ, and even God himself were brought on the stage. In those days it was all done very artlessly. In Victor Hugo's *Notre Dame de Paris*, an edifying play, to which the people were admitted without charge, was performed at the Paris town hall in the reign of Louis XI to celebrate the birth of the French Dauphin. It was called *Le bon jugement de la très sainte et gracieuse Vierge Marie*, and she appeared in person and pronounced her *bon jugement*. We occasionally had almost identical performances of plays, based on Old Testament stories, in Moscow before the time of Peter the Great. But in addition to plays, there were in those days a great many stories and "poems" in which, whenever required, holy angels and all the heavenly powers took part. In our monasteries monks were also occupied with translating, copying, and even composing such poems – and even under the Tartars. There is, for instance, one such monastery poem (translated from the Greek, of course): *The Holy Virgin's Journey Through Hell*, with descriptions as bold as those of Dante's. Our Lady visits hell and is shown round "the torments" by the archangel Michael. She sees the sinners and their sufferings. There is there, incidentally, a highly diverting category of sinners in a burning lake: those who are thrown into this lake can never swim out of it, and these "God forgets" – an expression of extraordinary depth and force. And so the Mother of God, shocked and weeping, kneels before the throne of God and begs for a free pardon for all in hell, for all she has seen there, without distinction. Her conversation with God is extraordinarily interesting. She beseeches, she refuses to go away, and when God points to the stigmata on the hands and feet of her Son and asks her: "How am I to forgive his torturers?" – she bids all the saints, all the martyrs, all the angels and archangels to kneel with her and pray for a free pardon for all without distinction. It ends by her obtaining from God a respite from torments every year from Good Friday to Trinity Sunday, and the sinners in hell at once give thanks to the Lord and cry out to him: "Thou art just, O Lord, in that judgement!" Well, then, my little poem would also have been of that kind had it appeared at that time. In my poem he appears, though, it is true, he says nothing, but only appears and passes on. Fifteen centuries have passed since he gave the promise to come into his kingdom, fifteen centuries since his prophet wrote: "Behold I come quickly." "Of that day and hour knoweth no man, not the angels of heaven, but my Father only," as he said himself while still on earth. But mankind awaits him with the same faith and the same yearning. Oh, with greater faith even, for fifteen centuries have passed since the pledges given to man from heaven have ceased:

> Trust what thy heart doth tell thee,
> Trust no pledges from above.

'And only the faith in what your heart tells you remains! It is true there were many miracles in those days. There were saints who worked miraculous cures; according to their "lives", the Holy Mother of God herself came to visit some holy men. But the devil does not slumber, and many people were already beginning to doubt the truth of those miracles. Just then there appeared in the north of Germany a dreadful new heresy. A great star, "burning as it were a lamp" (that is, the church), "fell upon the fountains of waters and they became wormwood". Those heresies began impiously to deny the existence of miracles. But those who remained faithful believed all the more ardently. The tears of mankind rose up to him as before, they waited for him, they loved him, they put their hope in him, they yearned to suffer and die for him as before. . . . And for countless ages mankind prayed with fiery faith, "Oh Lord our God, appear unto us." They called upon him for so many ages that he, in his infinite mercy, longed to come down to those who prayed to him. He had come down and had visited before that day some saints, martyrs, and holy hermits while they were still on earth, as is written in their "lives". In our own country, the poet Tyutchev, who believed sincerely in the truth of his words, proclaimed that:

> In slavish habit, the Heavenly King,
> By the burden of the Cross weighed down,
> Through my native land went wandering,
> Showering blessings upon village and town.

And I can assure you that it really was so. And now the time came when he wished to appear to the people, if only for a moment – to the tormented, suffering people, to the people sunk in filthy iniquity, but who loved him like innocent children. The action of my poem takes place in Spain, in Seville, during the most terrible time of the Inquisition, when fires were lighted every day throughout the land to the glory of God and

> In the splendid autos-da-fé
> Wicked heretics were burnt.

Oh, of course, this was not the second coming when, as he promised, he would appear at the end of time in all his heavenly glory, and which would be as sudden "as the lightning cometh out of the east, and shineth even unto the west". No, all he wanted was to visit his children only for a moment and just where the stakes of the heretics were crackling in the flames. In his infinite mercy he once more walked among men in the semblance of man as he had walked among men for thirty-three years fifteen centuries ago. He came down into the hot "streets and lanes" of the southern city just at the moment when, a day before, nearly a hundred heretics had been burnt all at once by the cardinal, the Grand Inquisitor, *ad majorem gloriam Dei* in "a magnificent auto da fé", in the presence of the king, the court, the knights, the cardinals, and the fairest ladies of the Court and the whole population of Seville. He appeared quietly, inconspicuously, but everyone – and that is why it is so strange – recognized him. That might have been one of the finest passages in my poem – I mean, why they recognized him. The people are drawn to him by an irresistible force, they surround him, they throng about him, they follow him. He walks among them in silence with a gentle smile of infinite compassion. The sun of love burns in his heart, rays of Light, of Enlightenment, and of Power stream from his eyes and, pouring over the people, stir their hearts with responsive love. He stretches forth his hands to them, blesses them, and a healing virtue comes from contact with him, even with his garments. An old man, blind from childhood, cries out to him from the midst of the crowd, "O Lord, heal me so that I may see thee", and it is as though scales fell from his eyes, and the blind man sees him. The people weep and kiss the ground upon which he walks. Children scatter flowers before him, sing and cry out to him: "Hosannah!" "It is he, it is he himself," they all repeat. "It must be he, it can be no one but he." He stops on the steps of the Cathedral of Seville at the moment when a child's little, open white coffin is brought in with weeping into the church: in it lies a girl of seven, the only daughter of a prominent citizen. The dead child is covered with flowers. "He will raise up your child", people shout from the crowd to the weeping mother. The canon, who has come out to meet the coffin, looks on perplexed and knits his brows. But presently a cry of the dead child's mother is heard. She throws herself at his feet. "If it is thou," she cries, holding out her hands to him, "then raise my child from the dead!" The funeral cortège halts. The coffin is lowered on to the steps at his feet. He gazes with compassion and his lips once again utter softly the words, "Talitha cumi" – "and the damsel arose". The little girl rises in the coffin, sits up, and looks around her with surprise in her smiling, wide-open eyes. In her hands she holds the nosegay of white roses with which she lay in her coffin. There are cries, sobs, and confusion among the people, and it is at that very moment that the Cardinal himself, the Grand Inquisitor, passes by the cathedral in the square. He is an old man of nearly ninety, tall and erect, with a shrivelled face and sunken eyes, from which, though, a light like a fiery spark still gleams. Oh, he is not wearing his splendid cardinal robes in which he appeared before the people the day before, when the enemies of the Roman faith were being burnt – no, at that moment he is wearing only his old, coarse, monk's cassock. He is followed at a distance by his sombre assistants and his slaves and his "sacred" guard. He stops in front of the crowd and watches from a distance. He sees everything. He sees the coffin set down at *his* feet, he sees the young girl raised from the dead, and his face darkens. He knits his grey, beetling brows and his eyes flash with an ominous fire. He stretches forth his finger and commands the guards to seize *him*. And so great is his power and so accustomed are the people to obey him, so humble and submissive are they to his will, that the crowd immediately makes way for the guards and, amid the death-like hush that descends upon the square, they lay hands upon *him* and lead him away. The crowd, like one man, at once bows down to the ground before the old Inquisitor, who blesses them in silence and passes on. The guards take their Prisoner to the dark, narrow, vaulted prison in the old building of the Sacred Court and lock him in there. The day passes and night falls, the dark, hot and "breathless" Seville night. The air is "heavy with the scent

THE GRAND INQUISITOR 293

of laurel and lemon". Amid the profound darkness, the iron door of the prison is suddenly opened and the old Grand Inquisitor himself slowly enters the prison with a light in his hand. He is alone and the door at once closes behind him. He stops in the doorway and gazes for a long time, for more than a minute, into his face. At last he approaches him slowly, puts the lamp on the table and says to him:

' "Is it you? You?"

'But, receiving no answer, he adds quickly: "Do not answer, be silent. And, indeed, what can you say? I know too well what you would say. Besides, you have no right to add anything to what you have said already in the days of old. Why, then, did you come to meddle with us? For you have come to meddle with us, and you know it. But do you know what is going to happen tomorrow? I know not who you are and I don't want to know: whether it is you or only someone who looks like him, I do not know, but tomorrow I shall condemn you and burn you at the stake as the vilest of heretics, and the same people who today kissed your feet, will at the first sign from me rush to rake up the coals at your stake tomorrow. Do you know that? Yes, perhaps you do know it," he added after a moment of deep reflection without taking his eyes off his prisoner for an instant.'

'I'm afraid I don't quite understand it, Ivan,' said Alyosha, who had been listening in silence all the time, with a smile. 'Is it just a wild fantasy, or has the old man made some mistake, some impossible *qui pro quo*?'

'You can assume it to be the latter,' laughed Ivan, 'if our modern realism has spoilt you so much that you can't bear anything fantastic. If you prefer a *qui pro quo*, then let it be so. It is true,' he laughed again, 'the old man was ninety and he might have long ago gone mad about his fixed idea. He might, too, have been struck by the Prisoner's appearance. It might, finally, have been simply delirium. A vision the ninety-year-old man had before his death, particularly as he had been greatly affected by the burning of a hundred heretics at the auto-da-fé the day before. What difference does it make to us whether it was a *qui pro quo* or a wild fantasy? The only thing that matters is that the old man should speak out, that at last he does speak out and says aloud what he has been thinking in silence for ninety years.'

'And is the Prisoner also silent? Does he look at him without uttering a word?'

'Yes,' Ivan laughed again, 'that's how it should be in all such cases. The old man himself tells him that *he* has no right to add anything to what had already been said before. If you like, this is the most fundamental feature of Roman Catholicism, in my opinion at any rate: "Everything," he tells him, "has been handed over by you to the Pope and, therefore, everything is now in the Pope's hands, and there's no need for you to come at all now — at any rate, do not interfere for the time being." They not only speak, but also write in that sense. The Jesuits do at any rate. I've read it myself in the works of their theologians. "Have you the right to reveal to us even one of the mysteries of the world you have come from?" my old man asks him and he replies for him himself. "No, you have not. So that you may not add anything to what has been said before and so as not to deprive men of the freedom which you upheld so strongly when you were on earth. All that you might reveal anew would encroach on men's freedom of faith, for it would come as a miracle, and their freedom of faith was dearer to you than anything even in those days, fifteen hundred years ago. Was it not you who said so often in those days, 'I shall make you free'? But now you have seen those 'free' men," the old man adds suddenly with a pensive smile. "Yes, this business has cost us a great deal," he goes on, looking sternly at him, "but we've completed it at last in your name. For fifteen centuries we've been troubled by this freedom, but now it's over and done with for good. You don't believe that it is all over? You look meekly at me and do not deign even to be indignant with me? I want you to know that now — yes, today — these men are more than ever convinced that they are absolutely free, and yet they themselves have brought their freedom to us and humbly laid it at our feet. But it was we who did it. And was that what you wanted? Was that the kind of freedom you wanted?" '

'I'm afraid I don't understand again,' Alyosha interrupted. 'Is he being ironical, is he laughing?'

'Not in the least. You see, he glories in the fact that he and his followers have at last vanquished freedom and have done so in order to make men happy. "For," he tells him, "it is only now (he is, of course, speaking of the Inquisition), that it has become possible for the first time to think of the happiness of men. Man is born a rebel, and can rebels be happy? You were warned," he says to him. "There has been no lack of warnings and signs, but you did not heed the warnings. You rejected the only way by which men might be made happy, but, fortunately, in departing, you handed on the work to us. You have promised and you have confirmed it by your own word. You have given us the right to bind and unbind, and of course you can't possibly think of depriving us of that right now. Why, then, have you come to interfere with us?" '

'And what's the meaning of "there has been no lack of warnings and signs"?' asked Alyosha.

'That, you see, is the chief thing about which the old man has to speak out.

' "The terrible and wise spirit, the spirit of self-destruction and non-existence," the old man went on, "the great spirit talked with you in the wilderness and we are told in the books that he apparently 'tempted' you. Is that so? And could anything truer have been said than what he revealed to you in his three questions and what you rejected, and what in the books are called 'temptations'? And yet if ever there has been on earth a real, prodigious miracle, it was on that day, on the day of the three temptations. Indeed, it was in the emergence of those three questions that the miracle lay. If it were possible to imagine, for the sake of argument, that those three questions of the terrible spirit had been lost without leaving a trace in the books and that we had to rediscover, restore, and invent them afresh and that to do so we had to gather together all the wise men of the earth — rulers, high priests, scholars, philosophers, poets — and set them the task of devising and inventing three questions which would not only correspond to the magnitude of the occasion, but, in addition, express in three words, in three short human sentences, the whole future history of the world and of mankind, do you think that the entire wisdom of the earth, gathered together, could have invented anything equal in depth and force to the three questions which were actually put to you at the time by the wise and mighty spirit in the wilderness? From those questions alone, from the miracle of their appearance, one can see that what one is dealing with here is not the human, transient mind, but the absolute and everlasting one. For in those three questions the whole future history of mankind is, as it were, anticipated and combined in one whole and three images are presented in which all the insoluble historical contradictions of human nature all over the world will meet. At the time it could not be so clearly seen, for the future was still unknown, but now, after fifteen centuries have gone by, we can see that everything in those three questions was so perfectly divined and foretold and has been so completely proved to be true that nothing can be added or taken from them.

' "Decide yourself who was right – you or he who questioned you then? Call to your mind the first question; its meaning, though not in these words, was this: 'You want to go into the world and you are going empty-handed, with some promise of freedom, which men in their simplicity and their innate lawlessness cannot even comprehend, which they fear and dread – for nothing has ever been more unendurable to man and to human society than freedom! And do you see the stones in this parched and barren desert? Turn them into loaves, and mankind will run after you like a flock of sheep, grateful and obedient, though for ever trembling with fear that you might withdraw your hand and they would no longer have your loaves.' But you did not want to deprive man of freedom and rejected the offer, for, you thought, what sort of freedom is it if obedience is bought with loaves of bread? You replied that man does not live by bread alone, but do you know that for the sake of that earthly bread the spirit of the earth will rise up against you and will join battle with you and conquer you, and all will follow him, crying 'Who is like this beast? He has given us fire from heaven!' Do you know that ages will pass and mankind will proclaim in its wisdom and science that there is no crime and, therefore, no sin, but that there are only hungry people. 'Feed them first and then demand virtue of them!' – that is what they will inscribe on their banner which they will raise against you and which will destroy your temple. A new building will rise where your temple stood, the dreadful Tower of Babel will rise up again, and though, like the first one, it will not be completed, yet you might have prevented the new tower and have shortened the sufferings of men by a thousand years – for it is to us that they will come at last, after breaking their hearts for a thousand years with their tower! Then they will look for us again under the ground, hidden in the catacombs (for we shall again

be persecuted and tortured), and they will find us and cry out to us,
'Feed us, for those who have promised us fire from heaven have not
given it to us!' And then we shall finish building their tower, for he
who feeds them will complete it, and we alone shall feed them in
your name, and we shall lie to them that it is in your name. Oh,
without us they will never, never feed themselves. No science will
give them bread so long as they remain free. But in the end they will
lay their freedom at our feet and say to us, 'We don't mind being
your slaves so long as you feed us!' They will, at last, realize themselves that there cannot be enough freedom and bread for everybody,
for they will never, never be able to let everyone have his fair share!
They will also be convinced that they can never be free because they
are weak, vicious, worthless, and rebellious. You promised them
bread from heaven, but, I repeat again, can it compare with earthly
bread in the eyes of the weak, always vicious and always ignoble
race of man? And if for the sake of the bread from heaven thousands
and tens of thousands will follow you, what is to become of the
millions and scores of thousands of millions of creatures who will
not have the strength to give up the earthly bread for the bread of
heaven? Or are only the scores of thousands of the great and strong
dear to you, and are the remaining millions, numerous as the sand
of the sea, who are weak but who love you, to serve only as the
material for the great and the strong? No, to us the weak, too, are
dear. They are vicious and rebellious, but in the end they will become
obedient too. They will marvel at us and they will regard us as gods
because, having become their masters, we consented to endure freedom and rule over them – so dreadful will freedom become to them
in the end! But we shall tell them that we do your bidding and rule
in your name. We shall deceive them again, for we shall not let you
come near us again. That deception will be our suffering, for we shall
be forced to lie. That was the meaning of the first question in the
wilderness, and that was what you rejected in the name of freedom,
which you put above everything else. And yet in that question lay
hidden the great secret of this world. By accepting 'the loaves', you
would have satisfied man's universal and everlasting craving, both as
an individual and as mankind as a whole, which can be summed up
in the words 'whom shall I worship?' Man, so long as he remains
free, has no more constant and agonizing anxiety than to find as

quickly as possible someone to worship. But man seeks to worship only what is incontestable, so incontestable, indeed, that all men at once agree to worship it all together. For the chief concern of those miserable creatures is not only to find something that I or someone else can worship, but to find something that all believe in and worship, and the absolutely essential thing is that they should do so *all together*. It is this need for *universal* worship that is the chief torment of every man individually and of mankind as a whole from the beginning of time. For the sake of that universal worship they have put each other to the sword. They have set up gods and called upon each other, 'Give up your gods and come and worship ours, or else death to you and to your gods!' And so it will be to the end of the world, even when the gods have vanished from the earth: they will prostrate themselves before idols just the same. You knew, you couldn't help knowing this fundamental mystery of human nature, but you rejected the only absolute banner, which was offered to you, to make all men worship you alone incontestably – the banner of earthly bread, which you rejected in the name of freedom and the bread from heaven. And look what you have done further – and all again in the name of freedom! I tell you man has no more agonizing anxiety than to find someone to whom he can hand over with all speed the gift of freedom with which the unhappy creature is born. But only he can gain possession of men's freedom who is able to set their conscience at ease. With the bread you were given an incontestable banner: give him bread and man will worship you, for there is nothing more incontestable than bread; but if at the same time someone besides yourself should gain possession of his conscience – oh, then he will even throw away your bread and follow him who has ensnared his conscience. You were right about that. For the mystery of human life is not only in living, but in knowing why one lives. Without a clear idea of what to live for man will not consent to live and will rather destroy himself than remain on the earth, though he were surrounded by loaves of bread. That is so, but what became of it? Instead of gaining possession of men's freedom, you gave them greater freedom than ever! Or did you forget that a tranquil mind and even death is dearer to man than the free choice in the knowledge of good and evil? There is nothing more alluring to man than this freedom of conscience, but there is nothing more tormenting, either. And instead of firm foundations for appeasing man's conscience once and for all, you chose everything that was exceptional, enigmatic, and vague, you chose everything that was beyond the strength of men, acting, consequently, as though you did not love them at all – you who came to give your life for them! Instead of taking possession of men's freedom you multiplied it and burdened the spiritual kingdom of man with its sufferings for ever. You wanted man's free love so that he should follow you freely, fascinated and captivated by you. Instead of the strict ancient law, man had in future to decide for himself with a free heart what is good and what is evil, having only your image before him for guidance. But did it never occur to you that he would at last reject and call in question even your image and your truth, if he were weighed down by so fearful a burden as freedom of choice? They will at last cry aloud that the truth is not in you, for it was impossible to leave them in greater confusion and suffering than you have done by leaving them with so many cares and insoluble problems. It was you yourself, therefore, who laid the foundation for the destruction of your kingdom and you ought not to blame anyone else for it. And yet, is that all that was offered to you? There are three forces, the only three forces that are able to conquer and hold captive for ever the conscience of these weak rebels for their own happiness – these forces are: miracle, mystery, and authority. You rejected all three and yourself set the example for doing so. When the wise and terrible spirit set you on a pinnacle of the temple and said to you: 'If thou be the Son of God, cast thyself down: for it is written, He shall give his angels charge concerning thee: and in their hands they shall bear thee up, lest at any time thou dash thy foot against a stone, and thou shalt prove then how great is thy faith in thy Father.' But, having heard him, you rejected his proposal and did not give way and did not cast yourself down. Oh, of course, you acted proudly and magnificently, like God. But men, the weak, rebellious race of men, are they gods? Oh, you understood perfectly then that in taking one step, in making a move to cast yourself down, you would at once have tempted God and have lost all your faith in him, and you would have been dashed to pieces against the earth which you came to save, and the wise spirit that tempted you would have rejoiced. But, I repeat, are there many like you? And could you really assume for a moment that men, too, could be equal to such a temptation? Is the nature of man such that he can reject a miracle and at the most fearful moments of life, the moments of his most fearful, fundamental, and agonizing spiritual problems, stick to the free decision of the heart? Oh, you knew that your great deed would be preserved in books, that it would go down to the end of time and the extreme ends of the earth, and you hoped that, following you, man would remain with God and ask for no miracle. But you did not know that as soon as man rejected miracle he would at once reject God as well, for what man seeks is not so much God as miracles. And since man is unable to carry on without a miracle, he will create new miracles for himself, miracles of his own, and will worship the miracle of the witch-doctor and the sorcery of the wise woman, rebel, heretic and infidel though he is a hundred times over. You did not come down from the cross when they shouted to you, mocking and deriding you: 'If thou be the Son of God, come down from the cross.' You did not come down because, again, you did not want to enslave man by a miracle and because you hungered for a faith based on free will and not on miracles. You hungered for freely given love and not for the servile raptures of the slave before the might that has terrified him once and for all. But here, too, your judgement of men was too high, for they are slaves, though rebels by nature. Look round and judge: fifteen centuries have passed, go and have a look at them: whom have you raised up to yourself? I swear, man has been created a weaker and baser creature than you thought him to be! Can he, can he do what you did? In respecting him so greatly, you acted as though you ceased to feel any compassion for him, for you asked too much of him – you who have loved him more than yourself! Had you respected him less, you would have asked less of him, and that would have been more like love, for his burden would have been lighter. He is weak and base. What does it matter if he does rebel against our authority everywhere now and is proud of his rebellion? It is the pride of a child and of a schoolboy. They are little children rioting in class and driving out their teacher. But an end will come to the transports of the children, too. They will pay dearly for it. They will tear down the temples and drench the earth with blood. But they will realize at last, the foolish children, that although they are rebels, they are impotent rebels who are unable to keep up with their rebellion. Dissolving into foolish tears, they will admit at last that he who created them rebels must undoubtedly have meant to laugh at them. They will say so in despair, and their utterance will be a blasphemy which will make them still more unhappy, for man's nature cannot endure blasphemy and in the end will always avenge it on itself. And so, unrest, confusion, and unhappiness – this is the present lot of men after all you suffered for their freedom! Your great prophet tells in a vision and in an allegory that he saw all those who took part in the first resurrection and that there were twelve thousand of them from each tribe. But if there were so many then, they, too, were not like men, but gods. They had borne your cross, they had endured scores of years of the hungry and barren wilderness, feeding on locusts and roots – and you can indeed point with pride to those children of freedom, freely given love, and free and magnificent sacrifice in your name. But remember that there were only a few thousand of them, and they, too, gods. But what of the rest? And why are the rest, the weak ones, to blame if they were not able to endure all that the mighty ones endured? Why is the weak soul to blame for being unable to receive gifts so terrible? Surely, you did not come only to the chosen and for the chosen? But if so, there is a mystery here and we cannot understand it. And if it is a mystery, then we, too, were entitled to preach a mystery and to teach them that it is neither the free verdict of their hearts nor love that matters, but the mystery which they must obey blindly, even against their conscience. So we have done. We have corrected your great work and have based it on *miracle, mystery, and authority*. And men rejoiced that they were once more led like sheep and that the terrible gift which had brought them so much suffering had at last been lifted from their hearts. Were we right in doing and teaching this? Tell me. Did we not love mankind when we admitted so humbly its impotence and lovingly lightened its burden and allowed men's weak nature even to sin, so long as it was with our permission? Why, then, have you come to meddle with us now? And why are you looking at me silently and so penetratingly with your gentle eyes? Get angry. I do not want your love because I do not love you myself. And what have I to hide from you? Or don't I know to whom I am speaking? All I have to tell you is already known to you. I can read it in your eyes. And would I conceal our secret from you? Perhaps it is just what you

want to hear from my lips. Well, then, listen. We are not with you
but with *him:* that is our secret! It's a long time – eight centuries –
since we left you and went over to *him.* Exactly eight centuries ago
we took from him what you rejected with scorn, the last gift he
offered you, after having shown you all the kingdoms of the earth:
we took from him Rome and the sword of Caesar and proclaimed
ourselves the rulers of the earth, the sole rulers, though to this day
we have not succeeded in bringing our work to total completion.
But whose fault is it? Oh, this work is only beginning, but it has
begun. We shall have to wait a long time for its completion and the
earth will have yet much to suffer, but we shall reach our goal and be
Caesars and it is then that we shall think about the universal happiness of man. And yet even in those days you could have taken up the
sword of Caesar. Why did you reject that last gift? By accepting
that third counsel of the mighty spirit, you would have accomplished
all that man seeks on earth, that is to say, whom to worship, to whom
to entrust his conscience and how at last to unite all in a common,
harmonious, and incontestable ant-hill, for the need of universal
unity is the third and last torment of men. Mankind as a whole has
always striven to organize itself into a world state. There have been
many great nations with great histories, but the more highly developed
they were, the more unhappy they were, for they were more acutely
conscious of the need for the world-wide union of men. The great
conquerors, the Timurs and Ghenghis-Khans, swept like a whirl-
wind over the earth, striving to conquer the world, but, though
unconsciously, they expressed the same great need of mankind for a
universal and world-wide union. By accepting the world and
Caesar's purple, you would have founded the world state and given
universal peace. For who is to wield dominion over men if not those
who have taken possession of their consciences and in whose hands
is their bread? And so we have taken the sword of Caesar and, having
taken it, we of course rejected you and followed *him.* Oh, many
more centuries are yet to pass of the excesses of their free mind, of
their science and cannibalism, for, having begun to build their
Tower of Babel without us, they will end up with cannibalism. But
then the beast will come crawling up to us and will lick our feet and
will bespatter them with tears of blood from its eyes. And we shall
sit upon the beast and raise the cup, and on it will be written:

'Mystery!' And then, and only then, will the reign of peace and happiness come to men. You pride yourself upon your chosen ones, but you have only the chosen ones, while we will bring peace to all. But that is not all: how many of those chosen ones, of those mighty ones who could have become the chosen ones, have at last grown tired of waiting for you and have carried and will go on carrying the powers of their spirit and the ardours of their hearts to another field and will end by raising their *free* banner against you? But you raised that banner yourself. With us, however, all will be happy and will no longer rise in rebellion nor exterminate one another, as they do everywhere under your freedom. Oh, we will convince them that only then will they become free when they have resigned their freedom to us and have submitted to us. And what do you think? Shall we be right or shall we be lying? They will themselves be convinced that we are right, for they will remember the horrors of slavery and confusion to which your freedom brought them. Freedom, a free mind and science will lead them into such a jungle and bring them face to face with such marvels and insoluble mysteries that some of them, the recalcitrant and the fierce, will destroy themselves, others, recalcitrant but weak, will destroy one another, and the rest, weak and unhappy, will come crawling to our feet and cry aloud: 'Yes, you were right, you alone possessed his mystery, and we come back to you – save us from ourselves!' In receiving loaves from us, they will, of course, see clearly that we are taking the loaves made by their own hands in order to distribute them among themselves, without any miracle. They will see that we have not made stones into loaves, but they will, in truth, be more pleased with receiving them from our hands than with the bread itself! For they will remember only too well that before, without us, the bread they made turned to stones in their hands, but that when they came back to us, the very stones turned to bread in their hands. They will appreciate only too well what it means to submit themselves to us for ever! And until men understand this, they will be unhappy. And who, pray, was more than anyone responsible for that lack of understanding? Who divided the flock and scattered it on unknown paths? But the flock will be gathered together again and will submit once more, and this time it will be for good. Then we shall give them quiet, humble happiness, the happiness of weak creatures, such as they were created. Oh, we shall at last persuade them not to be proud, for you raised them up and by virtue of that taught them to be proud; we shall prove to them that they are weak, that they are mere pitiable children, but that the happiness of a child is the sweetest of all. They will grow timid and begin looking up to us and cling to us in fear as chicks to the hen. They will marvel at us and be terrified of us and be proud that we are so mighty and so wise as to be able to tame such a turbulent flock of thousands of millions. They will be helpless and in constant fear of our wrath, their minds will grow timid, their eyes will always be shedding tears like women and children, but at the slightest sign from us they will be just as ready to pass to mirth and laughter, to bright-eyed gladness and happy childish song. Yes, we shall force them to work, but in their leisure hours we shall make their life like a children's game, with children's songs, in chorus, and with innocent dances. Oh, we shall permit them to sin, too, for they are weak and helpless, and they will love us like children for allowing them to sin. We shall tell them that every sin can be expiated, if committed with our permission; that we allow them to sin because we love them all and as for the punishment for their sins – oh well, we shall take it upon ourselves. And we shall take it upon ourselves, and they will adore us as benefactors who have taken their sins upon ourselves before God. And they will have no secrets from us. We shall allow or forbid them to live with their wives and mistresses, to have or not have children – everything according to the measure of their obedience – and they will submit themselves to us gladly and cheerfully. The most tormenting secrets of their conscience – everything, everything they will bring to us, and we shall give them our decision for it all, and they will be glad to believe in our decision, because it will relieve them of their great anxiety and of their present terrible torments of coming to a free decision themselves. And they will all be happy, all the millions of creatures, except the hundred thousand who rule over them. For we alone, we who guard the mystery, we alone shall be unhappy. There will be thousands of millions of happy infants and one hundred thousand sufferers who have taken upon themselves the curse of knowledge of good and evil. Peacefully they will die, peacefully will they pass away in your name, and beyond the grave they will find nothing but death. But we shall keep the secret and for their own happiness will entice them

with the reward of heaven and eternity. For even if there were anything at all in the next world, it would not of course be for such as they.
They declare and prophesy that you will come and be victorious
again, that you will come with your chosen ones, with your proud
and mighty ones, but we shall declare that they have only saved
themselves, while we have saved all. It is said that the whore, who sits
upon the beast and holds in her hands the *mystery*, will be put to
shame, that the weak will rise up again, that they will rend her
purple and strip naked her 'vile' body. But then I will rise and point
out to you the thousands of millions of happy babes who have known
no sin. And we who, for their happiness, have taken their sins upon
ourselves, we shall stand before you and say, 'Judge us if you can
and if you dare.' Know that I am not afraid of you. Know that I,
too, was in the wilderness, that I, too, fed upon locusts and roots,
that I, too, blessed freedom, with which you have blessed men, and
that I, too, was preparing to stand among your chosen ones, among
the strong and mighty, thirsting 'to make myself of the number'.
But I woke up and refused to serve madness. I went back and joined
the hosts of those who have *corrected your work*. I went away from
the proud and returned to the meek for the happiness of the meek.
What I say to you will come to pass and our kingdom will be established. I repeat, tomorrow you will behold the obedient flock which
at a mere sign from me will rush to heap up the hot coals against the
stake at which I shall burn you because you have come to meddle
with us. For if anyone has ever deserved our fire, it is you. Tomorrow I shall burn you. *Dixi!*" '

Ivan stopped. He had got worked up as he talked and he spoke
with enthusiasm; but when he had finished, he suddenly smiled.

Alyosha, who had listened to him in silence, tried many times
towards the end to interrupt him, restraining his great agitation with
an effort. But now he suddenly burst into speech, as though carried
away beyond control.

'But,' he cried, reddening, 'this is absurd! Your poem is in praise
of Jesus and not in his disparagement as – as you wanted it to be.
And who will believe you about freedom? Is that the way to understand it? Is that the way it is understood by the Greek Orthodox
Church? It's Rome, and not the whole of Rome, either – it's not
true. They are the worst among the Catholics – the Inquisitors, the

Jesuits! . . . And, besides, there could never have been such a fantastic person as your Inquisitor. What are those sins of men they take upon themselves? Who are these keepers of the mystery who have taken some sort of curse upon themselves for the happiness of men? When have they been seen? We know the Jesuits, people speak ill of them — do you really think they are the people in your poem? They are certainly not the same at all. . . . They are simply the Romish army for the future establishment of a universal government on earth, with the Emperor — the Pontiff of Rome — at its head. That is their ideal, but without any mystery or lofty sadness about it. . . . It's the most ordinary lust for power, for filthy earthly gains, enslavement — something like a future regime of serfdom with them as the land-owners — that is all they are after. Perhaps they don't even believe in God. Your suffering Inquisitor is nothing but a fantasy. . . . '

'Wait, wait,' Ivan laughed, 'don't be so excited! You say it's a fantasy — very well, I don't deny it. Of course it's a fantasy. But, look here, you don't really think that the Catholic movement in the last few centuries is really nothing but a lust for power for the sake of some filthy gains. . . . It isn't by any chance Father Paissy's teachings, is it?'

'No, no, on the contrary, Father Paissy once said something of the same kind as you, but,' Alyosha suddenly recollected himself, 'of course, it's not the same thing at all. Not the same thing at all!'

'A very valuable piece of information all the same in spite of your "not the same thing at all". What I'd like to ask you is why your Jesuits and Inquisitors have united only for some vile material gains? Why shouldn't there be among them a sufferer tormented by great sorrow and loving humanity? You see, let us suppose that among all those who are only out for filthy material gains there's one, just one, who is like my old Inquisitor, who had himself fed on roots in the wilderness, a man possessed, who was eager to mortify his flesh so as to become free and perfect; and yet one who had loved humanity all his life and whose eyes were suddenly opened and who saw that it was no great moral felicity to attain complete control over his will and at the same time achieve the conviction that millions of other God's creatures had been created as a mockery, that they would never be able to cope with their freedom, that no giants would ever arise from the pitiful rebels to complete the tower, that the great idealist had not in mind such boobies when he dreamt of his harmony. Realizing that, he returned and joined – the clever fellows. That could have happened, couldn't it?'

'Whom did he join? What clever fellows?' cried Alyosha, almost passionately. 'They are not so clever and they have no such mysteries and secrets. Except perhaps only godlessness, that's all their secret. Your inquisitor doesn't believe in God – that's all his secret!'

'Well, suppose it is so! At last you've guessed it! And, in fact, it really is so. That really is his whole secret. But is that not suffering, particularly for a man like him who had sacrificed his whole life for a great cause in the wilderness and has not cured himself of his love of humanity? In his last remaining years he comes to the clear conviction that it is only the advice of the great and terrible spirit that could bring some sort of supportable order into the life of the feeble rebels, "the unfinished experimental creatures created as a mockery". And so, convinced of that, he sees that one has to follow the instructions of the wise spirit, the terrible spirit of death and destruction. He therefore accepts lies and deceptions and leads men consciously to death and destruction. Keeps deceiving them all the way, so that they should not notice where they are being led, for he is anxious that those miserable, blind creatures should at least on the way think themselves happy. And, mind you, the deception is in the name of him in whose ideal the old man believed so passionately all his life! Is not that a calamity? And even if there were only one such man at the head of the whole army of men "craving for power for the sake of filthy gains" – would not even one such man be sufficient to make a tragedy? Moreover, one man like that, standing at the head of the movement, is enough for the emergence of a real leading idea of the entire Roman Church with all its armies and Jesuits – the highest idea of this Church. I tell you frankly it's my firm belief that there was never any scarcity of such single individuals among those who stood at the head of the movement. Who knows, there may have been many such individuals among the Roman Pontiffs, too. Who knows, perhaps this accursed old man, who loves humanity so obstinately in his own particular way, still exists even now in the form of a whole multitude of such individual old men, and not by chance, either, but by agreement, as a secret society formed long ago to guard the mystery. To guard it from the weak and unhappy, so as to make them happy. I'm sure it exists and, indeed, it must be so. I can't help feeling that something of the same kind of mystery exists also among the freemasons at the basis of their organization. That is why the Catholics hate the freemasons so much, for they regard them as their competitors who are breaking up the unity of their idea, while there should be only one flock and one shepherd. However, I feel that in defending my theory I must appear to you as an author who resents your criticism. Let's drop it.'

'You're probably a freemason yourself!' Alyosha cried, unable to restrain himself. 'You don't believe in God,' he added, but this time in great sorrow. He imagined, besides, that his brother was looking mockingly at him. 'How does your poem end?' he asked suddenly, his eyes fixed on the ground. 'Or was that the end?'

'I intended to end it as follows: when the Inquisitor finished speaking, he waited for some time for the Prisoner's reply. His silence distressed him. He saw that the Prisoner had been listening intently to him all the time, looking gently into his face and evidently not wishing to say anything in reply. The old man would have liked him to say something, however bitter and terrible. But he suddenly approached the old man and kissed him gently on his bloodless, aged lips. That was all his answer. The old man gave a start. There was an imperceptible movement at the corners of his mouth; he went to the door, opened it and said to him: "Go, and come no more – don't come at all – never, never!" And he let him out into "the dark streets and lanes of the city". The Prisoner went away.'

'And the old man?'

'The kiss glows in his heart, but the old man sticks to his idea.'

'And you together with him?' Alyosha cried sorrowfully. 'You too?'

Ivan laughed.

'Why, goodness me, Alyosha, it's all a lot of nonsense! It's only a stupid poem of a stupid student, who has never written two lines of poetry in his life. Why do you take it so seriously? You don't think I'm going to go straight there, to the Jesuits, to join the company of men who are correcting his work? Good Lord, what do I care? I told you all I want is to live to thirty and then – dash the cup to the floor!'

'And the sticky little leaves, the precious tombs, the blue sky, the woman you are in love with? How will you live? How will you love them?' Alyosha exclaimed sorrowfully. 'How could you with such a hell in your heart and your head? Oh no, that's just what you're going away for – to join them. And if you don't, you will kill yourself. You won't be able to endure it!'

'There is a force which can endure all!' said Ivan, this time with a cold smile.

'What force?'

'A Karamazov one – the force of the Karamazov baseness.'

'You don't mean to wallow in vice, to stifle your soul in corruption, do you?'

'I daresay, only till I'm thirty I'll perhaps escape it, and then —'

'Escape it? How will you escape it? It's impossible with your ideas.'

'That, too, à la Karamazov.'

'You mean, "everything is permitted"? Everything is allowed. That's it, isn't it?'

Ivan frowned and suddenly turned strangely pale.

'Oh, you're repeating the phrase I used yesterday which so offended Miusov and – and which Dmitry so naïvely and so eagerly repeated?' he asked with a wry smile. 'Yes, I daresay, "everything is permitted", since the words have been uttered. I won't deny it. And Mitya's version isn't bad, either.'

Alyosha looked at him in silence.

'You see, old man, I thought that when I went away I would have you at least in all the world,' Ivan said suddenly with unexpected feeling. 'But I can see now, my dear anchorite, that there's no place for me in your heart. I shall never repudiate the formula of "everything is permitted", but you will repudiate me for it, won't you?'

Alyosha got up and, without uttering a word, kissed him gently on the lips.

'Plagiarism!' cried Ivan, suddenly looking very delighted. 'You've stolen it from my poem! Thanks all the same. Get up, Alyosha, it's time we went, you and I.'

They went out, but stopped at the steps of the inn.

'Look here, Alyosha,' said Ivan in a firm voice, 'if I really have time enough to enjoy the sticky little leaves, I shall only love them in memory of you. It's enough for me that you're somewhere here, and I still shan't lose my desire for life. Does that satisfy you? If you like, take it as a declaration of love. And now you go to the right and I to the left – and that's enough – do you hear? – that's enough. What I mean is that if I do not go away tomorrow (I think I certainly shall), and we happen somehow or other to meet again, don't say a word to me on all these subjects. I ask you particularly. And, please, I ask you particularly, never even attempt to speak to me again about Dmitry,' he suddenly added irritably. 'We've got everything thrashed out. We've exhausted the subject, haven't we? And, for my part, I'll also make you a promise in return: when at the age of thirty I want "to dash the cup to the floor", I shall come once more to have a talk with you about it wherever you may be – even though it were from America. I want you to know that. I'll come on purpose. It will be very interesting to have a look at you, too, by that time – to see what sort of a chap you'll be then. You see, it's rather a solemn promise. For, as a matter of fact, we may be parting for seven or ten years. Well, go to your *Pater Seraphicus* now. I hear he's dying. If he dies without you, you will probably be angry with me for having detained you. Good-bye, kiss me once more – so – and now go. . . .'

Ivan turned suddenly and went his way without turning round. It was very similar to the way Dmitry had left Alyosha the day before, though the parting the day before had been quite different. This strange coincidence flashed like an arrow through Alyosha's wistful mind, sorrowful and grief-stricken at that moment. He waited a little, gazing after his brother. For some reason he noticed that Ivan swayed from side to side as he walked and that, when looked at from behind, his right shoulder appeared to be lower than his left. He had never noticed it before. But suddenly he, too, turned and almost ran to the monastery. It was getting very dark and he suddenly felt almost frightened; some new feeling was growing up inside him, something he could not explain. The wind had risen as on the previous evening, and the age-old pine-trees rustled gloomily round him when he entered the hermitage wood. He was almost running. '*Pater Seraphicus* – he must have got that name from somewhere – where from?' it flashed through Alyosha's mind. 'Ivan, poor Ivan, when shall I see you again? . . . Here's the hermitage. Good Lord! Yes, yes, it is he, it is *Pater Seraphicus*! He will save me – from him and for ever!'

Afterwards in his life he wondered several times in great perplexity how, after parting from Ivan, he could have entirely forgotten Dmitry whom only a few hours earlier that morning he had decided to find without fail and not to go back without having done so, even if he were unable to return to the monastery that night.

6

So Far Still a Very Obscure One

ON taking leave of Alyosha, Ivan went home to his father's house. But, strange to say, he suddenly felt terribly depressed and, what's more, his depression grew stronger and stronger with every step he took towards the house. It was not his depression that was so strange as the fact that Ivan could not for the life of him tell what was the cause of it. He had often been depressed before and it was not surprising that he felt like that at a moment when he had made a clean break with everything that had brought him here and was making ready to make a completely new start in life next day and enter upon a new and completely unknown future; he would again be as lonely as before, hoping for many things without any definite idea of what exactly he was hoping for, expecting many, too many things from life, but quite unable to give an account of his expectations or even his desires. And yet at that moment, though the apprehension of the new and unknown really did oppress his heart, it was not that at all that worried him. 'Is it disgust with my father's house?' he thought to himself. 'Looks like it. I loathe it so much, and though I shall cross its horrible threshold for the last time today, I can't help loathing it. . . . ' But no, it was not that, either. Was it his parting from Alyosha and the conversation he had had with him? 'I've kept silent for so many years with the whole world and thought it beneath my dignity to speak, and suddenly I've talked such a lot of rubbish. . . . ' And, as a matter of fact, it might have been a young man's annoyance at his youthful inexperience and youthful vanity. He was annoyed at having failed to speak frankly of his opinions and, particularly, to a fellow like Alyosha on whom he undoubtedly counted a great deal in his heart. Of course, that, too, that is, his annoyance had contributed to his depression. Indeed, it had to, but that was not it, either. No, it was not it. 'I feel sick with depression, but it's quite beyond my powers to tell what I want. Perhaps I'd better not think....'

Ivan tried 'not to think', but that, too, was of no avail. What was so annoying about that depression of his and what irritated him so much about it, was the odd feeling that it was accidental and had nothing whatever to do with him. It was as if some person or thing were standing and obtruding itself somewhere, just as sometimes something obtrudes itself on your eye, and, immersed in your work or in some heated conversation, you are not aware of it for a long time, and yet it is quite obviously getting on your nerves and worrying you till at last it occurs to you to remove the offending object, often a very trifling and ridiculous one, some article left lying about in the wrong place, a handkerchief on the floor, a book not replaced in the book-case, and so on. At last Ivan, in a most vile and irritable temper, reached his father's house and, suddenly, about fifteen paces from the gate, he looked up and all at once realized what was disturbing and worrying him so much.

On a bench by the gate sat the servant Smerdyakov enjoying the cool of the evening. As soon as he caught sight of him Ivan realized that Smerdyakov was at the back of his mind and that it was this man he could not stand. A sudden light flooded his mind and everything became clear. When Alyosha had been telling him about his meeting with Smerdyakov a short while before, something gloomy and loathsome suddenly filled his heart and immediately evoked a responsive feeling of anger. Afterwards, during their talk, he had forgotten about Smerdyakov for a time, but he had stayed in his mind, and as soon as he parted from Alyosha and went home alone, the forgotten sensation at once began to emerge quickly into his consciousness again. 'Surely this wretched blackguard cannot worry me so much!' he thought with unendurable exasperation.

As a matter of fact, Ivan had recently, and especially during the last few days, taken an intense dislike to this man. He even began noticing this growing feeling of almost hatred for the man. Perhaps the process of hatred had grown so acute just because at the beginning, just after the arrival of Ivan Karamazov in our town, something quite different had been happening. At that time Ivan had suddenly taken a particular interest in Smerdyakov and had even found him very original. He himself encouraged him to talk to him, always, however, feeling surprised at a certain incoherence or rather restlessness of Smerdyakov's mind and unable to understand what it was exactly that so constantly and persistently worried the 'contemplative fellow'. They discussed philosophical questions and even how there had been light on the first day when the sun, the moon, and the stars were only created on the fourth day, and how that was to be understood; but Ivan soon found out that what interested Smerdyakov was not the sun, the moon, and the stars, and that though he was undoubtedly interested in the subject, it was only of secondary importance to him and it was something else he was after. Whether that was so or not, he began to display quite an inordinate vanity and an injured vanity, too. Ivan disliked that very much and that was the beginning of his aversion to him. Later on there were all sorts of rowdy scenes in the house. Grushenka had made her appearance, the quarrels with Dmitry had begun, there were all sorts of troubles. They discussed that, too. Smerdyakov was always very agitated when talking about it, but, again, it was very difficult to find out what exactly he hoped to get out of it. Indeed, one could not help being surprised at the illogicality and the confusing character of some of his desires, which he involuntarily betrayed and which were always rather obscure. Smerdyakov was always trying to ferret out information. He put certain indirect, but obviously carefully thought out questions, but he never explained why, and usually suddenly fell silent at the most interesting point of his inquiries or changed the subject. But what at last angered Ivan most and filled him with such revulsion was the sort of peculiar and revolting familiarity which Smerdyakov began more and more undisguisedly to show towards him. Not that he ever forgot himself so much as to be rude; on the contrary he always spoke very respectfully. But Ivan got himself into such a position that Smerdyakov began, goodness only knows why, to consider himself in some sort of league with him. He always spoke in a tone of voice that suggested that the two of them had some secret understanding about something, something that had at some time been said on both sides and that was only known to the two of them and was quite beyond the comprehension of the other mortals who were crawling round them. But even then Ivan failed for a long time to understand the real cause of his growing revulsion, and it was only quite recently that he had realized what it was all about. With a feeling of disgust and irritation he now tried to pass through the gate without speaking and without looking at Smerdyakov. But Smerdyakov got up from the bench, and by the way he did it Ivan at once guessed that he wished to talk to him about something special. Ivan glanced at him and stopped, and the fact that he stopped so suddenly and did not walk past, as he had meant to only a moment before, infuriated him. He looked with disgust and anger at Smerdyakov's eunuch-like, haggard face with the hair combed back from his temples and the fluffed-up little tuft of hair on the top of his head. His left eye was screwed up, and it winked and smiled ironically, as if to say, 'Where are you going? You won't pass by. Don't you see that two clever people like us have something to discuss?' Ivan shook with fury.

'Away, you scoundrel! What sort of company do you think I am for you, you fool?' he was about to say, but, to his utter astonishment, what he did say was something quite different: 'Is Father asleep or is he awake?' he said softly and humbly to his own surprise, and suddenly, again quite unexpectedly, sat down on the bench.

For a moment he was almost frightened – he remembered that afterwards. Smerdyakov stood facing him, his hands clasped behind his back, and looking at him with self-assurance, almost severity.

'He's still asleep, sir,' he said unhurriedly. ('You were the first to speak, not I', he seemed to say.) 'I'm surprised at you, sir,' he added after a short pause, dropping his eyes demurely, putting his right foot forward and playing with the toe of his patent-leather boot.

'Why are you surprised at me?' Ivan asked abruptly and sternly, doing his utmost to restrain himself and realizing all of a sudden with disgust that he was feeling intense curiosity and that he would not go away without satisfying it.

'Why don't you go to Chermashnya, sir?' asked Smerdyakov, raising his eyes suddenly and smiling familiarly.

'And you ought to understand yourself why I smile, if you're a clever man,' his screwed-up left eye seemed to say.

'What do I want to go to Chermashnya for?' Ivan asked in surprise.

Smerdyakov was silent again.

'Why, sir, didn't your father himself ask you to go?' he said at last unhurriedly and as though not thinking very highly himself of his question: 'I'm putting you off,' as it were, 'with a secondary reason, just to say something.'

'Damn you, man, speak more clearly! What do you want?' Ivan cried at last angrily, passing from humility to rudeness.

Smerdyakov put his right foot to his left, drew himself up, but continued to look with the same calm air and the same sweet smile.

'I've nothing important to tell you, sir. I was just passing the time of day, sir.'

Again there was silence. They did not speak for almost a minute. Ivan knew perfectly well that he ought to get up at once and explode angrily, and Smerdyakov stood before him as though waiting to see whether he would be angry with him or not. So at least Ivan thought. At last he made a movement to get up. Smerdyakov seemed to seize the moment.

'I'm in a terrible position, sir, I don't know what to do,' he said suddenly, firmly and distinctly, heaving a sigh at his last words.

Ivan at once resumed his seat.

'Both of them are quite crazy, sir,' Smerdyakov went on. 'They seem to be behaving like a couple of kids. I'm speaking of your dad, sir, and your brother Dmitry. As soon as he gets up in the morning now, your dad, that is, sir, he at once starts pestering me every minute: "Hasn't she come? Why hasn't she come?" and he'll go on like that till midnight, and even later, I daresay, sir. And if Miss Svetlov don't come, for I don't think, sir, she intends to come at all, he'll be at me again next morning: "Why hasn't she come? What can have kept her away? When will she come?" as if, sir, I was to blame for it. And, on the other hand, sir, this is the sort of thing that happens: as soon as it gets dark, or even earlier, your brother comes from next door with a gun in his hands: "Take care," he says to me, "you dirty rogue, you broth-brewer, you, if you miss her and don't let me know she's come, I'll kill you before anyone else." When the night's over, in the morning, he, too, like your dad, sir, starts worrying me to death: "Why hasn't she come? When will she show up?" and here, too, sir, it's as if I was to blame that his lady-friend hasn't shown up. And every day and every hour, sir, they gets angrier and angrier, both of 'em, so that I begin to think, sir, sometimes, that I'd be better dead rather than be bullied like that. You see, sir, I can't trust them at all.'

'And why did you get mixed up with it?' Ivan said irritably. 'Why did you have to start spying for Dmitry?'

'And how could I help getting mixed up with it, sir? And I didn't get mixed up with it at all, if you wants to know the whole truth, sir. I never said a word from the very beginning, I didn't, sir. I daren't answer, you see. It was him, sir, who appointed me his page, in a manner of speaking. And since then all he says to me is, "I'll kill you, you dirty rogue," he says, "if you miss her!" I'm quite sure, sir, that I'm going to have a long epileptic fit tomorrow.'

'What's a long epileptic fit?'

'It's a long fit, sir. Goes on for a long time, it does, sir. For a couple of hours or more, or, as like as not, for a day or two. Once it went on for three days. I fell from the loft that time. The convulsions stop for a time, then start again. And for three days I didn't come back to my senses. Mr Karamazov, sir, sent for Herzenstube, our local doctor, and he put ice on my head and tried some other remedy, too. I might have died, I might, sir.'

'But I'm told with epilepsy it's impossible to tell beforehand at what time a fit is coming. What then makes you say that you'll have one tomorrow?' Ivan inquired with a peculiar and exasperated curiosity.

'That's right, sir. It's impossible to tell beforehand.'

'Besides, you fell from the loft then.'

'I climbs up to the loft every day, sir, and I might fall from the loft again tomorrow. And if it isn't from the loft, sir, I might fall down the cellar, for I have to go there every day, too, sir.'

Ivan gave him a long look.

'You're talking a lot of nonsense, I see, and I'm afraid I don't quite understand you,' he said quietly, but somehow menacingly. 'You don't mean to pretend tomorrow to have a fit lasting three days, do you?'

Smerdyakov, whose eyes were fixed on the ground and who was again playing with the toe of his right foot, set his foot down, putting his left foot forward instead, raised his head and said with a grin:

'Even if I was to play such a trick, sir, I mean, to pretend to have a fit, which isn't at all difficult for a man with experience of that sort of thing, I have a perfect right to use such means to save my life. For, you see, sir, even if Miss Svetlov comes to see his dad when I'm ill in bed, he can't very well come and ask a sick man why he hasn't told him. He'd be ashamed to.'

'Damn it,' cried Ivan, his face contorted with anger, 'why are you always in such a funk for your life? All my brother's threats are only words uttered in a passion and nothing more. He won't kill you. He will kill someone, but it won't be you!'

'He'll kill me like a fly, sir. Me first of all. But I'm more afraid of something else, sir. I'm afraid of being taken for an accomplice of his when he does something horrible to his dad.'

'Why should you be taken for his accomplice?'

'They'll take me for his accomplice, sir, because I told him the signals as a great secret!'

'What signals? Whom did you tell? Damn you, man, speak more plainly!'

'You see, sir, I must confess,' Smerdyakov drawled with pedantic composure, 'I've got a secret understanding with Mr Karamazov. As you knows yourself (if you do know it), he has for several days now locked himself in as soon as night or evening comes. Lately you've been going up to your room early every evening, sir, and yesterday you didn't go out at all and that's why perhaps you don't know how careful he's been to lock himself in at night. And though Grigory himself was to come, he'd only open the door if he recognized his voice. But Grigory, sir, never comes, and that's why I waits on him in his rooms alone – that's the arrangement he made himself ever since he started that business with Miss Svetlov. But at night, you see, sir, I goes away, by his orders, to the cottage as usual, but on condition that I don't go to bed till midnight, but keep watch, getting up and walking round the yard, waiting for Miss Svetlov to come, for he's been expecting her for the last few days, sir, just as if he was mad. He argues this way, sir: she's afraid of him, of your brother Dmitry, that is, of that puppy Mitya, as he calls him, and so she'll be coming the back way late at night. You look out for her, he says to me, till midnight and later. And if she comes, you run and knock on my door or on the window from the garden twice at first, very softly, so: one-two, then three times more quickly: knock-knock-knock. Then, he says, I'll understand at once that she's come and will open the door to you quietly. He told me of another signal in case something special happens: at first I have to knock quickly twice: knock-knock and then, after a short interval, knock again once, but much louder. Then he'll understand that something unexpected has happened and that I must see him at once, and he'll open the door and I'll go in and report to him. That's in case Miss Svetlov can't come herself but sends someone with a message. Besides, your brother Dmitry might also turn up, so I must let him know that he is near. He's terribly afraid of your brother Dmitry, sir, so that even if Miss Svetlov had come and was locked in the room with him and your brother Dmitry was in the meantime to turn up anywhere near, I have to report to him at once about it, knocking three times. So that the first signal of five knocks means: Miss Svetlov has come, the second signal of three knocks – "must see you at once". So he has taught me himself several times how to give the signals and explained them to me. And seeing as how it's only him and me in the whole world who knows about them signals, he will without the slightest doubt and without calling out (for he's terrified of calling out aloud), open the door. And it's them signals that your brother Dmitry knows all about now.'

'How does he know about them? Did you tell him? How dared you tell him?'

'It's because I'm so terrified, sir. And I would never dare hold it back from him, sir. Your brother Dmitry, sir, keeps bullying me every day. "You're deceiving me. You're hiding something from me, aren't you? I'll break both your legs for you, I will!" Well, sir, that's when I told him those most secret signals, so that he might at least see that I'm devoted to him like a slave and that he might be satisfied that I'm not deceiving him and that I'm doing my best to tell him everything I know, sir.'

'If you think he'll make use of the signals and try to get in, you mustn't let him.'

'But if I was to be laid up with a fit, sir, how am I not to let him in then, sir? Why, sir, I couldn't do nothing to stop him then even if I dare not let him in, knowing how desperate he is, sir.'

'Oh, hang it all! How can you be so sure that you're going to have a fit, damn you? You're not laughing at me, are you?'

'Why, sir, would I dare laugh at you? And, anyways, I don't feel like laughing, I can tell you, seeing as how I'm so frightened. I have a feeling I'm going to have a fit, sir. I have such a feeling. It will come from fright alone, sir.'

'Oh, hell! If you're laid up, Grigory will be keeping watch. Warn Grigory beforehand. He'll most certainly not let him in.'

'I'm afraid, sir, I'd never dare tell Grigory about the signals without master's orders. And as for Grigory hearing him and not letting him in, he's been ill ever since yesterday and Marfa intends to give him treatment tomorrow. They've arranged it today, sir. And her treatment, sir, is a fair treat. You see, sir, Marfa knows the recipe of a kind of infusion, and always keeps some. It's very strong, made from some herbs – she's got the secret of it. And she treats Grigory with this secret medicine of hers three times a year, sir, every time his lumbago gets so bad that he can't move, just as though he was paralysed, sir. Yes, sir, three times a year. When this happens, she takes a towel, dips it in the infusion and rubs his back with it for half an hour, till it's bone dry and goes quite red and swollen. Then what's left over in the bottle she gives him to drink with a special prayer, sir. Not all of it, though, for she leaves a drop or two over for herself, seeing as how it's such a rare occasion, sir, and she drinks it, too. And both being strictly teetotal, sir, they just drops off and they sleeps very soundly for a very long time. When Grigory wakes up, he's almost always well after it, but when Marfa wakes up she always has a headache from it, sir. So if Marfa carries out her plan tomorrow, sir, he won't hear nothing and he won't be able to stop your brother Dmitry from going in. He'll be asleep, sir.'

'What rot! And everything's going to happen all at once, as though on purpose! You'll have your epileptic fit and they'll both be unconscious!' cried Ivan. 'You're not by any chance planning it all to happen like that?' it escaped him suddenly and he knit his brows menacingly.

'How do you mean I've been planning it, sir? And how could I be planning such a thing if it all depends on your brother Dmitry and what he's a mind to do. If he has a mind to do something, he'll do it, and if he hasn't, I'm not going to bring him here on purpose to push him into your dad's room, am I?'

'But why should he go to father, and surreptitiously too, if as you say Miss Svetlov won't be coming at all?' Ivan went on, turning pale with anger. 'You say so yourself and all the time I've been living here I've felt sure that the old man was just imagining it all and that that slut will never come to him. Why, then, should Dmitry have to burst into the house if she doesn't come? Speak! I want to know what's at the back of your mind.'

'You knows yourself why he'll come, sir. It don't much matter what I'm thinking, does it? He'll come just out of spite or because he might get suspicious on account of my being ill, for instance. He'll think it's a trick and he'll come to search the rooms impatient-like, as he did yesterday, to make sure she hasn't slipped past him somehow or other. And, besides, sir, he knows very well that the master has a big envelope, sealed with three seals, with three thousand roubles in it. Tied round with a ribbon it is, sir, and on it is written in his own hand: "To my darling Grushenka, if she comes". Three days later, sir, he added: "And to my little chicken". So that's what makes me so suspicious, sir.'

'Nonsense!' cried Ivan, almost beside himself. 'Dmitry won't come to steal the money and kill father to get it. He could have killed him yesterday for Grushenka, like the crazy, frenzied fool he is, but he'll never steal!'

'He wants money very badly now, sir. He just has to have it. You've no idea, sir, how much he needs it,' Smerdyakov went on to explain with the utmost composure and with extraordinary explicitness. 'Besides, sir, he considers the three thousand roubles to be his own. He told me so himself. "My father," he says to me, "still owes me exactly three thousand," he says. And quite apart from that, sir, if you considers it carefully, that is, there's something else that's quite true. I mean, it's quite on the cards, if you don't mind my saying so, sir, that Miss Svetlov could, if she had a mind to, make the master himself, that is, your father, sir, marry her, if she had a mind to, of course. And for all you know, sir, she may have a mind to do just that. You see, sir, I've just said she won't come, but she, sir, may perhaps want something more than that. I mean, she may want to be the mistress, sir. I knows myself that her merchant Samsonov told her quite openly that it might not be such a bad thing at that, and he laughed, he did, as he said it. And she isn't such a fool, neither, sir. It's not in her interest to marry a beggar like your brother Dmitry, sir. And you've only to take this into account, sir, to see that if that was to happen neither your brother Dmitry, nor yourself, sir, nor your brother Alexey wouldn't get nothing after your dad's death. Not a penny, sir. For Miss Svetlov would only marry him to get everything settled on herself and have all his money made over in her name. Yes, sir. But if your dad was to die now, sir, while nothing of this has happened, each of you would get at least forty thousand at once. Even your brother Dmitry, sir, whom your dad hates. For, you see, sir, he hasn't made a will. And your brother Dmitry knows that, he does and all.'

A sort of spasm passed over Ivan's face. He suddenly flushed.

'So why in that case,' he interrupted Smerdyakov, 'do you advise me to go to Chermashnya? What did you mean by that? Suppose I go and all this happens here?'

Ivan drew his breath with difficulty.

'Quite right, sir,' Smerdyakov said, quietly and soberly, watching Ivan intently, however.

'What do you mean by "quite right"?' Ivan repeated, restraining himself with an effort, his eyes flashing menacingly.

'I said that because I feels sorry for you, sir. In your place, if I was here I'd chuck it all, sir, rather than stay on when such things might be happening,' replied Smerdyakov, looking with an air of the utmost frankness into Ivan's flashing eyes.

They were both silent.

'You seem to be a complete idiot and, of course, an – an awful blackguard!' said Ivan, rising suddenly from the bench.

He was about to pass straight through the gate, but he suddenly stopped and turned to Smerdyakov. What happened then was rather strange: Ivan, suddenly, as though in a spasm, bit his lips, clenched his fists and – in another moment would, of course, have flung himself on Smerdyakov. Smerdyakov, at any rate, noticed it at once. He gave a start and recoiled with his whole body. But the moment passed harmlessly for Smerdyakov, and Ivan turned back to the gate in silence, but as though in a sort of perplexity.

'I'm leaving for Moscow tomorrow, if you care to know – early tomorrow morning – that's all!' he said suddenly in a loud voice, spitefully and distinctly, surprised at himself afterwards that he had to tell Smerdyakov that at the time.

'That's the best thing you can do, sir,' Smerdyakov at once put in, as though he had expected to hear it. 'Except, of course, sir, that you might be summoned by telegram to come back, if anything happened.'

Ivan stopped again and again turned quickly to Smerdyakov. But something seemed to have happened to Smerdyakov. All his familiarity and casualness had gone completely; his whole face expressed extraordinary attention and expectation but this time timid and obsequious. 'You wouldn't say something more? You wouldn't add something, would you?' could be read in the intent look of his eyes fixed unblinkingly on Ivan.

'And wouldn't I be summoned from Chermashnya, too, if – if anything happened?' Ivan yelled suddenly, raising his voice to a shout for some unknown reason.

'Yes, sir, you would – er – be inconvenienced in Chermashnya, too,' muttered Smerdyakov almost in a whisper, as though he had lost his nerve, but continuing to look very intently into Ivan's eyes.

'Except that, I suppose, Moscow is further away and Chermashnya is nearer, and you are, no doubt, worried about my fares. That's why you're so keen on my going to Chermashnya, isn't it? Or do you take pity on me because I'll have to make such a long journey?'

'Quite right, sir,' Smerdyakov muttered in a faltering voice, with an odious smile and again making ready convulsively to jump back in time. But, to Smerdyakov's surprise, Ivan suddenly laughed and went quickly through the gate, continuing to laugh. If anyone had glanced at his face, he would most certainly have concluded that he was not laughing because he felt happy. Besides, he could not possibly have explained himself what he was feeling at that moment. He moved and walked as though he had no control over his actions.

7

'It's Nice to Have a Chat With a Clever Man'

AND he spoke like that, too. Meeting his father in the drawing-room, just as he entered it, he suddenly shouted at him, waving his arms: 'I'm going upstairs to my room, and I'm not coming in, good night!' and went past without even glancing at his father. Very possibly the

old man was too hateful to him at that moment, but such an uncere-
monious display of hostile feelings was most unexpected even to Mr
Karamazov. And the old man evidently wanted to tell him something at once, and that was why he had gone to meet him on purpose
in the drawing-room; but hearing himself addressed in so courteous
a manner, he stopped short in silence and followed with an ironical
look his darling son's progress upstairs to his room in the attic till
he passed out of sight.

'What's the matter with him?' he promptly asked Smerdyakov,
who had followed Ivan into the room.

'He's angry about something,' Smerdyakov muttered evasively.
'You never can tell with him, sir.'

'Oh, to hell with him! Let him be angry! Let's have the *samovar*
and clear out! Be quick about it! Any news?'

There followed a number of questions of the same kind as those
Smerdyakov had just complained of to Ivan, that is, all about the
expected visitor, and we will omit them here. Half an hour later the
house was locked up, and the crazy old man kept walking from one
room to another in tremulous expectation of hearing any minute the
five prearranged knocks, peering through the darkened windows
from time to time and seeing nothing but blackness outside.

It was very late, but Ivan was still not asleep. He lay awake thinking. He went to bed late that night, at two o'clock. But we will not
describe the trend of his thoughts, and, besides, this is not the time to
analyse his soul: its turn will come. And even if we attempted to
describe some of his thoughts, we should have found it very difficult,
because they were not really thoughts, but something very vague
and, above all, too excited. He felt himself that he had lost his bear-
ings. He was also worried by all sorts of strange and almost unexpected desires. For instance, after midnight he felt an insistent and
unbearable desire to go downstairs, open the front door, go to the
cottage and give Smerdyakov a good thrashing, but if he were asked
why, he would have been at a loss to give a precise reason, except
perhaps that the servant had become as hateful to him as a man who
had insulted him more mortally than anyone he could think of in the
whole world. On the other hand, he was overcome more than once
that night by a sort of inexplicable and humiliating timidity which –
and he felt it – seemed to deprive him suddenly of all his physical

strength. His head ached and swam. A feeling of hate kept gnawing at his heart, just as though he were preparing to avenge himself on someone. He even hated Alyosha, as he recalled the conversation he had had with him, and at moments he hated himself intensely, too. He almost forgot to think of Katerina, and was very greatly surprised at it afterwards, all the more so as he remembered distinctly how when he had boasted that morning so boldly at Katerina's that he would leave for Moscow next day, he had whispered to himself in his heart: 'But that's all nonsense! You won't go. It won't be so easy to tear yourself away as you're boasting now.' Remembering that night long afterwards, Ivan recalled with particular disgust how he would suddenly get up from the sofa and quietly, as though terribly afraid to be seen, open the door, go out on the landing and listen to his father moving about and walking in the rooms on the floor below – he had listened for a long time, for about five minutes, with a sort of strange curiosity, with bated breath and a thumping heart. But why he had done all this, why he was listening, he did not of course know himself. That 'action' of his he called 'contemptible' all his life afterwards; and deep inside him, in the most secret recesses of his heart, he thought of it as the vilest action of all his life. He did not even feel any particular hatred for his father at those moments, but was for some reason only intensely curious to know why he was walking about down there and what he would be doing in his room. He pictured to himself how he must be looking through the darkened windows and then suddenly stopping in the middle of the room and waiting, waiting to hear if anyone were knocking. Ivan went out twice on the landing to listen like that. When everything was quiet and his father had gone to bed, Ivan, too, went to bed about two o'clock, firmly determined to go to sleep at once, for he felt terribly exhausted. And, to be sure, he slept like a log and without dreams, but he woke up early, at about seven, when it was already daylight. On opening his eyes, he felt, to his amazement, such an extraordinary surge of energy in himself that he quickly jumped out of bed and, dressing quickly, pulled out his trunk and, without wasting any time, began hurriedly to pack. As luck would have it, he had got his linen back from the laundress the previous morning. Ivan even smiled at the thought of how perfectly everything had worked out and that there was no needless delay to prevent his sudden departure. And his departure certainly was sudden. Though Ivan had said the day before (to Katerina, Alyosha, and afterwards to Smerdyakov) that he would be leaving next day, when he went to bed – he remembered that well – he had not thought of going away, at least he had never thought that the first thing he would do on getting up in the morning would be to pack his trunk. At last the trunk and bag were ready. It was about nine o'clock when Marfa came in with her usual question: 'Where will you have your breakfast, sir, in your room or downstairs?' Ivan went downstairs, looking almost cheerful, though there was something hurried and distracted in his words and gestures. Greeting his father affably and even inquiring particularly after his health, he announced at once, without bothering to listen to the end of his father's answer, that he was leaving for Moscow in an hour for good and asked him to send for the carriage. The old man heard the announcement without betraying the slightest surprise, most indecently forgetting to say how sorry he was to hear of his darling son's departure; instead of doing that, he suddenly became very flustered, remembering in time a most important business of his own.

'Oh, dear, what a funny fellow you are, to be sure! You didn't tell me yesterday but– never mind, we'll manage it now all the same. Do me a great favour, dear boy, and stop at Chermashnya on the way. It's only about ten miles from Volovya station. Turn to the left and there it is – Chermashnya!'

'I'm sorry, I can't. It's about fifty miles from here to the railway station and the train leaves for Moscow at seven o'clock in the evening. I'll just be in time to catch my train.'

'You can catch your train tomorrow, or the day after, but please turn off to Chermashnya today! Won't cost you anything to put your father's mind at rest, will it now? If I hadn't business to attend to here, I'd have run over long ago, because, you see, it's rather an important deal and it has to be done in a hurry, and I can't leave here just now. You see, I have a wood there in two plots, in Begichov and in Dyachkina, on a waste plot of land. The merchants Maslov, father and son, are only offering me eight thousand for the timber, and only last year I happened to run across a customer who offered me twelve thousand for it, but then he wasn't a local man – that's the point! For you can't sell anything to the local fellows because old

Maslov and his son, who're worth hundreds of thousands, have a monopoly of everything here. With them it's take it or leave it, because no local man dares to compete with them. Now, the priest at Ilyinskoye wrote to me last Thursday that a man I know, Gorskin by name, also a lousy merchant, has just arrived there. The beauty of it is, you see, that he isn't a local man but from Pogrebov, and so he isn't afraid of the Maslovs, because, you see, he isn't a local merchant. He offers me eleven thousand for the timber. Eleven thousand, do you hear? And he'll only be there, the priest writes, for a week. So if you were to go, you'd be able to clinch the deal, see?'

'Why not write to the priest? He'll clinch the deal.'

'He can't, that's the trouble. He has no eye for business. An excellent fellow, mind you. I'd trust him with twenty thousand to take care of for me any time without a receipt, but he has no eye for business. Just as if he weren't a grown-up man at all. A crow could deceive him. And yet he's a learned man – can you imagine it? Now this Gorskin fellow looks like a peasant, walks about in a blue peasant coat, but he's a rogue, if ever there was one. That's the trouble with all of us. He's a liar – that's his chief characteristic. Sometimes he tells you such lies that you wonder why he does it. Told me a tall story the year before last about his wife having died and his having married another, and there wasn't a word of truth in it! His wife never died. She's still alive and she beats him regularly every other day. So, you see, what we have to find out now is whether he's lying or speaking the truth when he says that he wants to buy the timber and is ready to pay eleven thousand for it.'

'I'm afraid I, too, shan't be of any use to you. I've no eye for business, either.'

'Wait a minute, will you? You'll do all right because I'm going to tell you how to deal with him, with Gorskin, I mean. I've done business with him a long time. You see, you have to watch his beard. He's got a nasty, thin, reddish beard. If his beard shakes when he talks and gets cross, then it's all right: he's telling the truth and means business. But if he strokes his beard with his left hand and grins, well, then he's trying to cheat you, the swindler. Never look into his eyes. You won't find out anything from his eyes. It's like looking through muddy water – the damned rogue – look at his beard! I'll give you a note and you show it to him. His name's Gorskin, but he isn't really

Gorskin, but Lyagavy – a "kicker". Only don't tell him that he's nicknamed Lyagavy or he'll be offended. If you come to terms with him and see it's all right, drop me a line at once. All you have to write is that he's not lying. Hold out for eleven thousand, one thousand you can knock off, but no more. Just think of it, my boy: there's a difference of three thousand between eleven and eight thousand. It's as good as finding three thousand. It's not so easy to find a purchaser, and I'm in desperate need of money. When I hear from you that it's a deal, I'll run over myself and clinch it. I'll snatch the time somehow. But what's the use of my rushing off there now if the whole thing is just the priest's idea? Well, are you going or not?'

'I'm sorry, I've no time. I'd rather you didn't ask me.'

'Come, do your father a favour. I shan't forget it! You've no heart, any of you – that's what it is! What's a day or two to you? Where are you off to now? To Venice? Your Venice will keep for two days. I'd have sent Alyosha, but what does Alyosha know about such things? I'm asking you because you're a clever fellow. Do you think I don't realize that? You're not a dealer in timber, but you've got a pair of eyes. All you have to do is to find out whether the man is serious or not: look at his beard, if it shakes, he's serious.'

'You're driving me to that damned Chermashnya yourself, aren't you?' cried Ivan with a malicious smile.

Karamazov did not or would not notice the malice, but he seized on the smile.

'Then you will go, won't you? I'll scribble a note for you at once.'

'I don't know whether I'll go or not. I'll decide on the way.'

'Why on the way? Decide now. Come on, my boy, decide! If you clinch the deal, drop me a line. Give it to the priest, and he'll send on your note to me at once. After that I won't keep you any more – go to Venice, if you like. The priest will send you back to Volovya station in his own carriage.'

The old man was simply overjoyed. He scribbled the note and sent for the carriage. Some snacks and brandy were brought in. When the old man was pleased, he always became expansive, but this time he seemed to hold himself in. For instance, he did not say a word about Dmitry. Nor was he in the least moved by the parting. Indeed, he seemed to be at a loss what to say. Ivan noticed it at once: 'He must be thoroughly sick of me,' he thought. It was only when seeing his son off on the front steps that the old man seemed to get a little excited. He even tried to kiss him, but Ivan quickly held out his hand, obviously anxious to avoid his kisses. The old man understood at once and instantly checked himself.

'Well, good luck, good luck!' he kept repeating from the steps. 'Will you ever come back while I'm still alive, I wonder. Well, if you do, I'll always be glad to see you. Well, Christ be with you!'

Ivan got into the carriage.

'Good-bye, Ivan,' his father cried for the last time. 'Don't be too hard on me!'

All the servants came out to see him off: Smerdyakov, Marfa, and Grigory. Ivan gave them ten roubles each. When he had taken his seat in the carriage, Smerdyakov rushed up to put the rug straight.

'You see I – I am going to Chermashnya,' the words escaped Ivan suddenly, again as the day before, against his will, and with a sort of nervous little laugh. He remembered it long after.

'Yes, sir,' Smerdyakov replied firmly, looking meaningfully at Ivan, 'people are quite right when they say that it's nice to have a chat with a clever man.'

The carriage started and drove off. The traveller felt troubled in his mind, but he looked eagerly around him at the fields, the trees, the flock of wild geese flying high overhead across a cloudless sky. And all of a sudden he felt so happy. He tried to talk to the driver and something in the peasant's answer interested him immensely. But a moment later he realized that he had missed most of what the driver had said and that, as a matter of fact, he had not even understood his answer. He fell silent. It was pleasant as it was: the air was fresh, pure, and cool, the sky was clear. The faces of Alyosha and Katerina flashed through his mind – but he smiled gently and blew gently on the dear phantoms and they vanished; 'Their time will come,' he thought. They reached the post station quickly, changed horses and galloped off to Volovya. 'Why is it nice to have a chat with a clever man? What did he mean to say by that?' he thought, and suddenly his breath failed him. 'And why did I tell him that I was going to Chermashnya?' They arrived at Volovya station. Ivan got out of the carriage and the coachmen surrounded him. They bargained with him over the fares for the journey of ten miles to Chermashnya. He told them to harness the horses. He went into the station house, looked round, glanced at the station-master's wife, and suddenly went out again.

'I won't go to Chermashnya. I won't be late for the seven o'clock train, will I?'

'No, sir. We'll get you there in time. Shall we harness the horses?'

'Yes, at once. Will any of you be in town tomorrow?'

'Why, yes, sir. Mitry here will.'

'Can you do me a service, Mitry? Go to my father, Mr Fyodor Karamazov, and tell him I haven't gone to Chermashnya. Can you do it?'

'Of course I can, sir. I've known Mr Karamazov a long time.'

'Well, here's your tip, for I don't think he will give you anything,' Ivan laughed gaily.

'So he won't,' Mitry laughed too. 'Thank you, sir. I'll be sure to do it.'

At seven o'clock in the evening Ivan got into the train and set off for Moscow. 'Away with the past. I've finished for ever with my old life and I don't want to hear of it again. To a new world, to new places, and no looking back!' But instead of delight, his soul was suddenly filled with such gloom and his heart ached with such anguish as he had never known in his life before. He lay awake thinking all night; the train flew on, and it was only at daybreak, when he was entering Moscow, that he seemed suddenly to come to.

'I'm a blackguard!' he whispered to himself.

Meantime, Karamazov, having seen off his son, was very pleased with himself. For two whole hours he felt almost happy as he sipped his brandy; but suddenly a most annoying and disagreeable thing happened which at once threw him into utter confusion and dismay: Smerdyakov, who had gone to fetch something from the cellar, fell down from the top of the steps to the bottom. It was a good thing Marfa happened to be in the yard at the time and heard it in time. She did not see the fall, but she heard his scream – the strange, peculiar scream she had long known, the scream of the epileptic falling in a fit. It was impossible to say whether the fit had come on him when he was descending the steps, so that he must have fallen down at once unconscious, or whether it had been brought on as a result of the fall and the shock, Smerdyakov being well known to be liable to epileptic fits. They found him lying at the bottom of the cellar steps, writhing in convulsions and foaming at the mouth. At first they thought that he might have broken something – an arm or a leg – and hurt himself, but 'God has preserved him', as Marfa put it; nothing of the kind had happened, but it was difficult to get him out of the cellar. But they asked the neighbours to help and managed it somehow. Karamazov himself was present at the whole ceremony and lent a helping hand himself, looking frightened and rather lost. The sick man, however, did not recover consciousness: the attacks ceased for a time, but then began again, and they all concluded that the same thing would happen as had happened the year before when he accidentally fell from the loft. They remembered that ice had been put on his head that time. There was no ice in the cellar and Marfa took steps to get some, while towards the evening Karamazov sent for Dr Herzenstube, who arrived at once. After subjecting the patient to a thorough examination (Dr Herzenstube, an elderly and most estimable man, was the most careful and conscientious doctor in the province), he concluded that the fit was a very violent one and might have 'serious consequences', but that for the time being he, Herzenstube, could not quite make it out. If, however, the present remedies were of no avail, he would try something else next morning. The sick man was taken to the cottage and put to bed in the room next to Grigory's and Marfa's. But poor Mr Karamazov had to suffer one misfortune after another during the whole of that day. Marfa cooked the dinner, and compared with Smerdyakov's, the soup was 'just like slops' and the chicken was so dried up that it was quite impossible to chew it. In reply to her master's bitter, though justified, reproaches, Marfa maintained that the chicken was a very old one to begin with and that she had never been trained as a cook. In the evening more trouble came: Karamazov was informed that Grigory, who had been feeling ill for the last two days, was almost completely laid up with lumbago. Karamazov finished his tea as early as possible and locked himself in the house. He was in a state of terrible alarm and suspense. As a matter of fact, he was expecting Grushenka to arrive almost for certain; at least early that morning he had received an assurance from Smerdyakov that she 'had promised to come without fail'. The perverse old man's heart was beating uneasily. He kept pacing up and down his empty rooms and listening. He had to be on the alert: Dmitry might be on the watch for her somewhere and as soon as she knocked on the window (Smerdyakov had assured him two days before that he had told her where and how to knock), he had to open the door as quickly as possible and not keep her for a second longer in the hall, or else – which God forbid – she might get frightened and run away. It was a trying time for Karamazov, but never had his heart been full of such sweet hopes: why, this time it was practically certain that she would come!

I

The Elder Zossima and His Visitors

WHEN Alyosha entered the elder's cell with an anxious and aching heart, he stopped short almost in amazement: instead of a dying sick man, who was perhaps already unconscious, as he had feared to find him, he saw him sitting in his armchair, though looking weak and exhausted, but with a bright and cheerful face, surrounded by visitors and conversing quietly and lucidly with them. But actually he had only got up from his bed about a quarter of an hour before Alyosha's arrival; his visitors had gathered in his cell earlier and waited for him to wake, having received Father Paissy's firm assurance that 'the teacher will certainly get up to converse once again with those dear to his heart as he himself promised in the morning'. Father Paissy believed implicitly in this promise, and indeed in every word of the dying elder, so much so that if he had seen him unconscious and no longer breathing but had his promise to get up again to take leave of them, he would not perhaps have believed in death itself, but would still have expected the dying man to carry out his promise. In the morning, before he fell asleep, Father Zossima had told him positively: 'I shall not die without once again tasting to the full the joy of talking to you, beloved ones of my heart, looking at your dear faces and pouring out my heart to you once again.' The monks, who had gathered for this probably last conversation with the elder, were his oldest and most devoted friends. There were four of them: the senior monks Father Joseph and Father Paissy, Father Mikhail, the prior of the hermitage, and Brother Anfim. Father Mikhail was neither very old nor very learned. He was of humble origin, but steadfast of spirit and of firm and simple faith, outwardly stern, but of great tenderness of heart, though he obviously concealed it even to the point of being ashamed of it. Brother Anfim was a very old and ordinary little monk, of the poorest peasant class, almost illiterate, quiet and taciturn, very rarely speaking to anybody, the humblest among the most humble monks, who looked as though he had been frightened by something great and terrible beyond his comprehension. The elder Zossima was very fond of this man, who seemed always to walk in fear and trembling, and treated him all his life with extraordinary respect, though there was perhaps no other man to whom he had spoken less, in spite of the fact that he had spent many years wandering all over holy Russia with him. That was a long, long time ago, about forty years before, when Father Zossima first began his hard life as a monk in a poor and little-known monastery in the Kostroma province and when, shortly after that, he had accompanied Father Anfim on his wanderings to collect funds for their poor, small monastery. All of them, the host and his visitors, were sitting in the elder's second room, where his bed stood, a room which, as has been described before, was very small, so that there was scarcely room for the four monks (in addition to the novice Porfiry, who remained standing) to sit round the elder's armchair on chairs brought from the first room. It was already getting dark and the room was lighted by the lamps and wax candles before the icons. Seeing Alyosha, who stood in the doorway looking embarrassed, the elder smiled joyfully at him and held out his hand:

'Welcome, my gentle one, welcome, my dear boy, here you are at last. I knew you'd come.'

Alyosha went up to him, prostrated himself before him and wept. Something surged up in his heart, his soul trembled, he felt like sobbing.

'Come, come, it's too early to mourn for me,' the elder said, smiling and putting his right hand on his head. 'You see I'm sitting here and talking. Perhaps I shall live for another twenty years as the dear, kind woman from Vyshegorye, with her little girl Lizaveta in her arms, wished me yesterday. Bless, O Lord, the mother and the little girl Lizaveta!' (He crossed himself.) 'Porfiry, did you take her offering where I told you?'

He was referring to the sixty copecks donated by the cheerful woman for 'someone poorer than me'. Such donations are offered as a voluntarily imposed penance and always with money earned by one's own work. The elder had sent Porfiry the evening before to a poor widow with two children whose house had been burnt down lately and who had gone begging after the fire. Porfiry hastened to reply that he had carried out the elder's commission and that he had given the money, as instructed, 'from an unknown bene-factress'.

'Get up, my dear boy,' the elder went on to Alyosha. 'Let me have a look at you. Have you been home and seen your brother?'

It seemed strange to Alyosha that he asked so firmly and precisely about one of his brothers only – but which one? So it was for that brother that he had perhaps sent him out yesterday and today.

'I've seen one of my brothers,' replied Alyosha.

'I'm talking of your elder brother to whom I bowed down to the ground yesterday.'

'I only saw him yesterday,' said Alyosha. 'I could not find him today.'

'Make haste and find him. Go again tomorrow and make haste. Leave everything and make haste. Perhaps you'll still be in time to prevent something terrible happening. I bowed down yesterday to the great suffering that is in store for him.'

He fell silent suddenly and seemed to be pondering. His words were strange. Father Joseph, who had seen the elder's deep bow yesterday, exchanged glances with Father Paissy. Alyosha could not restrain himself.

'Father and teacher,' he said in great excitement, 'your words are too obscure. . . . What sort of suffering is in store for him?'

'Don't be too curious to know. I seemed to see something terrible yesterday, just as if his whole future were expressed in the look in his eyes. There was such a look in his eyes that I was instantly horri-fied at what that man is preparing for himself. Once or twice in my life I've seen such an expression on a man's face, an expression that seemed to foreshadow the fate of that man, and his fate, alas, came to pass. I sent you to him, Alexey, in the hope that your brotherly face would help him. But everything is from God and all our destinies. "Except a corn of wheat fall into the ground and die, it abideth alone: but if it die, it bringeth forth much fruit." Remember that. And you, Alexey, I have blessed in my mind many times in my life for your face, know that,' said the elder with a gentle smile. 'This is what I think of you: you will go forth from these walls, but you will live in the world like a monk. You will have many adversaries, but even your enemies will love you. Life will bring many misfortunes to you, but it is in them that you will find happiness and you will bless life and make others bless it – which is what matters most. But that is how you are. Fathers and teachers,' he turned to his visitors with a tender smile, 'I have never till this day told even him why the face of this youth is so dear to me. Now I will tell you: his face has been, as it were, a reminder and a prophecy to me. At the dawn of my days, when I was a little child, I had an elder brother who died before my eyes when he was only a boy of seventeen. And afterwards, in the course of my life, I came gradually to the conclusion that that brother of mine had been, as it were, a guidance and a predestination from above, for if he had not come into my life, if he had not existed at all, I should never perhaps, so I think, have followed the calling of a monk and not entered upon this precious path. He appeared to me at first in my childhood, and now at my journey's end there seems indeed to be a repetition of it. It is strange, fathers and teachers, that, while he bears but a remote resemblance to him, Alexey seemed to me to be so much like him in spirit that many times I looked on him as that young man, my brother, who had come back to me mysteriously at my journey's end as a reminder and an inspiration, so that I was even surprised at myself and at this strange dream of mine. Do you hear that, Porfiry?' he turned to the novice who waited on him. 'Many times I've noticed a look of distress in your face that I love Alexey more than you. Now you know why that was so, but I love you too, know that, and many times I grieved that you should be distressed. I should like to tell you, dear friends, about that young man, my brother, for there was nothing in my life more precious, more prophetic and touching. I feel deeply touched at heart and at this moment I am contemplating my whole life as though living it all over again. . . . '

*

Here I must note that this last conversation of the elder with his visitors on the last day of his life has been partly preserved in writing. It was written down from memory by Alexey Karamazov a short time after the elder's death. But whether it was all the conversation on that evening or whether he added to it from his notes of his former talks with his teacher, I cannot say for certain. Besides, the elder's speech in his account seems to go on without interruption, just as though, in addressing his friends, he had been telling his life in the form of a story, while from other accounts of it there can be no doubt that it all happened somewhat differently; for the conversation that evening was general, and though the visitors did not interrupt the elder frequently, they did occasionally speak up for themselves and intervene in the conversation. Indeed, it is quite likely that they told something of themselves, too. Moreover, there can be no question of any uninterrupted narrative on the part of the elder, for sometimes he was gasping for breath, his voice failed him, and he even lay down to rest on his bed, though he did not fall asleep and his visitors did not leave their seats. Once or twice the conversation was interrupted by the reading of the Gospel by Father Paissy. It is remarkable, too, that none of them thought that he would die that night, particularly as on that last evening of his life, after his profound sleep in the day, he seemed suddenly to have acquired new strength, which sustained him during the whole of this long conversation with his friends. It was, as it were, the last expression of his tender feelings for his friends which kept up his incredible animation, but only for a short time, for his life was cut short suddenly. . . . But of that later. Now I should like to add that I have preferred to confine myself to the elder's story according to Alexey Karamazov's manuscript, without giving a detailed account of the conversation. It will be shorter and not so fatiguing, either, though, of course, let me repeat, Alyosha took a great deal from previous conversations and added them to it.

2

From the Life of
the Departed Priest and Monk, The Elder Zossima,
taken down from his own words by
Alexey Karamazov

BIOGRAPHICAL DATA

(a) About Father Zossima's Young Brother

BELOVED fathers and teachers, I was born in a remote northern province, in the town of V. My father was a nobleman, but was neither a person of quality nor of high rank. He died when I was only two years old, and I do not remember him at all. He left my mother a small wooden house and some capital, not large, but sufficient to live on with her children without being in need. There were only two of us: my elder brother, Markel, and I, Zinovy. He was eight years older than I, short-tempered and irritable, but good-natured and not sarcastic, and quite unusually taciturn, especially at home, with my mother, myself, and the servants. He made good progress at school, but did not get on with his schoolmates, though he never quarrelled with them – so at least my mother remembered him. Six months before his death, when he was seventeen, he began visiting a man who led a very solitary life in our town, a political exile, who had been banished from Moscow for freethinking. That exile was a great scholar and a distinguished university philosopher. He got very fond of Markel for some reason and was glad to see him. Markel used to spend whole evenings with him all through that winter until he was summoned back, at his own request, to Petersburg to take up a post in the civil service, as he had influential friends there. It was the beginning of Lent, but Markel refused to fast. He swore and laughed at it: 'It's all nonsense,' he said, 'and there is no God,' so that my mother and the servants were horrified. And though I myself was only a small boy of nine, I too, hearing his words, was very frightened. Our servants were serfs, the four of them, all bought in the name of a landowner we knew. I can still remember how my mother sold one of the four, our cook Afimya, an elderly lame woman, for sixty roubles, and engaged a free servant in her place. In the sixth week of the fast my brother was taken seriously ill. He was never very well, he had a weak chest, a weak constitution, and a predisposition to consumption; he was rather tall, thin and delicate, but had a very handsome face. I don't know whether he caught a cold, but the doctor came and soon whispered to my mother that he had galloping consumption and that he wouldn't live through the spring. My mother began weeping and asking my brother very guardedly (chiefly so as not to alarm him) to fast and then go to church and take holy communion, for he was still walking about then. Hearing this, he got angry and swore at the church, but he grew thoughtful: he realized at once that he was seriously ill and that that was why his mother was sending him to church to confess and take the sacrament while he still had strength to go there. He had of course known that he had been ill for a long time and a year before had calmly observed to my mother at table: 'I shan't live long among you, perhaps I shan't last another year,' and it looked as though he had himself predicted it. Three days passed and Holy Week had come. And beginning with Tuesday my brother began fasting and going to church. 'I'm doing it really for your sake, Mother,' he said to her, 'to please you and set your mind at rest.' My mother wept with joy and with grief, too: 'His end must be near,' she thought, 'if there's such a sudden change in him.' But he was not able to go to church long. He took to his bed, and he confessed and was given extreme unction at home. Easter was late and the days were clear, sunny, and full of the fragrance of spring. I remember he used to cough and hardly slept all night, but in the morning he always dressed and tried to sit up in an armchair. And that's how I remember him: sitting in his chair, calm and gentle, smiling, looking cheerful and joyous, in spite of his illness. He was spiritually transformed — such a wonderful change suddenly took place in him! Our old nurse would come in and say: 'Let me light the lamp before the icon, dear.' Before he would not let her do it and he even used to blow it out. But now he would say to her: 'Light it, light it, my dear. I was a beast not to let you before. You pray to God when lighting the lamp, and I'm praying when I rejoice looking at you. So we are praying to one and the same God.' Those words of his sounded strange to us, and Mother would go to her room and weep, but coming back she would dry her tears and try to look cheerful. 'Don't cry, Mother darling,' he used to say, 'I shall live for a long time yet. I shall have lots of fun with you. Life is so joyful and gay!' 'Oh, my dear, how can you feel joyful when you are burning with fever at night, coughing as though your chest would burst?' 'Mother,' he replied to her, 'don't cry. Life is paradise and we are all in paradise, only we don't want to know it, and if we wanted to we'd have heaven on earth tomorrow.' And we all marvelled at his words, he spoke so strangely and so positively; we were deeply touched and wept. When friends came to see us, he would say to them: 'Dear ones, what did I do to deserve your love? Why do you love me, wretch that I am? And how is it I did not know and appreciate it before?' When our servants came in he would always say to them: 'Dear ones, why are you waiting on me? I don't deserve to be waited on. If God spared me and let me live, I'd wait on you, for we all must wait upon one another.' Listening to him, my mother would shake her head: 'Darling,' she would say, 'you talk like that because you're ill.' 'Darling Mother,' he would reply, 'there have to be masters and servants, but let me be the servant of my servants. Let me be the same as they are to me. And let me tell you this, too, Mother: every one of us is responsible for everyone else in every way, and I most of all.' Mother could not help smiling at that. She wept and smiled at the same time. 'How are you,' she said, 'most of all responsible for everyone? There are murderers and robbers in the world, and what terrible sin have you committed that you should accuse yourself before everyone else?' 'Mother, my dearest heart,' he said (he had begun using such caressing, such unexpected words just then), 'my dearest heart, my joy, you must realize that everyone is really responsible for everyone and everything. I don't know how to explain it to you, but I feel it so strongly that it hurts. And how could we have gone on living and getting angry without knowing anything about it?' So he used to get up every day, feeling more and more joyful and tender towards everyone and all vibrating with love. When the doctor, an old German called Eisenschmidt, called, 'Well, doctor,' he used to joke with him, 'how long do you give me? One more day?' 'Not one day,' the doctor would reply, 'you're good for many days yet, and for many months and years too.' 'Why years and months?' he would cry. 'Why count the days, when one day is sufficient for a man to experience all happiness. My dear ones, why do we quarrel? Why do we boast to one another? Why do we bear a grudge against each other? Why not go straight into the garden and walk and enjoy ourselves, love, praise and kiss one another, and bless our life?' 'Your son hasn't long to live,' the doctor said to my mother, when she saw him off at the front door. 'I'm afraid his illness is affecting his brain.' The windows of his bedroom looked out on to the garden, and our garden was full of shade, with old trees; the spring buds were beginning to swell on the trees, and the early birds had arrived and were chirruping and singing at the windows. And, looking at them and admiring them, he began suddenly to beg them, too, to forgive him: 'Heavenly birds, happy birds, forgive me, for I have sinned against you, too.'

That no one could understand at the time, but he wept with joy. 'Yes,' he said, 'there was such glory of God all around me: birds, trees, meadows, sky, only I lived in shame, I alone dishonoured everything, and did not notice the beauty and the glory of it all.' 'You take many sins upon yourself,' my mother used to say, weeping. 'Mother, joy of my heart, it's for joy, not for grief that I am crying. You see, I want to be responsible for them myself, only I can't explain it to you, for I don't know even how to love them. I may have sinned against everyone, but that is why they will all forgive me, and that is paradise. Am I not in paradise now?'

And there was a great deal more that I cannot remember or describe. I do remember going into his room one day when there was no one there. It was a bright evening, the sun was setting, and the whole room was lighted up by its slanting rays. He beckoned to me as soon as he saw me and I went up to him. He took me by the shoulders with both hands and looked tenderly and lovingly into my face. He said nothing, but just looked at me like that for a minute. 'Well,' he said, 'now run away and play, live for me!' I went then and ran to play. And many times afterwards in the course of my life I remembered with tears how he had told me to live for him. He said many more such wonderful and beautiful things, though we did not understand them at the time. He died in the third week after Easter. He was fully conscious, though he did not speak any more; but he did not change up to the last hour; he looked joyful, there was gladness in the eyes with which he sought us, smiled at us, called us. Even in our town they talked a great deal about his death. I was shaken by it all at the time, but not too much, though I did cry a lot at his funeral. I was very young then, a child, but it left an indelible impression in my heart, a feeling that lay dormant for years. It was to come to life and respond in time. And so it happened.

(b) Of the Holy Writ in the Life of Father Zossima

I was left alone with my mother. Soon her good friends advised her that, as she had only one son left and as we were not poor but had enough money, she ought to follow the example of other people and send me to Petersburg, for by keeping me with her she might deprive me of a brilliant future. And they persuaded my mother to send me to Petersburg and enter me in the Cadet Corps that I might afterwards join the Imperial Guard. My mother could not make up her mind for a long time: she could not bring herself to part with her only remaining son; but at last she decided to send me to Petersburg, though not without many tears, thinking that she was doing it for my good. She took me to Petersburg and entered me in the Cadet Corps, and after that I never saw her again; for three years later she died, grieving and mourning all during those three years for both of us. From the house of my parents I have brought nothing but precious memories, for there are no memories more precious than those of one's early childhood in one's own home, and that is almost always so, if there is any love and harmony in the family at all. Indeed, precious memories may be retained even from a bad home so long as your heart is capable of finding anything precious. To my memories at home I add also my memories of the stories from the Holy Scriptures, which, though a child, I was very eager to learn at home. I had a book of stories from the Holy Scriptures with beautiful illustrations called *One Hundred and Four Sacred Stories from the Old and New Testaments*, and I learnt to read from it. It is still lying on my shelf here, and I keep it as a precious keepsake of my childhood. But even before I learned to read, I remember how I was first moved by deep spiritual emotion when I was eight years old. My mother took me alone to church (I don't remember where my brother was at the time), to morning mass on the Monday before Easter. It was a sunny day, and I remember now, just as though I saw it again, how the incense rose from the censer and floated slowly upwards and how through a little window from the dome above the sunlight streamed down upon us and, rising in waves towards it, the incense seemed to dissolve in it. I looked and felt deeply moved and for the first time in my life I consciously received the first seed of the words of God in my soul. Then a boy stepped forth into the middle of the church carrying a big book, so big that I thought at the time that he could hardly carry it, and he laid it on the lectern, opened it, and began to read. And it was then that I suddenly understood for the first time, for the first time in my life, what they read in church. There was a man in the land of Uz, and that man was perfect and upright, and he had so much wealth, and so many camels, and so many sheep and asses, and his children feasted and he loved them very much and he prayed for them: perhaps they had sinned in their feasting. Now Satan came before the Lord among the sons of God, and he said to the Lord that he had been going to and fro in the earth and under the earth. 'And hast thou considered my servant Job?' God asked him. And God boasted to Satan, pointing to his great and holy servant. And Satan laughed at God's words. 'Hand him over to me and thou wilt see that thy servant will murmur against thee and curse thy name.' And God handed over the righteous man he loved so well to Satan, and Satan smote his children, and his cattle, and scattered his wealth, everything all at once, as with a thunderbolt from heaven. Then Job rent his mantle and fell down upon the ground and said, 'Naked came I out of my mother's womb, and naked shall I return into the earth: The Lord gave and the Lord hath taken away: blessed be the name of the Lord now and for ever!' Fathers and teachers, forgive my tears now, for my childhood days rise up again before me, and I breathe now as I breathed then, with the chest of a child of eight, and I feel, as I felt then, wonder and dismay and gladness. And my imagination was so forcibly struck by the camels, and by Satan who talked like that with God, and by God who gave up his servant to destruction, who cried, 'Blessed be thy name, though thou chastiseth me', and then the soft and sweet singing in the church: 'Hearken unto my prayer,' and again the incense from the priest's censer and the kneeling in prayer! Since then – even yesterday I took it up – I have never been able to read this sacred tale without tears. And how much that is great, mysterious, and inconceivable is there in it! Afterwards I heard the words of the scoffers and reprovers, proud words: how could God give up the most loved of his saints to Satan to play with, take his children from him, smite him with sore boils so that he scraped the corruption from his sores with a potsherd, and why? Just to be able to boast to Satan: 'See how much my saint can suffer for my sake!' But it *is* great – just because it is a mystery – just because the passing image of the earthly and eternal justice are brought together here. The act of eternal justice is accomplished before earthly justice. Here the Creator, just as in the first days of creation he ended each day with praise: 'That which I have created is good,' looks upon Job and again boasts of his creation. And Job, praising the Lord, serves not only him but all his creation for generations and generations and for ever and ever, since for that he was fore-ordained. Lord, what a

book it is and what lessons it contains! What a book the Holy Bible
is! What a miracle and what strength is given with it to man! Just
like a sculpture of the world and man and human characters, and
everything is named there and everything is shown for ever and ever.
And how many solved and revealed mysteries: God raises Job again,
gives him wealth again, and many years pass by and he has other
children and he loves them. Good Lord, but how could he love those
new ones when his old children were no more, when he had lost
them? Remembering them, how could he be completely happy as
before with the new ones, however dear they were to him? But he
could, he could: the old sorrow, through the great mystery of human
life, passes gradually into quiet, tender joy; the fiery blood of youth
gives place to the gentle serenity of old age: I bless the rising sun
each day, and my heart sings to it as of old, but I love its setting much
more, its long slanting rays and, with them, my quiet, gentle, tender
memories, the dear images of the whole of my long and blessed life –
and over it all Divine Justice, tender, reconciling and all-forgiving!
My life is drawing to a close. I know that, I feel it. But I also feel
every day that is left to me how my earthly life is already in touch
with a new, infinite, unknown but fast-approaching future life, the
anticipation of which sets my soul trembling with rapture, my mind
glowing, and my heart weeping with joy. . . . Friends and teachers,
I have heard more than once, and now for some time past it can be
heard more often, that our priests and, particularly, our village priests
are everywhere complaining bitterly of their small stipends and their
degradation, and they go so far as to declare plainly, even in print –
I have read it myself – that they are unable to expound the Scriptures
to the people now because their stipends are so small, and that if
Lutherans and heretics come and drive away the flock, then let them
do so, for their stipends, you see, are so small. Heavens above, I
think to myself, may the stipends that are so precious to them be
increased by all means (for their complaint is certainly just), but verily
I say: if anyone is to blame for it, half the fault is ours! For even if he
has no time to spare, if he is right in saying that he is overwhelmed all
the time with work and church services, it is not all the time, he still
has at least an hour a week in which to remember God. And his
work does not go on all the year round. If at first he gathered only
the children once a week, in the evening, their fathers would hear of

it and they, too, would begin to come. And there is no need to build marble halls for this work, let him simply take them into his cottage; he need not be afraid, they won't make a mess in his cottage, for he will only have them for one hour. Let him open the Book and begin reading it without learned words and without conceit, without any feeling of superiority towards them, but gently and tenderly, rejoicing that he is reading to them and that they are listening to him with understanding, loving those words himself, and pausing only from time to time to explain some words that simple peasants do not understand. Don't worry, they'll understand it all, the orthodox heart will understand it all. Read to them about Abraham and Sarah, about Isaac and Rebecca, about how Jacob went to Laban and wrestled with the Lord in his dream and said, 'How dreadful is this place', and you will greatly impress the devout mind of the peasant. Read to them, and especially to the children, how the brothers sold their own brother, the sweet youth Joseph, a dreamer of dreams and a great prophet, into bondage and told their father that a wild beast had devoured him and showed him his bloodstained coat. Read to them how his brothers afterwards went down to Egypt for corn, and Joseph, already a great courtier, unrecognized by them, tormented them, accused them, kept his brother Benjamin, and all the time loving them, loving them: 'I love you, and loving you, I torment you.' For he remembered his whole past life how they had sold him in the parched desert, by the well, to some merchants and how he, wringing his hands, wept and besought his brothers not to sell him as a slave in a foreign land, and now, seeing them again after so many years, he again loved them beyond measure, but he tormented and plagued them, loving them. And then he left them at last, unable to bear the suffering of his heart, flung himself upon his bed and wept; then he wiped his tears and went out to them looking bright and radiant, and announced to them: 'Brothers, I am your brother Joseph!' Let him read further how happy old Jacob was when he learnt that his darling boy was still alive, and how he went to Egypt, even leaving his own country, and how he died in a foreign land, having uttered in his testament a great prophecy, which lay hidden mysteriously in his gentle and timid heart all his life, that from his descendants, from Judah, will come the great hope of the world, its Peace-maker and Saviour! Fathers and teachers, forgive me and do not be angry with me for talking like a child about something you knew long ago and can teach me a hundred times better and more skilfully. I am saying this only from rapture, and forgive my tears, for I love that Book! Let him too weep, the priest of God, and he will see how the hearts of those who listen to him will be shaken in response. Only a little seed is needed, a tiny seed: drop it in the soul of a peasant and it will not die. It will live in his soul all his life. It will be hidden inside him amidst the darkness, amidst the stench of his sins, as a bright spot, as a great reminder. And it is not necessary, it is not necessary to teach and expound a lot. He will understand it all simply. Do you think the peasant will not understand? Try and read to him further the moving and pathetic story of the fair Esther and the haughty Vashti; or the wonderful story of the prophet Jonah in the whale's belly. Don't forget either the parables of Our Lord, mostly from the Gospel of St Luke (that is what I did), and then from the Acts of the Apostles the conversion of Saul (that above all, above all!) and, finally, from the Lives of the Saints, let us say, the Life of Alexey the man of God, and the greatest of the great, the happy martyr and the seer of God and the bearer of Christ, Mary of Egypt – and you will pierce his heart with these simple tales. And only one hour a week, regardless of his small stipend, only one hour. And he will see for himself that our people are kind and grateful and will repay him a hundredfold; mindful of the zeal of their priest and his moving words, they will voluntarily help him in his fields and in his house and will treat him with more respect than ever before – and in this way his stipend will be increased. It is so simple a matter that sometimes we are afraid even to mention it for fear of being laughed at, and yet how true it is! He who does not believe in God, will never believe in God's people. But he who has faith in God's people, will also behold his Glory, though he had not believed in it till then. Only the common people and their future spiritual power will convert our atheists, who have torn themselves away from their native soil. And what is Christ's word without an example? The people will perish without the word of God, for their hearts yearn for the Word and for all that is good and beautiful. In the days of my youth, a long time ago, almost forty years ago, Father Anfim and I wandered all over Russia, collecting alms for our monastery, and one night we spent on the bank of a big navigable river with some fishermen. A handsome-looking young peasant, a lad of about eighteen, joined us. He was in a hurry to get to his job next day, dragging a merchant's barge along the tow-path. I saw him looking before him with clear and tender eyes. It was a warm, bright, still July night. The river was broad, a mist was rising from it and from time to time we could hear the soft splash of a fish. The birds were silent. All was still and beautiful, all was praying to God. Only we two were not asleep, the peasant lad and I, and we began to talk of the beauty of God's world and the great mystery of it. Every blade of grass, every small insect, ant, golden bee, all of them knew so marvellously their path, and without possessing the faculty of reason, bore witness to the mystery of God, constantly partaking in it themselves. And I saw the dear lad's heart glowing with emotion. He told me that he loved the woods and the wild birds; he was a bird-catcher, could distinguish each bird-call and knew how to decoy each bird; 'I know nothing better than to be in a wood,' he said, 'though all things are good.' 'Truly,' I replied, 'all things are good and beautiful, because all is truth. Look,' I said to him, 'at the horse, that great animal that is so near to man, or at the sad and pensive ox which feeds him and works for him, look at their faces: what meekness, what devotion to man, who often beats them mercilessly, what gentleness, what trustfulness and what beauty! It is touching to know that there is no sin in them, for all but man is perfect and without sin, and Christ has been with them even before us.' 'But,' asked the lad, 'can Christ really be with them?' 'How could it be otherwise,' I said to him, 'since the Word is for all; all creation, all creatures, every leaf are striving towards the Lord, glorify the Lord, weep to Christ, and unknown to themselves, accomplish this by the mystery of their sinless life? Out there in the forest,' I said to him, 'wanders the terrible bear, menacing and ferocious, and yet innocent of it all.' And I told him how a bear once came to a great saint, who was seeking salvation in a little hut in a forest. And the great saint was filled with tenderness for it, went up to it fearlessly and gave it a piece of bread: 'Get along with you,' he said to the bear, 'Christ be with you.' And the ferocious beast went away obediently and meekly, without doing him any harm. And the lad was deeply moved that the bear had gone away without doing any harm and that Christ was with him, too. 'Oh, how good that is,' he said, 'how all God's work is good and beautiful!' He sat musing softly and sweetly. I could see that he understood. And he slept beside me and his sleep was light and sinless. May God bless youth! And I prayed for him before I went to sleep myself. O Lord, send peace and light to the men thou hast created!

(c) *Recollections of Father Zossima's Adolescence and Manhood while He was Still in the World. The Duel*

I spent a long time, almost eight years, in the Cadet Corps in Petersburg, and my new education there stifled a great many of the impressions of my childhood, though I forgot nothing. Instead, I picked up so many new habits and even opinions that I was transformed into a cruel, absurd and almost savage creature. I acquired a surface polish of politeness and society manners together with a knowledge of the French language, but all of us, myself included, treated the soldiers, who waited on us at the college, like brutes. I treated them perhaps worse than anyone, for I was more susceptible to everything than any of my fellow-cadets. When we received our commissions we were ready to shed our blood for the honour of our regiment, but scarcely any of us knew anything about the meaning of real honour, and if anyone had known it, he would have been the first to jeer at it. Drunkenness, debauchery and daredevilry we almost prided ourselves on. I don't say we were bad; all those young men were good fellows, but they behaved badly, and I worst of all. The trouble was that I had come into money and gave myself up to a life of pleasure with all the enthusiasm of youth, and threw myself headlong and without restraint into it. But the strange thing was that I read many books then and even derived great pleasure from them; the Bible, however, was the only book that I almost never opened at that time, though I never parted from it and always carried it about with me: in truth I was keeping the Book, without knowing it myself, 'for an hour, and a day, and a month and a year'. After four years of this kind of army life, I found myself at last in the town of K., where my regiment was stationed at the time. The social life in the town was varied and gay; there were many rich people there who entertained on a grand scale. I was well received everywhere, for I was by nature of a cheerful disposition and, besides, I was reputed to be well-off, which means not a little in society. Then something happened that was the beginning of everything. I formed an attachment to a young and beautiful girl, high-minded and intelligent, of a noble and serene character, the daughter of a highly respected family. They were well-to-do and influential people of good social position. They received me warmly and cordially. I imagined that the girl cared for me, and I worked myself up into a fever of excitement at the mere thought of it. Afterwards I realized myself, and, indeed, was quite sure that perhaps I was not so passionately in love with her at all, but only respected her intelligence and lofty character, which was quite natural. My selfishness, however, prevented me from proposing to her at the time: I felt it was hard and unfair to have to give up the temptations of my free and licentious bachelor life while I was still so young and, besides, had plenty of money. I did, however, drop a hint as to my intentions, though I put off taking any decisive step for a time. Then we were suddenly ordered off to another district for two months. On my return two months later I was astonished to learn that the girl had in the meantime married a rich landowner, who had an estate in the vicinity of the town, a man who was still quite young, though considerably older than I, with excellent connexions in Petersburg and in high society, which I did not possess. He was an exceedingly nice man and of excellent education, and education was something I lacked completely. I was so startled by this unexpected turn of events that I lost my senses. The worst of it was that, as I learned then, the young landowner had been engaged to her a long time and that I myself had often met him at her house, but, blinded by my high opinion of myself, I had noticed nothing. And it was this that hurt me most: what a fool I was! Everyone had known about it, only I knew nothing! That I could not bear: I was filled with sudden fury. With a flushed face I began recalling how many times I was on the point of telling her that I loved her, and as she never stopped me or warned me, I could only conclude that she must have been laughing at me. On thinking it over afterwards, I realized of course that she had not laughed at me at all; on the contrary, whenever I began talking to her about my feelings, she invariably broke off the conversation with a jest and changed the subject. But at the time I was quite unable to see it and I was overcome by a burning desire to revenge myself. I remember with astonishment that my anger and desire for revenge were extremely painful and repugnant to me because, being easy-going by nature, I never could be angry with anyone for long. For that reason I had to work myself up artificially and became revolting and absurd in the end. I bided my time till one day I succeeded in insulting my 'rival' among a large company for a supposedly quite different reason by ridiculing an opinion he had expressed on some rather important public event. (It was in the year 1826.) I managed to ridicule him, so people said, very cleverly and wittily. Then I demanded an explanation from him and treated him so rudely that he accepted my challenge in spite of the great difference in our social positions, for I was not only younger, but also a man of no consequence and of low rank. Later on I learnt positively that he had accepted my challenge because he, too, for some reason, had felt jealous of me: he had been a little jealous of me before on account of his wife, while she was still engaged to him; now he thought that if she got to know that he had put up with my insult and had not the courage to challenge me, she could not help despising him and would waver in her love for him. It did not take me long to get a second, a fellow-officer, a lieutenant of our regiment. Although duels were forbidden and severely punished in those days, they were rather in fashion among the military – to such an extent do savage prejudices sometimes spread and get firmly established among people. It was the end of June, and our meeting was to take place at seven o'clock next day on the outskirts of our town. But something happened to me just then that had a decisive influence on the whole of my future life. In the evening I returned home in an ugly and ferocious mood. I lost my temper with my batman Afanasy and slapped his face twice, as hard as I could, so that it was covered in blood. He had not been in my service long and I had sometimes struck him before, but never with such brutal ferocity. And, believe me, dear fathers, though forty years have passed since then, I remember it still with shame and pain. I went to bed, slept for three hours, and woke up when day was breaking. I did not want to sleep any more, got up immediately, went up to the window, opened it – it looked out on to the garden – and watched the sun rising. It was warm and beautiful, the birds began to sing. 'What,' I thought to myself, 'can be the meaning of that strange feeling of shame and disgrace in my heart? Is it because I am going to shed blood? No,' I thought, 'I don't think it's that at all. Am I afraid of death? Afraid to be killed? No, it is not that, it is not that, either.' And then I suddenly realized what it was: it was because I had given Afanasy a beating the evening before! And I saw it all happen again, as though for the second time: there he stood before me and I was slapping his face as hard as I could, and he was standing stiffly to attention, his head erect, his eyes fixed blankly on me as though on parade, shuddering at every blow but not daring to raise his hands to protect himself – and that was what a man had been brought to, that was a man beating a fellow-man! What a horrible crime! I felt as though my heart had been transfixed by a sharp needle. I stood there as though I had lost my reason, and the sun was shining, the leaves were rejoicing and reflecting the sunlight, and the birds – the birds were praising the Lord. . . . I covered my face with both my hands, flung myself on my bed and burst out sobbing. And then I remembered my brother Markel and his last words to our servants: 'My dear ones, why do you love me? Do I deserve to be waited on?' 'Yes, do I deserve it?' it flashed suddenly through my mind. And, really, what had I done to deserve that another man, a man like me created in God's image, should wait on me? So for the first time in my life this question pierced me to the core. 'Mother, my dearest heart, every man is responsible for everyone, only people don't know it. If they knew – it would be paradise at once!' Dear Lord, I thought as I wept, could that, too, be untrue? Yes, indeed, I was perhaps more responsible than anyone for all and certainly worse than any other man in the world! And I became suddenly aware of the whole truth in its full light: what was I about to do? I was about to kill a man, a good, intelligent and honourable man, who had done me no wrong, and by killing him I should deprive his wife of her happiness for ever, torture and kill her, too. I lay like that stretched out on the bed with my face buried in the pillow and did not notice how time was passing. Suddenly my second, the lieutenant, came in with the pistols to fetch me. 'Oh,' he said, 'I see you're up already. That's fine! It's time we were off. Come along!' I rushed about the room completely at a loss what to do, but we went out to get into the carriage. 'Wait here a minute,' I said to him, 'I'll be back in a moment. I forgot my purse.' And I rushed back alone to my flat and went straight to Afanasy's little room. 'Afanasy,' I said, 'I struck you twice in the face yesterday, please forgive me,' I said. He gave a violent start, as though he were frightened, and stared at me. I saw that it was not enough, not enough, and I suddenly threw myself down at his feet, in full uniform as I was, with my forehead touching the ground. 'Forgive me!' I said. At that he looked utterly confounded. 'Sir,' he stuttered, 'sir, you shouldn't – I – I'm not worth it . . .' and he burst into tears himself, as I had done before and, covering his face with his hands, turned to the window and shook all over with sobs. I ran out to my fellow-officer and jumped into the carriage. 'Lead on,' I cried. 'Ever seen a conquering hero? Well, look at him now!' I was in such an ecstasy that I went on laughing and talking, talking all the way. I don't remember what I was talking about. He looked at me: 'Well, old man,' he said, 'you've certainly got pluck. I can see you won't let the regiment down!' So we arrived at the place, and they were already there waiting for us. We took up our positions, twelve paces apart. He had the first shot. I stood facing him, looking happy, without batting an eyelid. I looked at him lovingly, for I knew what I was going to do. He fired and just grazed my cheek and ear. 'Thank God,' I cried, 'you haven't killed a man!' I seized my pistol, turned round and, flinging it high into the air, threw it into the wood. 'That's the place for you!' I cried. Then I turned to my opponent and said: 'Forgive a stupid young fellow, sir, for having insulted you without any provocation on your part and now forcing you to shoot at him. I'm ten times worse than you and, perhaps, even more. Tell that to the person whom you respect more than anyone in the world.' As soon as I said this, they all began shouting at me: 'Really,' said my opponent – he got angry in good earnest, 'if you didn't want to fight, why did you trouble me to come here?' 'Yesterday,' I replied gaily, 'I was still a fool, but I'm wiser today.' 'As to yesterday,' he said, 'I believe you, but as to today, I find it difficult to agree with your opinion.' 'Bravo,' I cried, clapping my hands, 'I agree with you there, too. I've deserved it!' 'Are you going to fire, sir, or not?' 'I'm not,' I replied, 'but if you like, you can fire at me again, but it would be better for you not to fire.' The seconds were shouting, too, mine especially. 'How can you disgrace your regiment like that, sir, facing your opponent and asking for his forgiveness? If I'd only known this!' So I stood there in front of them all, no longer laughing. 'Gentlemen,' I said, 'is it really so extraordinary in these days to find a man who will acknowledge his own stupidity and apologize in public for the wrong he has done?' 'But not during a duel,' my second cried again. 'Ah,' I said, 'that's right, that's what's so surprising, for I should have apologized as soon as we got here, before he had fired a shot, and not led him into a great and mortal sin. But,' I went on, 'we ourselves have brought things to such an awful pass in society that it was almost impossible to do that, for it was only after I had faced his shot at a distance of twelve paces that my words could have any meaning for him. Had I told him that as soon as we arrived here and before he had fired, he would have simply said that I was a coward, that I had taken fright at the pistols and that it was no use listening to me. Gentlemen,' I cried suddenly straight from my heart, 'look round you at God's gifts: the clear sky, the pure air, the tender grass, the birds. Nature is beautiful and without sin, and we, we alone, are godless and foolish and we don't understand that life is paradise, for we have only to want to understand and it will at once come in all its beauty and we shall embrace and weep.' I would have said more, but I couldn't. My breath failed me. Everything was so fresh and sweet, and my heart was full of such happiness as I had never felt before in my life. 'It's all very nice and proper,' my opponent said to me, 'and you certainly are a most original person.' 'You may laugh,' I said to him, laughing too, 'but afterwards I'm sure you'll approve of me yourself.' 'Why,' he said, 'I'm quite ready to approve of you now. Let's shake hands, for I believe you really are a sincere person.' 'No,' I said, 'not now, afterwards when I've become a better man and deserved your esteem, then shake hands with me and you'll do well.' We went home, my second swearing at me all the time, while I kept kissing him. As soon as my fellow-officers heard of it, they met to pass judgement on me the same day: 'He's disgraced the uniform,' they said, 'and now let him resign his commission.' There were some who defended my action: 'He did face the shot,' they said. 'Yes, he did, but he was afraid of other shots and apologized during a duel.' 'But,' my defenders retorted, 'if he'd been afraid of being shot, he'd have fired first himself before apologizing, but he threw his loaded pistol into the wood. No, there's something else here, something original.' I listened and felt happy looking at them. 'My dear friends and comrades,' I said, 'don't worry about my resigning my commission, because I've sent in my resignation already, and when I receive my discharge from the army I shall enter a monastery at once. That's why I've resigned my commission.' As soon as I said it, they all burst out into loud laughter. 'Why didn't you tell us that before? Well, that explains everything. We can't try a monk.' They laughed and could not stop themselves. Not sarcastically, but kindly and gaily. They all grew suddenly fond of me, even my most fierce accusers, and they seemed to make a fuss of me during the whole of the following month before my discharge came. 'Oh, you monk!' they said. And everyone said a kind word to me, tried to dissuade me from entering a monastery, even began to pity me: 'What are you doing to yourself?' 'No,' they said, 'he's a brave fellow, he faced the fire, and he could have fired himself, but the night before he dreamed that he became a monk, and that's why he did it.' Almost the same thing happened with the people of the town. Before, they were scarcely aware of my presence, though they received me cordially enough, but now they were all suddenly eager to know me and began inviting me to their houses: they laughed at me themselves, but they could not help loving me. I may observe here that although everyone in the town was discussing the duel, the army authorities hushed it up, for my opponent was a near relation of our general, and as the whole thing came to nothing, as no blood was shed and as I resigned my commission, they just looked upon the whole thing as a joke. And I began then to speak aloud and fearlessly, regardless of their laughter, for, after all, it was a kindly and not a malicious laughter. All these discussions took place mostly at parties, in the society of ladies, for it was the ladies who were most eager to listen to me and they made the men listen too. 'But how is it possible that I should be responsible for everyone?' they all would laugh in my face. 'Can I, for instance, be responsible for you?' 'But,' I replied, 'how can you possibly understand it when the whole world has long been following a different road and when we accept a downright lie as truth and, indeed, demand the same lie from others? Here I have for once in my life done something sincerely, and what happens? Why, you look upon me as though I were an imbecile. You may be fond of me,' I said, 'but you laugh at me all the same.' 'But how can we help being fond of you?' my hostess said, laughing. She had a great many visitors at the time. All of a sudden I caught sight of the young woman whose husband I had challenged and whom I had been planning to make my bride. I had not noticed that she had just arrived at the party. She rose, came up to me and held out her hand. 'Let me tell you,' she said, 'that I am the first not to laugh at you, but, on the contrary, I want to thank you humbly and express my respect to you for the way you acted then.' Her husband, too, came up, and then they all surrounded me and almost kissed me. I felt so happy then, but my attention was especially caught by a middle-aged man who also came up to me. Though I knew him by name, I had never made his acquaintance and never exchanged a word with him till that evening.

(d) The Mysterious Visitor

He had long been a member of the civil service in our town, where he occupied a very important position. He was respected by everyone, he was rich, he was well known for his charitable works, having donated a considerable sum to the almshouse and orphanage, and spent a great deal of money on charity in secret, without publicity, all of which came to light after his death. He was about fifty and had a rather forbidding appearance and was not very talkative. He had been married for about ten years. His wife, who was still young, had borne him three children. On the following evening I was sitting alone in my room when the door suddenly opened and this gentleman walked in.

I think I ought to explain that I was no longer living in my old lodgings, but had moved to others after sending in my resignation from the regiment. My new landlady was an old woman, the widow of a civil servant, who had let me a room in her house with service. I had moved from my old quarters simply because on my return from the duel I had sent Afanasy back to his company, for I was ashamed to look him in the face after the way I had apologized to him – so prone is an unprepared man of the world to be ashamed even of some of his most just actions.

'I've listened to you with great interest in different houses for the last few days,' said the gentleman who had just entered my room, 'and I'd like to make your personal acquaintance, as I am anxious to discuss things with you in greater detail. Can you do me such a great service, sir?' 'Why,' I said, 'with the greatest pleasure, sir. Indeed, I shall consider it an honour.' I said this, but I felt almost dismayed, so greatly did he impress me from the first moment of his appearance in my room. For although people listened to me and were interested in what I had to say, no one had ever approached me before with such a serious and stern air of deep, personal concern. And that man had come to see me of his own accord. He sat down. 'I can see,' he said, 'that you're a man of great strength of character, for you were not afraid to serve truth in a matter in which you risked incurring the contempt of all.' 'I think, sir,' I said, 'that you are greatly exaggerating the importance of what I've done.' 'No,' he said, 'I'm not exaggerating. Believe me, it is much more difficult to do a thing like that than you think. It's that really that impressed me so much and that's what I have come to see you about. Can you describe to me, please, if, that is, you don't think I'm being unduly inquisitive, what you felt at the moment when you decided to apologize at the duel, if you can still remember it? Don't think me frivolous. On the contrary, in asking you this question I have a secret motive of my own, which I will perhaps explain to you later on, if it please God to make us more intimately acquainted.'

All the while he was saying this I was looking him straight in the face, and I suddenly felt that I could trust him implicitly. Besides, my curiosity was powerfully aroused, for I realized that there was some peculiar secret in his soul.

'You asked me what exactly I felt at the moment when I apologized to my opponent,' I answered, 'but, to begin with, I'd better tell you something I haven't yet told anyone else.' And I told him all that had passed between Afanasy and me and how I had prostrated myself before him. 'From that you can see for yourself,' I concluded, 'that it was easier for me at the time of the duel, for I had made a beginning at home, and once I had started on that road, the rest was not only easy, but also a source of joy and happiness to me.'

After hearing me out, he gave me a very friendly look. 'All this,' he said, 'is extremely interesting and I'll come to see you again and again.' And after that he began visiting me almost every evening. We would have become very close friends if he had also talked to me about himself. But he scarcely ever said a word about himself, but always kept asking me about myself. In spite of that I became very fond of him and spoke to him with perfect frankness about my feelings, for, I thought to myself, 'What do I care about his secret when I can see that he's a righteous man?' He was, besides, such a serious-minded man and so much older than I, and yet he came to see a youngster like me and treated me as his equal. And I learned many useful things from him, for he was a man of high intelligence. 'That life is paradise,' he said to me suddenly, 'of that I've long been convinced.' And he added quickly: 'In fact, that's the only thing I am convinced of.' He looked at me and smiled. 'I'm more convinced of it than you,' he said. 'You'll find out why later.' 'I expect,' I thought to myself, 'he wants to reveal some secret to me.' 'Paradise,' he said, 'is hidden in every one of us. It is hidden in me, too, now, and I have only to wish and it will come to me in very truth and will remain with me for the rest of my life.' He was speaking with great feeling and looking mysteriously at me, as though questioning me. 'And as for every man being responsible for every other man and for everything, apart from his sins, you were perfectly right about that and it's remarkable how you could have grasped that idea in all its implications. And it is indeed true that when people grasp this idea the Kingdom of Heaven will become a reality to them and not just a dream.' 'But,' I cried bitterly, 'when will that come to pass, and will it ever come to pass? Isn't it just a dream?' 'Oh,' he said, 'I can see you don't believe it. You preach it and you don't believe it yourself. Know, then, that this dream, as you call it, will undoubtedly come to pass – you can be sure of that, but not now, for every action has its own law. It's a spiritual, a psychological process. To transform the world, it is necessary that men themselves should suffer a change of heart. Until you have actually become everyone's brother, the brotherhood of man will not come to pass. People will never be able to share their property and their rights fairly as a result of any scientific advance, however much it may be to their advantage to do so. Everything will be too little for them and they will always murmur, envy and destroy each other. You ask me when will it come to pass? It will come to pass, but first the period of human *isolation* will have to come to an end.' 'What sort of isolation do you have in mind?' I asked. 'Why,' he replied, 'the sort of isolation that exists everywhere now, and especially in our age, but which hasn't reached its final development. Its end is not yet in sight. For today everyone is still striving to keep his individuality as far apart as possible, everyone still wishes to experience the fullness of life in himself alone, and yet instead of achieving the fullness of life, all his efforts merely lead to the fullness of self-destruction, for instead of full self-realization they relapse into complete isolation. For in our age all men are separated into self-contained units, everyone crawls into his own hole, everyone separates himself from his neighbour, hides himself away and hides away everything he possesses, and ends up by keeping himself at a distance from people and keeping other people at a distance from him. He accumulates riches by himself and thinks how strong he is now and how secure, and does not realize, madman that he is, that the more he accumulates the more deeply does he sink into self-destroying impotence. For he is used to relying on himself alone and has separated himself as a self-contained unit from the whole. He has trained his mind not to believe in the help of other people, in men and mankind, and is in constant fear of losing his money and the rights he has won for himself. Everywhere today the mind of man has ceased, ironically, to understand that true security of the individual does not lie in isolated personal efforts but in general human solidarity. But an end will most certainly come to this dreadful isolation of man, and everyone will realize all at once how unnaturally they have separated themselves from one another. Such will be the spirit of the time, and everyone will be surprised at having remained so long in darkness and not having seen the light. And then the sign of the Son of Man will appear in the heavens. . . . But till then we must still keep the banner flying and, even if he has to do it alone, a man has to set an example at least once and draw his soul out of its isolation and work for some great act of human inter-course based on brotherly love, even if he is to be regarded as a saintly fool for his pains. He has to do so that the great idea may not die. . . . '

It was in such fervent and high-spirited talk that we spent our evenings, one after another. I even gave up my social calls and visited much less frequently the homes of my friends and acquaintances, apart from the fact that I was no longer in fashion to the same extent as before. I'm not saying this in condemnation of my friends, for they continued to like me and treat me good-humouredly, but simply to point out that fashion, in fact, wields no small sway in society, and that must be admitted, much as we may dislike doing so. But I began at last to regard my mysterious visitor with admiration, for, apart from enjoying his high intelligence, I could not help feeling that he was nourishing some secret plan in his heart and was perhaps preparing himself to do something great. Perhaps the thing he liked about me, too, was that I betrayed no curiosity about his secret and did not question him about it, either directly or indirectly. But at last I noticed that he himself seemed to be anxious to reveal something to me. At any rate, this became pretty obvious about a month after he first began visiting me. 'Do you know,' he asked me once, 'that people are beginning to be very curious about us in the town and are wondering why I'm visiting you so frequently. But let them wonder, for *soon everything will be explained.*' Sometimes he would suddenly become very agitated, and when that happened he would almost always get up and go away. Sometimes he would look, as it were, penetratingly at me for a long time and I could not help thinking that he was about to say something immediately, but he would suddenly avert his gaze and begin talking about something ordinary and familiar. He also began complaining frequently of headaches. And then one evening, after he had been talking with great fervour for a long time, he suddenly and to my great surprise turned pale, his face became contorted and he fixed me with a motionless stare.

'What's the matter?' I said. 'Are you ill?'

He had, in fact, been complaining of a headache.

'I – you know – I – I am a murderer!'

He said this and smiled, but was as white as chalk. 'Why is he smiling?' the thought pierced my heart suddenly before I had time to realize anything properly. I turned pale myself.

'What are you talking about?' I shouted at him.

'You see,' he said with the same pallid smile, 'how much it has cost me to utter the first word. Now I've uttered it and, I think, I'm on the right path. I'll follow it.'

For a long time I did not believe him, and I didn't believe him when he first told me about it, but only after he had been to see me three days running and told me everything in detail. My first thought was that he must be mad, but I ended by being at last convinced, to my great grief and astonishment, that what he had told me was true. He had committed a great and terrible crime fourteen years earlier. He had murdered the rich widow of a landowner, a young and beautiful woman, who owned a house in our town. He fell violently in love with her, made her a declaration of love, and tried to persuade her to marry him. But she had already given her heart to another, an army officer of high rank and good social position, who was on active service at the time, but whom, however, she was expecting to return soon. She rejected his proposal and asked him not to call on her again. Having ceased to visit her, but knowing his way about her house, he gained admission into it through the garden and by the roof with great daring, for he ran the risk of being discovered. But as so often happens, all crimes committed with extraordinary daring are more often than not successful. Entering the loft of the house through the skylight, he made his way downstairs by descending the ladder from the loft, knowing that the door at the bottom of the ladder was, through the carelessness of the servants, not always locked. He had relied on this oversight and so it happened. Having made his way to the inhabited part of the house, he went in the dark into her bedroom where a light was burning before the icon. And, as though on purpose, her two young maids had gone without asking permission to a birthday party in the same street. The other servants slept in the servants' quarters in the basement and in the kitchen. At the sight of her asleep, his passion was aroused in him and then his heart was overcome by vindictive, jealous anger and, beside himself, he went up to her bed like a drunken man and plunged a knife into her heart, so that she did not even utter a cry. Then with fiendish and criminal intent he contrived it so that the suspicion should fall on the servants: he did not scruple to take her purse, he opened the chest of drawers with the keys from under her pillow and took some things from it, just as some ignorant servant might have done, leaving the valuable securities and taking only money. He also took away some of the larger gold articles and left the smaller articles that were ten times more valuable. He took some other things, too, as keepsakes for himself, but of that later. Having done this dreadful thing, he went back the way he had come. Neither the next day, when the alarm was raised, nor at any time in his life, did it occur to anyone to suspect the real criminal! Besides, no one knew that he was in love with her, for he had always been of a taciturn and unsociable disposition and had no friend to whom he might open up his heart. He was simply regarded as an acquaintance of the murdered woman, and not even a close acquaintance, for he had not visited her during the previous fortnight. Suspicion fell at once on her serf-servant Peter and, as it happened, all the circumstantial evidence pointed to him, for he knew, and his mistress had made no secret of it, that, having to send a recruit to the army from her peasants, she intended to send him, as he had no relations, and his conduct, besides, was bad. People had heard him, when drunk in a public house, angrily threaten to kill her. Two days before her death he ran away and lived in town at some unknown address. On the day after the murder he was found lying dead drunk on the high road outside the town, with a knife in his pocket, and his right hand for some unknown reason was stained with blood. He claimed that his nose had been bleeding, but no one believed him. The two servant girls, on the other hand, confessed that they had gone to a party and that the front door had been left open till they returned. There were many other similar clues which pointed to the innocent servant and led to his arrest. He was put on trial for murder, but a week later he fell ill with a fever and died in hospital without regaining consciousness. That was the end of the matter, and everyone – the authorities, the judges, and society at large – was convinced that the crime had been committed by no one but the servant who had died during his trial. And after that the punishment began.

The mysterious visitor, now my friend, told me that at the beginning he was not in the least troubled by pangs of conscience. He was unhappy for a long time, but not because of that, but because he was sorry he had killed the woman he loved, a woman he would never see again and that, having killed her, he had also killed his love, while the fire of passion was still in his veins. But he never gave a thought at the time to the shedding of innocent blood and the murder of a human being. He could never reconcile himself to the thought that his victim could have become the wife of another man, and that was why he was for a long time convinced at heart that he could not have acted otherwise. He was worried at first by the arrest of the servant, but the prisoner's illness and death set his mind at rest, for, he argued at the time, the man quite obviously died not because of his arrest or his fright, but because of a chill he had contracted while he was on the run, when for a whole week he had lain dead drunk on the ground all night. The theft of the articles and the money troubled him little for (he argued again) the theft had been committed not for gain but to avert suspicion. The sum stolen was small and he even donated it all, and even more, to the almshouse which had been founded just then in our town. He did this on purpose to set his mind at rest about the theft, and the remarkable thing about it was that for a time, for a long time, in fact, he really was at peace with himself – he told me so himself. He began just then his very active career in the civil service. He volunteered for a very troublesome and difficult job, which occupied him for two years, and, being a man of strong character, he almost forgot about the crime he had committed; when he did remember it, he tried to dismiss it from his thoughts. He also did a great deal of philanthropic work, founded and endowed all sorts of charities in our town, became known in Moscow and Petersburg, too, and was elected a member of philanthropic societies there. But in spite of all that he fell to brooding painfully over his past and the strain of it was too great for him to bear. It was just then that he was attracted by a beautiful and sensible girl and soon married her in the vain hope that marriage would dispel his lonely desolation and that, by entering upon a new life and by zealously performing his duty towards his wife and children, he would escape his old memories altogether. But the opposite of what he expected happened. Already during the first month of his marriage he began to be worried continually by the thought: 'My wife loves me, but what if she knew?' When she told him that she was going to have a baby, their first child, he looked troubled: 'I'm giving life, but have taken life away.' Children came: 'How dare I love them, teach them, and bring them up? How can I speak to them of virtue, I who have shed blood?' His children were beautiful and he longed to caress them: 'But I can't look at their bright innocent faces: I'm not worthy of it.' At last he began to be bitterly and menacingly haunted by the blood of his murdered victim, by the young life he had destroyed, by the blood crying out for revenge. He began to have fearful dreams. But, being a man of stout heart, he bore his suffering a long time: 'I shall atone for everything by this secret agony of mine.' But that hope, too, was vain: the longer it went on, the more intense did his suffering become. In society he was beginning to be respected for his philanthropic work, though people were daunted by his stern and gloomy character, but the more they respected him, the more unendurable it was for him. He told me he had been thinking of killing himself. But instead of that, he became obsessed by another dream, a dream which he considered insane and impossible at first, but which finally gripped his heart so strongly that he could not shake it off. He dreamed of getting up, going out before the people and publicly confessing that he had committed a murder. For three years he nurtured that dream in his heart and he thought of all sorts of ways of carrying it out. At last he believed with all his heart that by making a public confession of his crime, he would most certainly restore his peace of mind and set it at rest once and for all. But, having come to this conclusion, his heart was filled with terror, for how was he to carry out his decision? And suddenly the incident at my duel took place. 'Looking at you I have made up my mind,' he said to me. I looked at him.

'But is it possible,' I cried, throwing up my hands, 'that such an unimportant incident could arouse such resolution in you?'

'My resolution has been growing for three years,' he replied. 'That incident of yours only supplied it with the necessary impetus. Looking at you, I reproached myself and envied you,' he said to me almost in a stern voice.

'But I don't think they'll believe you,' I observed. 'It happened fourteen years ago.'

'I have incontestable proofs. I'll present them.'

And I wept then and kissed him.

'Tell me one thing, one thing!' he said to me (as though everything depended on me now). 'What about my wife and children? My wife will probably die of grief, and though my children will not lose their rank as noblemen nor their estate, they'll be the children of a convict serving a life sentence in a Siberian prison. And what a memory, what a memory I shall leave in their hearts!'

I said nothing.

'And what about leaving them? Leaving them for ever? It is for ever, you know, for ever!'

I sat still, praying in silence. At last I rose to my feet. I felt frightened.

'Well?' he asked, looking at me.

'Go,' I said, 'and confess in public. Everything will pass, only the truth will remain. When they grow up your children will understand how much nobility there was in your great resolution.'

He left me that time and it looked as though he had really made up his mind. But for over a fortnight he kept visiting me every evening, still preparing himself, but unable to make up his mind. He worried me to death. One day he would come determined and say with deep feeling:

'I know it will be paradise for me, that it will come as soon as I confess. Fourteen years I've been in hell. I want to suffer. I shall accept suffering and begin to live. You can go through life under false colours and there's no turning back. Now I dare not love my neighbours, let alone my children. Dear Lord, surely my children will understand what I've been through and will not condemn me! God is not in strength but in truth.'

'Everyone will understand your great act of expiation,' I said, 'if not now, then afterwards. For you have served truth, the higher truth, not of the earth. . . . '

And he would go away, as though comforted, but next day he would come again, pale and angry, and say ironically:

'Every time I come into your room, you look at me with such curiosity, as though to say: "Not confessed yet?" Wait a little longer. Don't despise me too much. It's not as easy as you think. Perhaps I won't do it at all. You wouldn't denounce me then, would you?'

But, as a matter of fact, far from looking at him with foolish curiosity, I was afraid even to glance at him. I was so worn out that I felt ill, and my heart was full of tears. I even lost sleep at night.

'I've just come from my wife,' he went on. 'Do you understand what a wife is? My children shouted to me as I went out: "Good-bye, Daddy. Hurry back to read *The Children's Stories* to us." No, you don't understand that! Another man's misfortune cannot make anyone wiser.'

His eyes flashed and his lips quivered. Suddenly he struck the table with his fist so that the things on it jumped. He was such a mild man, it was the first time he had done such a thing.

'But is it necessary at all?' he cried. 'Must I do it? No one has been condemned. No one has been sentenced to hard labour for me. The servant died a natural death. And I've been punished by my suffering for the blood I shed. Besides, they'll never believe me. No proof will ever convince them. Must I confess? Must I? I'm ready to suffer all my life for the blood I've shed, if only my wife and children are spared. Will it be just to ruin them with me? Are you sure we're not making a mistake? Who can tell what's right? And will people recognize it? Will they appreciate it? Will they respect it?'

'Heavens,' I thought to myself, 'he's thinking of people's respect at such a moment!' And I felt so sorry for him then that I was almost ready to share his fate if only it would make it easier for him. I could see he was beside himself. I was appalled, realizing with the whole of my being and not only with my reason what such resolution meant.

'Decide my fate!' he exclaimed again.

'Go and confess,' I whispered to him. My voice failed me, but I whispered it firmly. Then I took up the New Testament from the table, the Russian translation, and showed him the Gospel of St John, Chapter 12, Verse 24: 'Verily, verily, I say unto you, Except a corn of wheat fall into the ground and die, it abideth alone; but if it die, it bringeth forth much fruit.'

I had read that verse before he came in. He read it.

'That's true,' he said, but he smiled bitterly. 'Yes,' he said after a short pause, 'it's awful the things you come across in these books. It's easy to push them under your nose. And who wrote them? Not men, surely?'

'The Holy Spirit wrote them,' I said.

'It's easy for you to talk,' he said, smiling again, but almost with hatred this time.

I took the book again, opened it in another place, and showed him the Epistle to the Hebrews, Chapter 10, Verse 31. He read: 'It is a fearful thing to fall into the hands of the living God.'

He read it and flung down the book. He was shaking all over.

'A dreadful verse,' he said. 'You've picked out a good one, I must say.' He got up from the chair. 'Well,' he said, 'farewell. Perhaps I shan't come again. . . . We shall meet in heaven. So it's fourteen years since I've "fallen into the hands of God". That is what we must call the fourteen years, mustn't we? Tomorrow I shall entreat those hands to let me go.'

I wanted to embrace and kiss him, but I did not dare – so distorted was his face and so sombre did he look. He went out. 'Dear Lord,' I thought, 'the things that man has to face now!' I fell on my knees before the icon and wept for him before the Holy Virgin, our swift mediator and helper. I had been kneeling like that for half an hour, praying in tears. It was already late, about midnight. Suddenly I saw the door open and he came in again. I was astounded.

'Where have you been?' I asked.

'I think,' he said, 'I – I've forgotten something – my handkerchief, I think. . . . Well, even if I haven't forgotten anything, you won't mind my sitting down, will you?'

He sat down on a chair. I stood over him. 'Won't you sit down, too?' he said. I sat down. We sat like that for two minutes. He looked at me intently and then he suddenly smiled – I remember that well. Then he got up, embraced me warmly and kissed me.

'Remember, old man,' he said, 'how I came to see you for a second time. Do you hear? Remember that!'

It was the first time he had addressed me so familiarly. And he went out. 'Tomorrow,' I thought.

And so it was. I had no idea that evening that the next day was his birthday. I had not been out for the last few days, so I couldn't have found it out from anyone. On that day he always gave a big party and the whole town went to it. They went to it now, too. And so after dinner, he walked into the middle of the room, a paper in his hand – a formal statement to the head of his department. And as the head of his department was present at his party, he read it there and then aloud to the whole gathering. It contained a full description of the crime, in all its details. 'I cast myself out from the society of men as a monster,' he concluded his statement. 'God has visited me – I want to suffer!'

Then he brought out and put on the table all the articles he thought would prove his crime, which he had kept for fourteen years: the gold articles that belonged to the murdered woman, which he had taken to avert suspicion from himself, her locket and cross he had taken from her neck – with a portrait of her fiancé in the locket, her diary and, finally, two letters: her fiancé's letter to her with the news of his speedy arrival and her reply to his letter, which she had begun but left unfinished on the table, intending to post it next day. He had carried off those two letters – why? Why had he kept them for fourteen years instead of destroying them as evidence against him? And now this is what happened: they were all amazed and horrified, but no one would believe it, though they all listened with intense curiosity. They all thought that he was ill, and a few days later it was definitely decided and agreed in every house that the unhappy man was mad. The legal authorities could not refuse to start criminal proceedings against him, but they soon dropped them, though the articles and letters he had produced gave them cause to think. But it was decided that even if they turned out to be authentic, it was impossible to prefer a charge of murder only on the basis of that evidence. Besides, he could have obtained all those things from her as a friend of hers and as a person who had acted as her legal adviser. I heard afterwards, however, that the authenticity of the articles was proved by many of the murdered woman's friends and acquaintances, and that there was no doubt about them. But, again, the whole thing came to nothing in the end. Five days later all had learnt that the poor man was ill and that his life was in danger. What he had fallen ill of, I can't say. It was rumoured that he had had a heart attack, but it also became known that, at the insistence of his wife, the doctors had examined his mental condition and had come to the conclusion that he showed signs of insanity. I disclosed nothing, though they rushed to question me, but for a long time they would not let me visit him, his wife especially. 'It is you,' she said to me, 'who have unsettled him. Before, too, he was melancholy, and last year everyone noticed that he was unusually excited and did strange things, and then you came and ruined him. It was your reading to him that drove him out of his mind. For the last month he never left your room.' And it was not only his wife. Everyone in town pounced upon me and blamed me. 'It's all your fault,' they said. I said nothing, and indeed I rejoiced in my heart, for I could plainly see God's mercy to the man who had turned against himself and punished himself. I could not believe in his insanity. At last they let me see him, for he insisted on taking leave of me. I went in and saw at once that not only his days but also his hours were numbered. He was weak, his face was sallow, his hands trembled. He gasped for breath, but he looked joyful and his eyes were full of deep emotion.

'It's done!' he said to me. 'I've long been yearning to see you. Why didn't you come?'

I did not tell him that I was not allowed to see him.

'God has had pity on me and is calling me to him. I know I'm dying, but I feel happy and at peace for the first time after so many years. As soon as I'd done what had to be done I felt paradise in my heart. Now I dare to love my children and kiss them. No one believes me. Neither my wife nor the judges believed me. Nor will my children ever believe me. I see in that a sign of God's mercy to my children. I shall die and my name will be without a stain for them. Now I feel that God is near, my heart rejoices as in paradise. . . . I have done my duty.'

He could not speak. He gasped for breath, but pressed my hand warmly, looking ardently at me. But we did not talk long. His wife kept looking into the room while I was there. But he managed to whisper to me:

'Do you remember how I came back to you for a second time at midnight? I told you to remember it. Do you know what I came back for? I came back to kill you!'

I gave a violent start.

'I went out from you that time in the darkness, walked about the streets, struggling with myself. And suddenly I hated you so much that I couldn't bear it. Now, I thought, he's the only one who stands in my way. He's my judge, and I can't refuse to face my punishment tomorrow because he knows everything. It wasn't that I was afraid you'd inform the police (I never even thought of that), but I kept thinking, how am I going to face him, if I don't make a clean breast of it? And even if you'd been at the other end of the world, so long as you were alive it would have made no difference to me. I couldn't have borne the thought that you were alive and condemning me. I hated you as though you were the cause of it all and were to blame for it all. I came back to you that time, for I remembered that you had a dagger lying on the table. I sat down, asked you to sit down, and turned it over in my mind for a whole minute. If I had killed you, I should have been done for even if I hadn't made known my first crime. But I was not thinking of that at all. I didn't want to think of it at that moment. I just hated you and longed to revenge myself on you for everything. But the Lord vanquished the devil in my heart. I want you to know, however, that you were never nearer death.'

He died a week later. The whole town followed his coffin to the grave. The priest made a moving speech. They all bewailed the terrible illness that cut short his days. But after the funeral the whole town turned against me and they even stopped receiving me. It is true that some, a few at first, but more later on, began to believe in the truth of his confession, and started visiting me often and questioning me with great interest and eagerness, for people love to see the downfall and disgrace of a righteous man. But I kept silent and soon left the town for good, and five months later I entered by the grace of God upon the straight and glorious path, blessing the unseen finger which had shown it to me. And the much-suffering servant of God Mikhail I have remembered daily in my prayers to this day.

3

From the Discourses and Sermons of Father Zossima

(e) Something about the Russian Monk and his Significance

FATHERS and teachers, what is a monk? Among the educated this word is nowadays uttered with derision by some people, and some even use it as a term of abuse. And it is getting worse as time goes on. It is true, alas, it is true that there are many parasites, gluttons, voluptuaries and insolent tramps among the monks. Educated men of the world point this out: 'You are idlers and useless members of society,' they say. 'You live on the labour of others. You are shameless beggars.' And yet think of the many meek and humble monks there are, monks who long for solitude and fervent prayer in peace and quiet. These attract their attention less and they even pass them over in silence, and how surprised they would be if I told them that the salvation of Russia would perhaps once more come from these meek monks who long for solitary prayer! For they are verily prepared in peace and quiet 'for an hour, and a day, and a month, and a year'. In their solitude they keep the image of Christ pure and undefiled for the time being, in the purity of God's truth, which they received from the Fathers of old, the apostles and martyrs, and when the time comes they will reveal it to the wavering righteousness of the world. That is a great thought. That star will shine forth from the East.

That is what I think of the monk, and is it false, is it arrogant? Look at the worldly and all those who set themselves up above God's people on earth, has not God's image and God's truth been distorted in them? They have science, but in science there is nothing but what is subject to the senses. The spiritual world, however, the higher half of man's being, is utterly rejected, dismissed with a sort of triumph, even with hatred. The world has proclaimed freedom, especially in recent times, but what do we see in this freedom of theirs? Nothing but slavery and self-destruction! For the world says: 'You have needs, and therefore satisfy them, for you have the same rights as the most rich and most noble. Do not be afraid of satisfying them, but multiply them even.' That is the modern doctrine of the world. In that they see freedom. And what is the outcome of this right of multiplication of needs? Among the rich *isolation* and spiritual suicide and among the poor envy and murder, for they have been given the rights, but have not been shown the means of satisfying their needs. We are assured that the world is getting more and more united and growing into a brotherly community by the reduction of distances and the transmission of ideas through the air. Alas, put no faith in such a union of peoples. By interpreting freedom as the multiplication and the rapid satisfaction of needs, they do violence to their own nature, for such an interpretation merely gives rise to many senseless and foolish desires, habits and most absurd inventions. They live only for mutual envy, for the satisfaction of their carnal desires and for showing off. To have dinners, horses, carriages, rank, and slaves to wait on them is considered by them as a necessity, and to satisfy it they sacrifice life, honour, and love of mankind. Why, they even commit suicide, if they cannot satisfy it. We see the same thing among those who are not rich, while the poor drown their unsatisfied needs and envy in drink. But soon they will drown it in blood instead of in drink – that's where they are being led. I ask you: is such a man free? I knew one 'fighter for an idea', who told me himself that when he was deprived of tobacco in prison he was so distressed by this privation that he nearly went and betrayed his 'idea' just to get a little tobacco! And it is such a man who says, 'I'm fighting for humanity'! How can such a man fight for anything and what is he fit for? For some rash action, perhaps, for he cannot hold out long. And it is no wonder that instead of gaining freedom, they have fallen into slavery, and instead of serving the cause of brotherly love and the union of humanity, they have, on the contrary, sunk into *separation* and isolation, as my mysterious visitor and teacher said to me in my youth. And that is why the idea of service to humanity, of brotherhood and of the solidarity of men is more and more dying out in the world. Indeed, this idea is even treated with derision, for how can a man give up his habits, where can such a slave go, if he is so used to satisfying his innumerable needs which he has himself created? He lives in isolation, and what does he care for the rest of mankind? And they have now reached the point of having more and more things and less and less joy in life.

The monastic way is different. People even laugh at obedience, fasting and prayer, and yet it is through them that the way lies to real, true freedom: I cut off all superfluous and unnecessary needs, I subdue my proud and ambitious will and chastise it with obedience, and, with God's help, attain freedom of spirit and with it spiritual joy! Which of them is more capable of conceiving a great idea and serving it – the rich man in his isolation or the man *freed* from the tyranny of material things and habits? The monk is reproached for his solitude: 'You have sought solitude to find salvation within the walls of the monastery, but you have forgotten the brotherly service of humanity.' But we shall see which will be more zealous in the cause of brotherly love. For it is they and not we who live in isolation, but they don't see that. In the olden times leaders of men came from our midst, so why cannot it happen again now? The same meek and humble monks, living a life of fasting and silence, will rise again and go forth to work for the great cause. The salvation of Russia comes from the people. And the Russian monastery has from time immemorial been on the side of the people. If the people are isolated, then we too are isolated. The people believe as we do. An unbelieving leader will never achieve anything in Russia, even if he were sincere at heart and a genius in intelligence. Remember that. The people will meet the atheist and overcome him, and Russia will be one and orthodox. Therefore, take care of the people and guard their heart. Educate them quietly. That is your great task as monks, for this people is a Godbearer.

(f) Something about Masters and Servants and whether it is possible for them to become Brothers in Spirit

Good Lord, no one can deny that there is sin in the common people too. And the fire of corruption is spreading visibly every hour, working its way from the top. Among the common people, too, isolation is coming: *kulaks* and village usurers are growing in number; the merchant, too, is getting more and more eager for honours and strives to show that he is an educated man, though he has no education whatever, and to prove it he basely scorns ancient customs and is even ashamed of the faith of his fathers. He pays visits to princes, though he is only a peasant spoilt. The common people are rotting in drunkenness and cannot give it up. And what cruelty to their families, their wives and even their children! All from drunkenness. I've seen in the factories children of nine years of age: weak, sickly, bent and already depraved. The stuffy workshop, the racket of machines, work all day long, bad language and drink, drink, and is that what the soul of a little child needs? He needs sunshine, games, a good example everywhere, and just a little bit of love. There must be no more of this, monks, no more torturing of children – rise up and preach that at once, at once! But God will save Russia, for though the ignorant peasant is corrupt and cannot give up his foul sins, he knows that his foul sin is cursed by God and that he does wrong in sinning. So that our people still believe in righteousness, have faith in God and shed tears of tender devotion. It is different with the upper classes. Following science, they wish to live a life based on justice by their reason alone, but without Christ as before, and they have already announced that there is no crime, there is no sin. And they are right according to their views: for if you have no God, then why worry about crime? In Europe the common people is already rising up against the rich with violence, and the leaders of the people lead them everywhere to bloodshed and teach them that their wrath is righteous. But 'cursed is their wrath, for it is cruel'. God will save Russia as he has saved her many times. Salvation will come from the people, from its faith and its meekness. Fathers and teachers, take care of the people's faith, and this is no dream: all my life I have been struck by the true and splendid sense of dignity in our great people. I have seen it myself and I can bear witness to it. I have seen it and I have marvelled. I have seen it in spite of the foul sins and the destitute appearance of our people. It is not servile, and that after two centuries of slavery. It is free in appearance and bearing, but without offence. It is neither revengeful nor envious. 'You are noble, you are rich, you are intelligent and talented – all right, may God bless you. I respect you, but I know that I too am a man. By respecting you without envy, I show you my dignity as a man.' And, truly, if they do not say this (for they don't know how to say this yet), they *act* like this. I have seen it myself, I have experienced it myself, and you would not believe it, but the lower and poorer our Russian peasant is, the more noticeable is that splendid truth in him, for the rich among them, the *kulaks* and the usurers, are to a large extent corrupted already, and our own negligence and oversight is responsible for a great deal of it! But God will save his people, for Russia is great in her meekness. I dream of seeing our future, and I seem to see it clearly already: for it will come to pass that even the most corrupt of our rich will end by being ashamed of his riches before the poor, and the poor, seeing his humility, will understand and yield to him, and respond with gladness and kindness to his magnificent shame. Believe me, it will end like that: everything points to it. Equality is to be found only in the spiritual dignity of man, and that will be understood only among us. Let there first be brothers, and there will be brotherhood also, and before we have brotherhood there can never be any fair share-out. We preserve the image of Christ and it will shine forth like a precious diamond over the whole world. . . . It will be so, it will be so! . . .

Fathers and teachers, a most moving incident befell me once. In my wanderings I came across my former batman Afanasy one day in the chief provincial town of K. This happened eight years after I had parted from him. He saw me accidentally in the market place. He recognized me, ran up to me and was so delighted to see me that he almost fell on my neck. 'Good gracious, sir, is it you? Is it really you I see?' He took me to his home. He had left the army, was married and had two little children. He and his wife earned their living as stallholders in the market. His room was poor, but clean and cheerful. He made me sit down, set the *samovar*, sent for his wife, just as though my visit called for a special celebration. He brought his children to me: 'Bless them, Father.' 'Who am I, an ordinary, humble monk, to bless them?' I replied. 'I'll say a prayer for them, and as for you, Afanasy, I've been praying for you every day since that very day, for you,' I said, 'are the cause of it all.' And I explained it to him as well as I could. And what do you think he did? He looked at me unable to believe that I, his former master, an army officer, was now before him in so humble a state and wearing such clothes: he cried even. 'What are you crying for,' I said to him, 'you who are always uppermost in my thoughts? Better rejoice over me, my dear fellow, for my way is bright and joyful!' He did not say much, but just sighed and shook his head over me tenderly. 'What did you do with all your money?' he asked. 'I gave it to the monastery,' I replied. 'We live a communal life there.' As I was taking leave of him after tea, he took out fifty copecks and gave them to me as an offering for the monastery, and I saw him thrusting another fifty copecks into my hand hurriedly. 'That's for you,' he said, 'the pilgrim; you may find it useful in your travels, Father.' I accepted his fifty copecks, bowed to him and to his wife and went away rejoicing, thinking on the way: 'I suppose both of us, he at home and I on the road, are sighing now, and yet we are smiling happily, in the gladness of our hearts, shaking our heads and remembering how God has brought us together.' And I never saw him again after that. I was his master and he my servant, but now when we had kissed each other lovingly and in the joy of our spirits, a great human bond had grown up between us. I have thought a great deal about it, and now what I think is: is it so inconceivable that the same kind of great and simple-hearted union could also occur everywhere in due time between all the Russian people? I believe that it will and that the time is near at hand.

And about servants I will add this: as a young man I was often angry with servants: 'The cook had served a meal too hot, the batman had not brushed my clothes.' But something I heard my brother say when I was a child suddenly came back to me: 'Do I, such as I am, deserve to be waited on by another and lord it over him because he is poor and ignorant?' And I marvelled at the time that such very simple and, indeed, obvious ideas should occur to our minds so late in life! It is impossible to carry on in the world without servants, but you must see to it that your servant should be freer in spirit than if he were not a servant. And why can't I be a servant to my servant and in such a way that he should see it, and that without any pride on my part and no scepticism on his? Why should not my servant be like a relation of mine, so that I may take him into my family at last and rejoice in doing so? Even now it can be done, and it may serve as the basis for the magnificent union among men in future, when man will no longer look for servants for himself and will no longer desire to turn men like himself into servants, as it is done nowadays, but, on the contrary, will long with all his heart to become every-body's servant himself, according to the Gospels. And is it really a dream that in the end man will find his joy only in great deeds of light and mercy and not in cruel pleasures as now – in gluttony, fornication, ostentation, boasting, and envious superiority of one over the other? I firmly believe that it is not, and that the time is near at hand. People laugh and ask: 'When will this time come and is it likely that it will ever come?' But I think that with Christ we shall accomplish this great work. And how many ideas have there not been on earth in the history of man which were unthinkable ten years before and which, when their mysterious hour struck, suddenly appeared, and spread all over the earth? So it will be with us too, and our people will shine forth in the world, and all men will say: 'The stone which the builders refused, the same is become the head stone of the corner.' And those who scoff at us, we shall ask: if our idea is a dream, then when are you going to erect your building and organize your life justly by your reason alone, without Christ? And if they them-selves assert that they, on the contrary, are advancing towards unity, it is the most simple-minded of them who really believe it, so that one cannot help marvelling at such simplicity. Truly, their imagina-tion is more romantic than ours. They think to organize their life justly, but by rejecting Christ they will end up by drowning the world in blood, for blood cries out for blood, and he who un-sheathes his sword will perish by the sword. And if it were not for Christ's solemn promise, they would have destroyed each other to the last two men on earth. And even those two would in their pride not have been able to restrain each other, so that the last man would have destroyed the one before the last, and then destroyed himself. And that would have come to pass but for Christ's solemn promise that for the sake of the meek and the humble this shall never happen. I began at that time, after my duel, while I was still wearing my officer's uniform, talking in society about servants and they were all, I remember, surprised at me. 'What do you want us to do?' they asked. 'Make our servants sit down on the sofa and offer them tea?' And I answered them: 'Why not? Even if you did it only once in a while.' They all laughed at the time. Their question was frivolous and my answer vague, but I can't help thinking that there was a grain of truth in it.

(g) Of Prayer, of Love and of Contact with Other Worlds

Young man, do not forget to say your prayers. If your prayer is sincere, there will be every time you pray a new feeling containing an idea in it, an idea you did not know before, which will give you fresh courage; you will then understand that prayer is education. Remember also: every day and whenever you can repeat to yourself, O Lord, have mercy upon all who appear before thee today. For thousands of people leave life on this earth every hour and every moment and their souls stand before God – and how many of them depart this life in solitude, unknown to anyone, in anguish and sorrow that no one feels sorry for them and does not even care whether they live or die. And so from the other end of the earth your prayer, too, will perhaps rise up to God that his soul may rest in peace though you knew him not nor he you. How deeply touching it will be to his soul, standing in fear before God, to feel at that moment that he has someone to utter a prayer for him, that there is one human being on earth left who loves him. And God also will look upon you both more benignly, for if you have had so much pity on him, how much greater will God's pity be on you, for God is infinitely more merciful and more loving than you. And he will forgive him for your sake.

Brothers, be not afraid of men's sins. Love man even in his sin, for that already bears the semblance of divine love and is the highest love on earth. Love all God's creation, the whole of it and every grain of sand. Love every leaf, every ray of God's light! Love the animals, love the plants, love everything. If you love everything, you will perceive the divine mystery in things. And once you have perceived it, you will begin to comprehend it ceaselessly more and more every day. And you will at last come to love the whole world with an abiding, universal love. Love the animals: God has given them the rudiments of thought and untroubled joy. Do not, therefore, trouble it, do not torture them, do not deprive them of their joy, do not go against God's intent. Man, do not exalt yourself above the animals: they are without sin, while you with your majesty defile the earth by your appearance on it and you leave the traces of your defilement behind you – alas, this is true of almost every one of us! Love children especially, for they, too, like the angels, are without sin, and live to arouse tender feelings in us and to purify our hearts, and are as a sort of a guidance to us. Woe to him who offends a child! Father Anfim taught me to love children: in our wanderings he, kind and silent man, would buy sweets and cakes for them with the farthings given to us; he could not pass a child without being deeply moved: that is the sort of man he is.

At some ideas you stand perplexed, especially at the sight of men's sins, asking yourself whether to combat it by force or by humble love. Always decide: 'I will combat it by humble love.' If you make up your mind about that once and for all, you may be able to conquer the whole world. Loving humility is a terrible force, the strongest of all, and there is nothing like it. Every day and every hour, every minute, examine yourself and watch over yourself to make sure that your appearance is seemly. You pass by a little child, you pass by spitefully, with foul language and a wrathful heart; you may not have noticed the child, but he has seen you, and your face, ugly and profane, will perhaps remain in his defenceless heart. You may not know it, but you have perhaps sown an evil seed in him and it may grow, and all because you did not exercise sufficient care before a child, because you did not foster in yourself a discreet, active love. Brothers, love is a teacher, but one must know how to acquire it, for it is acquired with difficulty, it is dearly bought, one must spend a great deal of labour and time on it, for we must love not only for a moment and fortuitously, but for ever. Anyone can love by accident, even the wicked can do that. My young brother asked forgiveness of the birds: it may seem absurd, but it is right nonetheless, for everything, like the ocean, flows and comes into contact with everything else: touch it in one place and it reverberates at the other end of the world. It may be madness to beg forgiveness of the birds, but, then, it would be easier for the birds, and for the child, and for every animal if you were yourself more pleasant than you are now – just a little easier, anyhow. Everything is like an ocean, I tell you. Then you would pray to the birds, too, consumed by a universal love, as though in a sort of ecstasy, and pray that they, too, should forgive your sin. Set great store by this ecstasy, however absurd people may think it.

My friends, ask God for gladness. Be glad as children, as the birds of heaven. And let not men's sins trouble you in your work. Fear not that it will obliterate your work and prevent it from being accomplished. Do not say: 'Sin is powerful, wickedness is powerful, bad environment is powerful, while we are lonely and helpless. Bad environment will destroy us and prevent our good work from being done.' Fly from that despondency, children! You have only one means of salvation: take hold of yourself and make yourself responsible for all men's sins. My friend, believe me, that really is so, for the moment you make yourself responsible in all sincerity for everyone and everything, you will see at once that it really is so and that you are, in fact, responsible for everyone and everything. And by throwing your own indolence and impotence on to others, you will end up by sharing Satan's pride and murmuring against God. As for Satan's pride, this is what I think of it: it is difficult for us on earth to grasp it, and that is why it is so easy to fall into error and share it, even imagining that we are doing something great and beautiful. Besides, many of the strongest feelings and forces of our nature we cannot so far comprehend on earth. But be not tempted by this, either, and do not think that this may serve as a justification for you for anything, for the Eternal Judge will call you to account for what you can comprehend and not for what you cannot. You will be convinced of that yourself hereafter, for then you will see everything in its true light and you will no longer argue about it. On earth, however, we seem, in truth, to be walking about blindly, and, but for the precious image of Christ before us, we should have perished and lost our way altogether, like the human race before the flood. Many things on earth are hidden from us, but in return for that we have been given a mysterious, inward sense of our living bond with the other world, with the higher, heavenly world, and the roots of our thoughts and feelings are not here but in other worlds. That is why philosophers say that it is impossible to comprehend the essential nature of things on earth. God took seeds from other worlds and sowed them on this earth, and made his garden grow, and everything that could come up came up, but what grows lives and is alive only through the feeling of its contact with other mysterious worlds; if that feeling grows weak or is destroyed in you, then what has grown up in you will also die. Then you will become indifferent to life and even grow to hate it. That is what I think.

(h) Can One be a Judge of One's Fellow-creatures? Of Faith to the End

Remember particularly that you cannot be a judge of anyone. For there can be no judge of a felon on earth, until the judge himself recognizes that he is just such a felon as the man standing before him, and that perhaps he is more than anyone responsible for the crime of the man in the dock. When he has grasped that, he will be able to be a judge. However absurd that may sound, it is true. For if I had been righteous myself, there would, perhaps, have been no criminal standing before me. If you are able to take upon yourself the crime of the man standing before you and whom your heart is judging, then take it upon yourself at once and suffer for him yourself, and let him go without reproach. And even if the law itself makes you his judge, then act in the same spirit as much as you can, for he will go away and condemn himself more bitterly than you have done. If, however, he goes away indifferent to your kisses and laughing at you, do not let that influence you, either; it merely means that his time has not yet come, but it will come in due course; and if it does not come, it makes no difference: if not he, then another in his place will understand and suffer, and will judge and condemn himself, and justice will be done. Believe that, believe it without a doubt, for therein lies all the hope and faith of the saints.

Carry on with your good work without ceasing. If you remember at night as you go to sleep that you have not done what you should have done, get up at once and do it. If the people around you are spiteful and callous and refuse to listen to you, fall down before them and ask them for forgiveness, for in truth you are responsible for their refusing to listen to you. And if you find it impossible to talk to the malevolent ones, serve them in silence and in humility, never giving up hope. But if they will all abandon you and drive you away by force, fall upon the earth, when left alone, and kiss it, drench it with your tears, and the earth will bring forth fruit from your tears even if no one has heard or seen you in your loneliness. Believe to the end, even if it should so happen that all men on earth were led astray and you were the only one to remain faithful: sacrifice yourself even then and give praise to God – you who are the only one to be left. And if two of you should meet – then that will be the world entire, the world of living love, and embrace each other with great tenderness and give praise to God: for though only in two of you, his truth has been manifested.

If you yourself have sinned and are grieved even unto death for your sins, or for your sudden sin, rejoice for others, rejoice for the righteous, rejoice that, though you have sinned, he is righteous and has not sinned.

But if the evil-doing of men should arouse your indignation and uncontrollable grief, even to make you wish to revenge yourself upon the evil-doers, fear most of all that feeling; go at once and seek suffering for yourself just as if you were yourself guilty of that villainy. Accept that suffering and bear it, and your heart will be appeased, and you will understand that you, too, are guilty, for you might have given light to the evil-doers, even as the one man without sin and you have not given them light. If you had, you would have lighted a path for them too, and he who had committed the felony would not have committed it if you had shown him a light. And even if you showed a light but saw that men are not saved even by your light, you must remain steadfast and doubt not the power of the heavenly light; believe that if they were not saved now, they will be saved afterwards. And if they are not saved afterwards, their sons will be saved, for your light will not die, though you were to die yourself. The righteous man departs, but his light remains. People are always saved after the death of him who came to save them. Men do not accept their prophets and slay them, but they love their martyrs and worship those whom they have tortured to death. You are working for the whole, you are acting for the future. Never seek reward, for your reward on earth is great as it is: your spiritual joy which only the righteous find. Fear not the great nor the powerful, but be wise and always worthy. Know the right measure, know the right time, get to know it. When you are left in solitude, pray. Love to fall upon the earth and kiss it. Kiss the earth ceaselessly and love it insatiably. Love all men, love everything, seek that rapture and ecstasy. Water the earth with the tears of your joy and love those tears. Be not ashamed of that ecstasy, prize it, for it is a gift of God, a great gift, and it is not given to many, but only to the chosen ones.

(i) Of Hell and Hell Fire, a Mystical Discourse

Fathers and teachers, I am thinking, 'What is hell?' And I am reasoning thus: 'The suffering that comes from the consciousness that one is no longer able to love.' Once, in the infinitude of existence, which cannot be measured by time or space, it was given to some spiritual being, on its appearance on earth, the ability to say: 'I am and I love.' Once, only once, was there given him a moment of active *living* love, and for that earthly life was given him, and with it times and seasons. And what happened? That happy being rejected the priceless gift, prized it not, loved it not, looked scornfully upon it and remained indifferent to it. Such a one, having left the earth, sees Abraham's bosom and talks with Abraham, as it is told in the parable of the rich man and Lazarus, and contemplates heaven, and can go up to the Lord, but what torments him so much is that he will go up to God without ever having loved and come in contact with those who love and whose love he has scorned. For he sees clearly and says to himself, 'Now I have the knowledge and though I yearn to love, there will be no great deed, no sacrifice in my love, for my earthly life is over, and Abraham will not come even with a drop of living water (that is to say, again with the gift of former active earthly life) to cool the fire of the yearning for spiritual love which burns in me now, having scorned it on earth; there is no more life and there is no more time! Though I would gladly give my life for others, I can do it no more, for the life I could have sacrificed for love is over and now there is a gulf between that life and this existence.' Men speak of material hell fire: I do not go into that mystery and I dread it, but I think that even if there were material fire, they would be genuinely glad of it, for I fancy that in material agony the much more terrible spiritual agony would be forgotten, even though for a moment. And, indeed, it is quite impossible to take that spiritual agony away from them, for it is not outside but within them. And even if it were possible to take it away, I cannot help thinking that their unhappiness would be more bitter because of it. For though the righteous ones in heaven, contemplating their torments, would have forgiven them, and called them to heaven in their infinite love, by doing so they would have multiplied their torments, for they would arouse in them still more strongly the fiery yearning for responsive, active, and grateful love, which is no longer possible. In the timidity of my heart, however, I cannot help thinking that the very consciousness of this impossibility would at last serve to alleviate their suffering, for by accepting the love of the righteous without the possibility of repaying it, by this submissiveness and the effect of this humility, they will at last acquire a certain semblance of that active love which they scorned in life, and a sort of activity which is similar to it. . . . I am sorry, my friends and brothers, that I cannot express it more clearly. But woe to those who have destroyed themselves on earth, woe to the suicides! I don't think there can be anyone more unhappy than they. We are told that it is a sin to pray for them, and outwardly the Church seems to reject them, but in my heart of hearts I think that we may pray even for them. For Christ cannot be angry with love. I have prayed inwardly all my life for such as those, I confess it to you, fathers and teachers, and I am still praying for them every day.

Oh, there are some who remain proud and fierce even in hell, in spite of their certain knowledge and contemplation of irrefutable truth; there are some fearsome ones who have joined Satan and his proud spirit entirely. For those hell is voluntary and they cannot have enough of it; they are martyrs of their own free will. For they have damned themselves, having damned God and life. They feed upon their wicked pride, like a starving man in the desert sucking his own blood from his body. They will never be satisfied and they reject forgiveness, and curse God who calls them. They cannot behold the living God without hatred and demand that there should be no God of life, that God should destroy himself and all his creation. And they will burn eternally in the fire of their wrath and yearn for death and non-existence. But they will not obtain death. . . .

*

Here Alexey Karamazov's manuscript ends. I repeat: it is incomplete and fragmentary. The biographical data, for instance, cover only the elder's early years. His teachings and views have been grouped together, as if they formed one whole, though it is obvious that they were uttered at different times and on different occasions. What the elder said during the last hours of his life is not stated precisely, but the spirit and character of his last talk can be gathered from what has been quoted in Alexey's manuscript of his former teachings. The elder's death came quite unexpectedly. For although those who had gathered in his room that last evening fully realized that his death was near, they never imagined that it would come so suddenly; on the contrary, his friends, as I have mentioned earlier, seeing him that night apparently so cheerful and talkative, were quite convinced that there had been a marked improvement in his health, for a short time at least. Even five minutes before his death, as they afterwards recounted with surprise, it was quite impossible to fore-see it. He seemed suddenly to feel an acute pain in his chest, he turned pale and pressed his hand to his heart. They all got up from their seats at once and rushed up to him; but though in great pain, he gazed at them with a smile, sank slowly from his chair on to the floor, knelt and then fell on the ground face downwards, stretched out his arms and, as though in joyful rapture, kissing the ground and praying (as he had bidden them do), quietly and joyfully gave up his soul to God. The news of his death spread immediately through the hermi-tage and reached the monastery. Those nearest to the departed one, as well as those whose duty it was in accordance with their monastic rank, began laying out his body according to the ancient rites, and all the monks gathered in the cathedral church. And even before dawn, as it was rumoured afterwards, the news of the elder's death reached the town. By the morning almost the entire town was talking of the event, and many citizens flocked to the monastery. But of this we shall tell in the next book; here we shall only add that before a day had passed, something so unexpected happened and, from the impression it made in the monastery and in the town, so strange, so disturbing and so confusing, that even after so many years that day, so upsetting to many people, is still vividly remembered in our town. . . .